BANSHEES

BANSHEES

MIKE BARON

WordFire Press
Colorado Springs, Colorado

BANSHEES
Copyright © 2016 Mike Baron

ISBN: 978-1-61475-394-0

Cover design by Bob Garcia

Art Director Kevin J. Anderson

Cover artwork images by Joe Comstock

Book Design by RuneWright, LLC
www.RuneWright.com

Published by
WordFire Press, an imprint of
WordFire, Inc.
PO Box 1840
Monument CO 80132

Kevin J. Anderson & Rebecca Moesta, Publishers

WordFire Press Trade Paperback Edition May 2016
Printed in the USA
wordfirepress.com

CHAPTER ONE

On a clear night in March, Kaspar Sinaiko coaxed his eleven-year-old Mercedes down a rutted dirt path that ended at an eight-foot hurricane fence topped with concertina wire. He turned off the engine, cutting short the Banshee's "One More for the Grave." One hundred feet inside the hurricane fence stood an old double-wide trailer that had once served as the construction HQ for a thriving shipbuilding factory.

But times changed. The shipbuilding factory had died in the 80s from poisoning, having sent thousands of workers to an early grave. Georgia had declared the site an environmental hazard, which hadn't stopped scavengers from removing everything but the concrete slabs and piles of slag. The parent company could no longer afford to guard the premises, so the vast industrial complex had been left to rot.

Kaspar got out of his car and stretched in the cool night air, inhaling the scent of chemicals and a hint of the salty Caspian Sea which lay on the other side of the blasted land. Despite the evening cool, Kaspar sweated through his white muscle shirt. Sweat beaded on his brow like rivets.

He was ripped like a cage-fighter, with a six-pack you could dig your nails into. Veins popped like cords on his muscular arms, blue/black from prison tattoos. He was clean-shaven, with small, close deep-set eyes of Arctic blue. His face had been flattened and his eyebrows scarred. His ears looked like tortellini. His torso was also covered in jailhouse tats, including the lifer's stars on each shoulder. The rose on his chest marked his initiation into the Russian Mafia. The executioner covering his gut indicated he was a killer. On his left bicep, a likeness of Rasputin. On his right, an edged saw. The barbed wire around his wrists were strictly decorative. The six Chinese characters on the left side of his skull meant, "True unto death."

Kaspar had visited this desolate hellhole, known as the Devil's Scab, a fortnight ago in preparation. Now all that remained was to transport the package from the car to the trailer and the ceremony itself. Kaspar looked down where the chain mesh fence met a steel stanchion. The mesh had been cut, but you couldn't tell unless you got right up to it.

Pulling a pair of heavy rubber gloves from the car, Kaspar knelt and bent back the corner, creating a triangle big enough to crawl through. God, what he wouldn't give for a snort of crystal. That could wait until he was inside the trailer. One misstep could result in his death. But if the texts were correct, if the dogma was solid, he was about to transform himself from a thug you'd avoid on the street into one of the most powerful and charismatic people on earth.

As head of the Mad Monks crime syndicate, he was already powerful. As president of the Skorzny Group, he traveled in rarefied circles. He was a natural leader. People looked up to him. He took over his cellblock day one. He'd hobnobbed with Trump, even attended Cannes in support of a Russian crime thriller he'd financed with drug money. A tux miraculously transformed him into a hard-nosed businessman. The long sleeves concealed his tats.

Kaspar knew business. He held no university degrees save the marks on his face from the School of Hard Knocks. He'd been a policeman once but stepped on the wrong toes and found himself in Lubyanka, and shortly after that at a labor camp above the Arctic Circle.

As a former cop his life expectancy in prison would have been infinitesimal save for one fact: the politician he'd offended was universally despised. Several gangs courted him, but he went with the Monks because their peculiar strain of evangelical mysticism and hands-on "spiritual ceremonies" satisfied a deep and twisted longing in his soul. He had always sensed this knot of perversity within himself. Always.

"You've got to believe in something, or you'll fall for anything," he sang atonally.

When I go to America I will see Mellencamp and the Boss.

Kaspar was a rocker and played a decent one-handed piano.

The car shifted and squeaked on its tired suspension. The package was coming out of it. Humming atonally Kaspar walked to the rear, sprung the hatch, and stared down at the thirty-seven-year-old woman, ankles and wrists bound with duct tape, her hair reduced to ragged stubble. He hadn't gagged her in case she had trouble breathing. She looked up at him with terrified eyes and croaked, "What…?"

Kaspar grabbed the roll of duct tape from the trunk, ripped off a piece and plastered it over her mouth. "Don't worry," he said in heavily accented English. "Will all be over soon." Bending at the knees, he gathered her into his arms and stood.

Her name was not important, although Kaspar had gone through her wallet with his usual efficiency. Fareeza Sollish was one of twelve known bastards sired by Paddy McGowan, lead singer of the Banshees. Fareeza was a teller for the Royal Bank of Scotland in London, unmarried, two cats.

It had taken Kaspar six years and a small fortune to track her down.

Kaspar had paid a contractor a thousand dollars to procure samples of Miss Sollish's hair from a salon. Using DNA from Paddy's discarded cigarette butts, saved by obsessive fans, Kaspar made his match, had found his key to a gate that would unlock another world.

Kaspar could not believe his luck when he learned (by following her tweets) that Fareeza planned to vacation in the Middle East. But it wasn't luck. The spheres were in alignment. The moon was in Capricorn. Civilization was unraveling. That Great Dread Thing that had lurked in the earth since time began was stirring. One need only look at the telly or the net. Food riots in China. War in the Middle East. Food riots in Greece and Ireland.

"In a time of mass confusion," he recited by rote, "When leaders fall, oceans rise, and men of goodwill are nowhere to be found, I shall come to lead my followers to the Kingdom of the Damned."

Like most Russians, Kaspar believed he was already damned. Nothing to lose and everything to gain.

He'd picked Miss Sollish up at a club in Istanbul. Kaspar could be quite charming. His tats covered with a cashmere sweater, he'd approached her at the bar.

"English?"

The tall, ungainly woman with short brown hair beamed, eager to show she wasn't one of "those" tourists who stayed with the pack and disdained locals. How was she to know he was Russian? Later, he'd bought her a drink. As Miss Sollish began feeling giddy, Kaspar "helped" her into his car. High on meth, he'd driven straight through.

The meth was wearing off, but it would have to wait.

Fareeza struggled feebly as Kaspar carried her effortlessly to the fence and set her on the ground next to the triangular opening. He crawled through, turned around and pulled Fareeza through by her ankles, causing her skirt to rise up around her midriff and expose sensible white cotton underpants.

Kaspar, a kidnapper, rapist, and murderer, felt a vague guilt for subjecting her to these indignities but shrugged it off as residual bourgeoisie tendencies. What was one more life to a man who had killed dozens? Inside the fence, Kaspar crouched, reaching beneath the bound woman's knees and shoulders, hoisted her up, and draped her over one shoulder like a rolled up carpet as he strode across the blackened concrete and soil that glittered like diamonds from broken glass, silicon, mercury, and PCBs.

The double-wide sat on cinderblocks, a broken wood stair led to an aluminum door. Kaspar found the key in his pocket, unlocked the door, and pushed it open with a hair-raising screech. He carried the package into the big, hollowed-out space and set her on the spring and fungal sofa, the only piece of furniture. A Sony boom box with fresh batteries sat on the built-in kitchen counter. Kaspar opened the lower cabinet six inches, reached in, and slowly disarmed his homemade claymore, set to discharge a half pound of double-ought shot into the face of anyone foolish enough to get this far.

Opening the cabinet all the way, he pulled out a black leather satchel and opened it. Inside lay a curved kukri of Damascus steel. He drew it out, fixating on the whorls and patterns in the steel until they began to swim.

Kaspar had chosen this spot for its isolation as well as the spiritual energy, which came from the thousands of lost souls who had perished in the factory. They died from heavy metal poisoning. Mesothelioma. They fell from catwalks. Killed by shrapnel from exploding propane tanks. Pushed, knifed, or shot. No sane person wanted to work in the Bilyanka Ship Factory, so the state exerted gentle persuasion. Many who had worked and died here had been criminals not expected to survive. The shipyard had a frighteningly high attrition rate.

Kaspar felt the spirits of the dead now. They were all around him, intensely excited over what he was about to do. And why not? The spirits hungered for revenge. It was the only thing keeping them "alive."

Kaspar took a paper bindle from his pants, quickly and efficiently deposited a mound of white crystal on the kitchen counter, and laid it out in a line using Miss Smollish's Royal Bank of Scotland credit card. He took a drinking straw from a drawer and cut off two inches with the kukri. With a sigh that almost sounded like pleasure he placed the straw to his nostril and hoovered up the line.

Wham, bam, thank you, ma'am.

Stripping off his shirt, shoes, and socks, wearing only cargo pants, Kaspar hit the start button on the boom box's cassette player. The Banshees' "Moloch Loves Me" blasted from the speakers.

Hear Moloch, fear Moloch, feed him another child!
Face Moloch, taste Moloch, this is going to be wild!

Sound quality was poor. It was a bootleg of their first album he'd bought in a bazaar in Uzbekistan for three rubles. Banshees' music was designed to overcome flawed equipment, designed to sound piercingly bright through a car radio, ceding the lower register to the wheels and wind.

Hardly anyone played the Banshees anymore, mostly Goths in thrall to Satanism, and most of them lived in the rural American South. Back in the day, Pope John Paul had issued a condemnation. Churches held Banshee record burnings, furious denunciations not only from the pulpit but from *Vanity Fair* and the *New York Times* as well. Johnny Carson had ridiculed them. A congressman from Maine introduced a bill forbidding them from entering the United States.

It seemed at the time that there was a limit to what the public would stomach. A flurry of Banshees-inspired suicides fed the flames and the pockets of trial lawyers right up to the moment when the Banshees all died in a plane crash on the Scottish moors, flying from Gatwick to Helsinki for a gig.

August 19, 1975. Long before the ship factory burned, the Banshees' twin-engine Cessna buried its nose in the bog killing all three band members, two birds along for the ride, and the pilot. "Rough justice," said the families of suicide victims. "Good riddance," cried the social arbiters and ministers of every persuasion.

> *Bind the tainted tarts and chop off all their hair-e-o*
> *Cut out their faithless hearts and throw them at the stereo!*

Although suicides and riots had been attributed to the band, and particularly their record *Beat the Manshees*, no one had taken literally the lyrics to "Moloch Loves Me," no more than they acted out "Street Fighting Man" or "Cop Killer."

No one until now.

Kaspar dragged the struggling, mewling woman to the center of the floor, onto a once-magnificent Persian carpet.

Eyes glittering like ice, heart palpitating from the meth, face a rictus mask, legs in horse stance, Kaspar gripped the knife overhead in both hands and plunged the blade into the woman's chest just below the collarbone. He had observed and even assisted in autopsies while in Lubyanka. Kaspar carefully carved the coroner's Y cut from the collarbone to the pubis. Blood pulsed from the still breathing victim, who began choking into the duct tape covering her mouth.

Kaspar was not a brute. He didn't intend for her to suffer. He swiftly inserted the blade beneath the woman's jaw and with steroid-enhanced strength drove it all the way through her palate into her skull. She died instantly, legs twitching. Kaspar reflexively recited a Russian orthodox prayer then laughed at himself for his hypocrisy.

"Kaspar!" he rasped. *"Tyi takoy zlobney!"*

Using the blade and his immense strength he peeled back the flesh of the upper torso, exposing the rib cage. Raw viscera seeped into the carpet. Kaspar dug his fingers beneath the ends of the fifth and sixth ribs on either side. It was slippery going. He pried back both sides of the rib cage like Samson bringing down the temple to the sound of bones cracking. He exposed the heart, like some obscene fruit. Using the blade with the utmost delicacy, he severed the heart from its moorings, cutting through the veins and the aorta until at last the slippery thing came free, not much bigger than a tennis ball.

He rose and hurled the heart overhand. It struck the Sony boom box with a resounding *thwap!* The music stopped.

Thousands of miles away, something stirred beneath the Scottish moor.

Chapter Two

The day didn't start well. Ian St. James sprawled in his hotel room, cheek glued to the floor in dried vomit. One eye fluttered open, revealing a red bull's eye. St. James emitted a low, animal noise. He lifted his head with a disturbing ripping sound, then set it back down again. Any movement caused his equilibrium to froth like the North Atlantic.

St. James waited a few minutes and tried again. Ever so slowly he sat with both hands on the floor to steady himself and watched the universe revolve around him. The floor felt like a Tilt-a-Whirl. Lovely.

The room was barely large enough to swing a dead cat. *Twenty-four CZKs a night. Oh snap! Where the fuck is my wallet?* St. James slapped his pockets and filthy fringed leather jacket until he located the emaciated folder in an inside pocket. He took it out and looked inside. He had 84 CZKs plus the forty bob hidden in his belt.

He'd come to Prague for a gig at the Zipper Club, five nights guaranteed, 100 CZK a night. When the proprietor didn't answer his phone, St. James took a taxi to the Zipper Club. Its blackened embers were sealed off from the sidewalk by hurricane fencing and plywood sheets. A busker, guitar case open at his feet, sang "All Along the Watchtower" in an adenoidal voice.

St. James dropped a note into the case and the busker nodded.

"When'd the club burn down?" St. James asked.

"Last night, buddy," the man replied in a Czech accent. "They think he did it for the insurance." The busker peered hard at St. James for a second, then shrugged and picked up where he'd left off.

Good.

Last thing St. James needed, some moon-eyed fan still hanging on any contribution to pop music he might have made in years past. Ian St. James was a pimple on the ass of pop music. No, less than that. He was that most dismal of creatures, the failed scion of a famous parent, in this case Oaian St. James, drummer for the late, unlamented, but indisputably great and destined to be a source of controversy forever, satanic metal band Banshees.

It was probably for the best. He could have used the money, but he had no desire to be gawked at by the same people who watched *Wetten, dass...?* His first record had been critically well received. Even sold a few. The second record was a disaster, and St. James now had the same appeal as a train wreck or Gloria Gaynor. People came to watch him make a fool of himself, cameras hovering.

He returned to the boarding house, which smelled of kraut.

"Fuck me," St. James muttered to the dismal room. *Uh oh, here come the heaves.* He couldn't even remember last night, but the feeling of waking up in the morning—or afternoon as the case may be—hammered and reeling from drinking, smoking, or snorting was not unfamiliar. Jayzus, he felt like shit! He hadn't felt this bad in weeks.

He needed to piss, throw up, and drink two gallons of water. The miserable room had no bath. There was a communal bath down the hall. It may as well have been at the summit of K1.

"Attitude," St. James snarled, feeling phlegm in his throat the consistency of Silly Putty.

Why were his knuckles bruised and bloody?

First step, get your skinny arse up off the floor. St. James got to one knee, head reeling, stomach flexing. *Breathe in,* he told himself. *Breathe out.* It was all about the breath control, or so a cute Belgian yoga instructor had once told him before leaving him for a football player. She had been lovely. Couldn't seem to hold onto anyone or anything these days.

Next: place your hand atop the cheap pressboard bureau and pray it can support your weight. Now slowly, slowly, let us rise to our feet like proper English gentlemen ... and VOILA! We are upright!

St. James' stomach spun in its grave. Wild-eyed, he looked around the room, settling on the cheap stamped metal wastebasket with white daisies on a rusted black background. He lurched forward and heaved, stomach tossing up a thin acidic gruel that was all that was left after last night's expectorations. St. James went down on his knees. "As I lay me down to sleep," he said. Another eight count. Gradually, he got the spasms under control.

Water. He needed water.

A rude, obnoxious pounding shook the ancient wooden door with metronomic regularity followed by the fishwife's shriek. "Past noon, Mr. St. James! Past noon! You stay, you pay!"

At times like these St. James wished Czechoslovakia had remained beneath the German boot. It would serve them right. First, they sucker him to Prague with a bogus gig, now this.

"I know you are in there, Mr. St. James! If you do not pay me, I am going to the police. You stay, you pay!"

St. James sat on the creaking bed with his legs splayed staring at the door. She'd given him the stink eye when he'd taken the room yesterday, but she liked the color of his money. Unfortunately, he'd blown his wad last night at—what was the name of that club? Who knew? Prague was suddenly filled with clubs blasting disco, jazz, rap, and rock. Seemed like half the Bright Young Things in England were here opening up web design or coffee shops.

The pounding continued a moment longer, resonating within his skull. St. James heard the woman shuffling away, muttering in Czech. He was in for it now. There wasn't a doubt in St. James' mind that she'd gone to get the cops. It had been St. James' experience that police had little use for transients and disrespected the rock community.

Using the steel bed frame, St. James hauled himself to his feet like a castaway climbing a rope ladder. He wobbled and nearly fell, one hand shooting out to grab the ancient bureau. For a second, like an optical illusion, he caught a glimpse of himself in the opaque mirror: a tall drink of water with long, unkempt hair, nose like a tomahawk, face of a hard drug user, wearing a tattered leather jacket from which much of the fringe was missing.

"I look like a child molester," St. James muttered, throwing his few belongings into his backpack. It hit him in the gut, and he had to sit on the bed, all the air going out of him like a deflating balloon. He was thirty-eight years old, living out of a knapsack. His only means of support were the royalties he received from his debut record which had come out eighteen years ago, plus the odd gig from clubs that liked to feature tribute bands.

Slipping into his backpack and grabbing his guitar case, St. James made a pit stop in the bathroom, where a man the shape and texture of a black bear squatted on the toilet grunting atonally and working up a storm. What kind of person puts the crapper right out in the open like that?

The man smiled cheerfully as St. James entered.

"Good morning!" he boomed in heavily accented English. St. James wished he would disappear.

"Good morning," St. James croaked, walking to the other toilet and unzipping his trou, then hovering over the bowl. *Come on, kidneys, come on.* Drinking will do that to you. His old man had been a world-class drunk, and so was he. St. James inherited Oaian's taste for liquor and his facility with musical instruments. That was about it. The sum total of Oaian's fortune.

Come on old thing. Dribble for Ian.

He tried holding his breath, then he tried breathing through his mouth.

The squatter thundered, releasing a stench from hell.

Leave, damn it!

"Having trouble?" the bear asked, wiping his ass.

St. James' head felt like a cement mixer. His mouth felt like a drain. He was in serious danger of dropping into the urinal. He made a gesture as if to say it's nothing. Would the man never pull up his pants and leave? The bear finally stood, buckled his belt and shuffled to one of three stained porcelain sinks where he performed noisy ablutions, cleaning his hairy armpits and splashing water all over. He finally concluded his toilet and prepared to depart.

"Well, goodbye!" he said.

"Goodbye," St. James said through gritted teeth, waiting. Almost reluctantly, the fellow left. Eventually St. James' bladder did its work. St. James did his best to wash his hands and face using paper towels made from recycled railroad timbers. Cupping one hand, he bent his head down to the faucet and slurped water. He left the bath and took the narrow stairs three flights down to street level, exiting the building just as the landlady approached with a cop in tow.

Thrusting one hand in his jacket pocket, St. James booked. The hand encountered a piece of paper. St. James hot-stepped it a block and turned the corner onto Uhelny Street where an outdoor cafe emitted the overwhelming odor of fresh coffee. He looked up at the clock on the bank across the street. It was one-thirty. He checked his pockets. Just enough cash for coffee and a pastry.

He waited for the frenzied traffic to die down. They all drove like madmen. He hot-footed across the street and slid onto one of the black wrought iron chairs chained to the wrought iron table which was chained to a wrought iron fence set in concrete. He set his guitar case on the chair next to him and slipped out of his backpack. A blue/black pigeon strutted his way with a hopeful gleam in its eye.

His hand found the piece of paper, and he drew it out. He was about to crumple it up and throw it away when he realized it might provide a clue as to where he'd been last night. Not that it was important. Strictly as a clinical exercise, the "Last Days of Ian St. James" and all that. He unfolded the sheet. It was a flyer for some place called the Phoenix Club; the date was for today. There was a graphic of a hand making the horned demon sign. The flyer said:

FOR ONE NIGHT ONLY
LEGENDARY ROCKERS
THE BANSHEES!

And then it hit him like a bunker buster. The Banshees died in 1975. He'd been two years old.

CHAPTER THREE

The Phoenix Club was on the second floor of a two story building on Strassburg Street, a narrow alley of trendy shops, cafes, and clubs off Platnerska Street, not far from the University. The doors opened at nine.

St. James spent the day hanging out at cafes and visiting the National Gallery, sitting for two hours before a little-known Hieronymus Bosch, which at first glance appeared to be a pastoral scene in a meadow but upon a closer look revealed scaly, pointed creatures lurking in the grass, feeding off the carcass of a crow, obscenely thrusting their spiked tongues at the viewer.

Metaphor for life, St. James thought. *It was best not to look too closely—in the gutter, at your fast food, at people's faces. You might not like what you see.* He did a few sketches. The uniformed guard gave him the hairy eyeball. At a quarter of seven, the guard came by and made a shooing motion with his hands.

"Out, out, museum is closing."

St. James wasted two hours over a cup of coffee in an Internet cafe surrounded by intense twenty-somethings hunched over iPads, Nooks, Blackberries, and Droids. St. James felt like a caveman. He'd been unable to check his Hotmail account in days, dependent as he was on the generosity of others. Usually, he would casually amble in through the side door of a big hotel, the kind with free Internet business center for its guests, hover and time his visit.

Occasionally, a man in uniform would inquire if he were a guest.

The Internet cafe was across the street from the Phoenix Club. St. James watched as a group began to gather beneath the small marquee advertising FOR ONE NIGHT ONLY! THE LEGENDARY BANSHEES! Soon there was quite a throng. St. James glanced at his cheap digital watch. Nine fifteen. They should have opened up by now.

As if reading his thoughts, a man appeared inside the glass door leading to the stairs and opened the door. There was a nip in the air despite being the middle of June, and the crowd hastily entered, forming a queue on the stairs. St. James left ten korunas, slipped into his backpack, grabbed his guitar case, and headed across the street.

He had no place to spend the night. At the moment, he wasn't concerned about that. What concerned him was that some band was illegally benefiting from his dead father's good name and work. Certainly there were no Banshees revival bands, but the songs still got played on college radio stations, there was still some attraction. Witness the crowd which continued to flow into the narrow stairs behind him until it backed out into the street.

Why were these kids there? The Banshees weren't their music or their generation. These kids dropped ecstasy and boogied to Mika or German electronica. Like jazz-rock, heavy metal had had its day. The attraction these days was mainly ironic, witness the Osbournes. The man who once snorted a line of ants reduced to mugging for Letterman. The stairwell smelled of hair spray and body odor. A sign near the top said in Czech, German, French, and English: "ABSOLUTELY NO RECORDING DEVICES OR CAMERAS."

The creature collecting money and stamping hands at the top of the stairs looked like an ex-con with his shaved head and jailhouse tats. He grinned wolfishly as St. James forked over fifty korunas.

The man stamped St. James' hand and said in a Russian accent, "I don't think they'll welcome anyone from the audience," indicating St. James' guitar case.

St. James smiled self-consciously. "I'm just lugging it around."

The ticket taker slowly waved a finger in the air. "No recording. Enjoy the show."

St. James entered the long, low-ceilinged club. He looked at his hand. The ink stamp was of a hand making the devil's horns—the Banshees' trademarked insignia. A dozen little round tables filled the floor with five booths at the back—toward the street—with windows looking out. The back of the room away from the street held the stage, which held three expectant black microphones, a drum kit, guitar, bass, and Yamaha electronic keyboard.

St. James quickly took the last empty booth, setting his guitar case and backpack on the bench seat across from him. He looked out on Strassberg. Tuner VWs and Hondas blipped up and down the street as kids continued to arrive, some by bicycle.

At nine-thirty a tall woman with lavender-colored, dandelion hair and a purple dress took one of the mics, which squealed like a stuck pig. Seconds later, the feedback died down. St. James glanced to his right where a man controlled the sound system from a small booth set against the far wall.

The woman spoke in Czech over the booming PA system which modulated before she finished a short statement. In English, she said, "Welcome to the Phoenix Club! I have a few announcements. Next week, Friday, we are featuring Pander Bear and Fool's Gerund. On Saturday, we are hosting a benefit for International Hunger Relief with five bands.

"Now I would like to present to you some very talented folks from right here in Prague, Greta and the Garbos!"

There was some clapping as three girls dressed in black with black eyeliner, one with jet-black hair, one with bright yellow hair, and one with orange hair took the stage. They carried their own instruments except for the drums. The lead singer and guitarist shrieked in Czech while the bass player and drummer struggled to keep time. St. James reached into his backpack and removed a set of Flent's Ear Stopples without which he would have lost all hearing by now.

St. James leaned back, pulled out his sketchpad and a pen, and sketched what he saw, which was the club. He worked his way methodically through three Zatec Pale Ales. He sketched an odd little fellow who looked like a troll, squat with a full gray beard, rimless glasses. The man wore a safari jacket stretched tight over his medicine ball belly and had to be in his sixties. Go figure. For the first time that day St. James began to feel better. His hangover had finally withdrawn. Hair of the dog.

Greta and the Garbos drove a dozen people from the club, and those that remained were not reluctant to share their opinions. Boos and catcalls filled the air. This only seemed to goad the three Goth girls to greater displays of sonic intransigence, until at last, the tall woman in the purple hair strode smiling to the lead singer and wrested the microphone away.

She spoke in Czech, then in English. "Let's hear it for Greta and the Garbos, ladies and gentlemen!"

A cacophony of boos and catcalls filled the room. Purple Hair tamped it down with her hands. "All right, we all know what you're waiting for. The Banshees will be up shortly."

Cheers and whistles.

It was past midnight, and the crowd was getting surly before Purple Hair reappeared with the same shit-eating grin plastered across her puss. "Thank you for your patience!" she said in Czech.

The audience hooted and cursed.

"Fuck you!" someone yelled.

Purple Hair smiled and said, "And now, the legendary Banshees!"

Everybody started whooping and got to their feet. Whistles, stomping, incoherent exhortations. St. James couldn't see the stage, but from the reaction of the audience, the Banshees were taking their places. A minute later, a deep electronic hum permeated the room and faded away. The drummer played a tight descending rhythm and the band launched into "Camel Toe," pure metal raunch as Paddy expertly stroked the keyboard and Cunar laid down bass as big as the Continental Shelf. They started off a little ragged, but by the time they hit the bridge they had it down.

They sounded exactly like the Banshees. St. James had only heard them on record and in old videos. When the band segued seamlessly into "Black Cat Fever," he heaved himself to his feet and tried to see over the bobbing heads, at least a hundred.

St. James got up on his bench seat and stared through the haze. Where was that smoke coming from? He saw the three Banshees bent over their axes, the drummer's head tilted back in ecstasy. The audience spontaneously clapped to the irresistible beat.

When the song ended, the audience responded with wild applause, whistles, fist pumps, and shouts of enthusiasm. For a moment, the drummer paused beaming at the audience. He could not have been older than twenty-seven.

That's him, St. James realized. *That's my father.*

CHAPTER FOUR

The visceral shock of recognition made St. James dizzy. He sat down.

How was it possible?

He'd heard all the stories. At school they'd teased him mercilessly about his dead druggie father, breathlessly repeating every rumor and sordid tale. The time Oaian hired three German hookers. The time Oaian rushed offstage to hospital to combat a virulent case of gonorrhea. In *I Slept with the Banshees*, Barbara Glieberman-Gronsky (1981) claimed both Paddy and Oaian had nine-inch units and compared them favorably with Mick Jagger.

The Banshees' dark and powerful music had filled Ian's youth. He read every scrap he could find on the band. A psychiatrist might suggest he was trying to compensate for the father he never knew by studying the man obsessively so as to build an idealized version in his imagination.

That wasn't it. St. James understood his old man had been a druggie and a lout. It went with the territory. St. James believed that he'd inherited his love for music and modest talents from Oaian, and for that reason alone, he was grateful.

Squaring what he saw with the rational world wasn't possible. Had Oaian lived, he'd be at least sixty-five. Yet the drummer was the spitting image. More than that, St. James felt a connection. He wasn't a mystical man, not even religious.

He reckoned Oaian was neither, as well. Nobody believed that Satanic rubbish! It was just to sell records.

His only recourse was to go backstage after the performance and see the man himself. St. James thought of a fourth pint, but he was already slippery and had hardly eaten all day. With 17 korunas in his pocket, he wasn't likely to be sleeping between clean sheets either. He settled back and enjoyed the show.

The Banshees tore through their set with verve and professionalism. Between songs, Paddy bantered with the audience. "Didn't think you'd see us lot again, did ya? 'Ow you like Cerberus, then?"

Dozens of hands thrust skyward showing the devil's horns. The band played another kinetic rocker with a terrific backbeat. Paddy's words were occasionally lost in the garble. Or he might have been speaking in tongues.

St. James wondered if Paddy would drop trou. It had been a bone of contention between the band and local municipalities.

Cunar leaned into his mike to add the high harmony to Paddy's rough wail. After a fast and furious forty-five minutes, Paddy panted, "That's all we got time for, you lot!"

"Moloch Loves Me!" shot back from the crowd. Others took up the chant. Soon the whole club was chanting "MOLOCH LOVES ME!"

Paddy shrugged and grinned. The will of the people. With a glance at Cunar and a tap of his foot, he tore into their signature song. St. James put his Flents back in. He hated the song. Hated what it stood for and what people said it stood for. They took it *accelerato*, and the crowd morphed into a frenzy of pogoing bodies. There were always a couple thugs in any audience who used the mosh pit as an excuse to slam into people. A scuffle broke out in front of the stage.

St. James was glad he was seated in the back of the room, observing the sudden spastic motion of people either trying to escape or joining the fray. The scuffle spilled onto the stage. The band stopped playing.

"'At's it, folks!" Paddy called. "See you next time!" The band filed offstage toward the dressing rooms in the rear.

Purple Hair took the mike. She stuttered something in Czech, repeated it in English, "Th-th-th-that's all folks! Thank you for coming."

The crowd was jacked up, exhilarated by the music, hungry for blood or sex or drugs. They poured down the stairs into the street and fanned out, some heading home, others heading toward clubs that stayed open all night. St. James remained seated at the booth looking out the window as the patrons flowed from the door like the Mississippi delta.

There was still some kind of disturbance in front of the stage. By the time the patrons had left, the band too had disappeared leaving Purple Hair, a swarthy Greek-looking guy in a white shirt with an open collar showing gold chains, and the skinhead ticket taker standing around a body directly in front of the stage. It appeared to be a young man, sprawled on his side and glassy-eyed. The skinhead prodded the man with his toe. There was no response.

St. James shouldered his backpack picked up his guitar and headed to the stage. The skinhead looked at him as he approached.

"What's up?" St. James said.

"No business of yours, sir," the skinhead said.

St. James went right up to them and joined the circle looking down at the dead man. He could see no visible signs of injury. A stroke?

"I'm Ian St. James. My Da is Oaian St. James, and I'd like to see him."

The skinhead assumed a guffaw without making a sound. His upper jaw thrust itself into a disbelieving overbite. "Sir, the drummer is twenty-eight years old. How can you be his son?"

Sighing, St. James unslung his backpack, set it on the ground and fished around in one of the pockets. He withdrew a well-creased ten by twelve glossy black and white photo of the band, the type press agencies released, and held it up. There was Oaian, not much different as he had just appeared, along with Paddy and Cunar. Across the bottom it read, "THE BANSHEES—copyright Melchior Management 1974."

"This band?"

The skinhead took the glossy gently from St. James' hand and stared at it. "I can't deny that's them."

"See the copyright? Nineteen seventy-four. So the question is, if he ain't my Da, who the hell is he? Who are those other guys? I mean what the fuck? They all died in a plane crash in 1975."

The Greek guy followed the conversation like a spectator at Wimbledon. St. James didn't think he understood English. The body at their feet was forgotten.

"Look," said Purple Hair, "We're closed. You have to leave."

St. James looked from her to the body. "You appear to have a dead man here. Has anyone notified the police?"

"We'll handle that," the woman said, and sprayed Czech at the Greek-looking guy.

"Look," St. James said. "Here's the deal. I'm tired. But I'm not leaving until I see that drummer guy. Otherwise, I go straight to the gendarmes."

Purple Hair exchanged a glance with the skinhead, who gave an imperceptible nod.

"Go with Kaspar," she said.

CHAPTER FIVE

ust my luck! Kaspar thought. He'd forgotten about Ian, the Banshees' sole legitimate heir, although all three had spread their seed from Berlin to Los Angeles. Ian had been a footnote in the Banshees' hagiography, the unlucky son of a notorious parent. Julian Lennon, Tal Bachman, Arlo Guthrie.

Well, at least this one hadn't killed anyone. Yet. The question was how was Kaspar to get rid of him? Bothering the band at this stage with family bullshit could derail the train. On the other hand, Oaian was just as likely to deny parentage no matter how much they resembled each other.

And they resembled each other. Even a blind man could see that.

Kaspar couldn't possibly tell him the truth. Then he'd have to kill him and that would be problematic. So Kaspar stalled.

He might have to kill him anyway.

"Well, ah, let's just give them a minute to decompress. Every band needs that."

St. James looked down at him with lugubrious eyes. Where had that Viking gene come from? "Are you the roadie?"

Kaspar flashed his wolfie grin. "Roadie, manager, wet nurse, and kapo."

"You ever done this before?"

Kaspar shrugged dramatically. "I've been managing bands for ten years. Solis, the Brocktons, Stanislaus?" He looked up at St.

James, his blue eyes searching for recognition. Nada.

"I could really use a shot of vodka. Can I buy you a drink?"

The tall man looked longingly at the bar where the bartender, a young man with a severe haircut, was wiping up.

"Why not?"

They went to the bar. "Manfred, my friend," Kaspar said, "how about a couple of White Russians?"

The bartender nodded and went to work, expertly blending the liquors in large cut glass tumblers. Kaspar watched in the mirror as the Greek looking guy and a rangy kid in blue jeans picked up the corpse and carried it back toward the dressing rooms where they would carry it down the back stairs, load it in a car, and dump it out in the countryside.

Idiot took too much ecstasy. Happened all the time. Kaspar really had managed bands, and the last thing he wanted was to cause trouble for the venue. It had been difficult enough getting the booking. And costly. Kaspar watched his companion, whose attention was riveted on the cocktail.

Manfred set the drinks on the bar. Kaspar and St. James picked them up.

"Cheers," Kaspar said, taking a sip and watching as St. James tilted the glass, his Adam's apple bobbing until the drink was gone. Kaspar signaled Manfred for another. The body was gone, and St. James hadn't even noticed.

"So what brings you to Prague?" Kaspar said.

"Fuckin' club offered me a gig. When I showed up, it had burned down."

"Ah, would that be the Zipper Club? Terrible, just terrible. Two people died, you know."

"I didn't hear 'at. So here I am, high and dry without two kopeks to rub together. I don't even know where I'm spendin' the night."

Kaspar nodded. Now he understood. St. James was looking to cash in, borrow a few bob from the old man. How much would it take for the troubadour to abandon his quest?

How had he heard about it in the first place? Their only advertising had been the handbills set out at other clubs. Of all the cursed luck! But wait a minute. Perhaps Kaspar could turn this goat fuck into stew. Who better to tell the world, "yes, they're back," than the drummer's own wee lad?

That raised all sorts of problems of the time travel sort. It made Kaspar's brain hurt. It would have been better if St. James had never shown up. It would have been better if St. James had never been born. As St. James drained half of his second drink, the answer came to Kaspar in a ray of light. Casually, he felt in his pocket for a rufie. He was no rock star and had to take what he could get.

Kaspar pointed toward the windows. "Look at that."

As St. James dutifully followed the finger, Kaspar dropped the rufie in his drink.

"What?"

"Didn't you see it? A pigeon trying to get in. Fellow like you, you shouldn't be scrabbling for gigs in dumps like this! Your name should be up in lights." Kaspar noted the hopeful gleam in St. James' eyes.

"You got that right. I'm writing a new album ... a new album ..."

Kaspar signaled for another drink.

Later, long after the band had left, Kaspar helped the tall troubadour down the rear stairs.

CHAPTER SIX

here was a mechanical swooshing sound followed by a bone-rattling impact, as of Thor's hammer striking the earth. It repeated at regular intervals along with the shriek of tortured metal. St. James got to where he dreaded the onset of the swoosh because he knew that within seconds it would be followed by the impact.

He just wanted to sleep.

St. James woke up. He was cramped and hot, head filled with cotton. A few beams of light barely illuminated the tight, cramped quarters in which he was confined. He looked at his watch. It was eleven AM. The last thing he remembered was going back to meet the band.

He never met the band.

After that it got hazy. He remembered the Russian. Kaspar. Kaspar Sinaiko. Giving him a ride? *Jesus*, he realized, *I'm in a trunk!* Another sound entered his befuddled confinement, some kind of tractor. It would approach, gears whining followed by adjustments and then it would roll away.

SWOOOSH—THWACK!

What the fuck was it?

St. James felt around. His guitar case and backpack had been thrown in with him. He adjusted himself as best he could and saw that the beams of light were entering through rust holes in the trunk lid.

"Hey!" he yelled. It came out a phlegmy croak. He pounded on the lid with his fists. The sound was blotted out by the tractor, and the *SWOOOSH—THWACK!* He suddenly felt nauseous. The tight confines, dust, and heat were unbearable. He kicked and screamed like a madman. He swiveled in the impossibly tight confines and kicked against the backs of the rear seat. No give there.

The tractor approached, and this time it was for him. Amid the stink of diesel, long metal arms slid beneath the chassis with a hair-raising screech. A second later, the chassis rose into the air to the accompaniment of whining hydraulics, the sudden motion making his gorge rise.

Frantic now, St. James swept the interior looking for something, anything. His hands encountered the jack, held in place by a spring grip. He worked it loose, searching for the jack handle. Oh, where was it? He was screaming quietly to himself now, breath grating in and out between clenched teeth. The car wobbled precariously as the tractor headed toward the source of the massive crushing sound.

St. James' hand slid beneath his guitar case and closed around a cool metal rod. The jack handle! No time to place the shoe which he couldn't find anyway. He planted the jack's narrow base just before the trunk opening, placed the handle in the ratchet and cranked. The jack went down!

The tractor delivered St. James' vehicle onto a scarred metal plate, which he could see through rust holes in the floor. Desperately fumbling, St. James reversed the ratchet, cutting his thumb open and bleeding profusely over his hands. Twisted in the tight confines, he cranked the jack and this time it rose. He cranked as fast as he could, cramps forming in his neck and shoulder.

The hydraulic intake of breath was deafening. If he was going to get out of there, he had to do it right away. He cranked and cranked. The trunk dimpled where the top of the jack forced its way up. Whimpering in frustration St. James continued to crank.

Suddenly there was light! The trunk sprang open. St. James sat up.

"STOP THE PRESSES!" he yelled.

A startled technician in coveralls and a hard hat goggled hard before lurching forward and ripping back the controls for the car press. St. James looked up. A metal slab the size of a handball court halted with a hiss of steam six inches above the car's roof. St. James threw out his guitar case and backpack, heaved himself over the bumper, and landed on the hot metal of the press. He looked up as the yellow forklift slid rails beneath another junker.

The tech ran forward, shouting in Czech, followed moments later by a man in hard hat, white shirt, and tie, his face a mask of shock. St. James could only lie there fearing to move, fearing another gagging bout.

Will I never learn?

The man in the white shirt said something in Czech with overtones of concern and anger. St. James couldn't blame him.

"English," St. James gasped. "I'm English."

"What are you doing here?!" the man shouted. Then, "Are you all right?"

St. James leaned over the lip of the slab and vomited up a thin yellow gruel. The man in the tie stepped back. St. James wiped his mouth on his sleeve.

"Aside from being sick to my stomach, yes, I think so. I don't know what I'm doing here. What is this place?"

"Mayerik Auto Salvagers. How did you get in the trunk?"

St. James watched horrific realization steal across the man's face.

"What do you think? Somebody put me there. They drugged me and put me in the trunk. It's a miracle I'm not a bloody pancake."

"You would have been had you not woken up. And we are running an hour late today, so you are very lucky."

St. James looked up at the vehicle he'd just escaped. A Mercedes. The trunk was by no means small.

"Do you know a Kaspar Sinaiko?" St. James asked. He'd written the name in his sketchpad during the night.

The manager looked confused. "Can you stand? Come with me. You can't stay here. We are behind schedule."

St. James slid on his pants to the edge of the steel platform and let himself slowly down. He could barely walk. The manager supported him as they stumbled toward the office of the salvage yard, located in the middle of towers of crushed steel.

"My guitar and backpack," St. James said.

"Yes, yes, I get them in a minute."

The office was a one-story pre-fab with a roof mounted air conditioner. The blessed cold revived St. James somewhat as he stumbled into a steel chair and accepted a cup of water. The manager was clearly concerned about the legal implications. St. James had no intention of calling the police. He would only draw attention to himself as an itinerant drunk. But the manager didn't know that. He drained the glass and held it out for more. The manager refilled it. He drained it.

"You say you don't know a Kaspar Sinaiko? Bald, all tatted up?"

The manager shook his head. He had a square head and black horn-rimmed glasses. "No, of course not. I'm the day manager. Jerzy Schimmel."

"How did that car get in the lot?"

"It was in loading dock this morning. The police frequently tow derelicts here if there is no crime involvement."

"I've got to get my things."

"Wait here." The manager rose and left the office. St. James looked around. Desk, fairly new flat-screen computer, rows of metal filing cabinets. He heaved himself up and over to the desk, files neatly stacked. He sat in the creaky steel office chair and riffled through the stack of papers on the left. He came to a promotional post card: "MAYERIK AUTO SALVAGE—A DIVISION OF THE SKORZNY GROUP."

He tucked it in his jacket, heaved himself up, and plopped back into the steel chair as the manager reentered the office carrying the guitar case and the backpack.

"You are musician?"

St. James took his backpack and opened it up. "I try to be." He rummaged around. "Oh, no. Oh, bloody hell, no! I don't fuckin' believe it!"

"What is the problem?"

"The fuckin' bastard that locked me in that trunk robbed me! I had one thousand korunas in here! May I borrow your phone?

I'm calling the police."

The manager held his hands up in a placating manner. "Let's not be hasty. What if we were to make it up to you?"

St. James did his best to look suspicious. "Why would you do that? Here this bastard tried to kill me. God knows how many other poor saps have been turned into pancakes." *Around here.*

"We're in a probationary period right now," the manager said. "We really can't afford any police involvement."

St. James noted that the manager had left out the word "more." As in, *We really can't afford any* more *police involvement.*

"Well, I don't know. I've been through absolute hell. I was supposed to leave for Berlin last night."

"What is your name?"

"Ian St. James."

"Mr. St. James, how would it be if we reimbursed you for the thousand koruna and took you wherever you want to go? Would you consider letting the matter go?"

St. James rubbed his head and looked rueful. "Do you know what it's like, being coshed on the head, shoved into a trunk, and left for dead?"

Schimmel steepled his fingers. "Two thousand koruna?"

CHAPTER SEVEN

From his second story bedroom hovering over Selden Canyon, Burke Melchior could see a slice of the blue Pacific between the hills. He stretched luxuriously, sitting up in his Louis XIV four-poster, inhaling the crisp scent of eucalyptus on the morning breeze. Like him, eucalyptus was not native to the United States. It had come from Australia and pretty much taken over the west-facing slopes of the state.

Melchior had come from England as a brash, twenty-eight-year-old hustler representing a handful of Brit bands and had clawed his way to the pinnacle. Melchior and Associates represented dozens of the most important acts in show biz, specializing in stadium rock. While Lilith Tour, and even the Rolling Stones, played to half-empty stadiums, Melchior's acts packed them in. His clients included Grimjack, Strontium 90, and Charon. Charon was currently embarked on a sixteen-city tour of Europe due to play Berlin the next evening.

Melchior used to go on the road with his acts, but he had fewer clients back then, less clout, and more time. Now he was an industry. A Godfather of Hollywood. A-list actors and top producers came to him hat in hand. "Godfather, be my friend?" An Oscar for Best Movie graced the Tudor bedroom's fireplace mantle beneath a pair of crossed cutlasses. *Disco*, the story of a boy and his dog. Melchior had enough gold records to tile a foyer larger than most people's apartments.

The enticing scent of fresh roast coffee drifted in on the morning breeze. Melchior glanced at the slight indentation made by Melissa, his twenty-four-year-old live-in girlfriend. A keeper. He had a nice little project lined up for her, a slasher film called *Helmet Head*, about a seven-foot-tall motorcyclist, dressed all in black leather, who slices off the heads of other cyclists with his samurai sword. Melchior didn't kid himself that Melissa was Katherine Hepburn or even Marisa Tomei, but in the right project, in the right costume, she would drive the fan boys crazy. He planned to unveil her at the San Diego Comic-Con International in July.

She could even sing a little.

"Melissa baby!" he called from the bed in a faint Cockney accent which he'd never bothered to disguise despite what Geffen told him. "Coffee?"

"Just a sec, hon," echoed from down the hall. Shivering in the morning chill, Melchior pulled on a Lakers' hoodie lying next to the bed. Even on the hottest days the house remained cool, manufacturing its own shadow. In the mild Southern California winter, the house verged on freezing. Melchior saved big-time on air conditioning bills but lost it during the winter.

Seconds later, Melissa appeared in a diaphanous blue kimono, pure sex, carrying a silver tray with two steaming mugs of shade-grown Sumatran coffee and a cell phone.

"Babe, there's a guy on the line, Ian St. James, says he's an old friend of yours, and he has to talk to you."

Melchior swung his hairy legs over the side of the bed. He was a fur-covered mesomorph of Serbian extraction. A gold Star of David nestled in his curly steel chest hair. Daily workouts with a personal trainer kept his sixty-five-year-old gut at bay. His perfect teeth represented state of the art dentistry. Not only were they the whitest white, they glowed in the dark. He had shaved his muscular bare skull, surrounded at ear level by a smoke-colored shadow.

His gray/green eyes widened in surprise. "Ian St. James? You're having me on." He reached for the phone. "Ian! How the fuck *are* you?"

"I'm in Berlin, Burke. The Banshees are back."

Mike Baron

Melchior pasted a silly grin across his face, default setting for
when he was gobsmacked. For an instant, his stomach lurched,
and he had that sick feeling he had once in Simpson's Lear trying
to land in Phoenix during a thunderstorm, when the plane hit a
downdraft and lost all gravity and control for a second, and
Melchior had been convinced he was going to die. He swallowed
the sick feeling and straightened his head.

"Excuse me?"

Melchior heard St. James take a breath. "I saw them last night
at the Phoenix Club in Prague. Go to their website. Look it up.
They're playing the K-99 Club tomorrow night in Friedrichshain.
I saw them, Burke. They bloody well looked like the band!"

"Looked like the band how?" Melchior asked, more to fill
space than from honest inquiry. St. James' absurd statement had
upset the delicate balance of spinning plates Melchior kept in his
head. It did not compute. The Banshees had been Melchior's first
act, the first astonishing success that led to everything else. Of
course, nothing good is ever free. The Banshees had also been the
source of unending grief over the years, from the church and
synagogue condemnations to the endless lawsuits. The League of
Decency for Christ's fucking sake! If they could come back from
the dead, why not the Banshees? Melchior tried not to think
about the Banshees. But, of course, he thought about them every
day.

Maybe he was still asleep. Unfortunately, Burke Melchior was
far too hard-nosed to fall for the old "it was all a dream"
sequence. That's why he'd passed on producing *Shelter Island*.

"I mean," St. James said through clenched teeth, "it was the
bloody band as if they hadn't aged a day! Either that or spittin'
fuckin' images of them."

"Did you take pictures?" Melchior said, trying to process this
information. The Banshees? Was it a joke? Had years of drug use
finally turned St. James into a full-bore paranoid schizophrenic?
What did he expect Melchior to do about it? Melchior had gone
to bat for St. James once too often. The man was a tosser and a
drug addict, and was stalling for an explanation. Melchior couldn't
go on bailing out this *schlimazel* forever, no matter what the boy's
father had meant to him.

"I don't have a cell phone anymore. I'm using a pay phone."

"Are you on drugs?"

"Some bastard slipped me a mickey last night, that's the only drug I'm on. Still can't shake the cotton."

"Are you drinking?"

"Come on, Burke! This isn't about my sad ass life! I know I sound crazy, but I'm not. I've never been crazy. Stupid and stubborn, maybe, but not crazy! There's something going on here—they looked like fuckin' clones! And the music, the music was perfect! You need to get your bum out here and take a look."

Melchior glanced at his watch. It was eleven. He had a one o'clock with Serafin at the Trai-San Asian Grill in Santa Monica. "Give me a number where you can be reached. I'll call you back in an hour."

"Okay, listen. I've got a little money, I'll buy a cell phone and give you the number. Who was that answered the phone? Your new bird?"

"Melissa. Are you all right, Ian? Seriously."

"I'm a bit hyper. Who wouldn't be, seeing their father as he was as a lad?"

"Do you realize how crazy that sounds?"

"There's something happening here. I don't understand it. Last night when I tried to get backstage to see if it was really them, this Russian fucker slipped me a mickey and set me up to get crushed in a fuckin' car compactor, if you can believe that. I barely escaped."

St. James' story just kept getting crazier. He'd never been one of those crash and burn sorts who, unable to exist in the glare of their celebrity fathers, either committed suicide or killed somebody in a car or boat crash. Ian had always struck Melchior as one of the more grounded celebrity scions, possibly because he'd been spared his father's drunken debauchery during his formative years. Melchior knew from personal experience that having a father was no guarantee of a happy childhood.

Was it better to have a drunk, irresponsible, drug-addicted and possibly Satan-worshiping father or no father at all?

"Are you all right?" Melchior said again.

"I'm fine. Listen. Write this down. Kaspar Sinaiko."

Melchior snapped his fingers at Melissa who sat in a salon chair sipping coffee from an enormous mug. Melchior mimed writing. Melissa picked up a pen from the dressing table next to her and tossed it to Melchior who caught it one-handed. He peeled off a Post-it note from a stack on the headrest. "Okay—go ahead."

St. James spelled the man's name.

"I'll look into it. In the meantime, hang tight."

"I'll be waiting," St. James said.

CHAPTER EIGHT

Melchior phoned his personal assistant, Stanton Bridger, who lived on premises in what had once been servants' quarters, and told him about St. James. Melchior showered in the oversized stall, dressed in sharp creased khakis, a Badger T-shirt, and Sketchers sandals. In Tinsel Town, the more successful you were the more casually you dressed.

He went online in his second floor office and checked out St. James' claim. A band called the Banshees had played the Phoenix Club in Prague last night. Melchior didn't read Czech, but judging from the exclamation marks, the crowd had loved it. There was one grainy photo of the band taken from the rear of the crowd. A Popsicle slid down Melchior's spine. His stomach churned and produced a nugget of fear instantly erased by the righteous flame of anger.

I found the Banshees. I made the Banshees.

Melchior googled Kaspar Sinaiko. Bupkus.

Bridger waited in the foyer when Melchior descended the broad, curving stair. Bridger was a thin, intense man of about fifty with a Dick Powell mustache, eager as a terrier. Bridger appeared to have no life of his own. He was on call 24/7. He handed Melchior a clipboard with the day's appointments and notes.

"Stanton, I want you to pick up my dry cleaning at Fung's and call your friend with the Hollywood PD. I can't have Melissa driving around without a license. Do you follow?"

"I follow, boss."

"Get hold of Freddie. Have him meet me at my office at three, and get hold of Stan Schaefer. Set up an appointment for tomorrow if you can." Freddie Guttierez was an ex-Mex gangbanger who did odd jobs for Melchior. Schaefer was one of his lawyers.

"I'm on it, boss."

"Okay. You know where to find me. Meet me at the office."

Carrying a leather backpack containing his laptop, Melchior walked to his free-standing four port garage. He chose the Boxster with the top down. He was not a flaunter, except for the house, of course. And that had been fate. The house had belonged to Melchior's mentor, teen producing sensation Chad Goodrich, who'd brought the Scottish manor house over from England in the sixties, stone by stone. Goodrich had installed a bowling alley and built a state of the art recording studio in the basement and once went eight years without leaving, sending out for meals, women, drugs, and talent.

Years ago they had walked these grounds, Goody's arm around the bigger man's shoulder. "Someday this will all be yours, Burke," Goody had joked.

And now it was. Tragedy, of course, that Goodrich had killed himself, but everything happens for a purpose. As Goodrich's heir apparent, it was only right and proper that Melchior purchase the estate from Goodrich's dry-eyed parents who had long ago washed their hands of their famous son. Melchior even bought the urn containing Goodie's ashes. Kept it in his bedroom. Long-standing rumors that Melchior had had an affair with his mentor faded as Melchior's career waxed. Anyone suggesting Melchior might be a poofter could expect a visit from Freddie.

A handful of guests had even claimed to see Goodie's ghost wandering the grounds at the height of one of Melchior's bacchanals. A fifth of vodka and an eight ball of coke will do that for you.

Melchior slipped into the gray Boxster's seat, put on his Gracie sunglasses and a Dodgers cap, pushed the starter button and slipped into gear. His long, curving driveway ended at

Siddhartha Boulevard, which he took to Selden Canyon where he turned west toward the freeway. He left the Bluetooth headset in the glove compartment. He had to think about this.

It could be as simple as St. James losing his tenuous grip on reality. That would be a tragedy, especially after what father and son had meant to Melchior. Part of him wished it were so. It would make things so much simpler.

Second most likely scenario: it was some kind of half-assed tribute band, and if that were the case, Melchior's lawyers would land on them like SEAL Team 6. Hence the meeting with Schaefer.

Beyond that Melchior had no idea. He did not believe in reincarnation. He considered more outré possibilities. Could it be some new reality show, an upscale version of *Punk'd*? No one in their right mind would build a reality show around a loser like St. James, nor did they have the guts to jerk Melchior's chain. Reality show—out.

That left some awful practical joke. Those with the 'nads to attempt such a thing could be counted on one hand. Richard Serafin, Editor and Publisher of *In Crowd*, was among them. Maybe that's why Serafin had called the meet—to stick the needle in. But where was the joke? What did Serafin expect, that Melchior would react like a jilted teenager and key the Banshees' car? Melchior couldn't see it. There was no humor angle. He didn't grok "Gotcha!" Melchior's critics had often accused him of being humorless, but that wasn't the case. Melchior saw humor, he just didn't think it was funny.

Traffic was glacial on the Pacific Coast Highway. Melchior pulled out the Bluetooth and reached out in 360: actors, agents, lawyers, producers, caterers. He had two ex-wives and six children, five of whom hated him. The sixth was an aspiring actor and couldn't afford to hate him. Melchior hadn't asked for parenthood. Those damn bitches had tricked him into it. He thought about phoning Jason, the actor. His private line beeped. It was Stanton.

"St. James called and gave me a number."

"Text me. I'm driving. Did you get a hold of Freddie?"

"Three-thirty, your office."

Several cars ahead two low-riders were banging into each other and exchanging shots. "Gotta go," Melchior said.

The Trai San was located on Montana just off Ocean, one of those trendy nouveau Oriental sushi con chili con carne joints with a striped awning and chauffeured parking.

"Good to see you, Mr. Melchior," said the Viet maître d' as the lot attendant chirped out the Porsche. "Mr. Serafin is on the private veranda."

Melchior bopped fists with the maître d' and wended his way back through the industrial décor—the turned aluminum walls, the open ductwork, the stainless steel sconces—up a short stair, and out a sliding glass door to a raised patio with a peek of the beach. Serafin sat at the lone table in black silk T-shirt, black blazer, and Gargoyle sunglasses reading something off his iPad, probably dummies for the new *In Crowd*.

Serafin put the iPad down, smiled, and stood as Melchior approached. They embraced like long-lost buddies, pounding each other on the back. "What up, dawg?" the sixty-four-year-old Serafin growled. He'd begun publishing *In Crowd* out of his Studio City garage in 1967. It had a circulation of 3.2 million and annual advertising revenues in excess of 130 million. The ostensible reason for the meet was a cover story on Charon, now a legacy act, Heavy Metal, Satanic Division. This would be the 4th time in 21 years that *In Crowd* featured Charon on the cover.

Charon was playing the Berlin Hippodrome that evening. The Rolling Stones were opening.

Melchior unslung his backpack, plopped himself into the cushioned teak chair and turned to the expectant dewy young Vietnamese waiter of indeterminate sex. "Tonic water with a slice of lime, please, and a glass of ice on the side. Do you follow?"

The waiter bowed and withdrew.

"The sea bass special looks good," Serafin said.

"Rich, Ian St. James just phoned me."

"Ian! He's not in trouble, is he?"

"No more than usual. He told me the damnedest thing. He said he saw the Banshees last night, and that they're playing Berlin tomorrow night."

Serafin perused the papyrus menu. "That sounds pretty serious. I'd like to help him, but really. I've done enough."

"No, Rich, you don't understand. He saw a band last night he's convinced is the Banshees. I went online. A band called the Banshees played the Phoenix Club in Prague. There's a graphic."

Melchior pulled out his laptop. Within seconds he reached the Phoenix Club's website. For several seconds he stared in consternation. "They took it down. Probably got a letter from a lawyer."

"Who? I'm the injured party here, and I haven't done anything."

"What about St. James? He might be pissed that someone's making hay off the family name."

Melchior considered it. St. James wasn't stupid. But if he'd threatened legal action, wouldn't he have told Melchior? It seemed to Melchior that St. James intended for him to take action. He logged on and sent the Phoenix Club an e-mail:

Why did you remove the graphic of the Banshees from your website?

Sincerely,
Burke Melchior
Century City, California, USA

There. That ought to put the fear of God in 'em. The removal of the graphic took some of the teeth out of St. James' account and Melchior felt relieved. It was some shitty tribute band, and they would never play again.

Then he remembered he was to call St. James to confirm the Berlin deal.

"This isn't Ian's style," Melchior said. "He's not confrontational, and where is he gonna find a Czech lawyer to take his case? You know, he says he's getting ready to record a new album."

"So's Sly Stone," Serafin said as the waiter returned with Melchior's tonic water.

"I'm supposed to call him. He's in Berlin. Suppose he's right. Suppose the Banshees—or whoever these fucks are—are really playing tomorrow night? That's a story, Rich. Banshees back from the dead, no matter how you cut it."

"You ready to order or would you like a little more time?" the waiter said.

"I'll have the sea bass," Serafin said.

"Perfect," the waiter said.

"I'd like a tossed salad," Melchior said, "red lettuce, no lettuce spines, cherry tomatoes, sliced leek and gorgonzola cheese with the house dressing on the side, and bring me an order of crab cakes, please, do you follow?"

"Perfect."

The waiter withdrew.

Serafin crunched down on a stalk of celery from his Virgin Mary. "If these guys really are playing tomorrow night, I'm surprised you're not trying to shut them down."

"Give 'em a little rope," Melchior said. "I'm curious. But seriously. Do you have anyone over there who could make the scene?"

Serafin shrugged. "Connie Cosgrove. She's with Charon right now. You know that."

"How 'bout Connie hooks up with St. James, and they give their perspective on this thing? No matter who these guys think they are, that would make an interesting story, don't you think? 'Son of Banshees Drummer Confronts Fake Banshees Band'?"

Serafin smiled. "I like 'Satanic Rock Band Returns from the Dead' even better."

CHAPTER NINE

Melchior's office overlooked the Warner Bros. lot. The bright, airy second story room resembled a successful artist's loft with skylights and glass facing north and west. Framed posters of Melchior's bands and movies decorated the walls. There was even a Banshees poster gathering dust in one corner. Stanton was waiting in the foyer when Melchior entered.

"Stan Schaefer confirmed you for eleven o'clock tomorrow at his office. Connie Cosgrove meets with Ian St. James at noon tomorrow at the Park Inn Alexanderplatz. Here are your calls in descending order of importance." Stanton handed over a riff of papers which Melchior stuffed in his slacks.

"Book a ticket for Freddie for Berlin, so that he arrives no later than five PM. tomorrow their time, do you follow?"

"I follow, boss."

Stanton followed Melchior into the office where Melchior sat behind his free-form walnut slab desk. "Get Dan Kennedy on the phone."

Stanton speed-dialed the number. Dan Kennedy was a federal agent who had advised on several Melchior thrillers including *Sniffers*. Melchior flipped through scripts. *The Manchurian Dog. Beverly Hills Chihuahua 4. Burlesque 2. Jurassic Park VII. Mamacitas VI. Die Hard with a Payback.* He looked at the latest BO and internal memos.

"Agent Kennedy is on the line, boss."

Melchior switched to head set. "Thanks for taking my call, Dan."

"What can I do you for?"

"You know I used to manage a band called the Banshees …"

"I was a big fan back when I was young, dumb, and full of cum."

They laughed.

"Seems they're back, Dan. Or somebody trading off the name. The manager's name is Kaspar Sinaiko, and my informant tells me he looks like a con, possibly Russian. Could you check that out for me?"

"It may take a while, especially if I have to go through Interpol, but I'll do my best. How do you spell that?"

Melchior told him and promised that they would get together for lunch next week to discuss Kennedy's possible involvement with *Helmet Head*.

Melchior waved Stanton away just as Freddie Guttierez burst through the door wearing a chartreuse and magenta Hawaiian shirt over baggy cargo pants, a leather bag hanging over one shoulder. He was six foot three of Latin goodness with twinkling brown eyes, slicked-back hair, a Zapata mustache, and telltale laser scars creeping up his neck.

"Padron!" he sang, sinking back onto the brown Spanish sofa and running his hand along the arm as he always did. "Rich Corinthian leather!"

"How's she hangin', Freddie?"

"Hangin' and clangin' since I quit bangin'. What I can do for choo?" Freddie laid it on a little thick. His English was perfect when he chose.

"I want you to fly to Berlin today. There's a band playing tomorrow night called the Banshees. I want you to go to the gig, talk to the manager, find out who the hell they are, and ask them why I wasn't notified, do you follow?"

Freddie whipped out a spiral pad and a pen. "Fly to Berlin. See Banshees. Ax 'em why the fuck they don't notify you they're ripping off your good name. Got it. You want me to make this a memorable visit?"

"Use your own discretion. Suffice it to say, I'm not happy."

"*Padron*, when you are unhappy, Freddie is unhappy. So I will make them unhappy."

"That's my Federico."

"What about this part you want me to play?"

"*Helmet Head.* A biker dressed all in black leather who rides the rural byways of Kentucky slicing off the heads of other bikers with his samurai sword. This could be a franchise operation, Freddie."

"Do they get to see my face?"

"Uh, no. Not technically. There's a reveal at the end, but it's not exactly your face. Still, it's an important part, an actor's part. You will have to convey a great deal of emotion without speaking."

Freddie looked crestfallen. "I don't speak?"

"You don't understand. This is job security! This story has winner written all over it. There will be sequels. You'll become a guest at comic and horror conventions and when they see how good looking and well-spoken you really are there will be other offers. Look at Hugo Weaving. *V for Vendetta*! This could be your *Terminator*."

Freddie smiled. "Well, of course, when you put it that way …"

Stanton knocked and entered. "I have a five-thirty out of LAX on Virgin-Atlantic nonstop to Berlin arrives two-thirty tomorrow."

Melchior rubbed his hands together. "Excellent! Freddie, do you have your passport?"

Freddie patted his leather bag. "Right here."

"Stanton, get a limo to take Freddie to the airport. You don't have anything you can't put off, do you Freddie?"

"No, *Padron*."

Melchior made calls. The limo came. Stanton stood in the doorway.

"What?" Melchior said without looking up.

"Chief, would it be all right if I took a few days off next week so I can go up to San Fran and see my little girl?"

"Absolutely out of the question," Melchior said without looking up. "I need you here until this Banshees thing is resolved, do you follow?"

"I follow, boss."

"And for God's sake, get rid of that shirt. You look like a salesman."

CHAPTER TEN

St. James looked up at the gleaming glass façade of Park Inn Alexanderplatz. It had been a long time since he'd stayed in a four-star hotel, or even a two-star hotel. Serafin was rolling in dough to put his reporters up in places like this. St. James saw European editions of *In Crowd* at every newsstand.

The liveried doorman beneath the broad portico frowned as St. James walked toward the main entrance. St. James looked like a refugee from *Nashville*, wearing a grimy leather-fringed jacket, his dirty brown hair down to his shoulders, the shades, the floppy hat, and carrying a guitar case. He counted on being mistaken for a rock star, the only positive explanation for his appearance.

The cavernous lobby was chock-a-block with tourists, business people, and a football team. St. James looked around and located a sign for Spagos, the restaurant in which he was supposed to meet Connie Cosgrove. St. James had read Cosgrove's stories in *In Crowd*. She interviewed musicians and wrote music reviews. Every review had a food reference. "They offered up a spicy bouillabaisse of Southern-fried blues ..."

Spago was a big, loud room with hardwood floors and a blue plastic ceiling. As St. James paused at the maître d's station, he noted many tables filled with business men and women shouting at each other, into hand-held devices, or simply into the air. The aroma of food made St. James' stomach search for something to surround. The maître d', a blond young man in jacket, tie, and severely styled hair, popped up behind the rosewood station.

"Sir?"

Must look English, St. James thought. "Ian St. James. I'm supposed to meet Connie Cosgrove here."

"Yes, sir. I'll take you to her table. Would you like me to put your guitar in a safe place while you are dining?"

St. James scrutinized the young man. The guitar was all he had. But this was the Park Inn Alexanderplatz. And the young man was German. "All right, thank you."

The maître d' took the guitar case and set it beneath his station, out of sight. He picked up a menu resembling the Rosetta Stone and led the way back through the vast sea of chattering wheeler-dealers to a square table in the rear where a young woman bent over her laptop pecking away.

She looked up as St. James arrived. The waiter pulled out a chair.

"Ian St. James. Lovely to meet you," St. James said.

An angel's face framed by a halo of gold hair; heart-shaped lips, impossibly young. She proffered a purple-nailed hand. "Well hello! I'm very excited about this. I've always been a big Banshees fan."

St. James took the menu from the waiter, who clicked his heels and walked away.

"Jawohl, mein obersturmbanfuhrer," St. James muttered.

Connie giggled. "They are a bit formal. By the way. I really liked your first record."

"Bless you, darling." St. James' stomach rumbled like the start of the Baja 1000. *She must have heard that.*

"When are you going to put out another record?"

A crimson tide of shame and humiliation crept from St. James' collar as he recalled his last disastrous gig at the Whiskey in Los Angeles, where he had forgotten the words to songs, stumbled off the stage, and landed on his face. A young writer named Rulon Wexler made his bones maliciously detailing the whole thing for *Rolling Stone*: "Shit-faced and oblivious, St. James finished his set by crawling to the men's room."

No producer would touch St. James after that. Not even Dre.

Thank Christ it happened before the Internet or cell phones.

St. James put the menu down and smiled with sealed lips. A tiny crease appeared on Connie's perfect brow rendering her even more adorable. She'd noticed his discomfort.

"That's the sixty-four-thousand-dollar question, innit? If I play my cards right with this story, I might get another grab at the brass ring. What do you know about the Banshees?"

"I've read everything *In Crowd* has done, including two interviews with Paddy MacGowan, plus everything else that's available. There's a book called *Praise the Lord and Pass the Stratocaster* that deals with the whole satanic thing in some detail. Allegations of ritual sacrifice, self-mutilation, heavy shit. They pretty much said it was a good thing the band died in a plane crash or there would have been hell to pay. Oh, I'm sorry. Real classy, Connie. I mean, it's hard to realize I'm sitting here with Oaian St. James' son."

St. James shrugged. "I didn't know him. I have no memories of him. I watch old films of the band and try to imagine him as me father. Never could. Just a figure behind the drum kit. I 'eard every nasty rumor there is about me dad at school. They used to call me 'Spawn of Satan.'"

Connie's emerald eyes peered into his soul. Everything else disappeared. "You're joking."

"Nope. Spawn of Satan, that's me."

"It's a miracle you turned out as well as you did."

St. James barked, "I suppose you could say that! What's good here? I'm a starving artist."

"Everything is good. By the way, Richard is comping you while you're working on the story. I checked with the desk, and at the moment there are no vacancies."

"That's all right, Luv. This place ain't my stoyle."

"One thing I've always wondered," Connie said.

St. James looked at her expectantly.

"Why did they call themselves the Banshees? A banshee is by definition a female spirit."

St. James shrugged. "Fuck if I know. I once asked Freddie Mercury why they called the band Queen, and he curled up regally and said, 'I don't know, darling, it was just the most awful name we could come up with.'"

The waiter came. St. James ordered Sauerbraten and a 20 oz. stein of Hacker-Pschorr. Connie, who offered a tantalizing hint of cleavage in her black and pink sweater, ordered chicken salad and cranberry juice.

Connie reached across the table and laid one elegant finger on the back of St. James' hand, sending an electric thrill up his arm. "Here's what I'd like—let's go to the club at the sound check and try to talk to the band. Ideally, you will ask that man posing as Oaian by what right does he presume to trade on your loss?"

"Like I said, I hardly knew Oaian."

"Whatever you feel comfortable with, but introduce yourself. I will have my trusty little vid cam. Later, we'll see the show, and I'll write a review. Your job, as I understand it, is to provide me with background detail and try to get them to admit they're a hoax and who put 'em up to it. You don't have a conflict do you?"

"I'm all yours."

CHAPTER ELEVEN

T he Law Offices of Mandell and Schaefer occupied their own glass cube in Century City, a cross between an aluminum water tower and the Russian Tea Room. Normally, a client of Melchior's stature did not visit his lawyer. His lawyer came to him. But showbiz lawyer Schaefer was in demand and had to shuffle appointments to make room for Melchior.

Melchior bulled by the helpful staff, holding up a palm to indicate he knew the way and was in a hurry. Schaefer's door was open, Schaefer talking to someone via headset, his tasseled loafers up on the battleship-gray desk. He motioned for Melchior to take a seat.

"I'm sorry Ms. Main," Schaefer said. "My client is adamant. Either you change the title or we will sue."

Beat. Schaefer winked at Melchior. Melchior found that trait irritating. He did not like to be winked at, not even by glamorous movie stars. He looked around the office. Nice impressionist—could it be a real Cézanne—law certificates, photos of Schaefer with his two daughters sailing on his 45-foot yacht, Schaefer with Arnold, Schaefer with Jerry Brown.

"All right," Schaefer said. "We look forward to hearing from you tomorrow. Good day."

Schaefer put his feet on the floor and stood to shake hands across the desk. He was a jovial man with curly red hair cropped short and big bifocals.

"'Preciate you're making time for me," Melchior said. He sat on the leather sofa diagonal to the desk.

Schaefer folded his hands on the desk in front of him. "We're dealing with intellectual property rights in the EU. Fortunately, the EU has very strong rules on that. Unfortunately, it can be a bear to enforce, especially in Czechoslovakia."

"They're playing Berlin tonight," Melchior said.

"Better. Obviously, it's too late to get an injunction, but maybe something as simple as a letter will get the job done. After all, these are kids, I mean, if the reports are accurate."

"I got something better than a letter," Melchior said. "I sent Freddie to deliver a message up close and personal. With any luck, there will be no performance tonight."

Schaefer pursed his lips. "What's Freddie going to do? Berlin isn't East L.A."

"He's just going to lean on them a little. Freddie can be surprisingly effective as a negotiator."

Schaefer took off his glasses and rubbed his eyes. "I'm not sure that's such a good idea."

Melchior spread his hands. "Too late. Done deal."

"What do you want me to do?"

"Get the legal thing in motion. I need a back-up plan in case Freddie falls through."

"Why don't you call Freddie off, and I'll see what I can do."

"No can do."

"Burke. Of course you can. Pick up the phone."

"I'm not going to do that, Stan. These people have got to learn that Burke Melchior is not someone you want to cross, do you follow?"

"That's your call. I just hope you're not creating more problems for yourself."

"Freddie's a professional. He knows just how far to lean."

"There are several people in the cemetery who might beg to differ."

"Freddie has paid his debt to society and turned over a new leaf. He's living proof of the power of redemption. Goes to Mass and confession every week. He's not going to do anything to fuck up the part I just offered."

"What part?"

Melchior stretched luxuriously like a big Persian cat. "*Helmet Head.*"

"The one about the homicidal biker."

"That's it."

"Miss Galindez is dropping her suit."

Melchior levitated. "Finally!"

"In exchange for ten thousand dollars."

Melchior made a flicking motion. "Take care of it."

"I will, but I have to tell you from what I learned in deposition there may be other time bombs out there. Burke, explain to me how a man in your position consistently hires illegals, and then tries to screw them out of their wages."

That was not all Melchior tried to screw. He had a thing for young Latin and Asian women. The younger the better. Ten years ago, he and Schaefer had flown to Thailand on a sex holiday. They never spoke of it, but it was part of the invisible bond that held them together. Schaefer was married to his childhood sweetheart and had two grown-up children. If the news ever became public, he was finished.

A producer could survive such a fall. A lawyer couldn't.

"I stopped using that agency."

"How's that hottie you're dating?"

"Melissa is cream pudding. We're going to have a party in July. You'll meet her then."

"Okay, great. I'll get the gears in motion on copyright and trademark infringement and let you know when something happens."

Melchior got to his feet. He had a tennis date at one. "Thanks, Stan. I'll be in touch."

CHAPTER TWELVE

The K-99 Club at Griefswalder Strasse 226 was a cavernous room with a hardwood floor and several steps down to the stage so that clubbers at the tables in back looked down at the band. The door was open when Connie and St. James arrived. A white Schumann's delivery van was parked in front, and a man in gray coveralls was loading crates of liquor onto a hand truck.

It was four-fifteen. Connie and St. James walked in through the propped-open glass door. The empty club stretched before them, the chairs upside down on the tables, a lingering aroma of beer, schnapps, sawdust, and sweat. A couple of men sat in shadow at the bar, talking softly with the redheaded female bartender. Tiny red lights gleamed from the Marshalls on the stage. A longhaired tech tuned the guitar guided by a sound man in a little booth at the center of the room, where the floor descended.

Connie walked up to the sound booth. St. James followed. Sensing her presence, the sound man turned. He was a prematurely balding and rotund man with a pale baby face and a bad comb-over. *"Kann ich Ihnen helfen?"* he said.

"Do you speak English?" Connie said.

The sound man stared at her and licked his lips. "Yes. How can I help you? We're not really open."

Flashing a dazzling smile, Connie held out her embossed and laminated *In Crowd* Reporter card, a purely ceremonial offering that nevertheless had a profound effect on people. "I'm Connie Cosgrove of *In Crowd* magazine, and this is my associate Ian St. James. Ian's father is Oaian St. James. We'd like to see him."

The man smiled nervously and sweated. "I have nothing to do with that. I'm just the sound man."

"Aren't they coming down to tune their own instruments?"

"We have someone to do that for them. That's what they wanted."

"Bollocks," St. James said. "They always tuned their own instruments. Now I don't think that bloke's me old man. How could he be?"

"You're welcome to purchase tickets and see the band. They start at eleven."

One of the men drinking on the other side of the room looked their way, got up, and came toward them with an easy-rolling prison stroll. St. James had his floppy hat on and was looking down at the set list taped to the sound man's board so was not aware of the man's approach until he was there.

"Excuse me," the man said in Russian accented English. "Is there a problem?"

St. James looked up. Kaspar Sinaiko's face went white and he took a step back.

"Well, hello, Kaspar. Surprised to see me?"

Kaspar slapped on a shit-eating grin. "My friend, it's you! I was so worried when you bolted from my car the other night before I was able to drop you off. I am so relieved you are all right! I was afraid you would be hit by a car. And who is this charming creature?"

Connie held out her hand. "Connie Cosgrove, *In Crowd* magazine."

Kaspar slobbered over her hand. "So you are here to see the band?"

"That's right."

"Well, come, come my friends! Let me buy you a drink." Kaspar turned back toward the bar. Connie and St. James followed.

"Are you the band's manager?" Connie said.

"Yes, yes, I'm the manager."

They sat at the bar. Kaspar introduced them to Udo, the club's owner, an aging hipster in a Perry Como sweater and Sinatra snap-brim fedora, and he introduced them to Brigid, the bartender, a pretty Nordic beauty with whom Kaspar obviously had a relationship.

Kaspar herded them to a table. "Come, come. Sit, sit, let us face each other like normal people. Tell Brigid what you want."

St. James looked longingly at the ranks of liquor behind the bar. "I'll have a Coke," he said lugubriously. Connie ordered a coffee. Udo and Kaspar sipped schnapps.

"We'd like to interview the band," Connie said.

Kaspar nodded. "We'll see. The plan is to tour and build a following. The boys really aren't into the cult of personality."

St. James barked. "Who's this wanker posing as me old man?"

Brigid brought the drinks. She pulled a chair over from another table and sat next to Kaspar massaging his neck. "His real name? I don't know."

"So you admit they're fakes," Connie said.

Kaspar shrugged. "I'm just the manager. I set up the gigs and make sure things go smoothly."

"Aren't you aware that you're breaking copyright and trademark laws?"

"Oh, I believe there's a statute of limitations on that."

"Well, no," Connie said. "Melchior has kept the copyright and trademark current. Aren't you afraid of legal repercussions?"

Kaspar shrugged. "That is for the lawyer to decide."

"What lawyer?" Connie said.

"Nadio Ninguna. He set up the deal."

"Well, where is he?"

Kaspar shrugged again. He reached into his hip pocket and pulled out his thick wallet which he went through until he found what he was looking for. He handed Connie a dog-eared business card belonging to Nadio Ninguna, Intellectual and Property Rights, Barcelona and La Coruna.

"May I have this?"

"Of course."

"May we meet the band?"

"You can see the band tonight at eleven like everybody else."

"Boyo." St. James gave him a bit of the old back alley. "We represent *In Crowd* magazine. Without *In Crowd*, you're just a backwater tribute act searching for a lawsuit. Besides," St. James smiled to let Kaspar know he was in on the joke, "that's me father we're talkin' about."

"Now, how can he possibly be your father when you are obviously older than he?" Kaspar asked sincerely.

"Well, if he's not me father, I'd like to ask 'im where he gets off using the name."

"You'll have to take that up with Señor Ninguna."

A force moved through the room, a sine wave of disturbance. St. James looked toward the door. Man. Big man striding straight at their table.

CHAPTER THIRTEEN

The man reached the table and smiled. He was over six feet with a full head of dark wavy hair and a Zapata mustache, quite handsome with excellent cheekbones and big brown eyes. He wore a leather bomber jacket with a lamb's wool collar and khakis. He looked like Captain Jack from the Scorchy Smith strip. He exuded the faint scent of some delicious alpine aroma.

"Gentlemen," he said in a deep voice. "Federico Guttierez at your service, special envoy to Mr. Burke Melchior."

St. James moved his chair over and indicated for the newcomer to bring a chair. "Sit down and join the party. What're you drinking?"

"Bar is closed," Udo said.

"Give the man a drink for Christ's bleedin' sake," St. James said.

Guttierez snagged a chair and pulled it up. He looked at Kaspar. "Are you the manager?"

Kaspar stood and stuck out his hand. "Kaspar Sinaiko."

They gripped, tight and white. Kaspar's hand went limp and Guttierez released it.

"What'll you have?" Kaspar said smiling and breathing hard.

"Choo got any Tecate or Dos Equis?" Guttierez said in an exaggerated Mexican accent.

"We have Tecate," Brigid piped up helpfully.

Kaspar squeezed Brigid's knee. "Do you mind, love?"

Brigid rose. "Of course not."

As all eyes followed Brigid's progress, Kaspar said, "Man comes to Berlin and orders a Mexican beer."

"That is right, my friend," Guttierez said with gusto. "And do you know why? Because we invented beer. No, no, I know what you're going to say. That the Saxons and the Romans invented beer, but there is positive proof that the Maya were making beer as early as 600 B.C."

St. James, who fancied himself an expert on hops, was mystified.

Kaspar gave Guttierez a hard prison look. "You are telling me that the Mexicans invented beer?"

"Not only that, my friend, we invented the modern calendar and the raised stone road eons before the Romans. You should look it up. As for the Russians, what have they invented but vodka and mass starvation?"

Kaspar responded to the insult by showing his teeth like a dog offering a warning snarl.

Brigid returned with a round tray holding an ice-cold Tecate and a glass. As she set them before Guttierez, he lightly grasped her wrist, looking into her face.

"You are very beautiful, chiquita. Are you a model?"

Brigid blushed charmingly. "No. Just a bartender."

"With your face and the way you move you could be a top model or a movie actress. Do you know who Burke Melchior is?"

"Not really."

"He's a movie producer in Hollywood. He also happens to be my boss. We are looking for a new face to cast in an exciting new picture."

Brigid was in no hurry to withdraw her arm from Guttierez' grasp.

"Brigid!" Kaspar snarled. "He's full of shit!"

Guttierez' eyes flattened into a horizontal gun slit leveled at Kaspar. "I am Mr. Melchior's employee. He sent me here to speak to you." Guttierez' hand dipped into his unzipped jacket and withdrew an ecru card which he slid contemptuously across the table. "Here is his card. Feel free to contact him."

He turned his attention back to Brigid who stood mesmerized, still as a statue. "Have you seen *Sniffers* starring Tom Hanks? *Weasels Ripped My Flesh?*"

Brigid nodded enthusiastically, smiling. "Yes! I've seen them both."

"Burke produced them. We're working on a thriller, and there's a part in it for a girl just like you. She's a bartender at a rural bar in the American south. Your English is very good. I suppose we could get around the accent by changing her backstory. No reason she didn't come over here to study, dropped out of school, fell in with a bad crowd ..."

Kaspar couldn't hide his disgust. St. James watched rapt. Guttierez wielded words the way a Ginsu master used his knives. Connie had a barely concealed smirk on her face, and Udo remained as still and withdrawn as a mausoleum carving.

On stage, the longhair emitted a series of ringing peals on the guitar which led to a round of feedback that buzzed around the room like a flying chainsaw before the sound man moved the dial to a more comfortable position.

Guttierez turned to Brigid. "I'm very serious, my dear. Burke trusts me on these things, particularly as I also will be in the movie. I could perhaps do a little interview right on my Blackberry and send it to him. What time do you go to work?"

Brigid hesitated, her lovely mouth half open. She looked like she was fifteen. She glanced at Udo.

Udo made a flicking motion with his hand. "Go. Be back at nine."

Kaspar sat back, arms crossed, quietly seething. St. James felt the malice on his skin like a cosmic ray.

"So," Guttierez said, standing. "Come to a coffee shop with me. Let me ask you a few questions. Can you do that?"

Brigid nodded enthusiastically, not looking at Kaspar.

Guttierez swung his chair back with an annoying screech. "Kaspar. I'm only going to say this once. Mr. Melchior owns the copyright and trademark to the Banshees. You can either change their name right now, or they don't go on. If they do go on, there will be serious consequences, do you follow?"

Kaspar didn't move. He remained hunched back in his chair with his arms crossed. A wry smile crept across his lips. "I get it."

"Good! And if you choose the former option, may I suggest a new name for the band? It's too bad the Genuine Fakes are taken. Why don't you call them the Sad Ass Motherfuckers?"

With a triumphant smile, Guttierez tapped St. James on the shoulder. "Thanks for the beer, Holmes."

He put a hand to the small of Brigid's back, and they walked out of the bar without a backward glance.

Chapter Fourteen

An awkward silence prevailed.

Connie sipped her coffee. She set down the cup. "So, can we talk to the band or not?"

"I will ask them," Kaspar said. "I am only the manager."

"I was under the impression that the manager managed the band's appearances, including the press," St. James said.

Kaspar looked at him with a hint of mischief. "Not in this case. They are the bosses."

"How'd you hook up with them, anyway?" St. James said.

"I answered an ad on Craigslist. 'Manager needed for heavy metal band.'" Kaspar seemed to take delight in the blatant lie, smiling broadly. "Listen. You come to the show. See the band perform. That is what they are all about. Maybe afterwards, we'll see."

"That's what you said last time," St. James reminded him.

"This time," Kaspar said, "I hope to do a better job."

Connie saw the dart pass between them. She put her hand on St. James' arm. "Come on. Let's go find dinner someplace. We'll come back for the show."

St. James and Connie stood and made their way toward the entrance. St. James retrieved his guitar case from behind the desk, and they walked out into the late afternoon, traffic moved in orderly fashion on the broad boulevard, trees from a park visible to their right. The avenue was rife with clubs and restaurants. They decided to walk. They made an odd couple, the hippie with his guitar case and the cover girl reporter in her pink sweater and trench coat.

The sidewalks were filled with well-dressed students, business persons, and hausfraus availing themselves of the June weather. Connie stopped at each restaurant and read the menu aloud. As she began to recite the seafood selections, St. James felt someone's gaze on the back of his head, but when he turned, no one stood out. People everywhere.

"This looks suitably fancy," Connie said. "Don't worry—it's all on *In Crowd*."

St. James followed her into the restaurant modeled on a bierskellar from the thirties, with white-washed walls, heavy exposed beams, and thick with the smell of heavy food. As the smiling hostess approached, the door opened behind them, admitting a whiff of dust that reminded St. James of a university library.

"Mr. St. James?"

St. James turned. The man was about 5'5" with a troll's long white beard, rotund belly, and round wire-rimmed glasses, toting a Gladstone that threatened to explode. Parts of his beard were braided with beads. Colored threads had been woven into the beard as well. He wore tweedy pants, a dark brown sweater and a tweed jacket with leather patches at the elbows. St. James experienced a moment of *déjàvu* and was about to dismiss it when an image snapped into focus. He had seen this man before—at the Phoenix Club.

"You were there," St. James said.

"Indeed, sir. We need to speak."

The hostess cleared her throat. "How many please?"

St. James glanced at Connie. "Three," she said.

The trio awkwardly followed the hostess to a booth with expansive screening boards decorated with a painting of mounted noblemen and hounds pursuing a stag so that the effect was semi-private. Connie and St. James took one side, the troll the other. He heaved his bursting Gladstone onto the bench next to him.

"I am Lothar Klapp. Please forgive my intruding like this, but it is of the utmost importance that we speak."

St. James watched Connie slip a tiny recorder from her bag, turn it on, take a napkin, wipe her mouth, then casually place the napkin on the table in front of her with the recorder underneath.

"About?" St. James prompted.

Klapp leaned forward clasping his hands on the table. "The Banshees. I fear they are the real thing, and their appearance portends a new Dark Age."

Connie poked St. James below the table with her elbow. "How is that possible?"

"Until recently, I was Professor Emeritus of Medieval History at the University of Dusseldorf. I specialize in ancient religions including Druidism and Satanism and the nexus between the two. I have always been interested in the Banshees. I saw them several times when I was a young man. I noted then the use of certain Druidic rituals and phrases in their music.

"As you know, Paddy, Oaian, and Cunar met at Sidcup Art College in '72 and shared their interest in rock and the occult. Burke Melchior heard them at the Quonset in Sudbury and signed them. Under Burke's direction, the Banshees recorded *Beat the Manshees*. There were rumors that Melchior was secretly in love with Paddy. Satan worship. Blood sacrifice. Churches burned their records. And the churches in turn burned."

"There were rumors that me old man deliberately smashed his Jaguar to kill me mother, too," St. James said softly.

"I have heard that, too. I enjoyed your first record very much."

"Thank you."

"What's so important, Mr. Klapp?" Connie said.

"Actually, it is Professor Klapp. I was quite obsessed with the Banshees as a young man, and their music has continued to haunt me through the years. I spent a summer sabbatical in Dunkeld in Scotland."

"Paddy's home town," St. James said.

"Ja, Paddy's home town. And do you know what else is there?"

"The moors?" St. James said.

"There was a village called Rathkroghen, named after Laird Rathkroghen, a priest who sought to merge Druidism and Satanism through the sacrifice of children. He was a cult leader like Jim Jones or Charlie Manson who held his flock in thrall, choosing whichever women he wished, sacrificing his own children to sing the praises of his dark and evil god. He had a marvelous voice and his songs hypnotized people."

Connie poked St. James again. *This is good stuff!*

An elderly gentleman in lederhosen approached to take their orders. Professor Klapp ordered the pork loin. Connie opted for a green salad. St. James ordered a beer, a Jägermeister, and knackwurst.

"That iss a good idea," the professor said. "I, too, would like a beer undt Jägermeister."

The waiter withdrew.

Connie leaned forward elbows on the table. "Please continue, Professor. We are in your thrall."

"Having exhausted his own brood, Laird Rathkroghen sent his minions to abduct children from other villages. They slaughtered the children and made a sausage while Laird Rathkroghen sang. It was the sausage that granted him the dark power. It was the music that granted immortality. The children's bones were made into flutes."

Connie swallowed.

"This was not a new concept. Baal, too, demanded sacrifice of children. At the time," Klapp continued, "six hundred years ago, there was really no way for news to spread except mouth to ear, and your average peasant did not travel far. The overwhelming majority of people in 17th century Scotland, indeed all of Europe, spent their entire lives within ten miles of their place of birth.

"Nevertheless someone, perhaps someone whose child had not been of Rathkroghen's seed, fled to nearby Melchior, to petition Laird Melchior to do something."

"Huh?" St. James said. "Any relation to Burke Melchior?"

Klapp held up a brat-like finger. "There is no doubt. Laird Melchior gathered a small army, and on a dark July night, they descended on Rathkroghen, putting Rathkroghen's followers to the sword. Laird Rathkroghen was burned at the stake. He died singing. He sang a curse to the entire world."

"Not so different from today, innit?"

"Lord Melchior tore down Castle Rathkroghen and used the stones to build his manor house. They say it was always cold, even in the heat of summer."

Their drinks came. St. James drained half his stein and shot back the Jäger. Klapp did likewise. Connie sipped iced tea.

"I got a good look at them," Klapp said. "They are the same band I remember as a young man."

St. James wanted to circle his ear with a finger, but he didn't want to offend the old man. "That's a terrible story. Did you write it up?"

"Ja, ja, I write it up, and they deny me tenure! Did I mention I am also a Druid?"

"They denied you tenure because of your theory regarding Laird Rathkroghen?" Connie said.

Klapp nodded his head. "Ja. But that is not important. We must stop the Banshees from reaching America. If they reach America, there will be a terrible tragedy."

Their food came. The waiter deposited a plate in front of St. James containing two steaming knackwurst and kraut. St. James stared at it wishing he'd ordered something else.

"So you're saying," Connie said, "that the Banshees are what? Representatives of Satan? Not human?"

"Do you believe in God?" Klapp said.

"No. I'm an atheist."

"That is too bad. What about you, St. James? Do you believe in God?"

St. James scratched his head. "Jury's still out on that one. I don't know what's happening, but I'm pretty certain this group is not the real Banshees."

Klapp could not immediately respond as he was stuffing his face. He held up one finger and drained the rest of his beer. "Well, we'll see tonight, won't we? This time you won't hover at the back of the room, will you? Do you think Oaian might know who you are?"

"I don't see how," St. James said, signaling the waiter for another round.

"Did you see the body the other night?"

"I saw it."

"Did you know that after the release of *Beat the Manshees*, there was a death at every single Banshees appearance?"

"Really," Connie said. "Why has no one mentioned that before?"

"One fellow fell off a speaker tower at the Isle of Wight. Another drove off a hairpin curve on his way home from the concert. Another was the victim of a hit-and-run accident, but because many of these events occurred after the concert, as people were on their way home, no one bothered to connect the dots."

"So if you're right," Connie said, "someone is going to die tonight."

"You said it, Fraulein. Not me. By the way, before I forget." Klapp rummaged in his Gladstone and produced an ancient scratched CD case, Ian St. James: *River of Blood*. He opened the CD case and slid it across the table toward St. James along with a pen. "If you don't mind. Please make it out to Professor Klapp."

St. James smiled ironically as he signed the CD booklet. He had a fan.

The waiter brought another round of drinks. Klapp quickly drained his Jägermeister and pushed himself away from the table. "Thank you very much for the supper. I will see you tonight, *nicht wahr?*"

"Wait," St. James said. "How do we get in touch with you?"

Klapp dipped into his tweedy jacket and handed St. James a card with his name, e-mail address, and cell phone number. Across the top was the embossed word 'Druids' in deep purple. "I play bass in a heavy metal band," Klapp explained. "What is your phone number?"

St. James told him. Klapp entered it into his cell phone.

They watched the strange little man walk toward the front with a sailor's gait, the heavy Gladstone causing him to tilt to the right.

CHAPTER FIFTEEN

After Klapp left, St. James reached over and helped himself to the professor's beer. Connie put the bill on her *In Crowd* card and led the way out front where she hailed a taxi. She noted that St. James was a little glassy-eyed. They got in the taxi. Connie told the driver to take them to the Park Inn.

They climbed out beneath the portico, and Connie paid the driver. "Do you want to meet me at the club at eleven?"

St. James smacked himself in the forehead. "We forgot to ask for press comps!"

"Don't worry. *In Crowd* will pay. I'm going to take a nap. See you at eleven."

Halfway across the lobby, she looked back. St. James stood in a forlorn posture like a dog waiting for its master. Well, that was too bad. She wasn't his minder. St. James was personable enough. Even droll. But he was a drunk. Connie knew the signs. Her father had been a drunk, the main reason Connie never imbibed. At least not alcohol.

She took the elevator to the sixth floor. Her room had been serviced, the bed neatly made, two foil-wrapped chocolates on the pillow. Connie wasn't tired. She went to the desk, pulled out her laptop, and logged on. She googled Kaspar Sinaiko. Nothing. She googled Federico Guttierez. He had his own web page with the following description:

Federico "Freddie" Guttierez was the fifth of six children born to Manual and Linda Guttierez in the Boyle Heights district of East L.A. Manual was a bus driver. Federico joined the Krazy Ass Mexicans at age fifteen, killed a rival gang member at seventeen, and served eight years in the penitentiary. Federico found Christ in prison and vowed to turn his life around. Upon his release, he went to an audition for a movie about gangs and landed a small part in Barrio. *Since then Federico has had speaking roles in four films including* The Massacre, One for My Baby, Machete, *and* To the Limit. *He has also appeared on* Sons of Anarchy.

Federico has since started the Barrio Project dedicated to saving kids from the gang life. Federico is active in community affairs and can be found on weekends coaching boys basketball at the Barrio Center.

There were numerous pictures: Freddie coaching the kids, Freddie as a movie star, stills from his films. It was dynamite stuff, Burke Melchior sending a real-life thug to straighten people out. Like everyone else at the table, she had been shocked at the ease with which Guttierez had pried Brigid away from Kaspar. There was something about the Russian manager that reminded her of Gollum from *Lord of the Rings*. If Gollum had muscles.

She bookmarked the page and googled Professor Lothar Klapp. There was a brief entry in university correspondence announcing Klapp's retirement at age sixty-five. There was also a teacher evaluation page on which Klapp was mentioned numerous times, but Connie could not read German. She recognized the words "Druid" and the German for disciplinary hearing. Herr Klapp had not been completely forthcoming. She copied several of the longer entries and sent them to her friend Gert, a reporter for *Der Stern*, with a request for translation.

She worried about St. James. As a girl she'd adored his first record, the sensitive songwriter shtick, even had a picture of him on her wall. The St. James she'd met that afternoon looked to be one drink away from the gutter. The way he'd eyed the liquor, like a starving dog through a restaurant window. His hands shook until he got a drink in him.

It was up to her to keep St. James sober enough to be useful. Connie knew well the effect she had on men. They looked and wanted to touch her. She'd used her looks since high school, manipulating teachers, boyfriends, employers. Connie was not a mean woman, but she was ambitious. She had to use the talents with which she was born, including her sharp intelligence, solid instincts, and, yes, her good looks.

All St. James needed was the slightest push to fall head over heels in love with her. She would use that to keep him in line. Connie had been married for six months to a good-looking drunk before she wised up, walked out, and took him to the cleaners.

She'd majored in journalism at UC Irvine, applied for an internship at *In Crowd* as a junior. She'd been with them ever since. She'd had to deal with horny editors and publishers—she'd even threatened to tell Serafin's wife if he didn't back off. She'd dealt with rock stars. She had even slept with a few and rumors got around, but Connie was not one of those girls who bloomed in the limelight. She did not allow herself to be photographed at industry functions, clubs, or parties, and avoided all personal publicity.

Keeping the Cosgrove brand viable.

Her stories were dynamic. She'd won a Lester Bangs for her coverage of Runcible Spoon. Her coverage of Charon would hit next week. It might be up sooner on the web if Richard chose.

As for the Banshees she already knew what she was going to say.

The world breathed a sigh of relief on August 13, 1975, upon learning of the death in a plane crash of every member of the Banshees. People never spoke of it, but the Banshees took their Satanism a little too literally for some, often cutting themselves onstage and bleeding onto their instruments. Their one and only album, Beat the Manshees, *is the only record ever singled out for a Papal denunciation.*

So when a band calling themselves the Banshees surfaced in Prague last week, In Crowd *was naturally interested.*

The rest would have to wait until later.

Chapter Sixteen

St. James was on his second Jäger of the evening—his fourth if you counted dinner—when Connie came through the crowd. He waved at her. Men turned toward her like sunflowers facing the dawn.

"I waited for you downstairs," she said, sliding on to the adjacent stool.

"I'm sorry. I should have gone down to greet you. I've been here since nine."

"All right. I told you *In Crowd* would pay. Did you save your receipt?"

St. James pulled the stub triumphantly from an inside jacket pocket. Connie took it and put in her handbag. She wore a white and yellow strapped summer dress with yellow flats. The purse was yellow vinyl. She looked stunning and emitted some disturbing tropical scent.

"Want a drink?" he asked.

Connie glanced at his shot glass. St. James could smell her disapproval. Well, fuck it. He was old enough to be her dad, had he impregnated her mother at age twelve. There was no sense in acting the fool because there was no payoff. But St. James, like millions of men before him, couldn't help it. Her beauty, her near-crazy sexiness forced him into ancient male patterns. "Oh, come on."

Connie sighed. "I'd like an Icelandic martini straight up with an olive."

As St. James conveyed this message to the bartender—a young man with jet-black hair, a stud through his chin, lip, eye, and ear piercings—Connie tugged on his sleeve. St. James swiveled to see Freddie Guttierez boppin' their way with a disco strut, throwing out his hands and shaking his hips followed by a mesmerized and laughing Brigid. Brigid had changed into a little black cocktail dress and black heels and looked sensational.

Guttierez saw them and waved. "How are you, my friend?" he said to St. James, sticking out his paw. St. James shook it. Guttierez wore a ridiculous Tyrolean hat with a little brush in the headband.

"Never better," St. James replied.

Guttierez turned to Connie. "Delightful to see you again, Connie."

Connie nodded. "You guys."

The bartender arrived with their drinks. Guttierez insisted on paying and ordered a Tecate and Brigid ordered a Depth Bomb, which was a shot of Jägermeister in a Red Bull. St. James had heard they led to strokes. Well, she was young.

"Mr. Guttierez," Connie had to yell to be heard. "What are you going to do if the band comes on?"

"Call me Freddie. If that band goes on, me and Kaspar are going to have a private talk. After the show."

"Melchior's trying to get an injunction, you know," St. James said holding his Jägermeister up to the light.

"You know, my friend," Guttierez said, "nobody in Germany drinks that swill. It's strictly for American college students."

"This from a man who orders Tecate," St. James said.

Guttierez laughed. "You're funny. I like you. Don't I know you from some place?"

"I used to be Ian St. James."

"Why does that name ring a bell?"

"Because, Freddie," Connie said, "Ian is a well-known musician. And his father Oaian was the Banshees' drummer."

Guttierez put an arm around Brigid and arched his highly expressive eyebrows. "Then you and I share a common interest. Neither one of us wants this band to go on."

"I'm not so sure," St. James said.

"What are you not so sure about?" Guttierez said.

"The drummer does look an awful lot like me father. I mean, I never knew him, but there are thousands of pictures. I used to stare at them for hours trying to convince myself that this grinning stranger was me father. He always had a pretty bird at hand."

"You don't really think he's your father. You're twice his age!"

"Not quite, but I get your point. I don't know. I'd like to talk to him. That's why I'm here. I tried to talk to him in Prague, but that fucker Kaspar spiked my drink and stuck me in the trunk of an auto due to be crushed. I barely escaped with me life."

"That is something else for which I will pay him back."

St. James shuddered. He would definitely not want Guttierez mad at him. He knew the type of person Melchior employed. True, Melchior had always been kind to him, possibly as a result of his never requited love for Oaian, possibly because he deemed it good politics. St. James was grateful for every bit of luck that fell his way. This was the biggest chunk in a long time. Melchior had promised him a recording contract if he helped Connie hype this into the story of the year.

Most likely they were a bunch of clever impostors, possibly surgically altered to resemble the originals. But who and why would anyone attempt such a thing? What was the point? Was the band incapable of writing new material? And why now?

A man appeared onstage in a ragged tuxedo, bowtie undone, stalking the stage like a meth addict. He took the mike.

"Meine Damen und Herren The Banshees!"

Three musicians loped onstage to thunderous applause and whistling. They all had military sidewalls. Oaian's right arm was now completely blanketed in an elaborate Oriental tattoo. St. James had missed it in Prague because Oaian had worn a long-sleeved shirt. The tat was new.

"Oll roight then," Paddy growled into the mike. "'Allo Berlin!" and he burst into the opening riff of "Race the Devil," Oaian providing a multi-faceted backbeat, Cunar thrumming on bass. The club was filled to capacity. Almost instantaneously, a number of clubbers gathered on the dance floor before the stage and began to gyrate like spastics in the grip of religious ecstasy.

Guttierez grinned fiercely at the stage. "Let's dance!" he said, pulling a laughing Brigid along behind him.

That proved to be a mistake.

CHAPTER SEVENTEEN

St. James stood and looked back toward the entrance.

"Who are you looking for?" Connie asked.

"The Professor. I hope nothing happened to him."

"He probably came to his senses and went home." They had to shout into each other's ears to be heard. "Is that your dad?"

"I don't know!" St. James yelled. "I'll have to get down there for a closer look!"

Connie yelled, "I'll save your seat!"

St. James downed his drink acutely aware of Connie's disapproving gaze. He'd taken Guttierez' words to heart. Henceforth, he would leave the Jägermeister to the college kids.

Getting to the stage presented certain difficulties. Mainly, the mob before him filled every available inch of space. St. James never was one for elbowing through a crowd. At least he could see over most of the heads when he stood on tiptoe. He found himself shuttled off to the left side in the third or fourth row. Further forward, progress was impossible. Between the leaping bodies, he concentrated on the drummer.

The drummer had one of those young/old faces that in their youth projected their seniority, and in their seniority projected their youth. He was the spitting image of Oaian St. James, eyes screwed shut, arms flailing, cymbals crashing, never losing the beat or the sense of forward propulsion. At one point, he looked up and seemed to stare straight at St. James.

He mouthed the words, "I love you."

Did he? Or was St. James just smashed?

"I am bloody smashed," he said, but of course no one heard him, not even himself. He turned his attention to the other Banshees. Save for the new wave haircut, Cunar and Paddy were dead ringers. Identical. Plastic surgery had entered its Golden Age.

Clones.

It popped into his head. They'd cloned a cow, a pig, and a dog. They'd been talking about cloning people forever. Could this be it? The cost of such an undertaking would be monumental. Surely someone who had mastered the science of cloning human beings wouldn't lavish his talents merely to bring forth a fake rock band.

But who was to say the Banshees represented the first fruit of this mysterious agency's labor? If they'd mastered cloning, might there not be dozens, if not hundreds of clones walking around? Their brains implanted with fictitious histories and synthetic personalities. Who was next? Jim Morrison? Elvis?

In that case, the Banshees were merely an artful exercise, amortized over years of secret production. Of course, only a madman would attempt such a feat, but many of the Banshees' followers were mad. St. James believed that was a study done to determine which Satanic heavy metal band had inspired the most suicides, homicides, and assaults, the Banshees would win hands down.

The band segued flawlessly into "Bo Diddley." God, they were good! St. James hadn't heard a band this hot in eons. Through a break in the crowd, he caught a momentary glimpse of Guttierez and Brigid dancing dirty. The sheer press of humanity chose the style for them.

More and more people continued to pack the floor until St. James was expelled from the fringes, like a splinter rejected by the body. He went to the men's room. Heavy snorting issued from the closed toilet booths.

I could use a whiff of something right about now, St. James thought. *Perish the thought, boyo.*

The band was playing "Honky Tonk Women" when St. James emerged from the restroom. St. James jigged and wedged his way back to the bar, extremely uncomfortable from the press of humanity. All the makings of a tragedy. All one had to do was light a match. The Station Nightclub fire in West Warwick, RI had killed a hundred people. Nice round number.

Stop it, boyo. You're creeping yourself out.

When St. James finally reached Connie at the bar, Kaspar was sitting in his seat. Kaspar rose as St. James reached them.

Kaspar stood. "I was saving it for you!"

Connie was bright-eyed and excited. "I was just telling Kaspar how good these guys sound. Even if they are fakes, they can bring it. Melchior should embrace these guys, not fight 'em."

"Excuse me," Kaspar said disappearing into the crowd.

St. James flopped down on the stool and looked for the bartender. Connie turned her back to the bar, disapproval evident in her posture and pursed lips. Well, fuck it. He was a grown man. She wasn't his keeper, and there was no point acting the swain. He'd only make a fool of himself.

St. James ordered another whiskey. The entire room thrummed to the Banshee's beat, the walls seeming to pulse in and out like a living thing. Beyond the sound booth was wall-to-wall humanity. If you fainted, you would not hit the floor.

The Banshees brought "Women" to a satisfying conclusion, and there was a momentary lull in the din.

"MOLOCH LOVES ME!" bellowed a man with buffalo lungs. Others took up the chant. "MOLOCH LOVES ME! MOLOCH LOVES ME!"

A smiling Paddy, face slick with sweat, nodded his head three times and hit it. Oaian scrambled a titanic riff and the band launched into their signature shocker. Red and blue lights strobed over the dance floor like a disaster scene. Heads pogoed furiously, bodies slamming sideways, all indistinguishable in the red/blue flashing light.

A queasy feeling developed in the pit of St. James' stomach. *Serves me right for drinking like a tosser,* he thought.

Impossibly, the band kicked it up a notch, Paddy ripping one monumental riff after another. They were *allegro* and *fortissimo*.

Paddy spat out words in Gaelic. At least, St. James thought it was Gaelic. He couldn't be sure. The audience responded like popping corn. As the band reached the chorus, the audience surged together in the middle of the dance floor, momentarily creating a mound of humanity. Hands flew up and down and for an instant St. James thought he saw the red/blue lights reflected in a knife. Out of nowhere, Paddy hit a dissonant chord. The crowd dropped all pretense of dance and turned on one another in a grunting, snarling, hair-pulling mass.

A woman's scream split the air, high, hysterical, nerve-grinding, and unending, a primordial cry of shock and pain shot into the lizard brain. The band stopped mid-chord, unplugged their axes and ran out the back. There was no chance of catching up with them. Only a greased snake could get through the mob.

Something wet and warm smacked St. James on the forehead. He used a napkin to mop it off.

Shouts of alarm, another earsplitting scream, and suddenly people were stampeding off the dance floor, running for the front exit. From his perch at the bar, St. James looked around for signs of fire. There was nothing. Nor did he smell smoke. Everyone at the bar took off like it was a raid, leaving St. James and Connie to themselves. The mash-up at the door looked like the Three Stooges times a hundred. Glass shattered. No one took control, no one grabbed the mic. It was an ugly free-for-all. It was Altamont.

Within minutes the club had emptied, people streaming out through the double doors, ripping their clothes and splattering blood from the broken glass. Somebody turned on the lights. St. James looked at the smeared red napkin in his hand.

The smell of sheared copper and charnel house protein was overwhelming. St. James was staring at the napkin when Connie touched his arm. Her face was a mask as she stared down at the stage. St. James followed her gaze. The dance floor was a lake of blood: blood tracked up the stairs, blood tracked to the front door. In the middle of the dance floor lay Guttierez' flattened hat.

CHAPTER EIGHTEEN

The room smelled like an abattoir, the lake of blood reflecting the overhead lights. St. James' stomach churned and rose like Mt. St. Helens erupting. He barely made it to the men's room in time, crouching over the bowl and heaving up knackwurst, sauerkraut, and three or four pints.

Gasping and drooling, he looked up. Someone had left a perfectly good line of coke on top of the white porcelain toilet tank.

One fuckin' line, what harm could it do? It wasn't as if he had access to an unlimited amount. He knew it would make him jangly and cost him sleep, but at that moment, on his knees before the porcelain bowl, he thanked God for providing him with the much-needed boost.

St. James surreptitiously rolled a Ten Euro note, leaned over the line and hoovered it up.

Idiot! It might be rat poison!

But it wasn't. It had that pure chem lab flavor of the finest pharmaceutical cocaine. An electric jolt spread through St. James' nervous system, restoring his self-esteem, increasing his strength, making him smarter.

Well, oll roight, then.

Checking himself in the mirror for tell-tale signs, St. James washed his hands and face and returned to the club. Udo and Kaspar furiously mopped the floor with industrial-sized mops, ringing them out in large corrugated steel pails. St. James stared, slack-jawed. He'd stumbled into a Uwe Boll movie.

"What the fuck, man!"

Udo looked up at him, eyes black as coal. "There's always a lot of blood after a good mosh."

St. James stared at the monstrous pool of blood. It looked like the entire contents of a body's circulatory system. Fucking gallons. Guttierez' hat was gone.

"Where's 'is 'at?" St. James wailed.

Kaspar grinned. "What hat?"

What happened to Guttierez and Brigid?

Guttierez wouldn't just run out, not without delivering his message.

St. James felt a touch on his arm.

"We have to get out of here," Connie said, shoving a digital camera into her purse.

St. James allowed her to lead him by the hand like a small child toward the front door where an employee was sweeping up broken glass.

Where were the police?

St. James could barely walk. Connie gripped him painfully at the bicep to keep him from falling. She was furious. "You're wasted," she hissed. "No point in talking about what happened tonight. Where are you staying?"

St. James dug in his pocket and found the room key attached to a large plastic fob. "Hotel Paradise. It's not far."

Connie could barely contain her disgust as she hailed a taxi and dropped St. James off in front of the narrow building sandwiched between an apartment block and an electronics store. St. James heaved himself from the rear seat, nearly falling into the gutter. He shuffled up to the front door, somehow got it open and went inside.

He checked his watch. It was one o'clock. At this hour, the lobby was empty except for a young man slouched behind the counter playing a video game on the booking computer. He had a shaved skull and barely acknowledged St. James.

St. James took the ancient creaking elevator to the seventh floor, went down the hall with one hand extended for balance. He double-checked his room number against the key—he'd stumbled into the wrong hotel room once too often. Wouldn't do to start a row now.

He got the door open, went in, and shut it behind him. His guitar case lay on the bed where he'd left it. Had the room been searched he had not the wherewithal to tell. The coke had left St. James jangly but exhausted, still suffering from the sleep deprivation of the previous two nights. Caused by drinking. Now he had beshat himself in front of Serafin's stunning reporter, further lowering him in her esteem.

Why not whip it out and piss on the floor while he's at it?

St. James growled low and guttural at the back of his threat, disgusted with himself. How could he be such a bloody wanker? How was it possible? After the first album, his future had looked so bright. There were appearances on SNL, Leno, and Letterman.

But when it came time to record a follow-up, St. James choked. Nothing left in the pipeline. He'd always assumed that artists manufacture art the way bricklayers lay brick—one brick at a time. He could never find the next brick. Twenty years of writers' block. "25 or 6 to 4" played constantly in the back of his mind drowning out his own melodies. If he ever had any.

He wanted badly to repair the harm he'd done to his reputation with Connie—not that he stood a chance with her. My God. Every man who met her felt the same thing. What a cliché. Maybe if he took one of the downers a girl had given him in Venice, if there were any left.

The bed squeaked as St. James sat and went through his pockets. Out came the wallet, miscellaneous change, matchbooks from a half a dozen dives, a pen, his cheap new cell phone.

It suddenly occurred to St. James to check his cell phone. It was a throwaway with a limited number of minutes he'd picked up the day before at the electronics store. He flipped it open. He had one voice mail. It took him four or five times before he was able to recall it. He suffered through the schoolmarm: "You have one voice mail. To listen to this voice mail ..."

He angrily pushed one.

"St. James," rasped Klapp in a German accent. "They're on to me—I don't know how they found out, but they're after me right now. It will be a miracle if I can escape them. You are our only hope. You must stop them before they reach Los Angeles! Learn the truth! Go to Rathkroghen! Dig up Paddy's grave …"

The call ended.

CHAPTER NINETEEN

I t was one-thirty local time when Connie got to her hotel room, nine-thirty in the morning in Los Angeles. She dialed Serafin.

"Serafin," he answered. She could tell by the sounds of traffic that he was on his commute and using a hands-free headset.

"Richard, it's Connie. Did you hear anything about the concert?"

"No. How did it go?"

"Something happened. Someone may have died, but there was no body. There was blood all over the floor—enough blood to fill a bathtub."

"What are you talking about ...?Oh great. What's the problem now?" he cursed, his voice further away and sounding distracted. She guessed it was something with the traffic.

"Richard?"

"Go ahead. I'm stuck in traffic. Tell me everything. How did your meeting with St. James go?"

"Rich, he's a drunk, and so far he hasn't been able to get close to these people. This is a bigger story than we thought." She told him everything that had happened since her meeting with St. James the day before, including Professor Klapp.

"Guttierez is dead?" he said incredulously.

"We don't know. He disappeared during the mêlée. They found his hat on the floor in a sea of blood?"

"A fucking Druid troll? Are you kidding me? Are you telling me Manny Guttierez and his date were butchered on the dance floor? Do you realize how crazy that sounds? And no bodies or body parts ...? Wait a minute. We're moving again. I'm about ten minutes away from the office. I'll call you as soon as I get in."

Connie took a hot shower, trying to wash the stench from her skin and hair. She was still shaking when she got out. She had considered herself a seasoned reporter—she'd covered a riot at a rock festival in Marin County once, and had drive-alongs in college with the Irvine Police. Nothing could have prepared her for that blinding red lake when the lights came on.

She dried herself off and dressed in a navy, velour tracksuit. She switched on the TV and flipped from news channel to news channel, searching for something on the massacre. But who had been massacred, and why?

And where were the bodies?

Connie realized that most of the crowd in front of the stage must have been in on it. They would have had to be. How else to account for the dismemberment and disappearance of two people in the middle of a dance floor? They could have spirited the body parts out—torsos and heads would be the most difficult, but it had been very dark when the crowd panicked and Connie hadn't noticed people carrying body parts. There had been a mass exodus of undifferentiated people.

How easy was it to dismember a body on a dance floor? A lot easier if helping hands secured them. But it could be done. If David Copperfield could vanish an airliner, the Banshees could disappear a couple of bodies.

Her phone rang. "I'm in my office," Serafin said. "Do you think Guttierez and his friend were murdered?"

"I don't know what to think, Richard. I've never been in a situation like that. It was harrowing."

"Did anybody notify the police?"

"No."

"Why not?"

"Rich, we were all in such a panic to get out of there. I didn't think it would do the magazine any good for me to be questioned about a crime that may or may not have taken place."

"Of course it would," Serafin said. "What's the matter with you?"

Connie knew he was right, but she hadn't been about to subject herself to intense police grilling just to spiff up a story! What had they actually seen? If the story ever got out people would wonder why Connie hadn't called the police.

I control the story.

She realized Serafin had been talking. "I'm sorry, what?"

"Are you listening to me? What's wrong with you?"

"Richard, I've been up for twenty hours, and I have just been through a traumatic experience."

"All right, okay. How's St. James holding up?"

"He's worthless. He's a hard-core alky."

Connie listened to Serafin sigh. "Does Melchior know?"

"I have no idea. That's not my responsibility."

"What are you going to write?"

"I don't know."

Beat.

"Rich."

"What?"

"I have photos of the dance floor and the trail of blood leading to the entrance."

"Send them."

"What do I do about St. James?"

"I feel he's valuable to the story. Hang with him. Make him part of the story."

"My albatross. I have to go to bed now."

"Will you be able to sleep?"

"I don't know."

CHAPTER TWENTY

Th
here was no escaping the banshee screams, a high-pitched atavistic vibration that shook the spine like a rag doll. St. James tried to flee, but it took overwhelming effort to lift his feet, mired as they were in peat bog. He felt weak as a baby duck. No matter how hard he struggled, he could not escape the hands that grasped at him from every side or flashed stainless steel blades reflecting lakes of blood.

St. James phase-shifted from restless sleep to full wakefulness. The bedside telephone rang with a panicky emergency wail only the Germans could love. St. James groaned.

Attaboy, boyo, you've done it again.

His head felt like the inside of a churning cement mixer. He had to piss and vomit. Piss, vomit, or answer the phone? He knew damn well who it was. Quite the impression he'd made last night. Then it hit him.

The lake of blood.

Sobriety arrived with the finality of a Mercedes door slamming shut. He picked up the phone.

"St. James," he croaked.

"Get up," Connie clipped. "It's two o'clock. I'm in the lobby."

"I'd better shower."

"You have fifteen minutes."

St. James hung up and bolted for the bathroom. He heaved his guts up in the toilet—there wasn't much left—drank three glasses of the tepid tap water, and took a hot shower. He put on his new clean jeans and an Oranjuly T-shirt, grabbed his backpack, and headed for the lobby.

Connie sat on one of the threadbare sofas, legs crossed, wearing hiking shorts and sensible shoes. She looked up from her laptop. She closed her laptop and put it in her backpack.

"Let's get some breakfast," she said, not waiting for St. James to acknowledge. He struggled to keep up. A half block down was a cafe featuring fresh-baked strudel. Connie went in, followed by St. James. The bakery smells triggered his stomach's growling mechanism. He was either stuffing it down or throwing it up.

St. James followed Connie to the counter, ordering hot coffee, orange juice, and Belgian waffles. Connie put her credit card down on the counter, looking out the window. They took a table by the window.

"Hell of a night, wa'nt it?" St. James said cheerfully.

Connie fixed him with green eyes turned cold as the North Atlantic. "Do you wish to remain on this story?"

"Huh?"

She bored in, furious. "I asked you if you wish to remain on this story, because last night you got drunk—again. I practically had to carry you out of that club. I'm not being paid to nursemaid some middle-aged alky has-been. If you intend to work with me on this story, you're not to have one more drop of alcohol, do you understand?"

"'Middle-aged alky has-been?'"

"You heard me."

"Ouch."

Moment of truth, boyo. Time to grow up.

Now he was hooked. He couldn't quit the story if he tried. If she booted him, he would continue to dog the band until he confronted the drummer. Much easier to do it with the backing of *In Crowd* than without.

"Oim in. I apologize for my behavior last night. I swear to you I won't have another dram of liquor until this is over."

Connie stared coldly. "I'd like to believe you, Ian. My old man was a drunk. I heard him swear to my mother a thousand times on the Bible that he would give it up. Guess what? He died in a

Veteran's hospital of cirrhosis of the liver. So I'm giving you one more chance. I smell liquor on your breath, I find one of those little servy-bar liquor bottles anywhere in your vicinity, you're off the story. You won't get a recording contract, and you'll end up drinking yourself to death."

God, she was beautiful. His boner could serve as the prow on a Spanish galleon.

"Why are you smiling? Do you think this is funny?"

"Not at all, luv. After last night, I don't think it's funny at all. Klapp phoned me while we were at the club. I want you to listen to the message."

St. James brought out his cell phone and cued it up. He handed it to Connie who listened with a look of intense concentration. When the message ended, Connie quietly folded the cell and handed it back. She opened her laptop and made notes.

"Maybe we should go to the police."

"Do you know what German police are like?"

Connie thought about it, touting up the costs. "You don't seriously think we should go to England and dig up Paddy MacGowan?"

"Oaian and Cunar left instructions to be cremated. Only Paddy had a proper burial. His father claimed the body."

"The father he hated."

"The very one."

A matronly woman in a light blue dress and white apron brought their meal. There was silence for several minutes while they ate. When Connie finished, she shoved the plate away replacing it with her laptop. "I'll book us tickets to London. We can rent a car. You can drive, assuming you have a valid license."

"That I do."

"Great." Connie focused on her keyboard.

St. James surreptitiously watched her. With her looks she could have been an actress. She seemed too smart to be an actress. Most of the actors St. James knew were self-absorbed morons.

"Did you call him?" she said without looking up.

"Who?"

"Klapp."

Chagrined, St. James took out his phone again and dialed the last number. One ring. "I'm sorry, that number is not in service at this time."

"His phone's offline. Says it isn't in service."

"Herr Professor becomes more interesting in his absence. That's it. I've booked us on Virgin out of Brandenburg at four PM. We'll arrive London a little before six."

"Should we call the cops or something?" St. James said.

"What? About Klapp? It's been less than twelve hours, and we're not his kin. It would just cause problems."

She continued to peck and stroke her laptop. She stared at the screen. "Oh, Jesus."

"What?"

"Now they've got a website. And they're playing Axton's in New York next Thursday."

CHAPTER TWENTY-ONE

Melchior stared at the image on computer as if he could burn a hole through the screen. He had snapped one of his prize Cohibas. He was that angry.

They had used the original logo. They were playing Axton's in NYC next week, a group of boys no older than the day they'd gone head first into the bog.

Melchior believed the world was conspiring to drive him mad.

He'd had a persecution complex since growing up Jewish in Blackpool, having to run home every day pursued by yobs. Nothing had ever come easy. Except talk. He could talk a sparrow out of a tree. He could talk starlets into his bed, sheiks out of their money, fleas off a dog. He could talk three provincial heavy metal belters to sign him as their manager thus becoming his vehicle for a lifetime ride to the top. Had they lived they might have shared that ride. It wasn't his fault they'd guessed wrong about the weather. It wasn't the first time, and it wouldn't be the last.

After a suitable period of mourning Melchior chose his next teen idols, those irrepressible power pups, Mayflower. There was an act you could market to young girls. And after that, Studley Bearcat, Serf City, a steady string of success stretching from Liverpool to Hollywood.

No one asked about the Banshees anymore. Fine with him. In retrospect, the imagery had been crude and obvious—something a biker gang would like.

And now they were back sticking their collective bums in his face. Mocking him. Daring him. According to Schaefer they were still under contract. Even if they weren't, Melchior had secured the rights to trademark and ownership from their grieving—and not so grieving—kin.

Well, they may look the same, but he was not the same Melchior as this gang of brigands was going to find out.

Serafin had phoned an hour earlier, catching Melchior at his morning workout with his trainer, Adolfo. Serafin insisted that Melchior take the call. As Melchior listened, he waved Adolfo off. There would be no workout.

He was in his office working damage control. The office was freezing. Melchior found a Lakers hoodie in the closet and put it on. He sat in front of the screen and looked in vain for some way to contact the Banshees' website. "Website under construction."

He'd called Guttierez four times, leaving a message each time. He'd left a message for Dan Kennedy describing Guttierez' disappearance. At this stage he could safely conclude that the Berlin police weren't going to do squat. No one had reported a crime. If the situation Serafin described was accurate, the whole crowd had been in on it. How do 250 people keep a secret? Especially when the secret is murder?

For the third time, he summoned the image Serafin had sent him. It was obscene, beyond belief. But only if you knew it was blood. You might think someone had spilled a bucket of paint on the floor. And the way it reflected the overhead lights … one of the most disturbing images he'd ever seen.

All that red.

The house was equipped with a 17th century bell and sash system to summon the servants. Melchior used it now. Seconds later Stanton appeared in the door carrying a clipboard. "Sir?"

"I need the Latitude Wednesday to fly to JFK. Thursday night I'll need VIP passes to Axton's in the Village."

"Sir, what is the event?"

"The fucking Banshees, if you can believe that shit. This time I'll nail 'em personally. Find out where they're staying. And get hold of Greg Eltaeb. I need to see him ASAP."

"What about Melissa?"

What about Melissa? Melchior had read in *Esquire* many years ago that the most powerful statement a man could make was to appear with a stunning girl on his arm.

"Yeah, why not."

CHAPTER TWENTY-TWO

T|he *In Crowd* building on Sunset Strip had once belonged to Miramax. Serafin's office looked down on the Strip from the third floor. A mock-up of the next issue was tacked to the wall. Connie's interview with Charon was featured.

Beneath it was a smaller mock-up: "ARE THE BANSHEES BACK?"

Melchior entered through the open door and stared in horror. "You can't run this!"

"I most certainly can. Why do you suppose I've got those two gallivanting around Europe?"

"I control the trademark and copyright! Those aren't the Banshees!"

"That remains to be seen."

Melchior stared at his old friend. "Come on, Richard!"

Serafin plopped onto a designer sofa: black leather, chrome legs. "I'm in the business of selling magazines. You're in the business of selling seats. This is rain from heaven. You should be happy."

"Happy? That lot are making fools of me! Everybody knows the Banshees were my first group. At the very least, this is an outrageous breach of intellectual property rights."

"The fans won't see it that way old chap. My advice to you is to get on the train or get out of the way."

"Have you seen the website?"

"I've seen it."

"I intend to shut it down."

"Rotsa ruck," Serafin said. "I asked my IT guys. It's virtually impossible to track down the actual place where a website was created. The only way to shut it down is to hack it."

There was a knock at the door. A cute Asian girl wheeled in a tray laden with stacked sandwiches and cans of Ogden's Cream Soda.

"From the Stratford Deli," Serafin explained scooping up a sandwich. "Thank you, Arlene."

The girl blew him a kiss and exited, shutting the door behind her. Outside, on the Strip, tourists ogled superheroes. Batman and Superman nearly came to blows.

Melchior sat in an Eames chair and surveyed the sandwiches. He wore a purple velvet jumpsuit with gold stripes. "Are you coming to New York with me?"

"Can't make it, Burke. Thursday we put the paper to bed, and I definitely want to be here. Besides. That's what Connie's for. Her and St. James."

"Has Ian been at all helpful?"

Serafin chewed and swallowed. He took several slugs of cream soda. "Not so's you would notice, but sooner or later they're going to catch up with the band, and that's why I want him there. Son confronts bogus father. You can't invent that shit."

"Where are they now, Connie and Ian?"

"England, I expect. They're heading up to Scotland tomorrow, take a peek in Paddy MacGowan's grave."

"You're joking."

"Nope. They got a tip. Wouldn't that be something, they open the coffin and it's empty?"

"They can't do that. Aren't their legalities? Don't they have to get a court order?"

"How the hell would I know? It's Scotland. I will tell you this, Connie is an unusually resourceful young lady."

Melchior gazed again at the mock-up about the band. "When's that going up? I don't suppose you could hold it until I have a chance to talk to them."

Serafin looked at the laptop on the coffee table in front of him. "Too late."

onnie got them adjacent rooms at the Anglish Hotel at Gatwick. St. James put in a wake-up call for six. He woke, stretched, and put on a pair of tennis and sweat pants. Taking the elevator down to the lobby, he pushed his way through the lobby doors, out onto the street, and ran. The sky was overcast with a promise of rain, ozone heavy from the airplanes. It was a bleak, gray industrial neighborhood. At first St. James felt awkward and stiff. He hadn't run in years.

As a pupil at Milford he'd been a star athlete at track. He'd run the hurdles, the relay, and the hundred meter. In his twenties, he'd run half-marathons.

St. James made it around the block before pushing back through the lobby doors, gasping and coughing, lungs burning. It was a big block. He went upstairs and showered, and was dressed and waiting when Connie came down at nine to arrange for a rental.

"We fly to New York Thursday morning. That gives us three days to get up there and look into this grave thing." She gave him the twice over, noticing his clear eyes and clean clothes. He'd slapped on some cologne named after a spy.

A shuttle bus deposited them at Avis where they rented a British Focus with right hand drive. St. James produced his driver's license. There was some kerfuffle as Connie tried to pay for it with her credit card. Rules required the driver to pay with his credit card. St. James dug up his one and only credit card.

"Richard will reimburse me, right?"

"Of course he will."

Another shuttle took them beneath gray and lowering skies to an iridescent green Focus into which they stuffed their luggage. Using the GPS, Connie guided them through the maze of round-abouts to the M23 heading north, and from there to the M26. She repeated every phrase given by the female robot which St. James found endearing.

St. James kept his eyes on the road except when they strayed to Connie's well-turned thigh on the seat next to him.

Don't think about it, boyo. Think of HIV, think of AIDS. Rotting away like a leper, yeah, that's the ticket. He'd had his share of groupies but the last groupie was long and long ago.

The Buzzcocks' "Ever Fallen in Love" taunted him from the speakers.

They stopped at the Crown Pub in Derby for lunch by which time a light rain had begun to fall. They crouched over steaming shepherd's pie in a booth. St. James drank Coke.

"What do we know about Paddy's father?" Connie said.

"Ah, old Peter. Tried to put the touch on me once. I don't know where he got the idea I'd give him money. As if I had some. Apparently Paddy didn't leave him a thing, and why would he? Paddy hated his old man. Peter forced Paddy to butcher lambs at age seven. Can you imagine?"

"I'm surprised the old man's still alive," Connie said. Her eyes were soft. Having seen them angry, St. James never wanted to see it again.

Fat chance, he thought. St. James had a tragic, Hobbesian view of life. He believed in Murphy's Law.

"Nothing in the obits. Someone would have noted if he'd died. *Melody Maker, NME,* somebody. He's a tosser. Like father like son, eh? Me old man was a tosser, too, but everybody knows that."

"I'm pleased to see you rested and sober for a change," Connie smiled.

"One day at a time."

"How are we going to convince Peter to let us dig up Paddy?"

"That'd be easy. We bring a bottle of Scotland's best, and if that doesn't do it, your boy Serafin could always throw him a hundred quid."

"Why do you drag that guitar around?" she asked abruptly.

"That's a good question. Maybe I'll show you."

"I'd like that."

They took off in the cold drizzle. Several blocks from the pub a flash of movement caught St. James' eye. He and Connie both looked to see two teenage boys dragging a struggling dog into an alley with a rope.

St. James immediately pulled to the left side of the road. "Fuck me," he spat, jumped out of the car, and dashed across the cobbled road in the rain, splashing through puddles. Connie waited a minute, dug around in the back for the brolly, opened it up and followed, automatically pulling out her iPhone.

By the time she caught up with St. James, the boys were gone. St. James was soaked through, holding a rope connected to some kind of mastiff that sat at his feet wagging its stubby tail and grinning up at him like an idiot.

St. James looked up. "Sorry 'bout that. Somethin' about that lot didn't look right. I know that type. They start out hurting animals."

Connie knelt to the grinning mastiff. The rope was tied cruelly tight around its neck. It had no collar. Connie struggled with the knot in the rain until she had loosened it sufficiently.

"Now what? We can't take it with us." She looked with distaste at the wet muddy dog.

"Well, we can't leave 'im here," St. James said. "Look. We'll drop 'im off at the police station on the way out of town."

The GPS showed the station was right on the way. The dog made itself comfortable in the back seat amid the bags, leaving a wet brown stain on the cloth upholstery when they led it into the cop shop.

St. James explained what had happened to a kindly, red-nosed desk sergeant.

"You did the roight thing, son. We have some roight villains in this town already cut up two dogs this spring."

Connie perked up. "What was their motive?"

The sergeant looked at her with sad brown eyes. "These young people believe all sorts of shite, excuse my French, and we think there's a bit of Satanism goin' on."

Connie looked like she wanted to say more. She thanked the officer, took St. James by the arm, and steered him back out into the street.

"Let's go. We're losing time."

Connie found a classic rock station out of Birmingham and left it pegged. Yes, Emerson, Lake and Palmer, Genesis, the Move, the Stones, the Attack. They drove for two hours when the skies broke and a zag of lightning pierced the earth so close they could smell the ozone. A second later caissons of thunder rolled across the land. The opening riff of the Banshees' "Shake Your Money Maker" blasted from the radio at full volume.

St. James nearly drove off the road. Connie clutched the side grip with white knuckles, reached out and turned the volume down. St. James hadn't heard the song in years. He never played his father's music. She pushed a button. A loud commercial came on.

St. James turned the volume down further. "That's the first time I've heard the Banshees on the radio in eons."

"Me, too …" The rain was getting worse. "I thought you were going to lose it back there."

"No sudden moves, that's the ticket."

"How far to Dunkeld?" Connie asked.

"You're the navigator."

Connie used the GPS. "Another hour at least. So. What does Ian St. James listen to?"

"Power Pop. Queen. Bryan Scary, the Plimsouls, Explorers Club, Marco Joachim, Farrah, the Foreign Films, Merrymakers, Jellyfish …"

"I've never heard of any of those."

"Well, you wouldn't, would you? The so-called music industry, guys like Burke are on their way out. They just don't know it yet. *In-Crowd?* They are clueless. When the industry dinosaurs go down they're taking Serafin with them.

"These bands I'm talking aboot record their own material at home and sell it through the Internet. Often there's no bloody packaging—nothing to hold in your hands. No liner notes. I don't like that. Fails to satisfy the collector's urges. But I can't complain about the music. We're livin' through a golden age of pop, but it's all underground."

"Would you repeat those names, please?"

St. James glanced over. Connie was taking notes.

CHAPTER TWENTY-FOUR

They stayed at the Corsican Inn, run by a Sicilian family. Dinner in the attached restaurant was robust. When the waitress extended the list of single malts, St. James declined. After dinner they ordered coffee and split a crème brûlée.

Connie waited until they had both dipped spoons in the dessert. "Back there with the dog, Ian, I never would have suspected that. What made you stop?"

"Oi don't know. Just a feelin' I had."

"You ever have a dog?"

"Not one of me own, not really. Some of the families I stayed with had dogs. Oi always liked 'em."

Connie gazed at him. "I had a dog. Bonnie." Her eyes filled with memories as they finished the dessert. And then she sighed and said, "Well, let's get some rest. Tomorrow's going to be a busy day."

St. James went up to his room. It was smaller than a typical US motel room, barely room enough to do push-ups. He looked at his battered guitar case on the bed. It was covered with stickers: Grateful Dead, Violent Femmes, Not Lame, various countries he'd visited. Inside lay his trusty Gibson which Brian May had signed in Magic Marker. Sitting on the bed he unsnapped the case, took out the guitar, and held it on his lap.

A riff had been rattling around inside his head for days. Tuning the guitar by ear, he worked the riff. It had Marshall Crenshaw chords. He played around with the melody for a few minutes, set the guitar aside, and took a pad and pen from the case.

My daddy died before I was born.
Some say that's for the best.

He was a rakehell bastard ripped and torn
Thought love was just a jest

St. James looked at the words. Good chords forgave a multitude of bad lyrics. Someone knocked at the door.

St. James was surprised to see Connie through the peephole. He opened the door.

"I thought you were going to play me your new stuff."

St. James shrugged, pleased and surprised. "I can't very well invite you in. There isn't room for the two of us."

"Let's go down to the lobby. They've got a fire going, and there's nobody there."

The lobby, with its tile floor, Persian rugs, and framed paintings of Venice and St. Peter's Basilica, was deserted. Rain drummed against the windows and the roof. St. James sat on an ottoman in front of the fire and played his song softly, pounding out a backbeat on the Gibson's hollow body with his hands. The song had good bones. He could feel it.

When he, finished Connie clapped in delight. "What else you got?"

"That's it."

"I thought you were writing songs."

St. James rubbed the bridge of his nose. "I've been having writer's block."

"Know any Dylan?"

St. James softly tiptoed through "All Along the Watchtower." When he finished, they both sat in silence for several minutes.

Connie stood. "Thank you for that. We'd better get some rest. It's going to rain all day tomorrow."

"Did I tell ya I worked one summer as a gravedigger?" St. James said.

Connie looked back with a half-smile. "Really?"

"For real," he said as they headed for their rooms. Once inside, he tossed his guitar on the sofa and collapsed on the bed.

O   O   O

St. James woke at six and looked outside. No way. He did fifty push-ups and a hundred sit-ups on the tiny floor, leaving him sweating and breathing hard. He took a shower, and, for the first time in God knew how long, did not feel like death warmed over. At eight he joined Connie for bangers and mash in the restaurant. At a quarter of nine they were on the road. The wipers could barely contend with the heavy rain. They drove for hours in the deluge, no faster than forty.

They pulled into Odoyle at seven-thirty. It was nearly full dark and the rain had settled into a steady drizzle. The only lights in the tiny village emanated from the Hog's Head Pub. The four regulars in the overheated pub stared at the unlikely couple, until St. James took Connie's hand and led her to the bar. She wore a baggy hoodie with the hood up.

The bartender, a ruddy-faced man with a curly gray beard, leaned on the bar. "Hell of a night. What can I get ye?"

"Oh, a couple of hot coffees I think," St. James said. "And is there any place to stay around here?" The GPS hadn't worked for the last three hours.

"Aye, there's the Bainbridge Inn about fifteen miles further on. I could phone 'em if you like."

"That's very kind of you," Connie said taking a stool next to St. James. The bartender got them two steaming coffees in oversized mugs and placed a bowl of sealed half-and-halfs and sugar in front of them. The bartender placed an ancient Bakelite phone on the bar and dialed. When the phone rang, he handed it to Connie, who reserved two rooms for them.

The regulars returned to their drinks and their stories.

As Connie hung up the phone the bartender came back and leaned on the bar. "So what brings you to Odoyle?"

"We're looking for Peter MacGowan."

The bartender leaned back as if he'd caught a whiff of the grave. "MacGowan? What do ye want with him?" Said in such a way as to suggest they were insane.

"We're working on a story about the Banshees," Connie said.

The bartender made an ugly face. "If ye call that music. Doubt you'll get much out of old MacGowan. Fried his brain years ago on the sauce, an' he's a nasty piece of business, that one. His boy Paddy lit out of there as soon as he was able. And good riddance, I say. He always was a nasty little prick."

"Do you know where we can find him?" St. James said.

"Och, aye. Aboot twelve mile out of town, ye'll see a road heading north. Look hard because it's easy to miss the sign. Rathkroghen Road. It's a rough road, not somethin' you'd be attempting at night. MacGowan lives in a cottage—an old shack, really—about six miles north, right where the road gives out."

Connie wrote it down in a pad. They finished their coffee and paid the tab.

"Good luck," the bartender said as they headed out. "Yer gonna need it."

CHAPTER TWENTY-FIVE

The hacker's name was George Lindenkugel, but he called himself Spyder. He arrived at Melchior's office on a Triumph motorcycle wearing a torn black-leather jacket and torn dungarees. His T-shirt was artfully ripped. He had a stud through his nose and a loop through his brow. His hair was dyed yellow.

He slouched in Melchior's office drinking a Red Bull. "How'd you hear about me?" Spyder asked, unimpressed with the trappings of greatness.

"Niles Poor," Melchior said.

"Ah, Niles, my favorite right-wing bastard. I wish he'd direct another movie."

"I bet you do. I hear you made out like a bandit on the last one."

"You want authenticity you come to Spyder."

"I will pay you ten thousand dollars."

"You want me to hack this website. Then what?"

"I want you to shut 'em down. Give 'em the stuxnet worm or whatever you've got. I want you to cause so much damage no one will ever think of putting up a bogus Banshees website ever again."

Spyder made a pistol of his thumb and forefinger. "Gotcha."

Melchior produced a three-page document. "I've drawn up a contract ..."

"Oh mannn, don't give me no fuckin' contract. Five thou now, five thou when the job is done."

"How do I know I can trust you?"

"What? Just watch the fuckin' net. They'll be down in twelve hours guaranteed."

"You can't talk about this."

Spyder looked pained. "Oh mannn. Do you know anything about the hacker underground?"

"No."

"Spyder's word is his bond, man. Go online. Ask anyone."

Melchior went to his desk and used a cylinder key to unlock a bottom drawer. He took out a metal cash box and opened it. It contained seventy grand for miscellaneous expenses. He counted out five thousand in Benjamins.

Spyder tucked them in his leather jacket. "I'll be back tomorrow for the other five."

"If I'm not here, I'll arrange for my secretary Betsy to give you the money."

Spyder stopped at the door. "Damned white of you, brother." He left Melchior's office and walked down the corridor and out through the reception area. Melchior's staff was used to far more outré characters than Spyder and barely took notice.

Spyder retrieved his Triumph from the Warner lot, where he worked off and on as a consultant for crime shows including *Law & Order* and *NCIS: Los Angeles*. He'd left the bike on its center stand, just inside the main gate under the watchful eye of Augie the gate guard, whom he'd tipped twenty.

Spyder waved to Augie, rolled the bike onto its wheels, started her up, and headed back to his place, a loft in West Hollywood he shared with Maggot Brain and Zimmy. Spyder took chances and split lanes. He rode around to the back alley entrance and rode the Triumph up a concrete ramp to a loading zone. Setting the kickstand and turning off the engine, Spyder got off the bike and flipped the cover up on a numerical keypad mounted on the brick wall. He glanced once at the video cam looking down on him from the third floor roof. He quickly entered the code, and the steel door retracted into the ceiling with a hair-raising screech.

Spyder dashed inside and turned off the security system. He rolled the Triumph into a broad industrial space which contained several automobiles shrouded in canvas. Spyder closed the garage door and reset the security system. Walking past the freight elevator, he took the stairs to the third floor landing with a steel door on either side, each with an eyehole. Spyder's was on the left. There was a camera on the wall covering both entrances.

He flipped up the cover on the keypad and entered a code. His door unlocked electronically. Spyder entered the vast space, arms spread wide. This was his domain. This is where he ruled. Maggot Brain and Zimmy had gone to Las Vegas for an electronic security convention, so Spyder had the place to himself.

The huge space had a hardwood floor, a ten-foot wall of cabinets and free-standing partitions. Motes of dust hovered in shafts of sunlight coming through the large vertical windows. There was a conversation cluster consisting of four beanbag chairs surrounding a discarded telephone company spool. There was a humongous water pipe on the spool table. Two working pinball machines gleamed against one wall. The room also contained a Hewlett-Packard Blade server with several cups, stacks of network hubs, and piles of Ethernet cable.

Spyder reached for a fat roach on the lip of an overloaded ashtray and lit it. He inhaled deeply. On the few square inches of desk space lay a pen, some Post-it notes, and a single-edged razor blade.

"Time to make the doughnuts," he said

He brought up the Banshees' home page. A black screen appeared accompanied by an ominous bass line. A red dot appeared in the center of the screen and expanded with explosive force into the bright red logo as the speakers blared "Welcome to Hell." He placed the cursor over the logo. A pop-up said "ENTER." He pushed the button.

A drumroll merged into thunder as he entered the website. A photo of the band bent over their axes taken from behind and above a madly pogoing crowd. When he placed the cursor on each individual band member a short bio popped up. Spyder didn't care about that. But he dug the band. His taste ran to death metal, and he worshiped the classics: Deep Purple, Judas Priest, Anthrax, and Tool.

Spyder tapped a few keys getting the Banshees' home page to spit out its operating system and version. He reached over to a media tower containing CDs and videos and grabbed a flash drive containing a program designed to crack the password. He entered the program.

The Banshees' logo wavered. The band played on. A slight whirring noise alerted him to the fact that the hard drive had ejected his disc. He pulled it out to make certain he'd entered it right side up. He had. He inserted it again. There was no visible effect.

"Hmmmmm," Spyder said. He initiated the wardialer which dialed thousands of his "bots," computers which, unbeknownst to their owners, were under his control. He entered a program instructing his bots to contact the website in an effort to overload the system.

"Jesus on a moped," Spyder muttered. "Welcome to Hell" ended and "Do the World a Favor (Off Yourself)" came on. It was a righteous jam! Spyder had never heard of the Banshees before Niles had contacted him on behalf of Melchior, but they were all right. And if Melchior produced them he was all right, although it seemed to Spyder that Melchior did not wish the band well.

High on weed and Red Bull, Spyder got up to do the funky chicken.

> *Stop takin' up space. Don't be a dope.*
> *Go to the kitchen and get you a rope.*

All of a sudden Spyder didn't feel well. A tendril of doubt wormed its way into his heart.

> *If you want to get to Hades,*
> *you've got to swallow razor blades.*

CHAPTER TWENTY-SIX

The Bainbridge Inn was as close to an American motel as Scotland was likely to offer, a series of rooms beneath a steeply pitched roof stretching from the office, each with parking outside its door. St. James rose at six. The sky was threatening, but there was no rain. Putting on his tennis shoes and sweats, he stretched and hit the road. Aches and pains manifested themselves from the previous day, but he sucked it in and ran it off. After ten minutes, the aches all merged into one.

He looped behind the Bainbridge up a rocky trail that rose sharply above the village. From the top he could see the tiny village, various farms, and outbuildings stretching out before him in the hilly gray earth. Visibility was limited to about a half mile because of the fog. He reckoned he'd done a mile by the time he got back to his room, gasping and sweating. Well, Rome wasn't built in a day.

Connie joined St. James for breakfast in the hotel's diner. They took a booth by the fogged window. "My friend Gert called me this morning," Connie said. "She works for *Der Stern*. She did a little digging and found that Klapp left the university under a cloud. Many student complaints, mostly from outraged feminists. Apparently his brand of patriarchal Druidism was not what they wanted to hear."

"They can't bounce the bloke just because the students don't like the facts."

"There were allegations of improper contact with female students."

St. James pinned his lower right eyelid with his index finger and pulled down, producing a lugubrious expression.

Connie laughed.

They checked out and drove to the nearest hardware store, in Selkirk, where they purchased two spade-tipped shovels, gloves, a pick, and buckets. "Relax," St. James said. "Oi've done this before."

Their departure had to wait until eleven when the local off-license opened. St. James suspected that Peter MacGowan really didn't give a damn what kind of Scotch they got him, but it was Richard Serafin's money so what the hell. They got him a bottle of Macallan. They headed back to Odoyle searching for the turnoff to MacGowan's place. They passed the nearly invisible road twice before Connie spotted an old wooden pole in the ditch and nearby the detached shingle pointing to Rathkroghen. The shingle was made of rotted wood, the black on white lettering barely legible. It was their first official confirmation that such a place existed.

The rocky rutted road wound up and over the hill, and within minutes, they were out of sight of the main road. Within a mile they were out of sight of civilization. The road wound before them through bleak gray hills overgrown with gorse. The fog had lifted and a pale sun rose, but you'd never know it was summer. A stone monolith jutted toward the sky, too symmetrical to be anything other than the work of man.

Several times the car scraped its frame on the rocks. "I hope we don't trash the bleedin' car," St. James said.

"Just as long as it gets us there."

Connie fiddled with the radio but was unable to find anything but static, which was odd, because they were in the south of Scotland within broadcast distance not only of most English stations but those on the continent as well. Nor did the GPS work.

"I think we're off the grid," she said.

They rode on in silence until it seemed they must have passed MacGowan's place or been given bogus direction.

"I think we should turn around," Connie said.

"We'll just go up to that next ridge, and if we don't see it, we'll go back." St. James shifted the car into first and ground up the rough surface. They stopped where the road leveled off for about ten yards before plunging down into the next valley. A gray building made of field stone lay a quarter mile ahead, a little off the path. It had a thatched roof and smoke issued from the chimney despite it being one-thirty in the afternoon.

Connie got out of the car and took pictures. "What a terrible place."

The only visible trees were twisted and devoid of leaves. The land looked like a frozen angry sea. Tiny lochs reflected the bleak sky. Connie got back in the car and they descended toward the cabin. Two forlorn gateposts marked a rock path leading to the cabin's front door. It had been fitted with frame windows. *Has to be absolute hell in the wintertime*, St. James thought.

Grabbing the bottle of Macallan from the back seat, St. James got out. Connie was already at the front door. She lifted the cast-iron knocker in the shape of a gremlin and let it fall with a clank. St. James joined her. There was no response. She let it fall again.

From inside the cottage, they heard sounds of movement, scraping furniture, a man cursing. Seconds later the door swung inward, revealing an old man who had once been tall but was now stooped, wild white hair flying in all directions, wearing grimy long johns, dungarees, and a pair of red suspenders. He was barefoot.

"What do ye fuckin' want?" he said in a gravelly voice.

"Mr. Peter MacGowan? Hello! I'm Connie Cosgrove from *In Crowd* magazine, and this is my associate Ian St. James."

The old man peered at St. James intensely. "St. James, eh? I remember you. And a fuckin' lot of good it done me."

St. James held up the bottle of Scotch. "My circumstances weren't much better than yours, Mr. MacGowan. We brought you a little something to atone for it."

MacGowan reached for the Scotch, a gleam in his eye. "Macallan, eh? Well, you done good with the selection, now what do ye want?"

Connie went doe-eyed. "Do you mind if we come inside, Mr. MacGowan?"

MacGowan melted like a Popsicle in a microwave at the sight of Connie. "Aye. Come in. It's a cold fuckin' day for June. A dram'll cheer us all up."

He ushered them into the main room which included a tiny corner kitchen. Two closed doors presumably led to the bedroom and water closet. The room had a wood floor and a few filthy scatter rugs. Two rough-hewn benches like you might find at a summer camp pulled up to an old wood table. A fat black tabby dozed in a pale beam of light. An ancient black and white photograph hung on the wall, depicting a much younger Peter, wife Abbie, and baby Paddy standing in front of a larger house with a picket fence. Next to it was a framed Banshees poster advertising their appearance at Albert Hall.

MacGowan sat on the bench and uncorked the Scotch. He reached over to the kitchen counter and grabbed three glasses, each touting a different beer. St. James held his hands up. "None for me, thanks."

MacGowan shrugged and poured. Connie stopped him at one finger.

MacGowan hoisted his glass. "Cheers."

Connie sipped.

MacGowan refilled his glass. "So what do ye want?"

"We'd like to dig up Paddy's grave. We understand you buried him yourself not far from here."

"That I did and I'd prefer he stayed buried. What in the world do ye want to do that for?"

"We have reason to believe that's not Paddy you buried there. I understand he was nearly incinerated in the crash. You never actually saw a body, did you?"

MacGowan looked at her through his hedgerow brows. "That I didn't. And what do ye hope to prove?"

"The Banshees are back, Mr. MacGowan," Connie said. "We saw them two nights ago in Berlin."

"Yer daft."

"Did you ever see them?" Connie asked.

"Never. I like Victor Borgia." MacGowan poured himself another drink.

"Do we have permission to take a look in the coffin? Will you show us where you buried him?"

MacGowan waved her away. "Ahhhhh! Do what ye like, but I'm not going over there. Not today. Too much to do."

St. James looked at the sleeping cat.

"Will you tell us how to get there?" Connie pressed in her most sincere and girlish voice.

MacGowan gestured again. "Just keep on this road another six miles. You'll see an iron gate by the side of the road. Falling down, it is. That's the entrance to the old Rathkroghen cemetery. Paddy's grave's the one with the guitar on the headstone. I didn't pay for it. Some fan paid for it. Only person who showed up at the burial. Paddy didn't leave many friends, did he?"

"May I take your picture Mr. MacGowan?"

The wave. "Ahhhh!"

Taking it for consent, Connie pulled out her little silver camera and carefully shot MacGowan as he sat at the table glowering. "Thank you, sir. We'll take no more of your time."

MacGowan didn't answer as he carefully poured another couple of fingers. Connie placed a Walter Scott on the table. "Thank you for your trouble."

MacGowan disappeared the bill into his pants as Connie and St. James headed out the door.

"Put it back the way ye found it," he called after them.

onnie and St. James got out of the car and stared at the burial ground in sickly fascination. A wrought iron fence enclosing several hundred square feet had long since collapsed. The gate hung at an angle from one hinge. The gravestones were as old and weathered as ancient steel.

People had planted shrubbery and trees over the years but little of it survived. Dead branches clawed out of the earth. In the middle distance, a dozen crows occupied a skeletal tree like Apache warriors on a hill. Even in the pale sunlight it was cold.

Connie took out her camera. "Could it possibly be any uglier?"

St. James opened the car's boot, took out the shovels, pails, gloves, and pick. "Come on. Help me with this stuff."

"Shouldn't we find the grave first?"

"Go ahead. Wave when you find it."

It wasn't difficult to locate. It was the newest and most elaborate of the headstones, a pink marble slab with

Paddy MacGowan
B. December 31, 1944
D. August 19, 1975

beneath a beautifully rendered Rickenbacker.

Connie waved. "Over here!"

St. James hung the pails from both ends of the two shovels which he placed across his shoulders. He set the tools next to the slight indentation in the spongy soil. The harsh landscape wore a coat of lichen. Connie took several photographs of the headstone.

"Who paid for this?"

St. James put on the heavy cotton work gloves and picked up a shovel. "Melchior."

"Did he buy headstones for the others?"

"They were cremated. He took out full page ads in *Billboard*, *Variety*, all those rags, lamenting the tragic deaths, young lives cut short, and so on."

"Brrrr. This place gives me the creeps. Were you really a gravedigger?"

"That I was, one summer at Falmouth. I'll start at this end, and you start at that end."

"You expect me to dig?"

"C'mon, love. Don't make a geezer do all the work."

Connie put on the pair of gloves and picked up a shovel. An eerie wind whistled through skeletal branches. "I expect the Hound of the Baskervilles to show up any second."

St. James placed the shovel's blade against the earth and stepped on the lip. "You dig sixteen tons and what do you get," he sang.

They worked in silence for an hour, excavating a foot down. They broke, drank bottled water, and ate pre-fab sandwiches they'd picked up in Selkirk. Connie put on a leather jacket with cinched waist and cuffs. The temperature continued to fall.

"You know what's funny?" Connie said.

"What?"

"Paddy's is the only headstone that's legible. I've looked at quite a few others, and it's almost as if they began to melt or something. You can make out a letter here, a number there, sometimes a whole name, but that's about it. Who were these people? Why are they buried in such a desolate spot?"

St. James shrugged. "Paupers. Gypsies. Who knows?"

"I mean, has this place always been here?"

"According to Herr Professor, this is the very place where the village of Rathkroghen stood."

"I googled it. There's nothing. The closest is an Irish Stone-henge."

St. James stretched and rose from the flat stone on which he'd been sitting. "Well, the proof is in the pudding. Shall we?"

It was twilight when St. James' shovel thumped against the coffin, six feet down. St. James was bone-weary and ached in every fiber of his body, but the hard physical labor had done him good. He wouldn't have to run tomorrow. Connie had done her share, taking the pails of dirt and depositing them next to the grave.

St. James bashed a trench out all around the coffin so he could get to the clasp. "Get the lantern from the boot, luv. It's too dark down here."

St. James stood atop the coffin, leaning on the shovel's handle while Connie returned to the car. Because of where he was standing and the intervening headstones, he could not see the car.

Something thumped against the lid from inside the coffin. St. James squealed and staggered, heart rocketing into his throat. Frantically, he scrambled out of the grave banging his knee on a rock. He knelt, wincing. Connie approached shining the big flashlight on the ground in front of her. The beam found St. James.

"What happened to you?"

St. James got to his feet. "Let me have that."

Connie handed him the flashlight. He shined it on the coffin lid. He listened. The *thump* of impact made him jump.

"What?" Connie asked again.

It was a clump of earth falling off the side of the excavation. There was nothing alive in Paddy MacGowan's grave. A crow dive-bombed them screeching. Connie yelled and waved her shovel. The crow flew back to its perch among the others.

"Let's get this over with," St. James said, picking up the shovel and the pick and jumping into the grave. It took him twenty minutes to remove the bulk of the dirt from the top. It was a steel coffin. The exposed lid had two sections, one from mid-thorax up. Crouching on the bottom section, St. James cleared the dirt off the top using his hands to clear dirt he couldn't lift with the shovel.

"Watch it," Connie said as he tossed a handful to the side. She'd set down the flashlight on the rim of the hole and picked up her gizmo. She moved around the grave snapping pictures, the strobe adding a surreal effect.

He undid the clasp, inserted the edge of the pick beneath the lid, and pried it open with a dry, ratcheting sound that made his hair stand on end. A whiff of eye-watering acid enveloped his head.

"Shine that lantern down here please."

Connie kneeled at the lip of the grave, fixing the beam on the coffin. St. James reached down and pried it all the way open with a desiccated grinding sound. They stared in befuddlement. Inside lay an organic knot of twisted fiber. Some kind of root. Connie snapped a picture.

Wearing gloves, St. James reached down and picked it up. It weighed about ten pounds and was a foot long. It smelled faintly of some exotic spice.

"What is it?"

"I don't know. Here. Take it."

He handed the root to Connie.

She sniffed at it as if it were a bottle of expensive cologne. "Sandalwood? Patchouli?" She set it on a patch of furze and photographed it.

By now it was full night, thousands of stars winking in the velvet sky. St. James turned his attention back to the coffin. The satin lining retained much of its red coloring. The visible part of the coffin was empty save for dust and dirt that had just tumbled in.

"Let's get out of here," Connie said.

"Hang on." St. James got on his knees, bent over and reached toward the bottom of the coffin, the unseen part. His hand closed around a smooth cylindrical object. He drew it out. At first he didn't know what he held—a delicate tube carved from bone with finger holes surrounded by intricate cuneiform.

The shock of recognition zapped him like an electric fence:
A flute.

Chapter Twenty-eight

Maggot Brain and Zimmy arrived home at 2 AM after driving straight through from Las Vegas. Their Dodge van was crammed with electronic equipment they'd wheedled, and in some cases actually purchased, at the electronic security convention. Cameras the size of lapel pins. Programs designed to elucidate a single speech from a crowd's babble. Sensors attuned to body heat.

They parked the van in the lot they shared with a dry cleaner and karate studio, set the alarms, and headed into the building through the front, an art deco entrance with bronze triangular door handles.

Zimmy pushed the button for the freight elevator. "I can't believe I got Charlie Sheen's autograph, man! That was so cool."

The elevator rumbled to a stop. They pulled open the brass gate and got in. Zimmy pushed the button for the third floor.

"No shit. Sitting there with that babe on his lap playing poker. He's my hero, man."

"Spyder's gonna shit when we tell him what he missed."

The elevator lurched to a stop. They got out on the third floor landing. Zimmy flipped up the cover on the keypad and entered the code. Nothing happened. Zimmy looked at the keypad.

"What the fuck. Nothing's lighting up."

Maggot Brain looked at the brightly lit wall sconce. "It's not a power outage. It must be local to the unit. Just bang on the door. He'll be up."

Zimmy banged on the door with the bottom of his fist. "Open up! Zimmy and Maggot Brain are in the house!"

He ceased pounding and they listened. Nothing.

Zimmy kicked the door with his steel-tipped Doc Martens with metronomic regularity.

A moment later the door to the other loft opened and Kim Rhee, the proprietor of the karate shop, stuck his head out. "What's wrong with you guys? It's two o'clock in the morning."

"Hey, oh, sorry, Kim. We're trying to get in our place. Have you seen Spyder?"

"No. Why can't you get in your place?"

"There's no power to the keypad. That's the only way to open the door."

"What about the fire escape?"

Zimmy and Maggot Brain looked at each other. Genius!

Problem: the windows were wired into the alarm system. Solution: the power was off there, too. It was all part of the same system.

Rhee watched Maggot Brain and Zimmy swivel toward the roof stairs. Quietly, he closed his door. Zimmy and Maggot Brain emerged on the flat tar roof of their industrial building and walked to the rear where the fire escape cantilevered out over the alley. Over the years, oxidation had turned once black wrought iron brick orange.

Maggot Brain, who was six four and weighed 350 pounds, looked over the edge. "I'm not sure this'll hold my weight."

"Bullshit, man. California building codes. What if Michael Moore gets caught in a fire here? They just gonna sacrifice him 'cause he's too fucking fat?"

"Get out there, you asshole. You're better at this shit than I am anyway."

Zimmy flexed his hands. "You want the ninja, you get the ninja." He stepped out onto the iron grid. It felt solid. "Okay, hang here for a minute."

Zimmy went down the iron steps to the small platform outside one of the vertical windows. The window opened outward but was clasped shut. Zimmy slapped his palm on the window several times.

"Yo! Spyder!"

He shaded his eyes with his hand and peered through the dark window. The servers and monitors had gone dark. A fluorescent Frisbee was the only visible object, a pale moon on the floor. Zimmy leaned back.

"Ahmina have to bust a window!"

"Do it!" Maggot Brain called.

Zimmy reached into his pocket and removed a folding knife with a mace-like tip. He took off his Army of Darkness T-shirt and wrapped it around his hand. He shattered the window with one blow. For a moment the sound of breaking glass reverberated up and down the alley. It was a mean, ugly sound, a lawless sound. The little industrial strip in which they lived backed up against a steep hill.

"I'm going back down," Maggot Brain called. "Let me in the front door."

"Check."

Zimmy shook out his T-shirt and tossed it through the broken window. Careful not to cut his ass on the ridge of glass sticking up from the frame, Zimmy crawled into the loft on hands and knees, emerging on a corduroy sofa like a big alley cat. All the monitors, including the SCTV, were dark. Zimmy stood just inside the window waiting for his eyes to adjust.

"Yo, dude! Where the fuck are ya?"

Nothing.

"Stupid asshole," Zimmy muttered, heading for the front door. He flipped on the overheads and suddenly the big room was flooded with cool fluorescent light. In the entry alcove, he flipped up the lid on the alarm system. Still no power. He unlocked the front door manually and let Maggot Brain in.

"He's not here," Zimmy said.

"Must be some chick," Maggot Brain said.

Each went straight to his station to check his e-mail. Zimmy checked Spyder's station. "What the fuck izzis?"

Spyder had swept his manuals, porn mags, and comic books off his work station leaving two pliers and the spines of several razor blades. A few shards of metal remained. Zimmy picked up the pliers and turned them around. One razor blade was only missing about a third. It looked to Zimmy as if Spyder had been methodically breaking up razor blades into smaller fragments using metal fatigue. The man was a genius. No telling what he'd invent.

A few minutes later, Maggot Brain went to the bathroom.

"OH FUCK!" he yelled.

Zimmy leaped out of his chair. "What?"

"COME IN HERE!"

Zimmy ran to the bathroom and wedged himself through the door beneath Maggot Brain's arm. Spyder lay twisted on the black and white tile floor, a fountain of blood flowing from his grotesquely slashed mouth. His bloody hand lay palm up clutching a handful of metal shards. A metal barb protruded from between Spyder's upper teeth. His tongue was blood pudding.

"If you want to get to Hades, you've got to swallow razor blades," Maggot Brain wheezed from somewhere back in his lizard brain.

CHAPTER TWENTY-NINE

St. James and nausea were old pals. The difference this time was that there was no drink involved.

"What is it?" Connie said.

St. James couldn't speak. He was afraid if he opened his mouth animal noises would come out. He handed the flute to Connie.

She looked at it for several seconds.

"Oh," she said dropping the flute. It landed on the spongy ground intact emitting a faint obscenely musical tone.

St. James closed the coffin lid and climbed out. He sat for a minute on the edge of the grave breathing hard. He got up and sank his shovel into the pile of dark flinty soil they'd unearthed. The first load hit the coffin with a *thunk* of finality.

"Help me," he said.

"Shouldn't we put it back?"

St. James stopped shoveling and looked at her. "The police might need it for the DNA."

Connie's mouth went round. "Are you suggesting the Banshees were Satanic murderers?"

"I don't know. Maybe it's an animal bone. Help me fill the bloody grave, and let's get the fuck outta here."

Connie picked up a shovel.

An hour later, they passed MacGowan's cottage in the car again. A single light burned through a slit in the drapes.

Connie gripped the handhold tightly. "If we go to the police with this, we'll most likely miss the Banshees' debut in New York."

"I know." St. James hunched over the wheel searching for obstacles in the Ford's flat headlights.

"We can do the DNA testing in New York. It will go a lot faster."

They barreled through the tunnel of night, minds furiously racing. Connie turned on the radio and roamed through FM until she found some chilly Finnish jazz.

Neither could sleep so they took turns driving, and by dawn they had reached Oxford.

"Praise Jesus!" Connie declared as her Internet access returned. Connie booked them into the Stoke on Trent Arms, an elegant old Victorian. They couldn't get to their rooms until one, so they found a breakfast place and hung over a large meal while Connie made airplane reservations. Their food arrived before she was done. St. James laid to with a vengeance.

Connie finalized the tickets and watched him eat for a minute before picking up her fork. She was thinking about the dog. She wouldn't date a guy who didn't love dogs. Not that she had any interest in dating this relic.

When they were allowed into their rooms, St. James collapsed on the bed and was almost instantaneously asleep. Connie went to her room. It was small but elegant. She checked her phone. Serafin had called three times during the past twenty-four hours.

She phoned him back.

"What's going on?" he answered.

"Rich, this just keeps getting weirder and weirder. I told you about Professor Klapp. He was right, Rich."

"Right about what? Don't tell me you actually exhumed the body."

"There was no body. There was some kind of root and a flute made out of bone. It might be human bone."

"Human bone?"

"Professor Klapp told us that Laird Rathkroghen sacrificed children and made flutes of their bones."

"Jesus! This is dynamite shit!"

Connie cringed. Serafin had said the same thing about really good coke.

"We'll be in New York tonight. I know people who can do a DNA study on the flute and tell us whether it's animal or human."

"You took the flute?"

"We've got it. We'll be in New York by nine PM Eastern. We're staying at the Raphael."

"When can we expect copy?"

"I'm exhausted. I've been up all night. I'm going to take a Xanax and go to sleep. I should have something by the time we land in New York."

"All right. Get some rest. And those pictures you sent? Dynamite. We just don't know how we're going to use them."

"Wait 'til you see the next batch."

Connie said goodbye, went into the bathroom, and took as hot a bath as she could stand. The Xanax did its work and she was asleep in fifteen minutes. She liked Xanax. It was a palindrome. It seemed she had just lay down when the telephone rang with her wake-up call. It was five PM. Their flight left Heathrow at seven.

St. James was waiting for her in the lobby with his backpack and guitar. The flute was in the guitar case. He was counting on airport security's ignorance. They weren't looking for bone artifacts and wouldn't recognize it as a national treasure.

They turned the rental in at Heathrow and took a shuttle to their terminal. Connie breezed right through, but as usual, airport security waved St. James aside for extra scrutiny. He got the wand and a pat-down and they opened up the guitar case.

A slim Indian with the nameplate Patrice Mukerjhee examined the bone flute under the terminals harsh lights. "You are a musician?"

"'At's right. Maybe you've heard of me."

"I can't say that I have, Mr. St. James."

"You should check out my website. You moight like it."

Mukerjhee smiled, replaced the flute, closed the guitar case, and waved St. James through. At the gate, Connie and St. James boarded early with the other first-class travelers. St. James hadn't flown first-class since he'd signed his first contract with Sony twenty years ago. The 747 took off on schedule. St. James tipped his chair back and went to sleep. Connie took out her laptop and began to write.

CHAPTER THIRTY

Melchior had not heard from Spyder in twenty-four hours. The Banshees' website continued as before. All of Melchior's phone messages went straight to Spyder's answering machine. Melchior began to think he'd been ripped off—the little shit had taken his five gees and left him in the wind. The more he thought about it, the angrier he got. Where did that fucking punk get the idea he could rip off Burke Melchior?

Melchior summoned Stanton to his office.

"Where's Eltaeb?"

"He'll be here in ten minutes, boss."

"Run down to Schlotsky's and get me a corned beef on rye. Just mustard. No mayo. Maybe a Coke or something."

Five minutes after Stanton left, Melchior's secretary opened the door. "Greg Eltaeb, boss."

"Thank you Betsy. Show him in."

Greg rolled into the room in slacks, blinding white T-shirt and a beige summer sports coat. He enclosed Melchior's hand in his giant meat hook. Greg was a celebrity detective of Mexican/Libyan descent, stood six four and weighed an even 300 pounds.

"How the hell are ya, Burke?"

"Fair to middling, Greg. Have a seat. I have two assignments for you."

Stanton knocked and entered carrying a Schlotzky's bag. He set it on the desk and retreated. Greg stared at the bag.

"You gonna eat?"

Melchior removed the bag from his desk and set it in the desk well, invisible to the detective. "It's for a sick pal."

Eltaeb took out a pen and pad. "Who do you want me to kill?"

"I hired this hacker, goes by the name of Spyder, but his real name is George Lindenkugel. I paid him five gees yesterday to take down the Banshees' website, and I got bupkus. Now he's not answering his calls. I want you to track him down and ask him what's his problem? I have a nasty suspicion he took the money and ran."

"Address? Phone number? SS number?"

Melchior slid a sheet of note paper across his desk. Melchior picked it up.

"No address."

"That's why I need you, Greg."

Eltaeb stuffed the note inside his jacket. "And the other?"

"This one's a little tricky. The Banshees are playing Axton's in the Village tomorrow night."

"What village?"

"Greenwich Village. New York. I need a lock of the lead singer's hair."

Eltaeb was nonplussed. "Why?"

"Because the bastard is claiming to be someone who died forty years ago, and I want to run a DNA test and shove it down his throat."

"I see."

"How's your show coming?"

The Discovery Channel had approached Eltaeb about doing a reality show that would follow him around much like *Dog the Bounty Hunter.*

Eltaeb grinned and stretched, moving the heavy leather sofa six inches. "The money's good, but once I sign on the dotted line, I can kiss real investigation goodbye. I'll cease to be a private eye and become a celebrity. I honestly don't know what to do. I love my job and I make a good living. The show pays a lot more, but what happens if it bombs and they cancel after a season or two? What am I going to do then? I'd look like a fool."

"Have you got a good lawyer?"

"Epstein."

"Epstein's the best. Listen to his advice." Melchior hit the intercom. "Betsy, write Mr. Eltaeb a five thousand dollar check as a retainer."

"Yes, boss."

Eltaeb smiled revealing a gold tooth. "You want to spend five gees to recover five gees?"

Melchior looked straight at him. "It's the principle. No one rips me off."

Eltaeb stood. Melchior stood. They shook hands. After Eltaeb had shut the door behind him, Melchior reached beneath the desk and retrieved his corned beef sandwich. He opened the sandwich up. He examined the condiments. He rang Stanton.

A minute later the assistant opened the door to his office. "Boss?"

Melchior threw the sandwich at his assistant. "Hey, asshole! I said no mayo. Now take it back and get me another one."

CHAPTER THIRTY-ONE

Knowing Spyder worked as a consultant at Warner's, Eltaeb asked Augie the gate guard what type of vehicle Spyder drove. Upon learning it was a late model Triumph Bonneville, Eltaeb approached a contact at the DMV and obtained a listing of all registered Triumph Bonnevilles in Los Angeles County. There was only one George Lindenkugel, and he lived at 323 Harrison in West Hollywood, a three block light industrial strip backed up against the hills.

Spyder's address was a three-story warehouse whose bottom floor housed a laundry and a karate studio. Eltaeb parked his Mercedes 350SL in front of the building. tae kwon do was in session, and he paused to watch a dozen eager students throwing punches and snapping into stances at their Korean instructor's commands.

Eltaeb examined the register. He pushed the button for Maggot Brain. There was no response. He tried the main door. It was unlocked. Students from the karate studio entered off the lobby. Eltaeb went up the stairs, careful to step next to the walls out of habit. So he wouldn't squeak. The steel door to Spyder's loft was covered with stickers: Grateful Dead, Dead Kennedys, AC/DC, Helmet, Green Day, Legalize Pot, Obama, the Lakers.

The lid on the security system keypad was up. It looked dead. He tried the door. It was unlocked. As soon as he swung it open, he knew something bad had happened. The heavy oppressive smell of congealed blood socked him in the kisser. The place vibed empty. Nevertheless Eltaeb took a small automatic pistol from his cargo pants and proceeded with caution.

He walked down a short hall into a vast space lit by girders of light slanting through the vertical windows. The place was a mess. Boxes, papers, electronic components scattered all over the floor. Furniture shoved into a corner. It looked like it had been abandoned under duress. Clean rectangles amid the dust on the tables indicated where hard drives, keyboards and servers had sat. Patches on the wall indicated where pictures had been removed. Most of the furniture remained. It was junk.

Eltaeb proceeded cautiously to the middle of the room and did a slow 360, sighting over his gun. Eltaeb stopped rotating with his eyes on the bathroom door. A tendril of blood extended from beneath the closed door. Eltaeb picked up a broom handle and used it to slowly ease the door open. A skylight in the bathroom's ceiling cast illumination. Eltaeb found the body lying in a puddle of blood.

Technically he should have called 911. But Eltaeb's clients came first. Careful not to step in the blood Eltaeb entered the bathroom as delicately as a fawn, sliding along the unmarked floor between the corpse and the bath. He noted the tiny metal chips in the blood and in the dead man's mouth. They didn't bother Eltaeb. In all his years as a cop, he had never encountered such a grisly method of suicide. The kid had to be out of his mind on drugs. PCP or Ecstasy maybe.

Gingerly, the big man crouched and dipped two fingers into the corpse's front pocket extracting his wallet. Eltaeb retraced his steps and sat in an office chair next to a table containing two pliers, some razor blade spines, and an ashtray full of Marlboro butts and roaches. The driver's license belonged to George Lindenkugel. He also had a medical marijuana card. What else would the ME find in Lindenkugel's system, Eltaeb wondered

He heard the sharp intake of breath behind him and swiveled his chair. The karate instructor from downstairs, still in his white gi, stood in the doorway to the bathroom.

Eltaeb stood up. "Did you know him?"

"He was my neighbor. Who are you?"

Eltaeb gave the karate instructor one of his cards.

The karate instructor stuck out a hand. "Kim Rhee. What do you think happened?"

"Mr. Lindenkugel was working on a project for my client. When Lindenkugel failed to check in, the client sent me over. I've never seen anything like this. It looks like he killed himself by swallowing and chewing razor blade shards. Who else lived here?"

"I only knew them as Maggot Brain and Zimmy. Always up late at night playing loud music. They told me they were computer security contractors."

"They were hackers, is what they were. Seems to be a lot of equipment missing. Do you remember what all they had?"

"This is the first time I've ever been in here."

"Did you notice anything unusual recently?"

"No more than usual. They were very odd young men. They had a security camera set up in the alcove. Maybe that can tell you something."

Eltaeb nodded. He would have anywhere from fifteen minutes to three hours to review the security tapes before the cops arrived from the time he called.

"Mr. Rhee, you've been very helpful. I'm calling the police now, and in a little while, this place is going to be crawling with cops. They'll probably want to talk to you. Just a heads up."

Rhee nodded. "I'm sure we'll see each other again."

Eltaeb nodded grimly. He waited until Rhee had left the loft before pulling out his cell phone and dialing 911.

CHAPTER THIRTY-TWO

St. James breezed through customs at Newark without a hitch. It was the first time in literally dozens of flights he hadn't been singled out for special attention. He waited ten minutes for Connie to clear customs.

Finally, she emerged from the line wearing her backpack and pulling her wheeled suitcase. "What are you grinning about?"

"They went through your backpack, didn't they?"

"So?"

"Nothin'. I think that inspector was crushin' on you."

Connie set out toward the main terminal. "Come on."

They took a shuttle into Manhattan, a taxi to the Raphael on West 69th St. It was past midnight by the time they got into their rooms. St. James conked right out and slept the sleep of the just. He woke at seven, put on his sweats, and hit the pavement. When he returned, the barbershop off the lobby had opened.

St. James entered the barbershop. The old barber in a white lab jacket looked up from his chair where he'd been reading the *Post*. He looked startled, frightened, and hopeful all at once.

"Yes, sir! Need a haircut?"

St. James untied his ponytail. "Take it all, mate. I want a buzz cut."

The clippers tingled as they mowed his skull. St. James felt as if a great weight had been lifted from his shoulders. He tipped the barber ten bucks and went shopping. He found a cunning little haberdashery around the corner where he purchased a black cotton sports jacket, white and ecru silk tees, and casual fit Dockers khakis.

When Connie exited the elevator off the lobby to join him for breakfast her eyes brushed right by him. *Wait a minute!* Connie did the biggest double-take St. James had ever seen. She stared dumbfounded. She smiled.

"Is it really you?"

St. James rose from the deep-seated leather chair. "None other. Hope you're hungry because I'm starving."

It was noon by the time they finished. Connie insisted they go to Axton's. She wanted some daylight pictures and to talk to the manager.

"I know Ron from when I lived in Manhattan," Connie said during the taxi ride.

Her phone rang. She looked. "It's Richard." She took the call. "Hi, Rich. We're in New York." She listened with creases radiating from the bridge of her nose. "What?" She looked horrified. "Oh, my God." She listened. "Of course. Of course." She hung up.

St. James waited. She turned to him. "Melchior hired some hacker to take down the Banshees' website. They found the hacker dead in his apartment yesterday. Apparently he swallowed some ground-up razor blades."

"'If you want to get to Hades you've got to swallow razor blades,'" St. James softly said.

"What?" Connie said.

"It's from 'Do the World a Favor.'"

The driver, a black man with dreadlocks and a green and red tam o'shanter, said, "That's fucked up, mon."

Axton's was at 176 7th Avenue in the Village, a large basement room beneath Del Toro's Restaurant. A black and white striped awning over the entrance said Axton's in bright red script. A cluster of Goths hovered around the door.

Connie paid the cabbie and got out. Connie shot a couple views of the club entrance. As they approached St. James saw that one of the boys wearing an ankle-length black duster like a *Matrix* geek was clutching a scuffed original copy of *Beat the Manshees.*

St. James put a hand on Connie's shoulder. "They're here for the band."

They reached the group. Connie's beauty seemed to penetrate their mulish gloom.

"You guys here for the Banshees?"

"What else?" said the kid with the record.

St. James pointed at the record. "Bet that's worth some money."

"No shit," the kid said. "I already been offered fifty bucks."

"They're not selling tickets," said a young Goth with a shaved skull and brow piercings.

"How did you hear about this?" Connie said.

"Net," said the dude with the record. "It's all over Twitter, and now there's a Banshees Facebook page."

"Have you seen their home page?" Connie said.

All nodded enthusiastically.

"Way bitchin'," said the kid with the shaved skull.

"Awesome."

"Sick."

Connie sliced through them with St. James following. The glass door was closed and locked. Connie leaned on the buzzer. Shortly a heavyset man wearing a striped sweater with the sleeves rolled up rumbled up the steps with a frown on his face. He had a ridiculous goatee and curly black hair, bald spot on the crown.

"What's the matter with you …?" he began.

He recognized Connie and grinned, unlocking the door. "Well, well. Lois Lane. What can I do for you, beautiful?"

"Talk to me for a few minutes, Ron. We're covering this for *In Crowd*. This is my associate Ian St. James."

"Ian St. James the folksinger?" Ron said extending his hand. *Ouch.*

"Pleased to meet you, Ron."

"Come inside, let me lock it back up."

Ron turned and walked down the stairs followed by Connie. St. James remained where he was. The stairs seem to lead into the very bowels of the earth. It was like looking into the wrong end of a telescope. St. James had had a problem with stairs and basements ever since his third foster family. Already his heart was quickening.

Halfway down the club stairs Connie stopped and turned. "Well?"

"Ahhh, just a minute, luv. I'm havin' a little trouble with these stairs."

Connie rolled her eyes. "Come on."

Breathing deeply and holding onto the rail, St. James grimly put one foot in front of another. *Don't embarrass the home team.* The vertigo rose in his gut and a giant hand constricted his throat. He stopped, eyes shut and drew a long, slow breath.

"YO," Connie called from the bottom, drawing out the "O." "Let's go! Chop, chop!"

Grimly St. James put one foot in front of another, eyes shut, until he reached the bottom. He opened his eyes.

"Wow," St. James said. "It's enormous."

He didn't say what he was thinking, that basement clubs were especially susceptible to a certain type of disaster.

"Is there a back entrance?"

"Oh, yeah. How else we gonna get all that shit in here?"

"Ron, we need to talk," Connie said.

"So talk."

Connie framed shots with her hands, figuring out where she would stand while the band was playing. She pulled out a pad.

"So Ron, how'd you land this gig? Did you contact them or did they contact you?"

"Fell into my lap, sugar. Guy calls out of the blue."

"Would that be Kaspar Sinaiko?"

"You're way ahead of me, Sugar. You know Kaspar?"

"I've met him. Seems a little sketchy."

"You're one up on me. I've only been dealing with him over the phone, and why he chose my club, I have no idea, but the buzz has been building all weekend. You should know—you wrote that article."

"I said they were fakes."

"Doesn't seem to matter. We sold out online in fifteen minutes! I'm trying to add a second show but all of a sudden this bird isn't returning my phone calls. I'm beginning to get a little worried."

"I will lay you nine to five they show," St. James said.

"I like them odds! You know how many press passes they want? Twenty-six! I ain't turning over twenty-six seats to those freeloaders! They can buy a ticket like everybody else. You and your friend excepted, of course."

"Why thank you, Ron."

"Ah, there you are!" a familiar voice called from the back of the room in a Russian accent.

Kaspar approached them from behind the bar, so pale he looked lit from within.

CHAPTER THIRTY-THREE

Who are you and how did you get in here?" Ron said.

"You know who I am. Who else speaks like me?"

"That's Kaspar, Ron," Connie said.

Kaspar approached with a rolling jailhouse gait. They shook hands.

"Connie and Ian! How nice to see you again."

"Paddy ain't gwinter expose himself like he did in Leeds, is he?" St. James innocently asked.

"We're covering the whole tour, Kaspar," Connie said. "We're going to be seeing quite a bit of each other."

"Brother," St. James said, "we got some questions. And this time you can't scoot like Speedy Gonzalez."

"But of course! Just let me take care of business with my good friend Ron and I will be with you in a jiffy, hokay?"

Connie and St. James sat at a table while Ron and Kaspar went up a flight of steps at the back of the room into Ron's office. St. James looked around. The room had a tiered floor like Klub-99. Black and white photos of musicians who had played there covered the walls, a Who's Who of jazz, blues, and pop. Miles Davis. Sonny Rollins. Rolling Stones. The Velvet Underground. The place smelled faintly of booze and disinfectant.

Muffled shouts issued from the closed office, but the words were indistinct. St. James went behind the bar and drew two Cokes, handing one to Connie. Ten minutes later Kaspar and Ron came out of the office smiling. Kaspar joined them at the bar.

"Hokay!" he said. "Is all set. Chopped Liver opens for us at nine, we go on at eleven."

"Kaspar," Connie said. "Are you aware of *In Crowd*?"

"Of course! Is very famous magazine."

"When can we interview the band?"

"I do not control those decisions."

"You're their manager," St. James said.

"If it's a hoax," Connie said, "let us in on it. That's all we ask. If the boys want to remain in character throughout the interview, that's fine. Although at some point you're going to have to tell us who they really are and who's behind this."

Kaspar spread his fingers on his chest. "What makes you think I'm not behind this?"

Connie just stared at him with the hint of a smile. "Where's the band staying?"

"The Kenny Arms," Kaspar said.

"Of course!" Connie sang. The Kenny Arms, aka the Vampire Hotel, was the first hotel devoted to the Goth ethic, with a cave-like restaurant, acres of purple and black velvet, flickering lights and spooky noises periodically issuing from the vents. Since opening its doors two years earlier it had become the hotel of choice for rockers of every stripe and persuasion.

Connie placed her recorder on the bar and turned it on. "Do you mind?"

Kaspar shrugged, grinning.

"Who's doing the booking?"

Kaspar pointed to himself.

"Have you ever managed a band before?"

"Sure, sure, lots of bands in Russia and Belarus."

"Don't you have a press kit?"

Kaspar looked puzzled.

"You know—photos, a biography, a record, something to give the press."

Kaspar shrugged. "In Russia, I don't need that stuff. Besides— there are no new recordings."

"Will there be new recordings?" Connie said.

Kaspar enthusiastically nodded his head. "Yes! We plan to record new album as we work our way west. By the time we reach Pacific, twelve tracks."

"How many dates have you mapped out?"

"Six, starting tonight. Band will play new songs. Record it live."

St. James looked around. "Who's your recording engineer?"

Kaspar pointed to himself.

St. James squinted at him. "Do you know what yer doin', mate? You ever done this sort of thing before?"

"I use Zoom R24. Is all set."

St. James' jaw hit his lap. "That's state of the art shit."

"Sure. I take one-day seminar in Berlin. Now I am recording guru."

St. James laughed. "You and me both, brother."

Ron stuck his head out. "Connie—you still want to talk?"

Connie got off the bar stool. "Don't go away, Kaspar."

"I'm not going anywhere."

St. James followed Connie to the back of the club, up three steps to Ron's office. They went inside. A one-way picture window looked out on the club. The room had oxblood shag carpeting, and the walls were completely covered with the usual autographed publicity pictures. A big flat screen TV in the corner showed water coursing through a town carrying cars, houses, everything, with Japanese sub-titles. The sound was off.

Connie and St. James sat on a plump black sofa.

"You guys want something to drink?" Ron offered.

"We're good," St. James said.

"Ron," Connie said, "are you aware that every time the Banshees play someone dies?"

"What are you talking about?"

"You can look it up. Go back to their initial tour in 1974. Isle of Wight—that guy fell off the tower speaker. The Horex in Berlin—guy was stabbed to death in the alley. At their last show in Berlin two people died."

Ron folded his arms. "Who? Where? What are you talking about? I haven't heard word one about it."

"We were there," St. James said. "We saw it happen."

"We didn't exactly see it happen," Connie said.

"What happened?"

Connie and St. James looked at one another. "Melchior sent Guttierez, this ex-gangbanger he uses as a gopher," Connie said. "Guttierez and his date disappeared beneath a sea of chopping moshers who cut them into a million little pieces and spirited them out of the club in the dark."

Ron stared at her with a twisted smile. "Is this some kind of gag?"

Connie and St. James didn't smile.

"So what do you expect me to do?"

"How's your security?"

"I've got three guys who've been with me for years. I trust them. Anybody starts anything they're eighty-sixed, swiftly, discreetly, and without the unnecessary infliction of pain."

"I would suggest hiring an off-duty cop and have an ambulance standing by."

Ron was no longer smiling. "Are you serious?

"Deadly serious," Connie said.

Ron frowned.

Someone knocked at the door.

"What?" Ron bellowed.

The door opened and a small balding man in a gray three-piece suit entered carrying a briefcase.

"Mr. Bonfiglio, I'm sorry to intrude like this. My name is Sam Drew, of Fairchild and Smith, Attorneys at Law." He removed a folded document from his inside jacket pocket and laid it on the desk. "This is a restraining order signed by Federal Judge Judith H. Monckton enjoining you from advertising or featuring any band called the Banshees."

CHAPTER THIRTY-FOUR

The Greyhound sawed its way through the outer boroughs. Walter Voinivich looked out the window and saw gray. Gray cars, gray tenements, gray streets, gray skies. Even the people were gray, or perhaps it was just the faded black they wore. More traffic, construction, and confusion than he had ever imagined. He'd been in New York once, in the early sixties, and he hadn't liked it then. He hated it now.

Forty-five years and the grief had only hardened like a cinder block in his gut. Forty-five years since his only son, Walt Jr., had hung himself from a basement rafter while listening to the Banshees. All those memories, holding the baby boy in his hands, Walter's first steps. Learning to ride a bike. The way that kid could throw and catch. He was a natural. The smell of his hair as Walter kissed him goodnight.

Sheryl had found the body. That good woman who had sacrificed so much already.

Walter could still recall the phone call from Deputy Frank Harmon. "Walt, there's no easy way to say this."

Big funeral, Walt Jr.'s entire baseball team and the coach. The school had let out for the day and offered grief counseling. Walter and Sheryl sought solace in the church, and Father Bishop tried to help. He was a good man, but his experience was limited. He'd never been a parent. His attempts at comfort were clumsy. He had no idea what it was like, seeing a reminder of your child every time you turned around. Every time you passed the school or the malt shop or the park. The pictures of Walt Jr. catching a deep one in left field, smiling self-consciously in his rented tux for the junior prom, beaming from the wheel of that old junker Ford Walter helped him buy.

It hurt every day. It hurt like a phantom limb.

Sheryl couldn't take it, not after all the other heartbreak. She died of grief six years later following a downward spiral of depression and alcoholism.

The Banshees had slaughtered his family.

Two months later God extracted his revenge, plunging the band face first into the Scots bog.

Walter felt cheated. Banshees-inspired suicides continued for a year or two and then the band was mercifully forgotten.

But not by Walter.

The terrible weight had almost taken him down, too. Voinivich was of that sturdy Polish peasant stock that never complained, never felt sorry for themselves. They rolled up their sleeves and did what had to be done. Walt was in his senior year at Indiana State when he got his draft notice. He didn't fake homosexuality or claim he was a drug addict, didn't seek a deferment as an only son to take care of his aging parents (who could damn well take care of themselves); he went and did his duty. One tour in Vietnam. He never talked about the things he saw there, except to Father Bishop.

He missed Walt Jr.'s birth by two weeks. That was all right with Walter. He wasn't one to stand around the birthing room mooning and holding hands. So Voinivich came home from the war, rolled up his sleeves, and went to work as an apprentice plumber. Two years later he took out a loan from the Muncie State Bank and started his own business, Voinivich Plumbing.

Three years later Sheryl gave still-birth to a daughter whom they named Maggie and buried in the Our Lady of the Redeemer Cemetery, next to the church. Now that cursed land held three Voinivichs in its cold embrace. Soon it would hold a fourth, and that would be all she wrote.

Walter might never have learned about the band's return if he hadn't happened to be sitting in the college barbershop last week waiting for his regular trim. He'd pawed through the eclectic stack of magazines and unearthed a recent issue of *In Crowd*. Walter had never paid attention to *In Crowd*. It was one of those "lifestyle" mags. The very word made Walter's skin crawl, suggestive as it was of monied jet-setters lounging around a pool trying to decide where to have supper.

There it was, a little headline along the top: "Are the Banshees Back?"

The headline struck Walter like a dum-dum right between the eyes. A vicious headache crawled to life. Walter looked around to make sure this wasn't some sicko's idea of a practical joke. The only other client was a retired postman whom Walter barely knew. Hands shaking, he flipped through the magazine until he found the article up front in their "What's Happening" news section.

Just who are these Banshees that played Berlin's Klub-99 June 14th, and are set to play Axton's in the Village on the 23rd? Connie Cosgrove writes, "They look and sound exactly like the Banshees. I wasn't around when the original Banshees tore up the heavy metal world, but I've seen the videos. But here's the deal: these guys look like they're no older than the day they died in 1975. Plastic surgery? Black magic? Come to the show and judge for yourselves."

Walter got a vibe. He spent one day thinking about it. The doctor gave him months to live. Lymphoma. For forty years he'd been a ghost, haunting his own house, going through the motions, enduring his friends' well-meaning solicitations until they tired of the gloom and left him alone.

Now only Father Bishop phoned, once a week.

Forty years sitting in his dark house watching football, baseball, and basketball. Forty years going room to room touching those things which Sheryl and Walt Jr. used to touch: the football trophies, the photographs, the quilt Sheryl made. He went to work every day but he was like a zombie. His employees knew it, his customers knew it. They wantedthe old jovial Walter back. But he was never coming back.

Work trickled off. Within a year he had no need for an assistant. He was able to handle all his accounts by himself. Most of them had been with him for decades and didn't call a plumber for conversation anyway.

There was an item on *Entertainment Tonight*, a gossipy tabloid show tracking celebrities' every move, reporting breathlessly on each smooch, each nightclub photo, and, in particular, on any hint of scandal or pathology. It was a throwaway line at the end of the show, an impossibly vivacious blond with a grin like the high beams on an Audi.

"What infamous heavy metal band is back from the dead and playing Axton's this week? That's right! Everybody's favorite bad boys, the Banshees!"

Her high beams penetrated Walter's grief. Didn't she realize what the Banshees were?

Besides. They were dead.

Walter had no Internet, only a cell phone. He didn't know what to believe. He phoned a Rotary pal, Win Houtkooper, who owned a radio station. Win confirmed that there was indeed some band calling themselves the Banshees.

A voice spoke to Walter.

"Walter, you're a good man and you've suffered enough. Every life has a purpose, and your time has come. Vengeance is mine sayeth the Lord, and you are my instrument. For your son and wife, and all those murdered by these spawn of Satan. Go forth Walter with my blessing."

The bus was now in Manhattan in its final stage. Walter could hardly believe the filth and chaos he saw through the bus window. Hustlers with fold-up tables swirling Three Card Monte. Two men holding hands and kissing. A big buck nigger handing a pasty-faced white boy something in a plastic bag.

The bus finally crawled into the Port Authority, a monstrous Bauhaus-inspired industrial edifice with massive crisscrossing girders. The bus parallel parked next to others from all over the East as the driver stood and opened the door.

"Last stop, folks. The porter will help you with luggage in the compartment. Please have your ticket stubs ready."

Walter had no luggage in the compartment. He wasn't planning a long visit. He had only his little overnighter which he'd been using for thirty years. He pulled the overnighter from beneath the seat in front of him, stood, and filed out with the other passengers. Nobody gave him a second glance.

Once out on the street not even the hustlers and hookers bothered him. He had that look about him. He went to a bus stand where several people waited and asked a woman in nurse's whites about catching a bus to the Village. She steered him to the proper bus stop.

Walter waited, the .44 Magnum heavy in his bag.

CHAPTER THIRTY-FIVE

Melchior and Melissa arrived JFK at six fifteen PM. Melchior could have given Eltaeb a ride, but he preferred the detective travel separately and was happy to pay for it.

Melissa was all a-twitter. "I can't believe it, Burke! Do you know who's going to be there?"

"Everybody who is anybody."

"Lady Gaga and Pink! It's all over the net! People are selling tickets for thousands of dollars!"

They were still strapped into their seats, Melissa clutching a copy of some gossip rag as the plane taxied to a stop in a part of the airport reserved for corporate jets. Looking out the window Melchior spotted John Travolta's Gulfstream 4 next to the distinctive turquoise blue of the Saudi Royal Family.

Stanton appeared from steerage in the back and raced ahead, down the gangplank to arrange for the transfer of their luggage to the approaching black limo. Stanton stood by as the ground tech unlatched the cargo area and began handing out matched luggage which Stanton hustled to the rear of the limo and stuffed into the cavernous maw. There were nine pieces.

The driver, a big black fellow in navy blue livery, held the door for them. "Sir, my name is Kent Washington and I'll be your driver while you're in the city."

"Excellent. Take us to the Abby on West 85th St."

Washington nodded toward Stanton heaving the last of the luggage into the trunk.

"Your assistant?"

"He can take a taxi."

Washington nodded and shut the door with the sound of a bank vault closing. Moments later they rolled in insulated splendor through Queens toward the city. Melissa had her iPad out and was Facebooking with her pals. Melchior's cell rang. He turned on his Bluetooth.

"Talk to me."

It was Eltaeb. "Boss, the lawyer delivered the injunction."

"And their response?"

"No immediate response. The club's consulting their attorney."

"Is that prick Sinaiko there?"

"Yes, sir, he's here."

"Where are you?"

"I'm on my way to the Kenny Arms where the band is staying."

"Excellent. We'll get together tomorrow."

"Looking forward to it."

Melchior turned his gaze out the window to the endless drab apartment complexes, the gang graffiti streaming past on bridge abutments and restraining walls. Kennedy had been unable to come up with anything about Kaspar Sinaiko. Interpol had never heard of him. He was not on any no-fly lists. Melchior looked forward to confronting the little *goniff*.

As to why Spyder killed himself by eating razor blades, it may have been the anti-acne medication he was taking. Since his cohorts had fled with all the hard drives there was no telling what Spyder had accessed on his computer. Examination of the boys' security tapes showed a guy the size of a refrigerator and his smaller companion carrying load after load of computer equipment out of the loft into the freight elevator.

Melchior tried to get the Feds involved but there was no proof that Spyder or his friends were involved in a federal crime. It had been officially ruled a suicide.

Meanwhile the Banshees website was garnering tens of thousands of hits. The Banshees were the subject of intense conversations around the globe. It was going to be one of those nights people talked about for years, like Truman Capote's Black and White Ball, or Woodstock.

News and gossip rags, reporters from many countries were tying up Melchior's publicist's lines. Everybody wanted the word from the Boss. Melchior preferred to let his lawyers do the talking. He actually wanted the band to play. He wanted to see them. It would be fun.

Of course what all the reporters really wanted was the band itself. GMA, Leno, Letterman, Fox, SNL all called. And they all thought Melchior could get it for them! Melchior wasn't talking. Not until he talked to the band.

Serafin had passed on Connie's warning. Melchior wasn't buying. It was the most brilliant media strategy he had ever observed. *Every time they play somebody dies.* It was only a matter of time before the Christian Right got word of this and mounted a counter-offensive, making the Banshees bigger than ever.

Fucking brilliant.

But without new material what was the point? All this anticipation for what? A big stadium show? No, there had to be more to it. There had to be "product". According to Connie they were going to record it live as they traveled west. Who did they think they were? Tower of Power? Tonight they would have to play new songs. Otherwise it was a forty-five-minute set.

Melissa turned toward him all aglow, shining her Droid at him like the All-Seeing Eye of Amagato. "Look, Burkey! Oh isn't he cute?"

A sullen-looking cat dressed as a taco.

"Fantastic," Melchior said.

They arrived at the Abby. While Washington held the door a doorman hurried out to help with the luggage.

"So glad to have you back, Mr. Melchior!"

"Thanks, Barney. It's good to be back."

Melchior eyed Melissa's ass all the way up in the elevator. Once they were in his co-op with the luggage and the doors locked, he slapped her butt. "Go put something slinky on and meet me in the bedroom."

Melchior went into the bath, splashed water on his face and gargled with mouthwash. Stripping off his shirt, he entered the bedroom and beheld Melissa beckoning enticingly from satin sheets.

Melchior's phone rang. It was the lawyer, what's-his-name, from Fairchild and Smith.

"Did you serve the restraining order?"

"Mr. Melchior, Sam Drew here. Yes, I did. Ten minutes ago another lawyer arrived with a letter signed by an Appeals Court judge overturning your restraining order."

CHAPTER THIRTY-SIX

ltaeb wore gray dungarees, a long-sleeved gray service shirt, and a Con-Ed cap and carried a clipboard as he walked through the Kenny Arms' service corridors. People smiled at him. Nobody said boo. He hovered outside the break room where the Guatemalan maids complained bitterly about the pay and conditions. Having grown up in an Hispanic household, Eltaeb spoke excellent Spanish.

He waited in the corridor. He followed a short brown maid as she exited and headed toward the laundry room.

"Señora," he said softly.

She turned, a look of apprehension on her round face. Her name tag said Lupe.

Eltaeb removed a wad of bills from his pocket and spoke in Spanish. "One thousand dollars, ma'am, if you can get me into Paddy MacGowan's room for ten minutes."

The woman was torn between greed and terror. One thou was probably more than she grossed in a month, and it wasn't as if she'd undergone a rigorous vetting procedure to land this job. Her eyes turned greedy as she calculated with whom she'd have to split the take. Motioning furtively for Eltaeb to follow, she led him to a large broom closet and turned on the light.

"Let me see the money."

Keeping a firm grip on the ten Benjamins Eltaeb let her fondle one end. "Half now, half when I come out."

"Do you swear to me on the life of your mother that you do not intend to steal anything or harm the guest in any way?"

Eltaeb reached down his shirt and withdrew a St. Christopher's medal. "I swear it on my mother's grave."

The little Guatemalan peered deeply into his eyes. "If you break this promise," she hissed, "the devil will rear up and strike you down!"

"I believe you, Lupe."

"Who is the guest?"

Eltaeb told her. "He'll be out of his room by eight. Ten minutes. That's all I need."

"If I do this I will have to leave."

"Not necessarily. No one will know I've been in there. I won't touch anything. I won't take anything. I won't leave anything."

"Meet me here, in the corridors. I will see what room he is in. Then I will tell you when to meet me on that floor."

Eltaeb peeled off five C-notes which Lupe tucked down her maid's dress. He gave her his card.

Eltaeb spent several hours reading magazines in a coffee shop. At eight o'clock his cell phone range. It was Lupe. At eight-fifteen he stepped off the elevator on the Kenny Arms' 11th floor. A maid's cart was parked outside the open door to 1129. The corridor was empty. Eltaeb quickly went to 1129 and stepped inside.

Lupe was wiping down the toilet. Eltaeb gently closed the door without quite latching it. "Did you empty the wastebasket?" he asked.

"Not yet."

Eltaeb looked around the room. The carpeting was dark gray, the design scheme shiny black and chrome. There was a black and white photograph of a creepy castle shrouded in mist over the bed, a wrought iron cemetery entrance over the desk. An ancient guitar case lay on the made bed. A battered suitcase was open. He quickly flipped through the garments, which were unremarkable. He checked the wastebasket next to the desk. Nothing in it.

He went into the bathroom. Toothbrush, Colgate, a package of floss, and a brush containing several long strands of brown hair. Taking an envelope from the desk Eltaeb quickly gathered the strands of hair and stuffed them inside. He licked the lid, sealed it, and stuck it in his dungarees.

He peeled off the remaining five hundred and gave it to Lupe, went to the door, looked out, and vamoosed.

CHAPTER THIRTY-SEVEN

S t. James and Connie were inside when Melchior and Melissa arrived at Axton's at nine-thirty. The line of freaks stretched half way down the block. Melissa wore a strapless black dress and stiletto heels, and trailed wolf whistles. Melchior wore gray twill trousers, a pink cotton T-shirt, and a black sport jacket. The power couple cut through the *hoi polloi* like an icebreaker. Melchior buttonholed the mesomorphic bouncer.

"I'm Burke Melchior!" he yelled over the ambient noise. The bouncer nodded and held the door for them. A sign just inside the entrance said, "ABSOLUTELY NO RECORDING DEVICES."

The Messerschmidts, a power-pop quartet, were tearing it up onstage. The joint was standing room only. Connie led the way down the stairs, around the tables, and up the stairs to Ron's office. All four went inside and St. James shut the door, shutting out the bombastic music. It was freezing inside. Ron sat behind his desk looking flummoxed. One wall was covered in photos and certificates of appreciation. Ron with Bill Graham. Ron with Steve Paul. Ron with Ed Koch. Ron with Madonna.

Two men whom Melchior had never seen before sat on one of the black leather sofas. The skinhead with the gold hoop and tats could only be the mysterious Sinaiko. The other man was tall, thin as a blade, with the dark good looks of a matador. His near-black hair was slicked back from a widow's peak, and he had a pencil-thin mustache. He wore a camel's hair suit.

St. James turned and shook Melchior's hand. "Long time, Burke."

"Looking good, St. James," Melchior replied and was surprised to realize it was true.

Sinaiko and the tall man stood.

"Kaspar Sinaiko, Banshees manager. And this is our attorney Nadio Ninguna."

Melchior grudgingly shook hands with them. A couple of *goniffs*.

"How do you assholes expect to get away with this?" he said.

Kaspar flopped back down on the sofa and picked up a bottle of Sam Adams. "With your cooperation."

"If you wanted my cooperation you would have approached me before taking this dog and pony show on the road."

"Mr. Melchior," Ninguna said. "There is a clause in your original contract stating that if you fail to exploit the Banshees image and product the rights revert to the band."

"I should think that death makes that bloody well null and void." Melchior looked around. Only one sofa left. He peeled out a hundred. "Melissa, baby, why don't you get something to drink?"

Wordlessly she took the bill and slunk out. Kaspar, St. James, and Ron watched her appreciatively.

"We have still not ascertained who these guys are," St. James said, accepting a canned root beer from Ron. He and Connie sat in a couple of random kitchen chairs.

"What are you trying to hide, Kaspar?" Connie asked.

Melchior stuck his feet up on the designer coffee table knocking over a stack of magazines including *Spin*, *Rolling Stone*, and *In Crowd*. "You want my cooperation? Bring these guys in here right now. If I don't meet the band right now I am going to take such measures as will cause you the utmost damned astonishment."

Everyone looked at Kaspar. Kaspar and Ninguna exchanged a look. Kaspar shrugged. "I go see if the boys want to come down." He pronounced it "boyce."

Kaspar left the room. For long moments the only sound was the faint thrumming of the band through the walls.

"Anybody want anything?" Ron said.

"Are you lot planning to record tonight?" St. James directed his question at the lawyer.

"That is the plan," Ninguna said in a sibilant Spanish accent. Their gaze fell on the window looking out on the club. With the strobe lights going and the mob jumping up and down it was impossible to make out individual faces. Shortly, however, Kaspar's distinctive dome could be seen bobbing their way with someone in tow.

Minutes later the door opened and Kaspar entered followed by Paddy MacGowan. The lead singer's long frizzy hair was tied in a ponytail. He was about five eight, thin as a reed, wearing a ribbed cotton shirt and tight jeans. Connie pulled out old publicity stills from her backpack as MacGowan smiled wolfishly.

His face seemed smooth and youthful except for the eyes which appeared somewhat shrunken and surrounded by crackle. Richard Corben eyes. "Well 'allo, mates! I have been so looking forward to this!"

Connie aimed her cell. "Mind if I snap a few?"

MacGowan spread his arms expansively and grinned like a wolf. "Fire away, Ducks!" He vogued across the floor turning to face Connie.

He went over to the desk. Ron stood. "Mr. Bonfiglio! Speakin' on behalf of me band mates I want to thank you for giving us this opportunity." He went around the room shaking hands. St. James stood.

"You must be Oaian's boy. I can see the resemblance."

MacGowan's hand was cold. "How come my father isn't here?"

"Oh, you know how 'e gets before a performance, all tingly-like and nervous. 'E'll see you after the show. 'E said to tell you personally, 'e's lookin' forward to it."

Paddy faced Melchior last. "'Allo, Burkey! Been a long time, innit?"

Melchior took his hand and shivered. "By God, I don't believe it. How did you do it?"

"Wot, my boyish looks?"

"The plastic surgery. It's flawless. Except for the eyes. The eyes give you away."

"Window to the soul and all that," Paddy said.

Ninguna leaned forward and put his arms on his knees. "You'll have to agree, Mr. Melchior, that publicity-wise the band seems to know what it's doing. Now if we were to announce a new contract with Melchior Productions that would only add fuel to the fire."

Melchior's mind spun like the national debt indicator. Serafin had played this like an expert. They were sitting on a publicity tsunami.

"What's the deal?" Melchior said.

CHAPTER THIRTY-EIGHT

During the intermission Melchior, St. James, Connie, and Ninguna filed out and took their seats in the VIP box, up and off to the side. The balustrade was finished in purple velvet. The club hadn't changed since disco's salad days. A big glitter ball hung from the ceiling, unlit during the show.

Melissa sat between Melchior and St. James while Kaspar went backstage. The seats were deluxe theater-style with plush purple upholstery and cup holders in the arms. A TV monitor mounted next to the booth showed a screaming mob in some Arab country. Onstage a couple of sketchy characters fiddled with instruments, making certain the drums were nailed down, the amps properly tuned. A silver flute stood incongruously onstage glittering like a diamond.

St. James wanted a drink so bad he could taste it. Taste that sweet alcohol on his tongue, feel the heat emanating from his belly. He could smell the juniper. A bolus of dread crouched in his gut, that back of the neck prickle he sometimes got when bad things were about to happen. He'd experienced it frequently growing up in foster homes, had it so bad once he'd refused to board the ferry for the Channel crossing. Sixteen passengers came down with food poisoning. It could have been worse.

Although there was no smoking in the club, some kind of haze hovered at head height playing tricks with the light. The club's alternating red and blue lights reminded him of a bust.

Like the time he got that skin-crawly feeling in Georgia moments before a highway trooper pulled them over for a doused headlight. Georgia didn't like long hairs. He'd spent a memorable night in the county lock-up.

Not that he had supernatural powers, merely a well-developed sense of self-preservation and the ability to see impending calamity—the multifarious ways in which things could go wrong. And a gloomy disposition. Facts were facts: someone had died at every Banshees concert thus far. St. James' eyes swept the room. He couldn't fault the club. Ron had five guys working security. No ambulance but this was New York. They could get an ambulance in a New York minute.

St. James had called Klapp several times each day. The last time he called the voice informed him that the number had been disconnected.

Melissa sat between St. James and Melchior. St. James leaned forward and shouted, "What happened to Guttierez?" Why did clubs insist on blasting music during the breaks?

"The police say there's no evidence of a crime," Melchior said.

"Are you shitting me? The floor was covered in blood! There was no way to clean it all up!"

Melchior shrugged. "Blood itself is not proof of a crime!"

Melissa tried to disappear into the back of her chair.

"Ian. I'm just as upset as you are. I'm just telling you what the cops told me. The next step is to hire a German private investigator. I don't know any!"

"We met a bloke, Professor Klapp. He knew shite about the Banshees, and he disappeared, too. He was supposed to make the Berlin show and he never showed." St. James didn't say what he feared, that Klapp was dead. Counting the stroke victim in Prague that was four deaths related to the Banshees' comeback—four of which he knew. And they hadn't even played their first gig in the States.

The crowd was overwhelmingly young and Goth. He leaned into Connie's ear. "What are all these kids doing here? It's not like heavy metal is the dominant life form!"

"It's Goth time. Vampires, werewolves, the kids can't get enough. This is just the thrill *du jour.* Tomorrow it will be something else."

St. James looked at the audience more closely. Black was their color of choice. More piercings than a quilting bee. Some in the crowd were truly disturbing, faces made up like zombies, carrying ugly little fetish dolls. Some with hideously realistic flesh wounds or made up to look like lepers. The floor was SRO.

Connie elbowed St. James in the ribs and pointed out reviewers from the *NYT* and *Billboard.* Ron appeared onstage wearing a black top hat, a white Axton's T-shirt, and a black leather vest. He looked like Ed "Big Daddy" Roth. He tapped the microphone and the crowd piped down.

"Axton's is very pleased to present the act you've known for all these years, THE BANSHEES!"

The shouting merged into one incoherent bellow as the musicians jogged onstage wearing black stovepipe jeans, white T-shirts, black leather vests, and black bowlers, a Clockwork Orange cycle gang. Paddy and Cunar had their axes slung around their shoulders. Oaian sat behind the kit and rolled out thunder as Paddy rounded on the mic and sang, "People say we're a little bit creepy—we don't mind, we don't mind ..."

The crowd roared back, "PEOPLE SAY WE'VE GOT BAD INTENTIONS! WE DON'T MIND, WE DON'T MIND ..."

St. James and Connie looked at one another. Connie took out her camera, stood, and took pictures. One of the security team noticed and approached making a broad swoop down with his arms. Connie put the camera away and mouthed, "Sorry."

"Crikey," St. James said. "That's off the first album." And he wondered not for the first time where were they getting this shit? Total sales on that first album may have tickled 50,000, but of those, how many survived? The record had never been issued on CD as far as he knew. Had to be alive on the Internet. The Banshees' home page had only been up for a few days.

The band flowed seamlessly from one crunching rocker to the next, Paddy releasing one epic riff after another. The sound was perfect. The final chord to "Kiss My Grits" died out.

"Folks," Paddy said, "we're recording tonight."

Whoops, hollers, whistles.

"'At's right! The boys and I have been workin' on some new material. Here's a little number I call "Makin' Bacon.""

Paddy's chord slashed the room in half. "WHEN PIGS FUCK, YOU KNOW WHAT IT'S CALLED—MAKIN' BACON, MAKIN' BACON!"

The crowd erupted like an angry sea, pogoing and slamming into one another. St. James' gaze fell to the TV monitor mounted at knee level below the balcony. A frenzied crowd in Arab dress burned an effigy of the President and stomped on an American flag.

St. James looked up to watch the band, Paddy nearly bent in two like a paper clip as he caressed his Stratocaster. St. James fixed on an anomalous motion, a tall man working his way determinedly through the moshing bodies. An older man judging by his steady pace and the way he turned his shoulder into the moshers. St. James glimpsed a gray head, a pair of spectacles momentarily reflecting the garish lights.

The hairs on the back of St. James' neck stood up, and he knew what was about to happen even as he felt powerless to stop it. He stood, cupped his hands and yelled "GUN!" as loud as he could, drawing the attention of his booth mates and no one else.

Melchior stared at him as if he were nuts. Ninguna paid no attention.

A woman's scream momentarily overpowered the sound system, and people began to run and stumble and crawl, trampling over one another in their panic as the tall man, dressed all in gray, raised an enormous chrome revolver in both hands, aimed at Paddy, and squeezed the trigger.

The report was gigantic, a sudden shocking *thwack* like a giant period stamped on the air itself. One of Oaian's cymbals *splanged* sideways. The ricochet's *kerranggg* occurred almost simultaneously, and St. James felt an impact to his left. Melissa flopped backward and slumped in her seat like a gallery duck, a glistening red hole in the middle of her forehead.

Chapter Thirty-nine

At eleven PM on a Saturday night the Hog's Head Pub crackled with warmth and heated discussion mostly centering on the upcoming football game between Glasgow and Edinburgh. A lively round of darts consumed several regulars, and the bar was chock-a-block. One corner of the pub remained cool and seemingly immune from the infectious bonhomie as two burly foreigners wearing black cardigans and watch caps, shunned by the vivacious bar girl, nursed vodka and beer in a booth.

The cardigans concealed arms and torsos covered in prison ink. The two men had received the call at the Nikolov Beria Reeducation Camp, one hundred acres of frozen tundra above the Arctic Circle surrounded by barbed wire and guard towers. Inside the barbed wire several thousand men slept in uninsulated log cabins and performed forced labor under the guns of hundreds of guards. Mostly, they cleared rights-of-way for rail lines that would never be built. There was a ten per cent monthly attrition rate. Thousands of corpses were stacked in a storage shed because it was impossible to penetrate the permafrost. The stacked corpses provided a human chronology, going all the way back to 1953, although those layers near the bottom couldn't be pried from the communal slab, not without heat, and nobody wanted that.

The theory was that when the railroad was finished, the corpses would be transported to a mammoth crematorium under construction in Zhilinda, a state-of-the-art facility that would employ hundreds of people. Zhilinda would stand at the nexus of hundreds of rail lines crisscrossing Russia, the final destination for the many thousands of corpses churned out daily by the Russian way of life. That was the theory. In reality, construction on the crematorium had stopped in 1988. Only the laying of useless track continued, and only because the labor and timber were free.

What was Russia but a vast empire of the dead? The average life expectancy for men was less than fifty-nine. The population had been declining since 1988. One had only to look at Lenin in his tomb to appreciate the deep brooding darkness of the Russian soul. They couldn't produce automobiles, telephones, or toilet paper, but they made corpses in abundance. Lebed and Yomnosko did likewise on a smaller scale.

Fyodor Lebed and Valm Yomnosko were members of the criminal syndicate безумные монахи; "Mad Monks" was the nearest English translation. The Mad Monks had its origins in the Czar's prisons where several inmates formed a pact to use any means necessary to gain power. They believed Rasputin had mastered certain dark arts—how else to account for the fact that he was extraordinarily difficult to kill? The syndicate had only grown stronger under the Reds. And now, in the new Russia, it had burst forth in full bloom as an international gang with several tentacles in legitimate business, mostly real estate holdings.

Several days ago Kaspar summoned Lebed and Yomnosko and told them to come to this Godforsaken corner of Scotland and prepare for the resurrection.

In December of 1916 anarchists dug up Rasputin's shot, strangled, poisoned, mutilated, and drowned body, took it into the woods and set it on fire.

Rasputin sat up sending his grave robbers screaming into the woods.

What happened next is not recorded in the history books. The Mad Monks had a relationship with Lord Sidney Turrington, a Scots fascist and Druid. Lord Turrington's agents spirited Rasputin's remains out of Russia and reburied them at an undisclosed location on the moors promising that the day would come when they would "sing him back to life."

Lebed looked at the TV hanging over the bar. Hundreds of riot cops holding huge plexiglass shields marched in lock-step toward a mob of screaming, bottle-throwing anarchists, many of them wearing face masks. A plate of pickled pigs' knuckles sat on the scarred table.

"That could never happen in Russia," Lebed said to Yomnosko. Yomnosko nodded and sipped his vodka.

"This country's been in the shitter since the sixties," Lebed said.

Gradually the regulars staggered home until only Lebed and Yomnosko were left. The proprietor called, "Gentlemen, we're closing."

Lebed waved, dropped a five-pound note on the table and got up. Yomnosko followed him out the door. Their rented Mercedes SUV was the only vehicle left in the lot. A lone street lamp provided the only illumination in either direction. Lebed slowly scanned the horizon. Saw tiny lights in the distance. Using the fob, he unlocked the car with a beep and a flash.

They got in. Lebed started the engine. Ignoring the high-tech GPS linked navigation system, he turned on the cabin light and examined an ancient map etched on lambskin. Six hundred years ago Linser Road had been known as Lenarch. The barely discernible black stripe twisted through the hills like a sidewinder. Some twelve miles past the turn off from the old coach road the map was marked with a horned demon skull.

Silently they drove off, Lebed watching the odometer carefully. Yomnosko reached into the back seat and retrieved a Yukon night vision monocular. He turned it on and held it to his eye. The world streamed by in iridescent green.

"Dunkeld," he said. "Forty-two klicks."

Lebed instinctively slowed the vehicle. "Watch left."

They almost missed it because the sign was down, but as they passed Yomnosko caught a glimpse of the pole. "Stop. Here it is."

Within ten minutes they passed Peter MacGowan's darkened cottage. The big Mercedes wallowed up the rutted trail. Another ten and they came upon the falling down cemetery. Lebed turned the wheel and coaxed the SUV around the wrought iron fence and kept on going. Soon they found themselves in a gelid, featureless depression beneath a starry sky. They got out of the vehicle. Although it was June they could see their breath as they exhaled. To the north they could just make out the tip of a stele protruding from behind the small hill.

Something happened. For a split second the air turned solid and then disappeared as if the whole world had been plunged into a vacuum. Lebed's and Yomnosko's ears popped, and each man had a frightening momentary glimpse of 240 grains of lead smacking through a young woman's flesh.

Lebed whipped his head around. "Did you feel that?"

Yomnosko nodded, unable to speak.

They retrieved their shovels and picks from the back of the vehicle.

CHAPTER FORTY

Two of Ron's bouncers tackled the gunman, who turned out to be a frail old man. He cracked two ribs when they took him down. He offered no resistance, tears streaming down his cheeks. The cops were there in five minutes. The shooter's name was Walter Voinivich, and he had come from Muncie. He declined legal representation and spoke freely about his intentions.

"They killed my boy."

Both the band and Melchior were gonesville. Melchior took one look at his dead girlfriend, got up and hustled out of the VIP box. St. James was too stunned to say anything. There was no point checking Melissa for vital signs. She gazed sightlessly upward, a growing pool of crimson beneath her blond locks.

The cops questioned St. James, Connie, and Ninguna. When the police learned the identity of Melissa's date a sergeant muttered, "Great. Another fuckin' prima donna."

It was two AM by the time the cops released them. St. James and Connie took a cab to their hotel.

"That's five," St. James said.

Connie was ashen-faced. She felt covered in filth and nauseated. "This is freaking me out."

"We still haven't talked to the fuckin' band."

Connie's phone sang the "My Generation." It was Serafin.

"I just heard. I need 2,500 words from you tomorrow. We're doing a special issue on the Banshees, and we're pulling out all the stops!"

"We haven't talked to the band yet, Richard!"

"There will be time. At this point we have to ask ourselves, are the Banshees for real? Is there a curse? Why do people go to their shows knowing that someone's going to get offed?"

"I think that's part of the appeal," Connie said. "They offered Melchior a new contract."

"Interview Burke. Get his take on this. And a side box with St. James' views."

Connie heard party noises in the background. She envisioned Serafin's Hollywood Hills party palace with the cantilevered swimming pool jutting out over the valley. She wished she were there.

They rode up together in the elevator. As St. James said goodnight outside his door she laid her head on his shoulder. "Hold me," she whispered.

Shocked, St. James' hands automatically encircled her. She breathed fast and ragged—delayed shock. All the shocks of the previous 72 hours piling up. Beneath the tough blond was a frightened little girl.

St. James held her awkwardly wishing his boner would just go away, but of course the thing had a mind of its own. Always had. He put a little distance between them, turning her awkwardly for a quasi-side embrace. Wouldn't do for Little Ian to spoil the mood. They stood that way for perhaps five minutes while her breathing gradually calmed and she stepped back shaking herself like a dog emerging from a pond. She stood on her tiptoes and kissed him on the cheek. She quick-walked down the hall and let herself into her room without looking back.

There was something endearing about the old hippy, like a stray dog with an ingratiating manner. His music intrigued her, but her professional interest was on hold until they put the Banshees to bed.

If the Banshees could be put to bed.

If the Banshees went to bed.

She'd talked to a hooker once in Amsterdam who claimed to have slept with Paddy. The woman was a drunk and a drug addict and barely tracked. She blamed Paddy. She would not describe the encounter except to say, "He can go fuck himself. No I mean literally. He can go fuck himself."

Connie swallowed a *clonazepam*, stripped in the bathroom, and stepped into the steaming shower trying to scrub the blood from her mind. Her father had wanted a boy. He would have named him Conor. However, dealt a curve ball, Mason Cosgrove rolled up his sleeves and went to work.

"If life hands you lemons, make lemonade!"

Yeah, she thought ruefully. With plenty of vodka.

Her father had her reading at the age of four. When she was twelve she read the *Encyclopedia Britannica* cover to cover. Sober, Mason was big on the Founding Fathers. He was not happy with trends in popular culture and had initially disapproved of her chosen profession—writing about rock and roll—until he saw her interviewed on *Good Morning America* at which point the phone calls started pouring in, and he belatedly realized that Connie was a success for which he took full credit.

She couldn't begin to describe the Banshees to him. Tomorrow was Sunday. They would talk as they did every Sunday, and she would fudge about her job, tell him it was boring and the bands sucked. Mason would pretend he was clean and sober.

Connie picked up a bottle of shampoo. It slipped through her hand like she was a ghost. As she bent to pick it up her hands were shaking. It seemed to her that something dark and seething, almost like an alien force had entered the culture, not fully understood, some new lurking sci-fi creature, like an untreatable new virus that had arisen from the socio-cultural-data-communication-pop-sex-celebrity-media overload.

Something her father taught her popped into her head. John Adams. "It should be your care, therefore, and mine," she recited from memory, "to elevate the minds of our children and exalt their courage; to accelerate and animate their industry and activity; to excite in them an habitual contempt of meanness, abhorrence of injustice and inhumanity, and an ambition to excel in every capacity, faculty, and virtue. If we suffer their minds to grovel and creep in infancy, they will grovel all their lives."

Saying it aloud made her feel better. By John Adams' standards ninety percent of pop culture was trash. Connie was more forgiving. She put the figure at eighty.

She toweled herself off, dried her hair, put on panties and a Not Lame T-shirt. It was two-thirty AM. To write or not to write? Fuck it. Not with a *clonazepam* already softening the rough edges. She'd write in the morning. She would sleep in late and spend the rest of the morning typing up her notes.

She crawled into bed and pulled the cool, crisp covers up and over her head. She began to settle into sleep like a feather falling to earth. She missed Mason. She would call him tomorrow. The world turned velvet.

DO THE WORLD A FAVOR! OFF YOURSELF—
OFF YOURSELF!
YOU KNOW YOU REALLY CRAVE HER! OFF
YOURSELF—OFF YOURSELF!

Connie's hand shot out and slammed down on top of the clock radio. The Banshees continued to blare at a volume that would surely wake the entire floor. Grunting frantically between her teeth Connie piled out of bed, pulled the night table forward and yanked out the plug. When the music finally stopped she sat on the edge of the bed crying and shaking.

CHAPTER FORTY-ONE

Melchior waited in the Plaza for Eltaeb, munching on a stalk of celery. He checked his phone. There was a voice mail from a Sargent Earl Hilbrick of the NYPD requesting he come in for an interview regarding the shooting at Axton's.

How had they got his phone number?

Someone was going to die for this. He called Stanton who answered immediately.

"Did you give the cops this phone number?"

"What? Boss! No! You know I would never do that!"

Melchior spotted Eltaeb cruising toward his table like an ocean liner with the wispy maître d' acting as a tug escort. He shut the phone and put it in his pocket, rising to shake hands with the hulking investigator. They sat. Eltaeb ordered coffee and a club sandwich. Melchior ordered an arugula salad with cucumbers to be sliced at a forty-five-degree angle, green tomatoes, and a bowl of Parmesan on the side.

"Any luck?" Melchior said.

He felt something tap against his leg. He looked down. Eltaeb handed him a sealed envelope from the Kenny Arms. "No sweat."

Melchior stuffed the envelope in his European man bag. "Excellent. I got a lock of his hair off eBay. We'll see if it matches."

"What makes you think it's authentic?" Eltaeb said.

Melchior handed him a slip of paper. "That's your job. Make sure it's authentic."

Eltaeb looked at the slip. It gave an address in Brighton, MA. The seller's name was Will Ballard. "You want me to go to Boston?"

"Yes. Of course. Although I did check, and he has an excellent rating."

"What can I do that a DNA analysis can't?"

Melchior squinted a little as if he couldn't believe what he just heard. "Greg. You're a big guy. Lean on him a little."

"You know, Burke, I try to stay on the up and up."

"Come on. Five gees for one day's work plus expenses. You won't have to touch him, believe me. I know the type. Lives in his parents' basement with his collection of action figures."

"What happens if it's a match?"

Melchior intertwined his fingers and touched them to his chin. "That opens up a whole new can of worms. Then we're in uncharted territory unless these clowns are working some massive con I can't see."

The waiter brought their dishes. Melchior took one look.

"I said the cucumbers had to be sliced at an angle! What's the matter with you? Are you stupid? Take it back."

Eltaeb averted his eyes and concentrated on his sandwich.

Chapter Forty-two

St. James left a wake-up call for nine. By nine-thirty he was in the gym working out on a treadmill, watching a man swinging a kettle bell. St. James did fifteen fast minutes on the treadmill—really ripping it, then cooled off with the elliptic machine. He preferred to run outdoors but there was too much work, plus this was Manhattan so anything could happen. A terrorist incident. Space aliens. Old girlfriends.

St. James would be happy when they got out of town. He'd never liked it. Too crowded, too noisy. He was a country boy at heart.

He had turned the kiss over in his mind a thousand times and it always came out the same: don't be a jackass! She likes you because you're a character. Her romantic interest in you is zero. Zip, zed, nada. Do not make a fool of yourself and queer the deal with *In Crowd*!

His stomach rumbled. There was a sit-up horse that could also be used for stomach crunches. St. James promised twenty crunches and then a shower followed by breakfast in the hotel restaurant. He positioned himself on the padded horse stomach down, feet wedged under an iron bar, torso extended over space, hands behind his head.

And … UP!

St. James felt a ripping sensation in his belly and knew instantly that he'd given himself a hernia. Carefully, he got off the horse and examined himself with his fingers. The tear was at his left waistline. He could feel the protruding gut like a cylindrical balloon.

Fuckin' great! Just what he needed. Ten years prior, he'd ripped the right side and had it stitched up before the National Health System descended into madness and harm. He could always go to an ER and stick the American taxpayers with the bill but that would take him out of circulation just when things were getting interesting. He decided to live with the hernia, at least until the story was done. He could live with that. He could practically poke it back in place with his fingers. Pharmacies sold devices that kept things nice and tidy until such time as he chose to visit a physician.

St. James went up to his room and showered, examining himself in the bathroom mirror. There was a telltale bulge if you looked sideways, nothing you'd see with clothes on. St. James sprayed himself with Axe, put on the khakis and a Von Dutch style Hawaiian shirt with flames and flying eyeballs.

His eyes fell on the bone flute wrapped in his sweater. They needed DNA testing. Rock band as serial killers. Connie said she knew someone. She'd left notice not to be disturbed. He'd bring her the flute when they met for lunch at two.

It might also be fruitful to go over the missing persons cases from 1974/75 to determine if any children had gone missing in or around Odoyle and Dunkeld. St. James left the hotel, had coffee and a bagel at a Chock Full 'o Nuts, and took a taxi to the New York Public Library. For two hours he searched the web for news of missing children. Twelve-year-old Siobhan McGregor bicycling home from school in Derby, disappeared without a trace, February 15, 1974. Nine-year-old Rob Fiesel of Odoyle, disappeared while playing on the moors, June 17, 1974. St. James cross-checked the disappearances with the Banshees' schedule and as near as he could tell MacGowan had been in England during both disappearances.

St. James used his credit card to print out the relevant stories and blessed whatever obscure soul had bothered to scan those ancient crime reports into the computer. A famous crime writer, now deceased, had written a book linking the Fiesel disappearance to Satanic cults. He was roundly ridiculed. There appeared to be no available copies of Ford Hanower's *Forbidden Rites* on Amazon or eBay.

It was noon by the time he finished at the library. He took a cab back to the hotel, fetched the flute from his room, and descended to the hotel restaurant which was off the lobby. He was fifteen minutes early so he bought a *New York Times* and sat on a deep-cushioned seat in the lobby. An article in *Arts* reviewed last night's show. "Unfortunately, as is so often the case, a madman with a gun ruined everybody's night and one young woman's life. This is sad because whether or not the Banshees are 'Rock Stars From Hell' or just clever imitators, they put on a hell of a show."

"Hi!" Connie said.

St. James looked up. She came toward him fresh-faced and bright-eyed, seemingly untouched by last night. St. James got up feeling old and awkward.

"How's the story?"

"I got my 2500 words. Richard is doubling the print order and sending out a press release. There was some talk on the morning news about last night."

They stood at the maître d's station.

"What are they saying?"

"Playing up the weird and grotesque although everyone seems to agree that the band's a fake."

The hostess, a slim black woman with a pageboy cut, arrived. "Two for lunch?"

"Yes, please," St. James said. He and Connie followed the woman to a corner booth. They slid in opposite one another as the hostess handed them menus. "Sylvia will be your waitress. She'll be with you in a minute."

St. James pushed the flute, wrapped in his *New York Times*, across the table. "You said you could get a DNA analysis on this."

Connie put the flute on the seat beside her. "I have friends in the Biology Department at Columbia. I'll get this to them today, but I don't know how long it's going to take."

The waitress brought them coffee.

"I went to the library." St. James told her what he'd learned about the missing children and showed her the print-outs.

Connie picked them up. "This just keeps getting better. The Banshees posted their schedule this morning. Their next gig is Madison, Wisconsin, Thursday."

"What?" St. James barked in consternation.

"Wait—it gets better. The following Saturday they play the Mishiwaka Amphitheater in Bellvue, Colorado."

St. James spit coffee. He'd played the Mish. It could maybe hold 300. "That's insane! Why would they do that when they could sell twenty times the tickets?"

"Sunday—Red Rocks. And on July 4, Pacific Arena in Long Beach."

Their waitress returned. "Before you decide, let me tell you about a couple specials we're running. In honor of the Dumfries Festival we're serving traditional Scottish haggis …"

St. James put hand to mouth and turned away.

CHAPTER FORTY-THREE

Connie made an appointment to see her old college pal and one-time roommate Professor Gretchen Haas in the Columbia Biology Department at four o'clock. She took a taxi to the Morningside Campus and trekked through the quad to Schermerhorn Hall where Gretchen was waiting on the steps, seated with her long plaid skirt folded under her long legs. She got up as Connie approached and spread her arms.

"Baby!" she declared, enclosing Connie in a tight hug. Connie hugged her back. They let go, looked at each other, and laughed.

"It's been too long!" Gretchen said.

"I know. I must have been in and out of New York a dozen times in the past five years."

"Can you at least come over for dinner?"

Connie sadly shook her head. "I can't, Gretch. I'm in the middle of a story."

Gretchen led the way into the Greek Revivalist temple of science. "Well, I'll take what I can get. You said you had a favor to ask."

"Yeah. Could you run a DNA test on a piece of bone and tell me where it came from?"

Gretchen stopped, turned, and smiled wryly. She had a lean, handsome face that would have been as home on a farm or a ranch. "What have you got?"

"Let's get to an office or something."

Gretchen led the way into the elevator, to the third floor, and they walked down an institutional yellow corridor that smelled of graphite and cleaning chemicals past bulletin boards hawking everything from summer jobs to satori, to Gretchen's tiny office, grey metal desk, picture of hubby and two adorable kids, bulletin board layered like a midden heap with notices, pamphlets, postcards, bills, receipts, and photos. The only other chair than the one behind the desk was buried a foot deep beneath reports, papers and journals.

"Oh, for gosh sake," Gretchen said, stooping and lifting the ungainly pile of paper which she unsuccessfully sought to transfer to the floor intact. As soon as she stood up the pile tilted and collapsed. Gretchen laughed and sat down behind her desk.

"You want coffee or something?"

"No, I can only stay a little while." Connie reached into her backpack, removed the bone flute, and handed it to Gretchen.

The scientist grasped it gingerly and with a slightly awed expression. "What is this … a flute made out of bone?"

"Human bone."

"Come on."

"Maybe. That's why I came to you. It's the strangest story and I really can't go into it right now. How soon can you do a DNA test?"

"I don't know. It might be a while; the process takes time. Inside a week?"

"That would be terrific, Gretch. And give me a bill. It's on *In Crowd.*"

"What are you working on? Gosh, everybody I know who knows you is soooo jealous! You get to hang out with rock stars."

"Most of them are jerks."

"Well what are you working on, in case you can't tell me?"

"The Banshees."

Gretchen's mouth went oval and she pulled back in surprise. "Were you at that club last night?"

Connie nodded. "Unfortunately. How do you know about it?"

"It was all over Facebook and Twitter this morning! And they talked about it on the news. I don't suppose you could get me tickets to one of their shows."

"Not unless you're willing to travel to Madison, WI."

Gretchen smiled ruefully. "The best I can do is break away on Sundays. Out of town is out of the question."

"Okay," Connie said. "The next time I'm in New York, you and me, the best seats in the house. I promise."

"What about the Banshees? I mean they'll be back, right? They're here to stay. I would really love to see them."

Connie was puzzled. "Since when do you like heavy metal?"

Gretchen blushed. "I don't know, I've been hearing them on the radio and there's just something about their music."

CHAPTER FORTY-FOUR

Will Ballard lived at 12 Ransom Road in Brighton. Eltaeb marked up one invisible point for Melchior as he got out of his rental car. Ballard lived in a basement apartment. But he lived alone. His was the only name on the mailbox and he had his own entrance directly to the street.

It was six PM, and Ballard saw lights through the drawn drapery. He had not telephoned. The idea was to surprise Ballard so that he would not have time to fabricate a story or vamoose. Eltaeb had not had time to delve into Ballard's background save for a contact at the DMV who told him that Ballard had been born in 1960.

Eltaeb descended three steps to the front door and rang the bell. Seconds later the door swung inward releasing a minute puff of marijuana and incense and revealing a man who appeared to be auditioning for the role of Cousin Itt. He was spindle-shaped and thatched on top with a shaggy beard that hung from his face like a grass skirt. He wore granny glasses on which Eltaeb could make out fingerprints.

"Will Ballard?"

Ballard hung behind the door looking wary. "Yes."

Eltaeb showed him his private investigator's license. "Greg Eltaeb. Sir, I'm sorry to bother you, but my client has asked me to ascertain the authenticity of an item he purchased from you on eBay."

"I sell a lot of stuff on eBay."

"You'll remember this. A lock of Paddy MacGowan's hair."

The aging hippy's eyes lit up like jack o' lanterns. He held the door wide. "Come in."

The moment Eltaeb stepped into the dark, cramped apartment he knew beyond any question that the lock of hair was authentic. Ballard's apartment was a shrine to pop culture, heavy on heavy metal and horror movies. Ballard gathered two stacks of comic books off one of two sprung sofas facing each other and placed them carefully on the floor next to other stacks of comics and books. Makeshift shelving ruled, cinderblocks and lumber filled to capacity with books, comics, DVDs, LPs, CDs, and action figures.

"I sold that hair to Stanton Bridger, but everybody knows he works for Burke Melchior."

Eltaeb's poker face did not twitch. "Not everybody knows that. How do you know?"

"Come on, man! TMZ, Perez Hilton, Celebrity Gossip—anybody who follows the trades! Can I get you something to drink?"

Eltaeb carefully lowered his bulk onto the aging sofa. "I would take a glass of water, thank you."

As Ballard went into the kitchen Eltaeb turned his attention to the walls. Framed comic book art: *Conan the Barbarian.* Framed movie posters: *Saw, Halloween, Pan's Labyrinth,* and in a place of honor, *I Eat Your Heart,* produced by Burke Melchior, a Kenny nominee and Scream winner. Ballard was a fan.

The skinny hippy returned with two *Star Wars* glasses of water, no ice, handed one to Eltaeb and vogued in the middle of his museum, one hand waspishly on hip. "What do you want to know?"

Eltaeb removed a small recording device from his pocket, held it up. Ballard nodded. Eltaeb turned it on and placed it carefully on top of *The Complete Bone* which rested on several other books on top of the overloaded coffee table.

"June 14, Brighton, Massachusetts. Greg Eltaeb visiting Will Ballard to authenticate a lock of hair allegedly belonging to Paddy MacGowan. Mr. Ballard, how did you acquire the hair?"

Ballard grinned goofily with crossed eyeteeth. "I ripped it off Paddy's head when they played the Garden in 1975!"

"Tell me about it."

"I would never do it today, but what the fuck, man, I was fifteen, it was my first big concert, and we were bugfuck for the Banshees. Me and all my friends. Four of us saw the show—we took the train. Fucking fantastic show! Still one of the greatest rock shows I've ever seen. Anyhow, we were seated right down by the stage on the side, and after the second encore we saw that they were gonna exit through the corridor right next to us. So Bill, Jim, Eric, and I jumped over the rail, just to get close to them, y'know? I didn't really plan it.

"About a hundred fans got back there before the cops stopped 'em, and it was like a little mini-riot in the corridor. All of a sudden here comes the band flanked by their bodyguards or whatever, coming right at us like a Pats offensive unit, and as they went by I just reached out and grabbed—I don't know why I did it. Snap! Got a tuft of hair. Paddy goes three feet, stops, puts his hand to his head, turns and winks at me! Man, it was the greatest moment of my life! Now they're back. I hope I get a chance to talk to him, man, so I can like apologize. Wouldn't that be cool?"

"Was that their only American appearance?"

"Yes. Yes, it was. Testing the waters so to speak. And then their plane crashed, but that was all a fake, obviously, like 'Paul is dead.'"

"Do you deal memorabilia full time?"

"Oh, hell no. I'm an orderly at Mass General. This is just my hobby. I should hang a sign in here: Nerds R Us."

Eltaeb smiled. "Do you have a lot of Banshees memorabilia?"

"I probably have the greatest collection in the world," Ballard proudly declared, puffing up a little. "I've been a life-long fan. I have all their recordings—the LP, five singles, two of which aren't on the LP, and a bootleg tape from a concert in Hamburg."

"May I see the LP?"

Ballard went to the front door and turned the dead bolt. He made sure the drapes were fully deployed and flicked on an overhead light which made the room look like the sad domain of a deranged hoarder. There was barely enough room for a person to walk sideways. Ballard went to a steel shelf holding at least a thousand vinyl LPs vertically, ran his forefinger along the sides until he found what he wanted. He carefully removed a vintage cardboard LP jacket sealed in a plastic sleeve.

Gently he handed it to Eltaeb who set it gingerly on his lap. The front bore the title *Beat the Manshees* and showed Paddy and Oaian. It was a wrap-around cover, the back depicting Cunar and a mysterious figure standing on a rock behind him.

Eltaeb pointed at the figure in the middle distance. "Who's this guy?"

"Some say it's the devil. Some say it's a Druid. That's one of the biggest questions about the album."

Eltaeb raised his eyebrows. "Only one?"

Ballard seemed almost feverish. "Oh yes! If you look at the liner notes it says it was recorded at DuPuy Studios in Soho in 1974. But there was no DuPuy Studios in Soho! Never was! And it says engineered by Burke Melchior, but he's never engineered another record in his life! And the mix is so good, it had to be someone who knew what they were doing. And finally, the biggest question, what the fuck are they saying when you play the record backwards?"

Eltaeb drew his head back in surprise. He had never even listened to Deep Purple, let alone the Banshees. His tastes ran toward Afro-Cuban jazz. "Would you mind playing that for me?"

Ballard's face clouded. "I don't know, man. Running the record backwards by hand is hard on the vinyl. Don't get me wrong—I have a great turntable—just a half gram of pressure on the stylus. That's the problem with vinyl—it wears out if you play it wrong or too often, but what are ya gonna do? The sound quality beats digital all to hell."

"Would you sell that record?"

Ballard snatched the LP out of Eltaeb's hands and stared at it. "Are you serious? Do you know what this is going for on eBay?"

"How much?"

"Five hundred dollars!"

"Will you take one thousand for it?"

Ballard twisted, mouth open in shock. "Are you serious?"

CHAPTER FORTY-FIVE

Melchior left New York without speaking to the police. It wasn't until they were over Kansas that Stanton suggested Melchior might want to call Melissa's parents. Melchior waved him away. "The cops already did that."

"Boss, it's the right thing to do, maybe pay for the funeral. It'll look good in the trades."

Melchior thought about it. "Yeah, okay, do it."

"What about attending?"

"Are you out of your mind? She was from Iowa! There's plenty more where she came from."

Stanton withdrew. Melchior gazed out the window. Ninguna had hinted at a new contract which would certainly be preferable to a long, drawn-out legal battle fought on TV and Twitter, as well as the courts. The Banshees juggernaut was gathering steam. The time to get on board was now. Every network, Internet gossip site, and trade publication had put in requests for interviews. Hucksters were already making fortunes off online rip-offs. Pirate Banshees merch had begun to appear on the streets.

The world was in meltdown. Tsunamis, riots, war, famine, pestilence, and death, but never mind because THE BANSHEES WERE BACK! Melchior retrieved the lawyer's card from his pocket and phoned him.

"This is the barrister Nadio Ninguna," said a recorded voice in a refined Spanish accent. "Please leave a message and I will get back to you."

"Nadio, you old pirate! Burke Melchior here. Let's talk about that deal! Your record will go a lot farther if it's on Melchior."

"Mr. Melchior," Ninguna suddenly picked up. "So good to hear from you. I trust you weren't unduly inconvenienced by last night's unpleasantness."

"I got outta Dodge. What about your boys?"

"The band deeply regrets Mr. Voinivich's loss and sympathizes with him, but we do not believe we are in any way responsible for either his son's death or his own actions."

That's because you weren't around when his son died.

"When you gonna be in L.A.?"LA?"

"I arrive two-thirty your time."

"Let's set something up for Wednesday. My assistant will be in touch."

"Very good. I look forward to hearing from you."

Melchior was on the ground heading home when Eltaeb called. Seated in the back seat of a Lincoln limo Melchior cued his headset. "What?"

"I met Ballard. The hair is genuine. He pulled it out of Paddy's scalp in 1975."

"Ha! Good work."

"There's more. I picked up a copy of their LP. Did you know there's a message when you play the record backward?"

"That old shtick! Sure, everybody knew that. It was just a bunch of gibberish."

"Maybe. Maybe not. Maybe you'd better have an expert evaluate it."

Eltaeb was no dummy. "Maybe you're right. When you winging home?"

"Tomorrow."

"Call me as soon as you get in. What kind of expert am I looking for?"

"I don't know—someone who speaks Druid?"

"Thanks so much, that's very helpful." Melchior cut the call. He turned to Stanton who was sitting opposite on the jump seat.

"Call UCLA tomorrow, find someone who speaks Druid, do you follow?"

"Boss?"

"Apparently the Banshees' LP has some backwards playing grooves. You know, like 'Paul is Dead.'"

"Are you sure it's Druid?"

"How would I know?"

"Didn't you engineer the album?"

"I left most of that shit to Paddy. He says he knew what he was doing, and the record sounded great."

"Okay, boss. I'll see what I can do."

The lights of the city fell away as they wound up Selden Canyon, reaching the house just as the sun was setting over the Pacific. Melchior opened the door as soon as the vehicle stopped moving and went straight upstairs to his office. As usual it was freezing inside. He eyed the huge fieldstone fireplace with longing, but the last time he'd fired it up his neighbor across the canyon had turned him in to the HuffPo which raised such a ruckus about his carbon footprint he'd been forced to donate a hundred thousand dollars to the Save the Androgynous Skink Foundation.

The housekeeper had neatly deposited his mail on his desktop. He swept it onto the floor, fell back into his hi-zoot mesh chair and called Serafin.

"Burke! I tried to reach you," Serafin greeted him. "Deepest condolences, buddy. That has to be rough."

Melchior momentarily drew a blank. "What? Oh. Oh! Yeah, thanks a lot."

"You'll let me know about the funeral arrangements? I'd like to send flowers."

"Yeah, sure, no problem. Listen. You play the record backwards it says something in Druid."

"Really. I wonder why no one has pointed this out before."

"Come to my office tomorrow at four. I'm going to have a language expert there."

"I don't know if I can make it. I might have to send somebody."

"Send that cute Chink served us sandwiches that one time."

"She's an intern, Burke."

"Send her anyway."

"Burke, I'll send the most qualified person for the job."

"Yeah. Right. Did you know they're playing Pacific Arena on the 4th?"

"I just found out. It's already sold out. You'd better have those boys under contract because they're going to make a billion dollars."

"Not a problem. Already talking to them."

"You're not the only one."

Melchior felt a sliver of betrayal like a Medici dagger through his heart. Hollywood was ruled by fear and greed. "Who?"

"I heard they were talking to Praeger."

"That little prick? Are they talking to him or is he talking to them?" Burke would not be surprised to learn the Banshees had already received dozens of offers ranging from recording to hawking life insurance. That was just the way the game was played. When you're hot, you're hot. Make hay while the sun shines. Praeger was a parvenu who rose from mailroom boy to the head of United Artists before he got booted for green lighting one of the biggest fiascos of all time, *Cantankerous* starring Tom Cruise and Julia Roberts.

Praeger was down, but not out. It took him six months to turn things around with his Oscar-winning independent, *Five Stars*, starring Stanley Tucci, about a restaurant critic who has to review a mob-owned joint.

Praeger was his own media brand with dozens of rock acts, a half dozen profitable movies, and a video game company.

"He's talking to them. Trying to. They're rather difficult to pin down as my team tells me. But you were there. You got to meet them."

"I met the manager, the lawyer, and Paddy."

"Well? Was it the real Paddy?"

Melchior gazed out his window down the valley at the ocean in the distance, an orange splash reaching from forever to the shore. "My mind says no, but my heart says yes. I'll know more once I get the results of a DNA test."

"Was there any truth to those rumors that you had the hots for him?"

"Richard. I'm devoutly hetero. Some would even say aggressively. You know that!"

"I was just asking."

CHAPTER FORTY-SIX

E ltaeb flew out of Logan Monday morning and arrived in L.A. at one PM. He took a taxi straight to Melchior's offices on Warner Blvd. By then it was two. Melchior had lunch catered from the Warner Commissary with a buffet table set up in his office. Also present were Stanton, a sound tech who had set up a turntable hooked up to a laptop and external speakers, and a gentleman in a seersucker suit, white shirt, and red bowtie. He had long silver hair and wore bifocals.

Melchior introduced Eltaeb. "Greg, this is Professor Daniel Frakke of the UCLA Department of History. Professor Frakke is an expert in medieval languages."

"Not quite an expert," Frakke phlegmed, giving Eltaeb the dead fish. "I just know a few things."

"We're hoping the Professor can identify whatever it is the Banshees are saying and what it means."

"Well, I don't know about that," the professor hoofed. "There are 137 known Druid dialects just going back to 600 A.D. Aleister Crowley did some very worthwhile research on the subject. Basically, there are two Druidic English groups ..."

Melchior held up his hand in a stop gesture.

Eltaeb unzipped his portfolio and removed the Banshees album still encased in its plastic sleeve. Melchior held out his hands.

"Let me see that puppy."

It was in excellent condition, the jacket barely frayed. Melchior turned it over and read, "Produced by Burke Melchior" down at the bottom. It brought forth bittersweet memories. He inhaled deeply. It smelled of old vinyl, a smell he'd grown to love. It used to hit him in the face every time he entered a record store. Now the record store was going the way of the passenger pigeon and the dodo bird. Even CDs were becoming scarce as time and tide turned to downloads.

Melchior held the album in both hands and looked at the painting of Paddy. For some reason the boys had insisted on a painting by an American comic book artist. Val Mayerik. The face that stared back at him was Paddy, all right. Indistinguishable from the face he'd seen the other night.

Except for that crackle around his eyes.

Eltaeb raided the groaning board building himself a towering corned beef and Swiss on rye. He sat on the sofa with a copy of the *Hollywood Reporter* open on his lap to catch the crumbs. Melchior sat at the other end.

"Very smart buying the record. Turn in a voucher. So this eBay character was the real deal, huh?"

Eltaeb chewed and swallowed. "Probably the world's greatest Banshees fan. Saw them on their first and only US appearance, had everything they put out, knows everything there is to know."

"Probably knows more than that old soak St. James. I should put him on retainer."

Eltaeb set his sandwich down. "I saw Ian perform at Grinnell College in 1998."

"Really. Was he any good?"

"The man has talent. I don't know what he's been doing all these years."

"Pissing it down the toilet along with enough booze, blow, and pills to kill everyone in Daytona Beach over Spring Break."

Professor Frakke sat in a black Barcalounger, back straight, going through some papers from his leather briefcase. Melchior waited until Eltaeb had finished his sandwich, which wasn't long. He stood.

"Okay, can we get this show on the road? Arnie, you want to do the honors?"

The sound man picked the sealed LP up off Melchior's desk. "Sure, boss." He used a pocket knife to slit the tape, removed the jacket from the plastic sleeve, turned it sideways and coaxed out the inner sleeve. He gently tapped out the LP, handling it only by the rim. He held it up to the light, tilted it slightly, and emitted a low whistle of admiration.

"Looks brand new."

Arnie set the LP on the turntable and turned on the amp, adjusting it via the laptop. Eltaeb took out his tape recorder, turned it on, and set it on the buffet table near the speakers. The Professor pulled out a notepad and set it on his knee. Arnie looked to Melchior. Melchior nodded.

Arnie gently placed the stylus in the grooves and rotated the disc counter clockwise by hand. Initially there was a low rip of noise, suddenly hushed, and then a voice spoke as from the end of a vast chamber with a slight echo effect, speaking in a guttural language with strange sibilants and harsh consonants. Frakke's pen moved then stopped as he looked up in astonishment.

The incantation assumed the cadences of an evangelical. It was mesmerizing, and at the same time frightening, like a swaying cobra or *Triumph of the Will*. Frakke made a lifting motion with his hand.

"Take it off. Take it off!"

Arnie glanced at Melchior who nodded. Arnie lifted the arm bringing silence to the room. For a moment nobody spoke.

Melchior looked at Frakke. "Well?"

"That's not Druid. It's not even Celtic! What we just heard is an ancient dialect from the Middle East, possibly Phoenician, but just as possibly Sumerian."

CHAPTER FORTY-SEVEN

Hannah Gold had been a stewardess for Virgin Atlantic for six years and had met plenty of celebrities, and still the man in seat C2 made her heart go pitter-pat. Veronica, with whom she roomed, peeked out of the stewards' galley at the handsome stranger reading the *Times of London* as their 747 streaked westward over the dark North Atlantic.

"Who is that guy?" Veronica said.

"Cyril Van Horn," Hannah replied, momentarily lost in her own daydreams. She told herself she didn't become a stew to meet guys. She told herself it was a good job with great benefits and you got to see the world. But everybody knew becoming a stewardess was like training to become a geisha. You did it to marry well.

Both Hannah and Veronica had seen plenty of engagements among their friends and even a few weddings. Van Horn, however, was a mystery man. He'd purchased his seat over the Internet at the last moment and offered very little in the way of personal information. He looked like a silent matinee idol in High Def. His dark hair was swept back from a proud forehead, black eyebrows over a piercing blue gaze. Black mustache just full enough to be enticing over a grin that radiated infectious glee. Devilish. Dark brown eyes that went straight to China. And his scent. No one had ever smelled it before—masculine yet delicate.

His bespoke silk suit came from Savile Row as well as the expertly cut Egyptian cotton shirt. His gleaming emerald tie was decorated with sky blue paisleys. He wore emerald cufflinks only visible when he shot his cuffs. He drank Balmenach neat. And that smile.

Hannah checked herself in the mirror. Pert twenty-eight-year-old brunette, curvy in all the right places, face like a cover girl, what's not to like? Someone like Cyril Van Horn, the way he looked, the way he handled himself, could have his pick of any woman in the world. Whom was she kidding? Someone like Cyril Van Horn was about as likely to ask her out as George Clooney, whom she'd seen once at a distance in the Sky Club Lounge at Heathrow.

A passenger call light went on. Hannah's heart skipped a beat. It was C2. "I'll take this," she said before Veronica could say anything.

Van Horn smiled at her with a hint of bad boy glee as she approached. His hands, she noticed, were large with black hair on the back. She imagined what he looked like naked; probably one of those guys with a hairy chest, but in all the right places, and it looked like he worked out. He smelled of paisleys, too. *Stop it, Hannah.*

"How can I help you, Mr. Van Horn?"

He held up an iPod. "Can you show me how this works?" he said in an intimate baritone. Forget the silents. He had a future in the talkies.

Hannah smiled, wondering if she was being set up. He continued to hold the little white device toward her. She took it and sat in the empty aisle seat next to him, turning the display face so he could see it. She began to scroll through the catalog, recognizing the names of mostly American bands as they went by.

"You stop the progression by doing this," she showed him with her finger. "Then you just hit the play button. And this is how you work the volume."

Does he have a Droid or something? she wondered. How can a man so obviously successful not know how to work an iPod?

She handed it over and he took it, his large hands lingering on hers for an instant, sending a chill up her arm and down her spine. "Thank you so much."

He had a deep, mellifluous voice with an indefinable accent, halfway between Austrian and Australian. It tickled something and she wanted to hear more. "Is this your first time flying with us?" Hannah said.

"This is my first time flying," Van Horn responded, eyes twinkling.

"Really. I find that hard to believe."

"There's a first time for everything," he said. "Also a second time."

"What brings you to New York?" *First time?* she wanted to ask. But that simply wasn't possible, was it?

"I'm meeting a couple of friends and we're driving to Los Angeles. I am going to see America." He spread his arms. "See it's beauteous bounty and bodacious beauty! From sea to shining sea, through purple mountain majesty."

Hannah could not stop from laughing. "Is it your first time in the States?"

"Yes. I have business in Los Angeles. City of Angels. Tinseltown. Hollyweird. All these years hearing about it, now I'm finally going to see it. See if it lives up to its billing! What rough beast slouches toward Jerusalem?"

Oh, Hannah, don't even think it. He reminded her of white yachts and white beaches.

"I fly to Los Angeles next week. If you need someone to show you around …"

"That's very kind of you, Hannah," he said reading her name tag. "How can I get in touch with you?"

Hardly daring to believe her luck, Hannah glanced around to make sure no one was watching, took a card out of her breast pocket and a pen from her pants and wrote down her cell phone number. "We usually stay at the Ramada near the airport, but if you let me know ahead of time I could trade with another stew and have maybe three days free."

"We'll see. It has been delightful to make your acquaintance."

Hannah got up and returned to the galley where Veronica was preparing to troll for trash up and down the aisle. "What?" she demanded.

Hannah felt a little high. "I gave him my phone number. He may phone me when he's in L.A."

Veronica's mouth stretched wide and she embraced her friend. "What does he do?"

"I don't know. Who cares? Maybe he's an international dope dealer."

"I watched him get on," Veronica said, maneuvering the steel cart toward the aisle. "He didn't have any carry on. No computer, no bag, nothing."

"He must have checked it through," Hannah said, preparing a beverage run for the other aisle.

Veronica raised her eyebrows. "Not even a cell phone?" She cruised from the galley with her trash pouch.

Chapter Forty-eight

onnie parked her rental on Atwood Avenue, across the street from the Barrymore Theater in Madison, Wisconsin, an old thirties movie house with a tower and a copper cupola turned green from oxidation. The jutting marquee proclaimed "BANSHEES!" and beneath that, "ONE NIGHT ONLY." The quadruple glass doors were occluded with posters advertising, among others, Emperors of Wyoming, Steve Earle and the Del McCoury Band, Richard Thompson, and, of course, the Banshees.

It was four PM. The manager of the Barrymore was only too happy to meet with rising journalista Cosgrove and Ian St. James, who had played the Barrymore in 1986. They walked in through the unlocked doors. The lobby contained a bar next to the snack stand, and the walls were decorated with demon masks which St. James found unnerving.

The manager was waiting in the lobby. He was young with a wild mane of curly black hair, a beard, and horn-rimmed glasses. "Ms. Cosgrove? Mr. St. James? I'm Randy Skeates, the manager. Mr. St. James, did you know your signed photograph is on the wall in my office?"

"You don't look old enough to have seen me the last time I was here."

"I'm not, but my parents were. Would either of you like a cup of coffee?"

Skeates went behind the snack stand and poured them both large cups of pungent coffee. St. James took his black. Connie went to the sideboard and added half and half and sugar. Skeates led them around the corner and up a flight of stairs to his office, a big square room fronting Atkinson through which they could see Monty's Blue Plate Special, a nouveau diner across the street.

"How can I help you?" Skeates said, settling behind his desk.

Connie and St. James both sat on the sofa—another student moving discard—diagonal to the desk. Connie placed her laptop on her knees.

"Actually," Connie said, "we're hoping we can help you."

"How's that?" Skeates said.

"You know about the shooting at Axton's Saturday night?"

"Yes, of course. Terrible. What does that have to do with us?"

"Someone has died at every Banshees performance so far," Connie said. "We don't want it to happen here."

Skeates looked at them bemused for a second. "Is this a joke?"

St. James leaned forward. "It's no joke. I saw them in Prague, the first stop on their come-back tour. Huh. Bloke dropped dead from a stroke. Connie and I were both at their next gig in Berlin. Two people were stabbed to death in the middle of the dance floor."

Skeates looked interested. "I didn't hear about that."

"The whole thing was swept under the carpet," St. James said.

"How many does the theater hold?" Connie said.

"Counting you, me, and the employees, 971. Six hundred seats."

"Do you have a dance floor?" Connie said.

Skeates nodded. "A small one. We're mostly a sit-down concert venue."

"We suggest," Connie said, "that you hire a couple off-duty policemen to keep an eye on the crowd and have an ambulance standing by."

Skeates' mouth hung open as if he were on the verge of getting it. "Don't be absurd. This is the Barrymore. This is Madison. We haven't had a lick of trouble since we opened up over thirty years ago."

"How many press requests have you received?" Connie said.

Skeates started counting them off on his fingers but he ran out of fingers. "It's incredible. We have journalists flying in from both coasts. Even the *New York Times* is here. We've got requests from filmmakers. We turned them all down of course. No one shoots without the Banshee's permission."

"You've been dealing with Kaspar Sinaiko?" St. James said.

"Him and the lawyer, Ninguna. I begged them to add a second show. No can do they said. They're bringing their own security. I'm sure they don't want trouble any more than we do."

"Yeah, right," St. James mumbled.

Skeates caught it. "What are you intimating?"

"You know that Banshees drummer Oaian St. James was me father."

Skeates' mouth and eyes expanded exponentially. "I didn't know that! I never listened to the Banshees until last week when they approached us about playing here. But wait a minute. These guys are a re-creation, right? They're not supposed to be the original band—they all died in a plane crash."

"Randy," St. James said, "there's something fishy about this whole operation. I've tried to speak to the drummer several times and each time they shut me out."

"Well, of course!" Skeates said. "If the dude's not your old man he's probably too embarrassed to speak to you!"

"These guys look exactly like the original Banshees," Connie said. "Like they had plastic surgery or something. And they never bothered to clear it with Burke Melchior, their original manager, who still owns the copyright and trademark."

Connie took her laptop and placed it on Skeates' desk facing him. "Look—all sorts of conspiracy sites are talking about the Banshees' deaths."

Onscreen was the results of a Google search for "Banshees deaths (the band)". They ran to 75 pages.

"You're going to get a lot of bottom feeders and ghouls tonight," St. James said.

Skeates was already shaking his head. "This is Madison, not New York or Berlin. We're going to get a lot of aging hippies and kids who have been raised by aging hippies. They're about as violent as a roll of toilet paper."

"Consider who's playing," Connie said. "This is not your usual indie rock crowd."

Skeates crossed his arms. "Guys, I appreciate the head's up and I'll take it under advisement, but trust me, nothing's going to happen but a great show. The police are always attentive and cooperative. If there's any trouble they'll be here within minutes, if not seconds. I wouldn't be surprised to find several off-duty policemen among the audience with their families."

"Isn't this adults only?" Connie said.

Skeates smacked his forehead. "Right, right."

"Who's the opening act?" St. James said.

"The Wickershams. Local indie with lead girl violinist and singer. If we'd known you were available we could have worked something out. Mr. St. James, if you're performing, I think we should get together and see if we can't schedule you sometime this summer."

"Tell you wot," St. James said. "We get through tonight's show with nobody getting killed, we'll sit down."

Skeates stood and offered his hand. "Shake on it."

CHAPTER FORTY-NINE

The burgundy Cadillac rolled west on blue highways. Elmira. Titusville. Napoleon. Inside, Yomnosko and Lebed took turns driving as Van Horn sat in the back seat with the window open, head in the wind like a dog. Inhaling it all. Asking endless questions which the two Russkis were hard-pressed to answer, this being their first time in the United States.

No motels. One slept while the other drove. Van Horn never slept. He read a great deal. He learned how to access the Internet on Lebed's laptop and commandeered it. When he wasn't hanging his head out the window he was speed-reading *Wikipedia*.

Neither Yomnosko nor Lebed dared mention their hunger, but their stomachs occasionally growled so loudly that Van Horn suggested a food stop. They ate one real meal a day, snacking all day long on 7/11 booty: Weasel Peters, Doritos, shelled pistachios, dollar bananas, energy drinks, and nacho cheese dip, dutifully depositing all trash in a large bag which they disposed of when fueling.

Lebed and Yomnosko didn't speak. They played the radio. Van Horn didn't care as long as it was music. Song after song he listened with cocked head like Nipper, the RCA dog. "Listen to that!" he exclaimed often. Once he heard a song, he could sing it back flawlessly, often improving on the original singer's locution and phrasing. Van Horn had an exquisite voice with an unbelievable range. His version of "Midnights in Moscow" made them weep. He was particularly fond of Mellencamp and the Boss.

They circled Chicago, Van Horn's head in the wind, picking up the scent of gasoline, diesel, ozone, rotting garbage, perspirants, perfumes, the aromas of 2,600 restaurants in the Greater Chicagoland Area. He inhaled deeply, breathing in five centuries of civilization. He listened to the hum of tires on pavement, the scream of jets landing and taking off from O'Hare, the sounds of thousands of radios blasting through open car and apartment windows, the voices of people on the street, a Tower of Babel shaped like an endless stack of forty-fives on the world's biggest jukebox.

He inhaled the scent of their souls, raw and jejune. After the Transformation the world would smell sweeter to him.

I will cleanse this verminous land with fire.

America—a bedlam of egotism and twisted spirituality, from the dregs of the so-called church to the hive-mind of the Islamists to the prideful vanity of the Jews to the feigned peace of the Buddhists to the empty dreams of the Greens—the modern Druids. Even the Satanists disgusted him. He saw their signs on the over- and underpasses—the upside-down crosses, the racial crosses, the gross drawings of genitalia, symbols that had passed down intact from the Sumerians, and before them the Vaas.

How easy it was to turn neighbor against neighbor, black against white, rich against poor, gay against straight, Lutherans against Episcopalians, and it was all being done for the most venal of purposes.

Amateurs.

Yomnosko drove. He had the air conditioning on high to counteract the heat and humidity Van Horn admitted through the open window.

"How are we doing, boys?" Van Horn said in English in his odd accent.

"Madison by seven," Lebed answered, stomach rumbling.

"I see you boys require provender," Van Horn said, picking up the by-now well-used and dog-eared copy of the *Rand McNally Road Atlas* they'd been given at the Cadillac agency in Queens. Normally one had to produce a valid American driver's license when purchasing a vehicle, but Braun Cadillac happened to be owned by the Skorzny Group so they got around that. Van Horn had paid cash for the new Cadillac. Impeccable forgeries testified to his ownership and insurance. It was for his assistants.

Van Horn himself did not require a passport or a driver's license. He had merely to convince authority he was legit, and he was good at that.

It was just past six. "Can you boys hold out 'til Madison?"

"Sure boss," Yomnosko said, stomach churning. America made him hungry. He was always hungry. As a boy he had killed an old woman for a bag of potatoes.

They rolled through the green Wisconsin countryside, Van Horn breathed deeply of fertilizer and pollen. As they topped a promontory heading north, Wisconsin's capital city stood before them, the white capital prominent between the deep blue of two lakes. Yomnosko had the Barrymore's location dialed in on the GPS and had already located a cheap motel nearby for him and Lebed.

The cool feminine voice of OnStar guided Lebed unerringly to Monty's Blue Plate Special. They pulled in at five after seven, snagging a parking spot in the back of the lot just as a Prius was pulling out. The scene across the street bordered on chaos, people lining up to get in, drug and ticket dealers working the alleys and the shadows.

Inside the diner the three men, all dressed in dark suits, drew a few quizzical stares. A hostess quickly seated them in a booth and handed them menus.

Van Horn remained standing. "Boys, get me a glass of water. I'll go across the street and get the tickets."

Yomnosko looked up, mouth watering. "Do you know how to do that, boss? Do you need any help?"

Van Horn smiled. His teeth were perfect. "Give me a little credit, boys. I've been cramming for two days."

As Van Horn strode out of the diner the hostess gazed after him with undisguised interest. Van Horn walked across Atkinson where he stood out among the crowd of shabbily genteel East Siders, pierced board punks, and professional therapists. He stood with his hands clasped behind his back gazing up at the marquee while a soft voice wheedled, "Tickets, tickets, who needs tickets?"

Van Horn whirled, startling the hawker, a stooped skinny dude in an ancient letter jacket, shades, and platinum blond pompadour.

"I need tickets," Van Horn said.

The man made a shushing motion. "Okay, be cool, my man, follow me. We need to do this right." The seller ambled along the sidewalk past a pet shop and a Vietnamese restaurant, Van Horn following. The man turned left at the corner and walked halfway up the block then turned into a narrow alley between a garage and a commercial building.

Once in shadow the seller pulled out two tickets from his jacket. "Second row, balcony. Two fifty a piece."

"I only need one."

"Three hundred."

Van Horn removed his ostrich skin wallet, purchased in a mall in New York, and peeled off three Benjamins. They exchanged.

"Pleasure doing business with you, my man," the seller said truckin' on out of there.

Van Horn stuck the ticket inside his jacket. As members of the Banshees' security detail Lebed and Yomnosko had backstage passes. It was warm when he emerged from the alley, the west side bathed in the glow of the setting sun, lighting up the red brick buildings, the Barrymore's ornate facade. Motorcycles and pick-up trucks slunk up and down the avenue in heavy traffic. Van Horn waited until there was a break before walking quickly across the street.

As he was about to reenter the diner he glanced toward their car at the back of the lot and noticed a flicker of motion, a shadow really, someone bending over the far rear bumper. Van Horn hot-footed it to the rear of the lot so silently the young man bent over the Cadillac's flank intent on his work did not even notice until Van Horn stood directly behind him.

The young man, who wore Birkenstocks and a black, red, and yellow knit cap, had scratched "CAPITALIST PIG" with a knife on the Cadillac's rear fender.

Van Horn leaned forward and crooned in the man's ear. "Hello."

Dude jumped and shit his pants at the same time. He started to book but Van Horn's hand shot out and caught the scratcher by the back of his Che T-shirt and pinned him effortlessly against the car. The knife fell from his numb fingers hitting the ground with a soft clank.

"What are you doing?" Van Horn said calmly, coolly, in a smooth low voice.

"Man, don't give me that shit! Is this your Cadillac? Do you know what your carbon footprint is? Cadillacs aren't welcome on the East Side you fucking capitalist pig. You wanna do something about it? Call a cop. Go ahead. I dare ya."

But the vandal's eyes told the real story.

Van Horn switched his grip to the man's throat. The vandal's eyes bulged and he tried to pry Van Horn's hand away, but it was like trying to bend a horseshoe. Van Horn gazed into the man's soul and loosened his grip ever so slightly.

"Who … are … you …?" the scratcher croaked.

"I am the god of hellfire," Van Horn crooned. "And I bid you to burn."

And then he let his guard slip and showed the scratcher his true face.

Van Horn let go. The man gasped wordlessly, stumbled, and ran toward Atwood as fast as his long legs could carry him, right out into the middle of the street, smack into an East Side bus, which rolled over him like road kill.

CHAPTER FIFTY

The traffic fatality in front of the Barrymore resulted in Total Goat Fuck. The cops cordoned off the street and redirected traffic maze-like through the Atwood neighborhood. Gawkers added to the problem. Witnesses had seen the deceased race blindly out of Monty's parking lot, but they searched in vain for the reason. He had to have been higher than a kite.

St. James and Connie were inside the Barrymore. It did not take long for them to learn what had happened from the beat cop, who agreed that the doors would stay open. Madison police had coped with much worse, including angry mobs ransacking the capitol building for weeks on end. By seven-thirty the Barrymore was filled to capacity and still hundreds of people milled outside as if awaiting word from the Prophet.

A big sign on the door read, "ABSOLUTELY NO RECORDING DEVICES."

Skeates found St. James and Connie two seats on the far right next to the wall on the main floor, and they were happy to have them. Even with the AC on the air felt viscous. The Banshees had negated the agreement the Barrymore had with WORT to broadcast performances live, ostensibly to protect their new material.

The Wickershams began playing at eight. St. James could not imagine a more inappropriate opening act. The Wickershams played cheerful, multi-harmonic power pop. The crowd was clearly impatient. As St. James stood with his back to the wall and surveyed the crowd, he concluded that Skeates had been wrong about the demographics.

Certainly the East Side was well-represented, but there were at least as many Goths and headbangers in Doc Martens, as well as bikers and a group of self-avowed atheists handing out pamphlets titled "THERE IS NO GOD."

The Wickershams left the stage to lukewarm applause. Kaspar briefly appeared in the wings.

"There's the fucker," St. James said, easing himself down the row to the aisle. He headed toward the stage, but when he sought to step up his way was blocked by two thick-looking men with Slavic faces.

"Aw, not this shit again," St. James groused. "I know Kaspar. Me dad's in the band!"

The men grunted and blocked his way. Disgusted, St. James made his way up the aisle toward the lobby. It was slow going with people everywhere. It took him fifteen minutes to wend his way to the front door and out into the street. The police had taken down the barricades. As St. James stepped outside, a hair-raising rumble rattled down the road, and he looked up to see a dozen motorcycles coming at him, straight out of *Mad Max Fury Road*. They parked directly in front of the theater in violation of the no-parking zone the police had set up. Their colors showed a horned demon and said, "INSANE ASSHOLES/JOLIET."

St. James thought about going around to the stage entrance but it would probably only result in another rebuff. He smelled marijuana smoke. *Must be mad,* he thought, *wanting to be stoned for what comes next.* He felt the hernia. Every now and then it would remind him it was there with a little tweak. *Careful, boyo. Just keep stuffin' it back in,* he told himself. *Hang on. Recording contract coming.* Then maybe he could afford some medical treatment.

There was an organization that helped down and out rock and rollers, but it was for old people. Geezers who'd rendered themselves useless with too many acid trips, trashed their kidneys with a lifetime of drinking. St. James couldn't bear the thought of seeing his picture on TMZ over the caption, "Guess which pathetic rock and roll has-been seeks medical treatment?"

At least, he thought, *we've got the killing out of the way and can get on with the concert.* But he knew it wasn't going to be that simple. The others had died during or after the performance. This vehicular death was coincidence and nothing more. Or so he told himself.

People began moving back inside. Some ticketless bikers headed across the street and down the block toward the Harmony, a corner bar. There were more bikes parked outside the bar. St. James joined the concertgoers streaming back into the auditorium. The lights went down as he took his seat next to Connie against the wall.

"Talk to him?" she said.

St. James shook his head. "It's a mob scene outside."

"What's going on outside?" she said.

"We are joined by the Insane Assholes, a motorcycle club out of Joliet, Illinois."

A beloved Madison deejay took the stage, his brand new Banshees T-shirt stretched taut over his medicine ball gut. "Hellooooo Madison!"

Incoherent screaming, whistling, applause, stamping, and hooting.

"Well, we've lucked out again! Not only are we getting the Banshees on their first world tour in FORTY YEARS ..."

Wall of noise.

"They're also recording tonight! We're going to be part of history! I want to remind everyone there will be no photos or recording during the performance. You do, and they'll put a hex on you!"

White noise.

"Here they are, THE GODFATHERS OF HEAVY METAL, THE BANSHEES!"

Not even that crowd could outmuscle the power chord that ripped from the massive amplifier as Paddy, Cunar, and Oaian came onstage, Paddy and Cunar playing their axes like strolling minstrels. Paddy's guitar had three necks protruding from the body at angles like a trident. His hands roamed Vishnu-like from one neck to another. Oaian perched behind the drums, and they dove into "Whistle Past the Graveyard," a little known single that was not included on their album. People immediately filled the small dance area in front of the stage gyrating in place under the watchful eye of Banshee's security, a pan of popcorn heating up.

Everywhere St. James looked people were taking notes. Half the audience was media. He recognized several faces from television and the Internet. A Borsalino hat bobbed among journalists, and St. James felt sick to his stomach. It was Rulon Wexler who'd made his bones savaging St. James' last disastrous concert appearance. At that instant Wexler turned toward him, and his face lit. He tipped his hat at St. James and smirked.

Paddy's power chord whipsawed Wexler's eyeballs back toward the stage.

The Banshees burned through four songs without pause, leaving the crowd breathless and exhilarated.

Barely breathing hard Paddy took the mike. "'ALLO MADISON!"

Jet engine roar from the crowd.

"'Speakin' on behalf of Oaian, Cunar, an' me, I want to say what a pleasure and an honor it is to play for you tonight in this 'istoric venue. Oaian, you got something to say?"

Paddy handed the wireless mike to Oaian. "Hiya, son! Be talkin' to you soon." Paddy took the mike back.

Connie looked at St. James whose mouth was agape. *Son?*

"'At's roight!" Paddy roared. He held up one finger. The audience hushed and looked around trying to spot Oaian's son. He'd have to be a child judging from the man on stage. Of course they could do miracles with make-up and lighting, but no one believed these were the originals. It was a post ironic world, and they were all in on the joke.

Paddy sat on a hardwood stool, a single spot lighting him up. Cunar and Oaian fell back, grabbing bottles of beer. "Paddy, woy don't you play something noice once in a while? Oi hear that all the toim. So 'ere's something noice for the ladies."

Hands flew from neck to neck like sparrows. Segovia's "Chaconne." Each note crystalline and limpid, a jewel hovering in the air. Time stopped. So this was Heaven—a sound so haunting and beautiful it erased all pain and suffering. People wept with joy. They wanted it to go on forever. Only St. James glanced impatiently at his watch. Paddy was setting something up. He was sure of it.

Paddy braked on the Beatle chord, letting it reverberate through the room like the afterglow of a perfect dream.

"'Ow you loik Cerberus then?" he asked, dipping his guitar. "Made special for me by a very demented craftsman. I mean devoted!"

Laughter.

"You loik that classical stuff?"

He casually ripped off several stanzas of a Bach cantata. A snatch of "Toccata and Fugue in D Minor" that made St. James' hair stand on end.

"Now Oi 'ear some bird named Clapton is ripping off me riffs!" Smiling at the audience like a young swain, Paddy unleashed a series of climbing arpeggios like the Swiss Alps.

"Now as you know, we're recording here tonight."

Jet engine.

"Now afore I introduce our next song, I want to know, ARE THERE ANY ATHEISTS IN THE HOUSE?"

St. James was surprised the ceiling didn't crumble at the resultant roar. A sick feeling began to build in his gullet and a prickle of fear sunk fangs into the base of his spine. At least here against the wall no one could blindside them.

"'Cause this next one is going out to all you atheists in the crowd! Never give up! Never give in! And don't you keep that faith, baby! I call this one ... 'There is No God, But There is a Head Nigger in Charge.'"

A collective gasp scraped the ceiling. They cringed in apprehension that the band might go the wrong way. Paddy bent over Cerberus and insouciantly ripped off a riff that raised Kurt Cobain.

> *He ain't loved and he ain't feared*
> *He ain't no old guy in a beard*
> *He's the man who wasn't there*
> *The one they pray to on the stair*

The words changed. They sounded like English but it wasn't English. Paddy's clear tenor became hoarse and guttural, hands a blur as they worked his three necks, Oaian laying down thunder, and just as the tension became unbearable, Paddy hit the sweet bridge with a swooning release that could be felt throughout the auditorium.

Over Oaian's and Cunar's granite solid bass Paddy began peeling off revelatory power chords that climbed the scale, and the higher it got the louder it got. People clapped their hands to their ears and turned away. People stood and screamed at the stage and then people screamed throughout the auditorium and especially from the balcony until there was no rock and roll, just screaming.

Something moist struck St. James on the top of his head. He stood and turned around. A woman danced grotesquely on the balcony banister, hands to her head trying to stanch the flow, blood spewing from her eyes, ears, nose and mouth. The house lights went on. The tightrope walker's screams drowned out all else like a chainsaw through the skull. More and more of the audience stood, turned and gasped. All hell broke loose and the stampede began.

Just before the woman pitched onto the seats below St. James saw standing a row behind her, a man in Silva-thin shades, black jacket, and gray shirt, smiling.

n Crowd's special Banshees issue came out the next day, too late to include the latest fatality. But what they had was enough. It sold out within two hours of hitting the street. In a frenzied late-night phone call Serafin had instructed Connie how to talk to the press. She and St. James had booked rooms at the Edgewater. The press was camped out in the lobby.

They'd spent an hour talking to the police after Skeates had told the cops about the conversation he'd had earlier in the day. Once again the band had fled too quickly for the police to question. It was unclear how they traveled as they had no bus.

St. James and Connie found eight news services waiting for them in the lobby, Rulon Wexler among them, dressed like Bruno Mars. St. James referred all questions to Connie who delivered a sanitized version of events, no mention of Paddy's grave or Professor Klapp. She left them with the distinct impression that the Banshees' tour was the cleverest media exploitation since Lady Gaga. It didn't matter whether the band was real or not, the *idea* of the band had captured the zeitgeist of the nation.

Connie held up a hand. "Really, folks. We're going to have to cut this short. We've got a plane to catch."

"I have a question for Mr. St. James!" piped up Rulon. The other journalists eyed him with adoring puppy eyes. *Rolling Stone!* St. James wanted to puke.

Rulon was giddy. "Ian, if that's your dad playing drums, how can he be so young? How much are they paying you to do this? Is Connie in on it?"

"You're full of shite, Rulon," St. James said getting up.

"I don't believe anyone died in Berlin or Krakow or wherever the fuck you say they did. It's a big dog and pony show, isn't it? Come clean, Ian! Come clean!" He sniggered at his double entendre.

St. James and Connie headed for the lobby. Rulon followed, but St. James wheeled on him so abruptly they nearly collided, and said softly between gritted teeth, "Back off, or I'll feed you your eye teeth."

Rulon hopped around wide-eyed. "Did anyone hear that? Did anyone hear that? I need a witness!"

o o o

Connie and St. James were on their way to the airport when the radio breathlessly announced the medical examiner's preliminary results. The woman who had danced along the banister and plunged to the floor below breaking her neck had suffered a massive stroke. She had a high blood pressure condition and her friends and family had begged her to skip the concert, as she was to avoid high-stress situations. However, for reasons that soon became apparent, she could not be talked out of attending.

The radio announcer was the self-same soul who had welcomed the Banshees to the stage. The decedent's name, released after notifying her next-of-kin, was Hella Fensterman-Pritchard, President and Founder of the Religion Is Evil Foundation, headquartered in Madison. Her organization sought the removal of any mention or symbol of God in the public arena. They had caused a thirty-foot steel cross memorial to fallen soldiers in the Arizona wilderness to be removed even though it was on private lands because it could be seen from a nearby road. They had successfully had the Ten Commandments removed from thirty-six courthouses. They sponsored a squad of vandals who rearranged the letters in church signs at night into obscenities.

Ian's and Connie's bewhiskered cab driver, who had hung his PhD. in Philosophy next to his license, said, "Holy moly, dudes. That's heavy. Dig it—the head of the Religion is Evil Foundation drops dead in the middle of 'There Is No God!'"

"'But There is a Head Nigger in Charge,'" St. James reminded him.

Connie hit him on the arm. Hard.

The Doctor of Philosophy looked in the rearview. "Were you guys there? You were there, weren't you? You're that reporter from *In Crowd*, aren't you?" He picked up the latest issue of *In Crowd* and waved it.

"Yessssss."

"How do you know?" St. James said.

"Are you kidding? Your picture's all over the news. Famous reporter been on the case since Berlin! Christ, would I loved to have been there! I had to work! You know what's fucked? You can't get the record anywhere!"

"I'm surprised somebody hasn't put it on the web," St. James said.

"I heard you could find it, but when I looked I couldn't find anything."

They pulled up in front of the Frank Lloyd Wright terminal. Connie paid the man.

"Good luck with your story!" he said.

"Thanks," St. James said, grabbing the luggage. Connie pressed her lips together and didn't look back.

Naturally they gave St. James the full treatment. As they waited in the plane St. James said, "I thought Rulon was gointer seize a piston when Oi got in his face."

"That little shit," Connie said. "He dropped acid in the punch bowl at one of Richard's parties. Richard's convinced Wenner put him up to it."

"'E's a regular Westbrook Pegler, ain't 'e?"

The plane started to taxi. She laid a hand on St. James' wrist. "You were good at the press conference. I would have liked to punch the little shit in the face myself."

"Now Con, can't 'ave reporters punching out reporters, can we?"

They laughed. For a moment time stood still like the Segovia, only better.

They were somewhere over Nebraska when Connie checked her messages, which were stacked up like flights over O'Hare. There were twelve from other media outlets. There was one from Gretchen Haas.

Connie listened to the message. "Call me."

St. James saw something in her face. "What?"

"My scientist friend at Columbia."

St. James watched her dial. Connie made a face, waited impatiently for the message to end. "Finally! I can't wait to hear what you found ..."

Connie's expression changed to one of delight as Gretchen picked up the phone. "Okay, I don't have much time, so I'll make this short. The bone is that of a young girl, maybe ten to fifteen years old. Now the question is what do I do with it? Is this evidence of a crime?"

"If it is, it's a very old crime. Centuries. Please don't tell anyone, Gretchen. I promise you, we're working on this."

"What do you want me to do with it?"

"Can you FedEx it to me at the *In Crowd* offices?" Connie recited the address and the FedEx account number, which she knew by heart, thanked Gretchen profusely, and hung up.

"What?" St. James said.

Connie told him.

"Bloody hell," he muttered, looking out the window. Thirty thousand feet below he spotted a tiny vermilion automobile heading west on a deserted highway.

Chapter Fifty-two

Mr. Burke Melchior
Melchior Productions
1497 West Olympic Boulevard, Suite 309
Los Angeles, CA
90067

Elwood Bonner, Professor Emeritus
Middle Eastern Language Department
University of Florida
Brixton Hall
1492 Tamiani Drive Suite 210
Gainesville, FL
32611

June 20

Dear Mr. Melchior:

I have listened to the recording you sent and these are my findings:
Although there are phrases and words with which I am not
familiar I believe the language used to be Archaic Sumerian which
dates from the 26th century BC. The structure is not so clear to me
but I have been able to identify a number of recurring phrases,
particularly the word **reth**, which roughly translates to "wrath"

and is used in conjunction with an ancient deity heretofore mentioned in only two known documents.

The word rethkrorg *translates roughly as Rathkrogh and refers to a deity worshiped by the Nippur, a people who surfaced briefly in Southern Mesopotamia approximately 2400 BC. The text mentions a "white-robed challenger" several times as a threat to Rathkrogh and predicts the rise of this challenger approximately two and a half millennia in the future. The "white-robed challenger" could refer to Jesus or Muhammad.*

The text uses the word (————————) which translates to "music," and declares that through music the challenger and his followers may be defeated. This is interesting because according to my colleague Prof. Natalie Bowman of the Department of Ancient Music, the Sumerians were not known for their musicianship. The text also refers to (————————) which we know to mean bone flutes, the oldest known musical instruments.

Taken altogether I believe the speaker to say, "Turn their bones into flutes. Turn their flesh into pudding. Strike down the unbelievers and let darkness rule."

I hope this has been of some help to you. In lieu of my consulting fee, I am asking you to make a donation to the American Jazz Society.

Thank you.

I remain your obedient servant,

Elwood Bonner, Professor Emeritus
Middle Eastern Language Department

CHAPTER FIFTY-THREE

Special to *Variety* by Chris Morris: MELCHIOR, BANSHEES INK DEAL. Everything old is new again as entertainment powerhouse Burke Melchior reunites with his first band (or is it?), the legendary Banshees who have embarked on a new Brit Invasion, threatening to dominate the American music landscape as never before.

Melchior Productions announced an agreement today with Skorzny Group President Kaspar Sinaiko to represent the band worldwide. The Banshees are currently on the first leg of their American tour which has been SRO since their initial appearance at Axton's in New York City. They are recording a new album which Melchior plans to release in the fall. Melchior also promises a re-issue of *Beat the Manshees* with added bonus material.

The big question is just who are these bad boys of rock? As we all know, the Banshees died in a plane crash on August 19, 1975. Graphics of the band today have a curious habit of appearing and disappearing on the Internet, but those who have seen the current band say that they're young—mid-to-late twenties. So who are they really?

The Skorzny Group is a property management consortium headquartered in the Cayman Islands with branches in Moscow and Los Angeles. Although rumors have linked Skorzny to the Russian Mafia, the FBI has no information on the group or knowledge of any ties to organized crime. There is speculation that the three band members, "Paddy MacGowan," "Cunar Odoyle," and "Oaian St. James" are Russians surgically altered to look like the originals.

Variety notes the involvement of Ian St. James, Banshees drummer Oaian St. James' son, with *In Crowd's* coverage. Ian St. James launched his own musical career in 1996, initially meeting with modest success, but has been absent from the scene for several decades. Is Junior in on it? What's the payoff? Thus far Ian St. James isn't talking. He is following the Banshees along with *In Crowd's* ace reporter Connie Cosgrove.

Given the Banshees' reputation and oeuvre, *Variety* believes we are witnessing a brilliant PR campaign—a satanic rock band that went down in flames, that preached immortality and human sacrifice, back from the dead. *Variety* must ask if these guys are so smart, why isn't the record available? Why do they choose venues with such limited seating?

Tonight they are playing the Mishawaka Amphitheater in Bellvue, Colorado, capacity: 325. Their final concert will take place July 4 at Pacific Arena in Long Beach. The 62,000 seats sold out within two hours. *Variety* promises full coverage of the event.

Variety hears that the FBI has begun an investigation into the deaths attendant to the two American concerts along with claims of deaths at the Banshees' two European appearances, in Prague and Berlin. *Variety* has found no substantiation to claims that people died at the European concerts.

Chapter Fifty-four

ear Mr. Melchior: *The two hair samples you submitted share the same DNA. There is a 99.45% likelihood they came from the same person.*

Yours,

Emily Wipperfurth
Research Director
DNA Testing Truth 4 U
Los Angeles.

Melchior stared at the e-mail as if he could will it to disappear backwards down the memory hole. He deleted it. The information was his and his alone. He'd paid for it. He'd use it as he saw fit.

He sat for long seconds gazing out the window wondering what it meant. Well it was fucking *impossible*, wasn't it?

Melchior pushed the intercom. "Stanton, get in here."

Seconds later his assistant appeared in the doorway to his office quivering like a pointer. "What's up, chief?"

"I'm throwing a party for the Banshees at my place. Get hold of Gruber BBQ. I want the whole nine yards: ribs, shredded pork, brisket, and I'll need the party tent from the lot. We'll need ten waiters and two parking lot attendants. We'll have to run cars across the street and park on the canyon, do you follow?"

"Music, chief?"

"What are you, stupid? I'm going to have somebody play for the Banshees? We'll need instrumentation, amplifiers, get hold of Hollywood Sound. The Banshees are gonna play."

"Guest list?"

"I'm working on it. Expect around eighty. Have we heard anything from Kennedy?"

"No, chief."

"Put him on the list." Melchior went back to his monitor. Interview over.

"Chief, your two o'clock is here."

"What? Oh. Oh! Show her in."

Stanton withdrew. Seconds later the door opened and a svelte redhead entered smiling ingratiatingly.

"Close the door, Rachel. Have a seat."

"This is such an honor, Mr. Melchior. I've been a fan all my life."

Where did they come from, this endless supply of nubile young things drawn to Hollywood like journalists to an open bar? This one came from Muscatine, Iowa according to her publicity package, had starred in her high school production of *Oliver!*, done dinner theater for a couple years, and had a walk-on on *The Chicago Way*.

Was there a greater racket in the world than making movies? If so, Melchior had not heard of it. Rachel Kropenski, twenty-three years old, dying to break into movies, moist as the morning dew. Tall. Melchior liked that. He loved the look of raw lust and envy every time he entered a room with some fresh beauty on his arm.

"I've watched your screen tests and you show promise. The project is called *Helmet Head* and you would be playing the part of a waitress at a roadhouse with a biker boyfriend with whom you have a stormy relationship."

"I read the script, Mr. Melchior."

Melchior raised his eyebrows.

"I asked Mr. Manning for a copy and he gave it to me. I signed a confidentiality agreement."

"Smart as well as beautiful. I like that."

"I've also had biker boyfriends."

"What about now? Do you have a boyfriend?"

"Free and unattached."

"You know, I'm having a little gathering at my place on the 3rd in honor of the Banshees. Would you like to come?"

Rachel clapped her hands together and squealed with glee. "I'd love to come!"

"I'll tell my assistant to send a car."

Melchior's head unit softly chimed. "What?" he barked, irritated.

"Dan Kennedy on the line, chief."

Melchior smiled apologetically. "Excuse me one minute." He switched on the Bluetooth. "Dan?"

"I have a friend in the Federal Security Service says Kaspar Sinaiko is serving life at hard labor for murder at the Nikolov Beria Camp in Siberia."

"Is there any way to substantiate that?"

"I'll try."

"So the guy's a killer."

"He's also wanted for bear baiting."

"Excuse me?"

"Yeah. It still goes on in Russia. They trap bears and use them in carnivals. It's been outlawed by every civilized nation and the International Wildlife Treaty. If it's your guy, I can pick him up soon as Interpol or GRP shoots me a request."

That would be awkward, if the Banshees' manager turned out to be a convicted murderer. On the other hand, Melchior couldn't buy that kind of publicity.

"What about Ninguna?"

"Member of the Spanish Bar, argued before the International Court at The Hague, specializes in intellectual properties, very highly respected. Clients include Antonio Banderas and Phillipe Germaine."

Melchior made a mental note to make certain Ninguna got an invite. "Dan, I'm having a little get-together on the third."

CHAPTER FIFTY-FIVE

C onnie and St. James headed north in their rented Chevy. Connie drove. "When did you play the Mish?"

"Back in '99. Just before I imploded. Probably my last decent concert."

Connie glanced over. "What happened?"

"Same old story. Drugs, alcohol, lack of focus. Used to stay up all night wondering where it all went. I mean I 'ad it, and then all of a sudden it was gone." He snapped his fingers. "Like that. In retrospect, I could write a book. Nobody's fault but me own. But you know, I think I'm coming out of it. I mean, I haven't had a drink since Berlin ..."

Self-consciously he touched the protrusion at his beltline. It was asserting itself with little tweaks. Not to the point of pain, but to the point of him being constantly aware a piece of his gut was hanging out the window.

"Judging from what I heard, it's back. Don't sell yourself short, Ian. You've got talent. The other night when you played me that song ..."

"Oim no Paddy."

"Your guitar playing is excellent, the way you sustain a bass with one hand and play all those multi-faceted runs with the other. And I don't think Paddy conveys the emotion that you do."

The emotion that he felt right now.

"Oi've had a lot of time to practice." He turned and reached into the back seat, laying his hand on his guitar case as if feeling for a pulse.

"They're running a shuttle from Ted's Place. We'll check in before we head out. Be prepared for a long night."

"Oi've played there before."

A minute buzz permeated the sealed automobile and grew into a mighty roar as a dozen chopped Harleys with straight pipes shredded by.

St. James saw the familiar horned demon on the backs of their grimy denim vests. "Our old friends the Insane Assholes. Somehow, it just oin't a party without 'em."

They checked into the Fort Collins Marriott and went to their rooms. When they linked up again in the lobby St. James had his guitar case. Connie was flushed with excitement, her short blond hair swinging wildly as she sashayed across the lobby toward him.

Keep coming. Right into my arms.

Stop it. Old fool.

"Are you ready to freak out?" she asked with dancing green eyes.

"What?" Bemused.

"Serafin just called. Melchior got a lock of Paddy's hair from the New York gig and matched it with a lock some fan pulled off his head in 1975. They're the same."

St. James experienced a sudden vertigo and had to put a hand out against a pillar to steady himself. His hernia sent a little jolt up his gut.

"Are you okay?"

"Jayzus. I mean, what can I say? How is that possible?"

"I don't know. I don't believe in ghosts or ghoulies and I don't believe this is some satanic rock band back from the dead."

"Is 'e sure? I mean, what if it's a con?"

"Burke Melchior has no sense of humor. Zero. And he is not someone given to false statements, nor is he anyone you want to cross. If Richard says it's a match it's a match."

They ate a late lunch at the hotel and rode north on 287 to Ted's Place, the entrance to Poudre Canyon. It was six PM. They parked their car next to several dozen others on a field behind the gas station/convenience store, went inside and stocked up on bottled water and almonds from the aging hippy behind the counter.

At six-thirty, a bus belonging to Poudre Canyon Outfitters and Adventures pulled into Ted's parking lot and St. James and Connie joined a dozen others on the long trek up the canyon. Although it was a hot and sunny day the canyon's steep walls threw the western slopes into shadow. Connie leaned her face out the open window.

"Wow."

"Yeah," St. James said. "You can see why the Mish is such a popular drinking spot—twenty-six miles west of Ted's Place and 350 hairpin turns. Hardly a week goes by some poor jasper doesn't put his bike or his cycle or his car in the river. One woman slid off her Harley up by the Narrows in April and they didn't find her body until June."

The bus ground gears as the driver downshifted for another hairpin turn which he took dead slow. A Corvette in the opposite lane nearly collided with them. The bus driver laid on the horn.

"Asshole!" he shouted throwing the bird through his open side window. "Sorry, folks! Just another flatlander."

Everybody laughed. It was a picnic atmosphere with some riders passing flasks and brown-bagged bottles. A whiff of marijuana wafted forward.

A hour later the bus wheezed to a stop in front of Mishawaka, a rambling wood-frame structure on the Poudre River with two tiny parking lots on either side. All the space in front of the restaurant for 100 feet was filled with chopped Harleys. Insane Assholes stood by the walled compound smoking cigarettes, a cluster outside the main entrance. Posters tacked to the rough wood wall advertised upcoming concerts. Opening for the Banshees was Dead Floyd, "specializing in the music of the Grateful Dead and Pink Floyd."

A police car with its red and blue flashers on stood by the side of the road, the cop directing traffic.

A sign just inside the entrance said, "ABSOLUTELY NO RECORDING DEVICES."

The place was jammed. The young woman at the door had St. James' and Connie's names on a list and let them in after affixing a yellow wrist band to each. The bar was SRO with Assholes, Deadheads, metal heads, board punks, college kids, slackers, hackers, and Packer backers lined up three deep at the bar.

Connie and St. James made their way through the crowd to the sun-drenched deck cantilevered over the fast-running Poudre. "I'm starving," Connie said.

A young woman with long kinky blond hair in a tie-dyed dress met them at the door. "Two for lunch? It'll probably be about an hour."

Connie produced a fifty-dollar bill held low. "Can you shorten that a little?"

The woman took the bill. "Wait here."

Fifteen minutes later the woman led them to a corner table jutting over the river. Connie ordered a Coke and a hamburger. St. James ordered an iced tea and a hamburger. He looked out over the river which rushed downstream at a forty-five-degree angle.

"This is one of the last untamed wild rivers in the country. I was up here once and I looked over there was a bighorn sheep right down there in front of the stage."

Connie twisted in her seat to look at the half-shell concert stage which backed up against the river.

"Wild as all get out, just wandered in and wandered out."

Connie got up and took out her little silver camera. "I'm going to take some shots of the river."

St. James lifted a finger. "Ta."

He watched her walk down the wooden stairs to the concert area where several dozen people were seated at picnic tables drinking beer from plastic cups. Every man on deck watched.

St. James felt a cold hand on his shoulder. "Noice crumpet, i'n't she?"

Paddy MacGowan sat down with his back to the river.

CHAPTER FIFTY-SIX

Paddy," St. James said, extending his hand.

Paddy's grip was glacial. "Sorry we been, loik, givin' you the cold shoulder, mate. It's not by desoign. Things have been so crazy since we came back …"

St. James looked into eyes the color of arctic ice. "Are you a ghost, Paddy?"

Paddy grinned showing bad teeth. No excuse for it in this day and age. "Flesh and blood!" He punched St. James playfully on the arm.

"How'd you do it then?"

Paddy clasped his hands and looked down. "All praise our lord and master."

"And who might that be, Paddy?"

Paddy smiled. "You know who. That old scarper Klapp 'as 'is theories, don't 'e?"

"What happened to Klapp?"

"'Ow should I know?"

"Who's Lord Rathkroghen?"

Paddy feigned surprise. "'Oo?"

"Don't you think you're carrying this Satan thing a bit far?"

Paddy chuckled. Others on deck realized who he was and there was much whispering and finger-pointing, but no one bothered them. The phone cams came out. The waitress returned with their drinks.

"What about me Dad?"

"Oaian loves you. He has always loved you."

St. James barked. "He's got a funny way of showing it, don't he?"

"You'll have your talk, about that there is no doubt."

"So why ain't he out here talkin' to me now?"

"Oaian 'as his reasons. Now listen. Me and the boys 'ave a little ritual we always perform before a concert an' it don't leave us much time."

St. James shuddered.

"You fancy 'er, oi? Can't blame you. She's a real crumpet, she is. Write what I tell you and she's yours."

"Bollocks."

"Ah, you're a doubter, Ian. We was afraid of this. Well listen. Dead Floyd had a bit of trouble and 'ad to cancel. 'Ow would you like to open for us?"

St. James grinned and shook his head. "You're good."

"Oi ain't lyin'." Paddy looked around, spotted someone and waved his arm. A plump middle-aged man with curly white hair and beard wearing denim coveralls made his way sideways through the revelers and joined them at the table.

"Matt Sherkoff, Mr. St. James. I'm the owner."

St. James shook hands. "Pleased to meet you, Mr. Sherkoff. What happened to Bob Anderson?"

"Mr. Anderson was caught with a mammoth grow op in his house on Stovepipe and has been arrested by the DEA. I bought the place from him last April."

Paddy turned to Sherkoff. "Wot about my boy Ian 'ere opening up for us?"

Sherkoff spread his hands. "Fine with me. We were going to pay Dead Floyd $500. It's yours if you can put on a forty-five-minute set."

A violent storm of emotions swept through St. James. Fear. Hope. An unexpected thrill of anticipation that surged like hot water through ancient steam pipes, pipes that had lain cold for far too long. An electric thrill ran from his chin to his fingertips which curled and played air guitar below the table's rim. He began to assemble a play list in his head.

Did he have enough songs? Were his chops up to it? Would his voice hold up? *Good Christ, man! There were reviewers in the audience from both coasts!* He searched his pockets for a pen. Paddy handed him one.

"Use this. Write on the back of the menu."

"How about it, Mr. St. James?" Sherkoff said.

St. James felt a surge of energy. He had just gone from bystander to player. He was once again being invited into the halls of the elite. All the doors would open: wealth, fame, love. If he didn't find a way to muck it up. A profound unease pulled at his soul but he flashed his smile. His teeth were good.

"Whoi not?"

Sherkoff grinned and clapped him on the shoulder. "Great! We run a little early here to give people time to get down off the mountain, so you go on at eight."

St. James nodded, stunned and elated. Kerchoff excused himself and went inside the bar.

"Now there is one thing Oi have to mention," Paddy said.

"What's that?"

"This 'ere's wild country. The bleedin' Wild West, innit? Sure, the redskins are gone and you gotcher Starbucks on every corner of every town, but up 'ere, up the canyon it's a different story. This is serious, dangerous country."

St. James stared at the Banshees' front man as if Paddy were insane. And of course he was. "So?"

"Just this. Did you know that every year Colorado sees a half dozen mountain lion attacks and that some of these prove fatal?"

St. James peered at Paddy with his mouth open. "Wot?"

"Oi, look," Paddy said rising. "'Ere comes your bird." And before Connie could reach them Paddy walked back into the bar. St. James turned to watch and as he did so, a smirking face smiled at him from across the deck tipping his Borsalino in St. James' direction.

Chapter Fifty-seven

Connie sat down as the waitress delivered their burgers. "Was that Paddy?"

"Oi. They want me to open."

"*What?*"

"Evidently the opening act couldn't make it. I told 'em I'd go on. I start at eight."

Connie smiled in delight. "I can't believe it! Wow! I'm so happy for you! How do you feel?"

"I don't know. Excited. Nervous. Scared shiteless, frankly."

"Let me know if there's anything I can do to help!" Connie addressed her burger. "Finally!" She slapped a two-handed grip on the plump disc and chowed down.

St. James looked at his hamburger with no appetite. Butterflies swirled through his stomach. Worms of apprehension as well. What if he blew it? Rulon Wexler would gleefully describe his failure to the world. Thank Christ there were no recording devices permitted.

Yah, roight, with every person there toting some kind of smart phone.

St. James looked across the river hoping to catch a fleeting glimpse of some big predator.

"What?" Connie demanded.

"Nothing. I'd better go get ready." He rose and picked up his guitar case. Connie stood, too.

"Let me give you a kiss for good luck."

He bent down expecting a peck on the cheek. Connie kissed him sweetly on the mouth. "Break a guitar string!"

Stunned and confused St. James made his way back into the bar looking for some private space to tune his guitar, put together a list, and get the quaver out of his voice. As he pushed open the screen door an adenoidal voice trailed after him.

"You'll fuck it up. You always do."

St. James felt that familiar flush of shame and rage, but this time he beat it. It was an almost physical struggle, and it only lasted a split second, long enough for him to realize Rulon was a fart in the wind and the power lay within him. His whole life had been building to this point. All those years woodshedding in coffee houses and cheap apartments, practicing his scales over and over again, singing in empty men's rooms and into home tape recorders, it was all coming together. He had the songs, technique, and voice. He was his father's son. Success was preparation meeting opportunity.

Say what you will about Oaian, he was one of the great rock drummers. Ginger Baker said so after seeing the Banshees at the Odeon. St. James inserted himself sideways through the crowded bar, easing between human boulders. Sherkoff was behind the bar.

"Mr. Sherkoff! Is there some place I can tune up in private?"

Sherkoff motioned St. James to follow him into an office behind the bar with a window looking out on the river. "You'll be okay in here. How do you want me to introduce you?"

St. James shrugged. "Ian St. James."

"He ain't gonna drop his pants, is he?"

St. James laughed. "I have no oidea. Where're the Banshees warming up?"

"They're in a cabin over by the amphitheater."

Sherkoff excused himself closing the door behind him. A dull conversational roar penetrated the wall along with the deep throbbing bass of the jukebox. St. James removed his treasured Gibson, sat on a wooden kitchen chair, and used a pitch pipe to tune the strings. He sat at the desk and wrote out a list of ten songs which he hoped would fill forty-five minutes including banter. Five of the songs were covers. Five were his.

Crikey. Me heart must be pumpin' 160.

He practiced a deep breathing exercise taught to him by the long-departed yoga instructor. He sang "Do Re Mi" from *The Sound of Music*. He sang "Hellhound On My Trail" with a gullet full of grit and a Mississippi drawl, using a glass bottleneck to wring glistening blue glissandos from his guitar. He lined up his picks.

Setting the guitar on the desk St. James knelt on the thread-bare scatter rug over the hard wood floor and bent his head. "Dear Lord, please don't let me fuck up tonight. Wait a minute. I take that back. I don't want to sound selfish, Lord. I am grateful for the opportunities you have given me so, uh, I just want to say thank you. Thank you for everything so far."

> *And please make Connie fall in love with me.*
> *And I wouldn't squawk if Wexler got sick and had to leave.*
> *What a miserable wretch I am.*
> *Amen.*

Three sharp raps on the door. Sherkoff stuck his head in. "You ready?"

St. James hurriedly got to his feet, embarrassed to have been seen praying. "Roight as oil ever be."

"Five minutes."

Sherkoff turned to go.

"Mister Sherkoff!"

"What?"

"What about the curse?"

Sherkoff waved in dismissal. "We have taken every precaution short of canceling. I can't worry about rock and roll bullshit. I'm trying to run a business here."

Sherkoff left the door open. Slinging his guitar over his shoulder St. James followed him through the packed bar, out onto the packed deck, down the packed stairs, across the SRO concert ground to the edge of the stage. The last shafts of sunlight played golden tones across the west facing rock as the river itself fell into shadow. Spotlights came on from the amphitheater ceiling and from a station behind the sound booth, a wooden structure at the back of the crowd toward the highway.

Sherkoff appeared onstage to shouts and applause. "Welcome, campers, to a very special Mishawaka performance! As you know tonight we are featuring the legendary Banshees ..."

Crowd noise led by the Insane Assholes grew to boiler factory proportions. Sherkoff waited for it to die down before continuing. "Are they real or are they Memorex? Folks, I don't know! Judge for yourselves! Now I have some bad news and some good news."

Groans, shouts.

"The bad news is Dead Floyd had to cancel."

A smattering of boos punctuated by a stentorian, "WHO GIVES A SHIT?"

"The good news is that opening up for the Banshees we have none other than Ian St. James, son of Banshees drummer Oaian St. James, making his second Mishawaka appearance!"

The response was mostly enthusiastic but as the applause and shouting died down one pair of hands continued to clap sarcastically. St. James was not surprised to spot Rulon Wexler standing at the deck rail smirking at him.

CHAPTER FIFTY-EIGHT

Feeling as if he were a rat in a maze St. James took the stage and sat on a lone wooden stool set up before the mike. As he sat, one of the Banshees' Slavic bully boys hustled onstage with another mike mounted on a stand which he set up at guitar level.

St. James played an exploratory chord. Excellent feedback from a pair of small speakers on the edge of the stage facing him. He made the "OK" symbol to the sound man back in the little booth.

"'Allo Colorado!" St. James said with more enthusiasm than he felt. The result was gratifying although he could not help glancing in Wexler's direction. Wexler stood with his arms crossed, his plump face glowing with bemused contempt.

Ignore him. Find some bird in the audience and play to her. And there was Connie, shining like a three-quarter moon. A rainbow flickered across his happy heart. He'd sung to her before.

"Been a long time 'tween engagements, innit? Here's a little song by a good friend o' mine, Mark Wiley called 'The Badger.'" He hit the chord.

> *This used to be a real nice town.*
> *You could walk the streets at night.*
> *No bums to get you down.*
> *No drunks to start a fight.*
> *Then weirdoes started hangin 'round*

Hangin' 'round and talkin' trash.
Talkin' trash and hangin' 'round.
Livin' on welfare cash.

Things progressed from bad to worse.
This town was filled with dread.
Who's got the guts to crack crime's curse?
There appeared a man in red.

He hit the bridge and unbelievably the audience began to clap along.

Germs. Bacteria. Crime. Decay
Germs. Bacteria. Crime. Decay
The Badger is on his way
Norbert Sykes got his walking papers just the other day.
He's out on the street now and there's hell to pay.

Back to the main verse. Down in front of the stage kids were jukin' and jivin', clapping their hands and doing crazy jitterbug maneuvers. Insane Assholes clapped along and stomped their feet. St. James ended the song and the applause was long and lasting and as refreshing as a summer rain.

His voice was back. He could feel the range and the confidence deep down in his belly and he realized that there was no place on Earth he would rather be. Why had it taken him so long?

He sang Shazam's "Falling All Round Me" and the audience lapped it up like a six-week-old St. Bernard pup. He sang "Don't Rush the Beat," "Stoke On Trent," "The Lizard Song," and "Try Me," all his own. The audience responded with such unexpected enthusiasm St. James choked up and tugged his hat low to hide the tears in his eyes.

Get a grip, boyo!

Forty-five minutes flew by in the twinkling of an eye. The next time St. James looked up Sherkoff was at the side of the stage making a throat-slitting motion and the audience was on its feet cheering, clapping, shouting "More!"

"I hate to wrap it up folks, but me Dad wants the stage back. I promised him I'd only take it around the block."

There were laughs, groans, yells, applause, and calls for an encore. St. James looked at Sherkoff who smiled and shrugged. He held up one finger.

"All right I got time for one more."

"Stairway to Heaven!" bellowed an Insane Asshole.

St. James stood and played "All Shook Up" in his best Elvis imitation shimmying his hips. The crowd went crazy. When he finished they whooped and hollered for more but Sherkoff was at the side of the stage shaking his head.

St. James waved to the crowd. "Th-th-that's all folks!"

He looked up at the edge of the deck where the odious Wexler had been standing stone-faced throughout his performance. The critic was nowhere to be seen, his place taken by a man with slicked back black hair, Silva-thin shades, hairline mustache, a black sports jacket, and a white turtleneck. Beaming like a proud parent.

It wasn't until he was back in the manager's office putting his guitar back into its case that he realized something was different. His hernia was gone.

CHAPTER FIFTY-NINE

The Banshees' modest equipment had grown into two massive speaker towers glowering at the crowd like the grills of two Dodge Ram pick-up trucks. Steel canisters connected by wire had been placed around the perimeter. While the crowd milled and swilled, the two Slavic roadies checked connections, gaffe tape, and made certain the drum kit was nailed down. Despite the evening chill rushing down the canyon, both men wore Mish T-shirts, ugly prison tats creeping below the sleeves.

In the temporary lull between sets the river rushed and gurgled.

St. James came back out shaking hands and accepting congratulations until he had made his way to where Connie stood not far from the Silva-thins Man. One of the roadies went by carting a heavy piece of equipment. Rasputin's face stared from his bicep beneath the rolled up sleeve which held a pack of American Spirits.

Connie hugged St. James clutching her little silver camera. "You were great! I got you on video!"

"Careful, luv. You know how they are about recording."

Connie winked. "I'm discreet."

The roadie with the rolled up sleeves worked his way toward them with his shoulders eliciting shouts and muffled curses. An Insane Asshole said, "Hey, motherfucker!" The roadie turned a flat dead face on him, and the Insane Asshole quailed.

The Slav bumped his way to where Connie and St. James stood and reached for the camera in Connie's hand. Surprised, Connie held it up and away like a game of keep-away.

"Giff me the camera," the roadie grunted.

"No way! Don't worry—I'm not shooting your precious Banshees. I'm only shooting my friend Ian."

The Slav seized Connie's neck in a steel clamp, other hand reaching for the camera. Without thinking St. James pivoted, throwing a short upper cut into the man's midriff. The thug *whoofed* as the air went out of him and he bent over gasping, looking up at St. James with angry little pig eyes.

St. James read his intentions and delivered a swift kick to the crotch and the man went down groaning. Was that a cup St. James felt? People screamed and edged away. Insane Assholes gathered 'round. One huge bearded Asshole with a blue bandanna covering his forehead gave him the thumbs-up. St. James was appalled to find himself at the center of a fracas. He looked around fearfully for Wexler. Thank Christ the weasel had missed it. He hoped.

Crikey, what if someone got it on film?

Sherkoff and two beefy bouncers rolled through the crowd to find the Slav writhing on the ground, St. James with one arm around Connie. Her camera was back in the pack.

"What happened?" Sherkoff said.

"This yob tried to paw her," St. James said.

The Slav got to his knees, both hands on his crotch, and spit through gritted teeth. "She has *camera*! She has taken *pictures*!"

Connie held her hand up. "Only my friend Ian. No more, I swear!"

Sherkoff looked worried. He stepped in and spoke softly, "Come on, you guys! Don't fuck this up for me. These dudes are touchier than meth freaks. You have a camera?"

"It's gone. No pictures."

The bouncers helped the roadie to his feet and led him toward the building. Sherkoff waved a finger at St. James. "You fuck this up there will be hell to pay."

Connie put her hand over her heart. "No fuck-ups, swear to God."

"There better not be." Sherkoff headed toward the stair leading down to the amphitheater.

Connie put her hand on St. James' chest and looked at him with glowing eyes. "That was awfully brave of you."

St. James felt an uneasy mixture of testosterone-fueled pride and intense shame at the cheap shot he'd taken.

But come on, Ian. Why the shame? Isn't that merely a vestige of the political correctness that's crippled society? Sometimes a man's gotta do what a man's gotta do. Damn it felt good to sink his footstep into that yob's bollocks.

"I acted instinctively."

"It was very brave. Thank you." She kissed him on the mouth.

That was thrice in three days. He didn't know what to think. It simply wasn't possible that a certified ten could view him romantically. All sorts of craziness had been happening. Rock bands back from the dead! St. James thrilling an audience! A pulsing gleam snatched his eye. St. James looked over Connie's shoulder and saw the silver flute leaning in its rack, gleaming hypnotically in the spot. It filled him with a sense of dread, ice pouring over his shoulders. Like a cocked gun.

Connie shook his shoulder. "Hey. Hey."

St. James snapped to. "What?"

"Where were you just now, Ian?"

"Lost in the ozone."

"Don't freak out on me. We've still got a job to do."

"Oim here."

Sherkoff was onstage tamping down the noise. The microphone emitted an obligatory squeal before the sound man got it under control.

"Okay folks! I want to thank you all for coming out tonight. Before we get to the show I have a few announcements. The police are all over the canyon so if you've had a couple drinks don't even think about driving. That goes double for you bikers. The shuttle bus will run until everyone is down the mountain no matter how long it takes.

"Also, if you parked on the other side of the road be aware that Larimer County is towing. We're posting the number of the impound yard on our website.

"Next week the Mishawaka Amphitheater is very proud to present, all the way from Toronto, the Foreign Films …"

An Insane Asshole shaped like a haystack cupped his hands and bellowed, "BANSHEES!"

Other Insane Assholes joined in. "BANSHEES! BANSHEES! BANSHEES!"

Sherkoff threw his hands up in mock despair. "LADIES AND GENTLEMEN! THE BANSHEES!"

The theme from "Also Sprach Zarathustra" blasted from the speakers. The steel canisters erupted into fountains of flame, Roman candles shooting zillions of multi-colored embers into the sky. The wind was out of the northwest and the embers trailed over the river and died.

Paddy, Oaian, and Cunar ran onstage, Paddy and Cunar holding their axes. They stopped and pirouetted as one. Paddy and Cunar took identical A-frame stances and with the explosive report of a starting pistol, sang "Please allow me to introduce myself—I'm a man of wealth and taste …"

The audience responded like pyrotechnics. They leaped, they screamed, they cheered, they held Zippos to the sky. They forgot the Rolling Stones.

St. James looked around. Wexler and the Silva-thins Man were gone. The Banshees' next song snapped his head around like a Mike Tyson punch. The Banshees played something he'd never heard before called "Armies of the Night." The lyrics dealt hellish imagery of a city in flames, rioters and looters running amok through the streets. At the climax Paddy turned away from the crowd, helped himself to a small metal flask and turned back. Holding a lighter before his mouth he belched flame like a dragon. The audience screamed with delight. St. James had seen the trick several times over the years. You filled your mouth with kerosene. You were all right as long as you didn't inhale.

The Banshees burned through 110 minutes of original material like Sherman's march to the sea driving the crowd into a frenzy. St. James didn't understand how the cops didn't shut them down they were so loud. They must have heard it in Fort Collins, forty miles away. And the pyrotechnics during a very dry summer.

That had to be illegal.

Nobody touched the flute. It sat there like an unexploded bomb.

At half past midnight an exhausted and sweating Paddy said, "We're finished! Good night you lot and droive safely!"

Not even the entreaties of the Insane Assholes could coax another encore out of the band which rushed toward their cabin protected from the crowd by the two Serbs and Sinaiko. Sherkoff turned on the lights. Sounds from traffic being directed around the club filtered through and people drifted toward the exits.

St. James and Connie looked at each other.

Was it possible?

St. James took Connie's hand and headed toward the exit. "Crikey, what a disappointment! Nobody died!"

CHAPTER SIXTY

I t was just past two by the time they reached their rooms at the Marriott. Connie hugged St. James and pecked him on the cheek. "Don't call me before ten."

St. James lingered at his door to watch Connie walk down the corridor.

It was a long time before he fell asleep.

In the morning he was the first guest in the business center logging on to check the reviews. The Banshees blogs were ecstatic.

"THE CURSE HAS BEEN BROKEN!" headlined a very long discussion. All agreed "Armies of the Night" was a worthy addition to the Banshees oeuvre. People took several stabs at the lyrics.

Next he checked in vain on all the Banshees' websites for sound bites. Not a single Banshees chord could be found anywhere on the web. There were several discussions about the Banshees' curse, this time aimed at the seeming inability for the Banshees' music to transmit in electronic form. The chats searched in vain for ancient YouTube clips that had existed before the Return. In an age where you could find video of everyone from the Moscow Philharmonic playing Tchaikovsky to the Ramones and the Fugs, not one byte of YouTube was devoted to the Banshees.

St. James checked his e-mail. Over three hundred messages, mostly congratulating him on his "comeback." Inquiries from several venues, including those he'd played before. Requests for interviews from *Rolling Stone* and *MOJO*. He would have to update his website, presuming his webmaster was still alive. He hadn't heard from the guy in years.

St. James bought a *Coloradoan* and sat in the lobby waiting for Connie. "BANSHEES BREAK CURSE!" was the headline along with a gushing review.

"Ian St. James surprised the crowd with a surprisingly bold and moving set. Of course his appearance puts the lie to any claim that these are the original Banshees, but who cares? If they're not the originals, they're just as good, if not better."

Huh, St. James thought. This from a writer who wasn't born when the Banshees died.

Curiously, Rulon Wexler's blog had not been updated since announcing his trip to the Mish two days ago.

Maybe he broke his fuckin' neck. Ha. I should be so lucky.

But that wouldn't be so good, would it? Because that would mean the curse was not broken.

At ten-thirty St. James felt a disturbance in the Force and looked up to see Connie walking toward him with a big smile toting her backpack.

"Come on," she said. "Let's eat. I'm starving."

They got seated in the cheerful Cooper Creek restaurant and ordered orange juice, coffee, an omelet for St. James, a Belgian waffle for Connie.

"Richard is throwing a huge party for the Banshees at Hotel Crabbe on the first! I booked you a room."

"No bungalow?"

"No," Connie said stuffing her face. "But your star is rising. I told Richard about your performance. He heard about it online too."

St. James puffed.

"And you're walking better, too. You know, it almost seems as if you're getting younger!"

"Fat chance o' that. I just chose me parents really well."

"What are you going to say to that guy when you finally talk to him?"

"Hello, Dad!"

"Seriously."

"I don't know, Con. What do you say to someone who impersonates your father?"

"I want you to write up your interview with Paddy."

"It weren't an interview."

Connie looked at him funny. "Oh, yes it was. Richard wants an interview. I saw you talking to him. It looked intense. What were you talking about?"

"He asked me to play the opening set."

"Did you discuss Oaian?"

St. James' glance fell on a silent TV monitor hanging on the wall. A mob in *kaffiyehs* rioting, burning vehicles. The scene switched to a portion of Japan devastated by a tsunami.

"No, we did not discuss Oaian. I'd like to see that video you shot of me."

"You can watch it in the car."

"Is it any good?"

Mouth full she shrugged, fork hovering over a strawberry. She chewed. She swallowed. "I haven't done a playback. I want to get to Englewood and write. Richard needs copy by five. Can you be ready in a half hour?"

"Oim ready now, luv. I was born ready."

Forty-five minutes later they passed the Loveland Outlet Mall heading south, St. James watching himself on Connie's smart phone. He always got a weird sense of displacement when he watched himself. Who is that bloke? He sounded so different through a mike than he did in his own head. However, he had to admit the clip did him no harm.

"Not bad," he said.

"Find some news, willya?"

St. James found KCOL out of Fort Collins. The perky hosts shat all over Shia LaBoeuf's reboot of *The Incredible Two-Headed Transplant*, a Burke Melchior Production. The news came on. Rioters in Afghanistan killed sixty-six people because a pastor in Florida burned a Koran. The President's nominee for Secretary of the Treasury was found to have paid no income tax during the previous five years. A new strain of influenza was proving remarkably resistant to antibiotics.

The weather was good. The hosts began a lively discussion of the miraculous resurrection at Mishawaka. "They said when Bob Anderson was arrested that the Mish was finished. We're glad to see that's not the case."

"You know, Bill," said the hostess, "the real resurrection is this band, the Banshees. I mean, had you ever heard of them before?"

"I was aware of them, sure. But I never listened to them."

"We have Terry on the line. What's up, Terry? Did you see the show last night?"

"No. This band is the devil's spawn. What is the matter with people that they go out of their way to embrace this type of hateful, death-worshiping noise?"

"Whoa," said the hostess. "I think you have to take them with a grain of salt, Terry. Like Deep Purple, Alice Cooper, and Black Sabbath. It's all done in a spirit of fun."

"No. It's not," the caller said hanging up.

Urgent news music marched through the speakers accompanied by the sound of a Morse code transmitter. "Forest rangers are reporting the discovery of a body in the Poudre Canyon near the Mishawaka Amphitheater. The victim appears to have been mauled to death by a mountain lion. Forest rangers are tracking the animal now. Those who live in the area are advised to stay indoors. Identification of the victim is being withheld pending notification of relatives."

St. James punched it off. They rode in silence for several minutes, dread clawing its way up his gullet like some nightmare creature that wouldn't stay in the basement. Squeezing his heart, stroking nausea from churning stomach acid like the aftermath of a coke binge. It wasn't over. It had only just begun.

"That's eight," St. James said.

Chapter Sixty-one

AVID LETTERMAN'S TOP TEN REASONS TO ATTEND A BANSHEES CONCERT:

10. Your recipe calls for a pint of human blood.

9. Your kids think you're cool with a pitchfork piercing your upper lip.

8. You never have to worry that the venue is over-capacity.

7. Human ribs—the other white meat!

6. Where else can you meet a nice girl?

5. You missed them the first time they toured—in 1574.

4. You are a direct descendant of Alferd Packer.

3. You are the love child of Aleister Crowley and Lady Gaga.

2. You want to be part of the Guinness Book of World Records' Greatest Rock Disaster.

1. And the number one reason to attend a Banshees concert, YOU HAVE JUST GIVEN YOUR LIFE TO SATAN!

Chapter Sixty-two

Kenny Grace fumed. He went to bed mad and he got up mad. He hardly slept even with the pills Doc Addison laid on him. The lead singer for Charon had been informed five days ago that on the 4th of July, Charon was opening for the Banshees at Pacific Arena.

For the first time in eleven years Charon was not the headlining act. Melchior hadn't even had the human decency to tell him personally. He left that up to his little weasel Stanton. A text message.

A text message.

Grace paced the plain of his Zen-seeking living room in his woodsy multi-leveled bungalow up Laurel Canyon while his lifelong friend and Charon's bass player Woody Nuringer rolled a doobie on the couch, the latest issue of *In Crowd* on his lap.

"Now that motherfucker wants us to show up and kiss the hem of his new darlings! I'd like to give him a tune-up."

"Chill, dude," low-toned the always steady Woody. "Those last two shows sucked. We only filled half the room."

Grace wheeled. He wore artfully torn blue jeans and a muscle shirt exposing his cut bod, kept in shape at enormous expense with the aid of two trainers, the curly black hair, the gold upside-down cross around his neck, his strong chin, the cleft, the brooding eyes surrounded with kohl, the thick black uni-brow like a mutant caterpillar, and that leonine mane of hair.

"Don't 'dude' me, dude! Whose record's in the Top Ten? The Banshees? Noooooo. They don't even have a record. We're certified platinum, man! Where are the Banshees? Nowhere! They're gonna melt like fuckin' lemon Jell-O when they get out here, man, I'm tellin' ya, and that's the time we should pounce on that fucker and renegotiate."

Woody inserted the entire zeppelin-shaped joint in his mouth and pulled it out with a light coating of saliva. He blew on it. "I don't know, dude. The biz is in the crapper."

"I've always said I could manage this band. It's time to step up. Come on, Woody! You don't like that cocksucker any more than I do. You know he screwed us out of royalties on the first album, man!"

Woody's gaze became unfocused as he stared into the void, smoke issuing from his nostrils. There was no denying the truth of Grace's words. "Take a toke of this, man. It'll make you feel better."

"I don't want to feel better!" Nevertheless, Grace strode over to Woody and took the joint. He paced the room with his hands behind his back, doobie jutting like a Bizarro Groucho Marx. "Why aren't we recording? I'll tell you why—Burkie's all a-flutter over his new boy toys. That's why."

"Come on, dude. At least admit Melchior's straight."

"He can fuck BMWs far's I'm concerned. He can fuck Courtney Love."

"Whoah, dude."

"I'm thinking of not going."

"Whoah, you can't do that, dude."

"Sure I can. I'm exhausted from that fuckin' tour, fourteen cities in seventeen days, do you think the fuckin' Banshees could pull that off? Look at those pussies! Look at where they're playing!"

"Pacific Arena's pretty big, dude."

"I mean before that! Little piss-ant places! What's up with that? And if these guys are so bad, how come we never hear anything from or about any groupies? What are they, celibate? Are they fags? Like a *ménage à trois* or something?"

"Don't do that, dude. I get itchy when you talk that frog shit."

"Do you know who's opening up for them tonight at Red Rocks?"

Woody gazed out the window at verdant growth. "I have a feeling you're going to tell me."

"A fucking illusionist! It's a fucking freak show! And how come the great Burke Melchior won't re-release the album? And how come every time somebody puts up a picture from one of these piss-ant places, their hard drive melts down?"

"What?"

"You'd know these things if you went online."

Woody waved away a cumulus of reefer smoke. "It steals your soul, dude."

A girl with long blond hair, who could not have been older than twenty, wearing satin purple bikini panties and matching bra oozed around the corner from the hall.

"Kenny, when are you coming back to bed?"

"Just chill! Watch Leno. I'll be there in a minute."

The girl remained, stroking the wall. "Come on, Kenny, I need to ask you about something."

"Just take whatever you like. Jesus, Shelly. Woody and I are trying to have a conversation!"

"Come on, Kenny. You're ranting."

Grace turned toward his bass player and shrugged. Whaddaya gonna do? Woody waved him away with his fingers. Grace followed Shelly around the corner, down the hall to the master bedroom, which cantilevered over the canyon and featured a 51-inch flat screen television and an enormous bathroom with a sauna, shower for two, and whirlpool.

Shelly rolled onto the big bed, grabbed a cut soda straw and bent over a line of white powder arranged on a hand mirror.

"Is that why you called me in here? I thought you wanted to fuck."

"Of course I want to fuck, Kenny! I heard you're invited to a party at Burke Melchior's for the Banshees."

"Jesus! So what?"

"I want to go, that's what."

Grace felt an overwhelming urge to slap her. He drew back his hand and she flinched. He sat down on the bed next to her and started chopping up another line out of Shelly's little baggie.

"Fuck it! Yeah, all right. In fact, you might be able to help me out."

CHAPTER SIXTY-THREE

C onnie gleefully turned toward St. James. "We're getting the whole interview! As soon as we get to L.A."

Ian looked at her from the passenger seat. "Everybody?"

"All three band members. We'll do it at the hotel before the party."

Connie started the engine and edged out of the Wingate parking lot. It was six-thirty. The show was in one hour. They headed west on Alameda Parkway joining a long line of cars headed into the mountains. Traffic slowed to a crawl as they wound their way up 74, several police cars flashing lights by the side of the road. They passed a grim looking Old Testament type—long beard, wide-brimmed hat, holding a sign: "PRAISE THE LORD! PRAY FOR FORGIVENESS!"

We'll be seeing a lot more of that, St. James thought.

It was a warm summer evening and everybody had their car windows rolled down. Everybody seemed to be tuned into the same radio station as the Banshees blasted from thousands of automobile speakers: "This is How It Ends," one of their least offensive and hookiest songs.

Crimson fingers scratch the sky
The city lies in flames.
Children bleed and mothers cry
A deep and lasting shame

"If you didn't know the lyrics you'd think it was a joyous celebration of life", St. James said. Neither moved to change the station. It seemed right.

Dusk fell early in the mountains, and all the cars turned on their lights forming a many-eyed serpent crawling toward the sky. The opening act was an illusionist called Maribel Merino. While Connie drove St. James accessed the magician's web page. This was Merino's first American performance. Indeed, this was Merino's first trip to America. He had previously toured in a small carnival throughout Eastern Europe, headquartered in Romania.

"Dig it," St. James said. "Merino's specialties included 'The Iron Maiden' (sawing a woman in half), the disappearance of a circus elephant named Gris-Gris, single hypnosis, mass hypnosis, and his *pièce de résistance*, something called 'The Human Meteor.'"

"They are really going for it," Connie said.

"I'm shocked Grand Guignol isn't opening."

"Is that a band?" Connie said.

"Yeah. Bunch o' posers out of Waverly. Really quite pathetic, actually. I saw them once at the Isle of Wight. Bad songs, bad hair. Lead singer sodomized a baby doll, all quite predictable."

Police directed traffic into the parking lots, which were rapidly filling up. Connie parked the car at the back of the Lower North Lot behind a half-dozen choppers. Insane Assholes held a tailgate party on their bikes, quaffing beer and grilling brats in the back of a pick-up.

St. James and Connie joined a festive crowd heading toward the amphitheater including many pierced board punks, Goths, illustrated men and women, even young families rolling strollers. St. James shuddered when he noticed a scorpion tat on a six-year-old's ankle.

"What kind of parent takes a six-year-old to see the Banshees?" St. James said out of the side of his mouth.

"Sick puppies," Connie agreed.

Uniformed security guards checked backpacks at the security checks next to which a big sign was mounted on a tripod: "ABSOLUTELY NO RECORDING DEVICES." This time Connie had left her camera at the hotel. Occasionally the wind stirred up a whiff of vomit that the custodians hadn't found. Their seats were a third of the way back, center on flat benches. Foot lamps added to the magic of the evening casting a warm glow across the aisles. The last rays of the setting sun lit up the spectacular red rock formations which reminded St. James of a stack of magazines sliding to the floor. Two ten-foot speaker towers faced the audience from either side of the stage.

Insane Assholes formed a solid block of black leather on the left side. No cops were visible, although they'd seen three county cars and a private ambulance in the parking lot.

At least, St. James thought, *they're taking this seriously.* A cheerful young usher showed them to their seats in the middle of a bunch of *BoBo* journalists. Connie paused to greet several and introduce St. James. A few of them made nice comments about St. James' performance the previous night and all agreed Wexler's death was a senseless tragedy.

St. James touched his miraculously healed hernia. They sat as the amphitheater filled to its almost ten thousand seat capacity. As the sun dipped behind the Rockies a popular Denver DJ walked onstage.

"Good evening, folks! Ted Paxton of KCLU, Denver, that's 1200 on your AM radio dial. What a night, huh?"

The crowd responded enthusiastically.

"Before we get to tonight's entertainment, a few announcements."

Six Insane Assholes rose as one, cupped their hands and bellowed "BANSHEES!"

The acoustics were such that it reverberated off the back of the amphitheater and echoed up the aisles. Paxton looked upset.

"They're coming! They're coming! Just let me get these announcements out of the way."

"BANSHEES! BANSHEES! BANSHEES!" the Insane Assholes chanted. Six County deputies in khaki uniforms walked down the outside aisle and took up position next to Insane Assholes' Row. The Insane Assholes sat down.

"I want to thank our biker friends for bearing with us."

The audience groaned at his servility.

"All the way from the Belarus Republic, Master Illusionist Mirabel Merino!" Paxton shouted and beat it offstage. Vast clouds of dense smoke billowed at either edge, and soon the stage was enclosed in an impenetrable fog. The fog lit up: pink, yellow, blue! Cotton candy! Khachaturian's "Sabre Dance" blared from the PA system.

A wind blew up out of nowhere whipping the fog offstage like a snatched curtain. Merino the Magnificent stood among his tools wearing white jodhpurs stuffed into knee-high black cavalry boots, a red velvet waistcoat trimmed with gold frogs and epaulets, and a black silk top hat. He had a black handlebar mustache waxed to needle-like points and a neat Van Dyke. He stood with hands slightly raised like a martyr and bowed.

Even the Insane Assholes applauded.

Speaking through a throat mic the magician said, "Ladies and gentlemen, mademoiselles, madams and monsieurs, señors y señoritas, I am the illusionist Merino! This is Isabelle, my lovely assistant." He had the same East European accent as Kaspar Sinaiko.

A woman with long glistening black hair and a dancer's body wearing a black leotard, yellow sash, and high heels strode from the wings waving gracefully. She paused with one hand on what appeared to be a lacquered wood cabinet—a gaily decorated coffin, really—resting on four sawhorses. A double-handled saw lay atop the cabinet. She held it up and displayed it to the crowd like a Claymore.

"For my first illusion, I will need a volunteer! A young lady, preferably, with a spirit of adventure who is not afraid of appearing before an audience and won't go to pieces!"

Connie rose. St. James' hand snapped out and pulled her down. She turned on him angrily, "Don't!" She rose and waved her arm.

"You there!" Mirabel responded. "Very good! Come up, come up!"

Connie turned toward St. James. "Don't worry! This'll be great!"

She sidled out to the aisle and quick-stepped down and up onto the stage.

CHAPTER SIXTY-FOUR

Connie was pretty damned sure the Banshees weren't about to queer their comeback by butchering their interviewer. She knew for a fact that the police had talked to Sinaiko about the killings and warned the band not to do anything that could exacerbate the situation. The Banshees—and their handpicked opening act—would do nothing to jeopardize their march to the sea.

Merino's touch was soft and cool as he led her to the cabinet. "And what is your name, my brave young friend?"

"Connie Cosgrove."

"And you are a reporter for *In Crowd* magazine! I read *In Crowd*! Everybody should read *In Crowd*!"

Connie was momentarily speechless as Merino led her behind the cabinet. Isabelle whipped up the saw in both hands, bending it and causing it to howl. Up close Isabelle was not as young as she looked. From the well-pancaked crow's feet and slight sag in the neck Connie judged her to be in her late forties. Fantastic shape for an old dame. She held one end of the saw down with her feet, bent the other hand with her free hand used a violin bow with a thick rubber band to saw a wobbly "Theme to Star Trek."

The audience lapped it up like puppy dogs.

Merino opened the casket whose lid hinged toward the audience. The interior was lined with pink satin and contained a fresh pillow. A wood stepping stool came out from beneath. Up close, Connie could see the vertical lines cut into the wood.

Holding her hand, Merino said, "If Madame would be so kind as to step into the cabinet?"

Connie looked inside. It appeared to be a straightforward coffin. "What's the trick?" she whispered.

"There is no trick, dear lady," Merino said in a hypnotic voice. "Only magic. Trust me. Do you think I would harm a hair on your lovely head?"

The old goat was charming. He wore Alpish cologne. Connie let him lead her up the step so that she laid down in the coffin. Merino shut the lid sealing off all light and sound. *This can't be right*, Connie thought. *How does he expect me to breathe?* As if in response she felt a minute stirring of air. At least there was circulation.

It was weird. One moment she was onstage in front of ten thousand people beneath harsh lights. Now she was in a sensory deprivation chamber. Seconds stretched into minutes. She was sorry she'd snapped at Ian, but she couldn't stand men telling her what to do. All her life they'd been telling her what to do.

But Ian was different. He was comfortable in his own skin and without a trace of arrogance. She found him increasingly attractive. She had no idea what he'd been like before. Other children of celebrities she'd met had struggled with their identities. A lot of them didn't make it. It was fucking hell to be the child of a superstar. Particularly a self-centered superstar, as most of them were. They put on a great show of compassion. Their publicists worked steadily to inform the media of their good deeds; the UN expeditions, the children's hospitals, shows for the troops. But it all came wrapped in a prickly ego and a stunning lack of empathy.

Success might have spoiled Ian. She couldn't deny the attraction, but no way was she going to derail her career by taking him on as her beau! Her questionable availability was one of her most marketable commodities.

Connie began to wonder what Merino was doing. The interior smelled faintly of perfume and sweat. Isabelle's perfume. Connie was suddenly certain that Merino and Isabelle made love in the coffin.

"Yuck," she said in the enclosed space, and her thoughts turned inevitably back to St. James. She would have been a fool to deny the attraction, but he was simply all wrong for her. Too old and his future was sketchy, although his performance at the Mish last night was an encouraging sign. Connie was certain that she could manage him better than he could. And every day he looked better. Ever since he'd stopped drinking and started running. Yes, he'd been walking with a slight limp for a few days but that seemed to have cleared up. His teeth were good for a Brit's.

But little Connie had plans and couldn't afford to hook up with someone perceived as a has-been, even if he wasn't. Connie had set her sights on her own talk show. The Banshees couldn't have come along at a better time. She would be eternally grateful to Richard and Ian for drawing her into what looked like one of the biggest stories of the year.

In five years, she thought, *I want a daily syndicated show. I'll do in-depth celebrity interviews. Someday I'll get married to my successful, handsome soulmate, and we'll have two kids. But not to a rock star. God no. Never a rock star.*

Abruptly her silent world was shattered by the rasp of a saw, a cage-rattling sound that admitted a sliver of light as sawdust rained down on her belly.

This can't be right, she thought. It was a professional magic show. What could go wrong? The whisking blade descended slowly toward her stomach as choking sawdust filled the confined space. Connie coughed. She lifted her fist and banged on the roof.

"Hey! This isn't working!" Her voice seemed tiny and weak, unable to penetrate the stout oak and satin. The saw was now within two inches of her belly. Connie found herself flattening out, trying to sink into the base but there was no place to go! Who was this supposed to impress? Her or the audience?

Connie banged on the lid with both hands. "LET ME OUT!" she screamed and even to herself her voice sounded impotent. She watched in horror as the rapidly oscillating blade descended to one inch. Surely they were going to stop now, let her out, and all have a good laugh at her expense.

The ripping violation of her flesh stunned and shocked her, instantly transforming her from a rational human being into a trapped and screaming animal. The pain was all consuming. Millions of shredding nerves overloaded her system, a wall of agony that shoved reason out the window. Systems failure. Shut down.

Oh, God! The agony!

Her breath came in high wheezing gasps. Tears poured from her eyes. She felt the jagged teeth grinding through gristle and meat, heard the soul-crushing rasp of metal through bone, felt her bodily fluids spurt wetly out of her, smelled the acrid stomach acids, the contents of her abdomen. She lost all feeling below the waist. The top half of her torso was a raw sucking wound. She put her hands down, felt the soaked and severed bottom half of her like a side of dead meat in blue jeans. She pushed it away simultaneously screaming and laughing. How could she still be alive?

It can't be me, she thought. *I can't die! Not now! Certainly not in some ridiculous magic show! Not when everything is going so well!*

Connie went into shock. She viewed herself trapped and bleeding in the coffin as if she were an angel hovering above the scene. The rasping stopped. All sound and light vanished.

Why did her consciousness survive?

Let oblivion take me! she prayed.

Light flooded the cabinet as Merino threw back the lid. Connie gasped. She looked down. She was intact. Nothing had touched her. Such golden relief flooded through her veins she wept. Her armpits were wet from sweat. She had pissed herself. She looked up. A smiling Merino extended his hand. She wanted to slap him. The coffin lid was intact—no cut lines.

Unsteadily she took his hand, sat up, got to her knees and stepped out of the cabinet. Snot ran down her upper lip and her cheeks and her voice was hoarse from shouting. Isabelle handed her a tissue without looking at her. Merino led her to the side, still unsteady, and held one arm toward Connie, the other to the sky.

"A big hand for the brave and beautiful Connie, ladies and gentlemen!"

The audience responded enthusiastically. Connie looked out at the clapping whistling audience as if they were from another planet. Didn't they understand what had just happened to her?

Crimson with shame she stood sideways to hide the stain in her crotch.

What had happened? Connie was still in a state of shock as Isabelle led her to the edge of the stage. Connie gripped the banister in both hands as she unsteadily descended.

She stumbled and nearly went down. Someone gasped. St. James got up, sidled out into the aisle and went to her, holding her arm and helping her back to her seat.

People started to say something as Connie passed but one look at her face shut them up. She collapsed on the seat next to St. James and leaned on him weeping.

"What's wrong?" he said softly. "You've been crying. Are you all right?"

"What happened?" she gasped.

"He cut all the way through the cabinet," St. James said. "Quite a trick! What happened to you?"

Connie tried to answer but couldn't find the words. St. James saw the stain but said nothing.

Onstage the magician Merino announced, "And now for the vanishing!"

CHAPTER SIXTY-FIVE

It was full dark, and the performance took place beneath a glittering tapestry, a million points of light set in a velvet sea. Connie was trembling. St. James put his arm around her. "Do you want to go?" he whispered.

She shook her head.

"What happened?"

"I'll tell you later. It's all right. I have to go to the ladies' room. I'll be right back."

But it wasn't all right. Not by a long shot. Something had happened to her in the coffin. Something that went beyond virtual reality. She could effortlessly summon the excruciating pain as the saw teeth ripped through her abdomen. It made her sick to her stomach, and she bent over between her knees and practiced the tantric breathing she'd been taught in yoga.

Unable to help, St. James could only place his hand on her back in a feeble attempt at comfort. Resolutely she shook her blond locks like a fighter shaking off a punch and stood up. She was there to cover the show for *In Crowd*.

She eased out into the aisle and walked up the stairs toward the facilities. Once inside, she shut herself in a stall, removed her pants and wet panties and dried herself off as best she could. Naked from the waist up she stood in front of the hot air blower until her jeans were dry. A Latino woman with a small child came in, looked once and looked away.

She knew she would never write about what had just happened. It would haunt her as long as she lived. Shivering in the cool mountain air, she deposited the soiled panties in the waste receptacle and returned to her seat. St. James' arm felt comforting around her, and she reached up and grasped his hand.

The PA system switched to Mussorgsky's "Night on Bald Mountain" as Isabelle drove an enormous black and yellow Hummer up a ramp and onto the stage. Acting like a runway traffic director Merino motioned her toward him, held his hands up when he wanted her to stop. Merino turned toward the audience, cheeks bulging, lit a pocket lighter in front of his mouth and belched flame. The Insane Assholes stood and applauded. Connie would have been impressed if she hadn't seen a dozen rock stars do the same thing.

Merino walked around and opened the driver's door. "The beautiful Isabelle, ladies and gentlemen!" He bowed as he helped her from the vehicle and the audience applauded.

"BANSHEES!" yelled an Insane Asshole. A county deputy shined his flashlight on the offender.

Isabelle retreated. Merino took center stage. "They wouldn't let me bring Gris-Gris into the country," he said petulantly. "Gris-Gris is my elephant, a talented thespian with whom I have worked for many years." He glanced all around, covered his mouth as if imparting a secret, and stage whispered, "She works for peanuts!"

The audience erupted in hilarity. It was the way he said it. Connie looked around. Everywhere the audience leaned forward with eager, almost childlike anticipation. Even the Insane Assholes were rapt. No one gave her a second glance.

"When I first discovered Gris-Gris she was doing dinner theater in Fort Lauderdale. *The Elephant Man*! Later some Neil Simon. In any case she is not here, they would not let her in the country so I am forced to make do with a substitute! This Hummer, ladies and gentlemen, will be our stand-in. Now with your belief and participation, I shall vanish the vehicle before your very eyes!"

Merino motioned to his assistant and Isabelle appeared onstage carrying a light blue nylon car sock folded into a massive triangle. Merino joined her, and together, they unfolded a vast rectangle of nylon, enough to completely cover the vehicle. Isabelle and Merino brought the long flowing item out in front of the vehicle.

"Is very simple. Isabelle and I will cover the vehicle momentarily with this nylon tarp. When I ask you to blow, please everyone blow as hard as they can at the stage, and hopefully you will blow that big black Hummer out of here!"

Merino stomped his cavalry boot! "The ground, she is solid oak! They do not allow trick trap doors or rotating walls at Red Rocks!"

In sync with the music Merino and Isabelle ran away from the audience toward the Hummer, holding up the blue nylon which billowed behind them like a Christo installation. Up and over the vehicle it went in a smooth, practiced flow.

With a flourish, Merino took off his top hat and bowed deeply showing the audience the gleaming crown of his brilliantined hair. Smoke billowed from the corners of the stage and seemingly from beneath the floor. The smoke congealed in the center of the stage into a towering cumulus through which the dark figure of Merino was barely visible, still holding his bow.

He straightened up. "Blow, ladies and gentlemen! Blow as if your life depended on it!"

Everywhere Connie looked grown men and women were puffing their cheeks and blowing toward the stage. It sounded like ten thousand frogs breaking wind. Magically, a cool breeze fell upon them dissipating the smoke and revealing the blue tarp bunched up to twice its previous height.

Merino grabbed one corner at the back and Isabelle grabbed the other. With a practiced sweep they yanked the tarp back revealing Gris-Gris the elephant.

"Gris-Gris!" Merino exclaimed, ran up and kissed the elephant on the trunk.

The crowd was delirious with joy. Little children sat up squealing and clapping. Men and women laughed, marveled, looked at one another, and scratched their heads. Merino had them eating out of the palm of his hand. Even St. James stared at the elephant with a goofy grin which Connie found endearing.

Isabelle instructed Gris-Gris to kneel, took her place relaxing in the crook of Gris-Gris' trunk like Rita Hayworth. The elephant got to its feet and walked slowly offstage to Henry Mancini's "Elephant Walk."

Merino gestured after them. "A big hand for Isabelle and Gris-Gris, ladies and gentlemen! Two lovelier creatures you will ne'er behold!"

Merino turned serious. "The final illusion, ladies and gentlemen, is not for the faint of heart nor those who flee from the natural functions of the human body. The Human Meteor can only be performed by Merino! No one else in all the world knows the ancient Tibetan secrets of gastric, tantric, and glandular control that permit me to fly through the air. Yes, ladies and gentlemen, I will fly through the air on a rocket of my own making!"

As he spoke, Isabelle reappeared at the edge of the stage rolling out a peculiar object that appeared to be scaffolding made of wrought iron, three feet high with a slightly pyramidal shape. It looked like a stool with a steel tractor seat.

"The percentage of human beings who produce methane in their gastric system is twenty percent! I am fortunate to be among that number. I have studied the ancient Tibetan secret of human rocket propulsion. I have cultivated the extremely rare manicotto root, mangrove hearts, and a certain beetle known to reside only in the Serengeti."

St. James leaned over and whispered, "He's going to light his farts."

She just glared. No buffoonery was going to make up for the pain and horror she had just experienced. The sham act did not fool her. Something evil was going on. She no longer doubted it.

Merino stepped behind a dressing screen. His white jodhpurs slapped over the top. He stepped out from behind the screen wearing black cycling pants, his feet bare. He seated himself on the contraption and held up a golden Zippo, turning it so as to catch the lights and reflect them back at the audience.

"Ladies and gentlemen, with the help of this ignition device I will fly straight up in the air and hover for up to ten seconds!"

The crowd tittered uneasily. Parents squirmed as their kids turned to them and said, "Is he going to light his farts?"

St. James bumped Connie. "There was a French performer at the turn of the century, Le Petomaine. He farted musically. *Rolling Stone* did a book on him."

Connie could not take her eyes off Merino the Magnificent. With Isabelle looking adoringly on, he flicked the Zippo offering the flame to the audience. He composed himself and elaborately held the flame directly below his anus on the tractor seat.

There was a minute flash, a delay of perhaps a second, and then a loud, moist pop as Merino exploded, pieces of flesh, bone and clothing splattering the stage and the first five rows. For an instant there was silence. Merino's head landed with a resounding thump next to the frozen Isabelle.

The screaming began.

CHAPTER SIXTY-SIX

People began to leave the amphitheater. Cops ran onstage. The deejay ran out, followed by Kaspar. There was a lot of gesticulating and shouting. The smoke generators erupted and within seconds the stage was enveloped in impenetrable fog.

From out of the fog spoke Isabelle in an East European accent. "It's an illusion, folks! Look! Look at his head!"

The breeze responded as if it belonged to the union. The fog trailed sideways revealing Isabelle standing with her statuesque legs spread holding Merino's head by the long black ponytail. Up close it was obviously a well-detailed prop. Arms and legs were revealed to be made of plastic but realistically weighted.

The Banshees' thug roadies raced onstage with brooms and dustpans. Kaspar checked the gaffer's tape holding down electrical cords, made sure Oaian's kit was solidly mounted to the floor. Paxton took the stage.

"A big hand for the Magnificent Merino!" Paxton said.

St. James turned to Connie. "Where is the Magnificent Merino?"

Connie shrugged. It was all an act. The Banshees were milking this for maximum shock value. How could anyone possibly top this tour? Several Congressmen had suggested looking into the Banshees and the possibility of revoking their visas.

Kaspar came back onstage carrying something that gleamed evilly at St. James' eye. He had been dreading this moment all evening. Kaspar set the flute on a small plastic base leaning against a stand. St. James could not take his eyes off it. It taunted him, whispering, *Wait until you hear me play.*

St. James never wanted to hear the flute. It reminded him of that other flute which would be waiting for them in L.A.

The Insane Assholes stood as one. "BANSHEES! BANSHEES! BANSHEES!"

The cops watched apprehensively.

Paxton pointed to the wings. "LADIES AND GENTLEMEN, THE BANSHEES!"

The boys ran onstage, Oaian rhythmically whacking a cowbell with a stick, kept it up until he was seated behind his kit, dropped the cowbell and flawlessly picked up the beat without losing a step.

They began with "Sympathy for the Devil." St. James felt a chill run up his spine in spite of himself—a genuine rock and roll chill like the first time he saw the Who or the Rolling Stones. The sound was enormous—St. James heard a Farfisa swell. They had to be using a pre-recorded tape but there was nothing canned about the boys' performance. The spotlight drifted to a dark corner revealing Kaspar on keyboards.

St. James was impressed in spite of himself.

They finished "Sympathy" with Oaian tapering the beat down to a disappearing marching band. The audience was on its feet. People down front showered the stage with plastic skulls and voodoo dolls.

Paddy smiled triumphantly. "Well that was a bit of oll roight, wasn't it?"

Paddy basked in the audience's adoration for a minute. "Now as some of you know, we're recording tonight ..."

Eruption.

"This 'ere's something new that Cunar and I wrote. It's called 'Live Evil.'"

Paddy unleashed a riff, and the crushing sound rolled off the stage, over the audience, and on into the hills. Even the cops were shaking their butts. They segued seamlessly from "Live Evil" to "Smoke My Knob," "I Just Called to Say I Hate You," "Do the World a Favor," "The Devil Came from Kansas," "Devil and Daughter," and "Cold Shot."

"You all know Mozart was Austrian, right?" Paddy said into the mic. "The Krauts 'ave spent seventy years trying to convince the world Mozart was Kraut and 'Itler was Austrian. Oi say to the Krauts, own him you fuckin' bastards! It's nothing to be ashamed of. This is Mozart's piano concerto #19."

Even the Insane Assholes were hushed into silence. The Banshees played Mozart's composition with allegro and brio, the master's sweeping melody rising up to grace the sky, Kaspar's Korg sounding like a harpsichord. When they finished the audience waited until the last throbbing vibe of Cunar's bass faded until leaping to their feet and making noise with every instrument at their disposal. One sick puppy held up his screaming eighteen-month old infant and aimed him at the stage, a joyous celebration to be sure.

"'Ow you like Cerberus, then?" Paddy said turning the trident guitar this way and that. The crowd responded with an enthusiastic roar.

The band finished with "Makin' Bacon." The crowd screamed for an encore and they came back for "Harley to Hell." That was it. It was eleven PM. The lights came on and the cops stood in formation looking at the Insane Assholes.

St. James and Connie joined the throngs heading toward the parking lots. Cops directed traffic with flashlights and whistles. Vehicles dribbled out of Red Rocks onto the winding mountain road leading to the highway.

Connie handed St. James the keys. "Would you mind driving?"

"Of course not, but feel free to speak out if I should drift into the left lane."

For a long time neither St. James nor Connie spoke, each lost in his own thoughts. St. James could see that something had happened while Connie was onstage. Gone was her usual bubbly, sarcastic, self-deprecating self, replaced by a brooder.

They were halfway to the hotel when he finally broke. "What happened?"

"I died up there, Ian. They locked me in that coffin and sawed through me. I saw it. I felt it. I didn't know it was possible to experience that much pain …"

She shut up and bit her lip. St. James glanced at her to see her staring out the window and sniffling.

He handed her a napkin from the door pocket and waited.

"I don't know how they did it. It wasn't some kind of mind trip or virtual reality. They sawed me in half. I felt it. God! I can still feel it! I'll feel it for the rest of my life!"

"Do you think you should talk to the police?"

"And say what? People will think I'm insane. But something happened back there. Something evil. Ian, what's happening?"

St. James patted her thigh, one hand on the wheel. "Okay, Oi know. I mean you're not supposed to think such things, not in this day and age."

"I keep telling myself this can't be happening. It's like some nightmare we can't escape."

"We could always scupper, tell *In Crowd* to find another scribbler."

"I can't! My whole career is riding on this story!"

"Okay, luv, okay. I hear you. We'll ride it out. I mean, it's not as if me old man is gonna off me, is it?"

"You think he really is your father?"

"What else am Oi supposed to think? Oi'll know when we talk to him on Monday."

"Because the only logical conclusion we can draw from all this shit is that the Banshees really are back from the dead with the help of Satan. I mean, that's gonna be a little hard to report with a straight face, y'know?"

"They say Satan, but maybe that's just a term, a synonym."

"What do you mean?"

"Maybe this Lord Rathkroghen is the deal."

"I don't know, Ian. I just don't know." She slid across the bench seat so he could put his arm around her.

At the hotel she didn't move on when St. James unlocked his door. She took his arm and said, "I want to be with you tonight. I'll be right back." She stood on tiptoes to kiss him on the mouth.

CHAPTER SIXTY-SEVEN

St. James closed the door

Oi can't believe this is happening to me.

But it was happening. He stood in front of the bureau and addressed himself in the mirror. He combed his hair—it made no difference. It was so short it just bounced back into its natural shape. He went into the bathroom, stripped off his shirt and sniffed his pits. He ran hot water, soaped up a washcloth and sudsed them, drying off with a towel. He dug out the Axe body spray, stripped off his shirt and anointed himself. He tried to catch his breath in his hand but that never worked. He flossed, brushed his teeth, looked around wildly to see if anything was out of order.

He put his shirt back on. It was lurid Hawaiian he'd purchased at an airport shop and given the bill to Connie.

It had been a long time, and he was out of practice. He didn't know whether to shit or go blind. The room had been neatly made-up, his guitar leaning against the wall in the corner. Should he strip? *Don't be an ass! Don't be presumptuous!* This wasn't some twenty-year-old groupie infatuated with an image. She knew him.

Which made it all the more miraculous.

He sat on the bed and flipped on the television. It was the hotel's home page playing inane music and hawking room service and OnDemand. He began marching through the channels. Disney. Weather. CNN. Fox. AMC. St. James snorted. He remembered when American Movie Classics played real movie classics like *Rebel Without a Cause* and *Yankee Doodle Dandy* without commercial interruption. Now a ninety-minute movie was likely to take two and a half hours and was just as likely to be *Mamacitas IV* as *Home Alone Two*.

It was twelve-thirty. What was she doing? For a freezing instant he thought she'd forgot—or worse yet was playing a cruel joke.

There was a knock at the door. St. James leaped off the bed and nearly tripped. He opened the door. Connie slipped inside wearing the trench coat she'd had in England.

She turned toward him and let the trench coat open. She wore a diaphanous black teddy with a pink bow. Tentatively he put his arms around her and she circled his waist and jammed herself tight against him.

Liberated, he whirled her around and deposited her on the bed with a bounce and a chuckle of glee.

O   O   O

They lay in bed, she snugged beneath his arm tracing his chest hair. They lay like that for ten minutes without speaking, St. James afraid to move for fear of startling her away like some wild animal. Enjoying the closeness. He'd forgotten how good it was.

"Fancy something from the serve bar?"

"I could use a Coke if they have one," she said.

St. James disentangled himself, pulled on his jockey shorts and went to the serve bar. He grabbed the red can, popped it, and poured the fizzy stuff into one of the plastic bar glasses.

"Pure class," he said handing it to her.

"Thank you." She lugged. "Mom."

"So are we loik goin' steady or what?"

She laughed, and silver coins spilled from her mouth. She put her hand on his. "Not likely, old bloke! But I do like you and we may do this again."

Careful, boyo. Keep it inside.

"We'd do it roight now if Oi had me some diagram!"

"I haven't had a lot of boyfriends. You may find that hard to believe."

"Oi don't."

"My daddy taught me about boys. I've been lucky and I've been careful. I never slept with any of those rockers they said I did except one, and I ain't talkin'."

"Fair enough."

"Now I'm going to tiptoe back to my room 'cause I can't sleep in a bed with others and I need to get up and write at the crack."

"Okay."

She stood, put on her trench coat, kissed St. James long and hard on the mouth and slipped out the door.

It was a long time before he fell asleep.

CHAPTER SIXTY-EIGHT

T he curse is broken!" Little Steven declared.

BANSHEES PERFORM, NOBODY DIES! blared the tabloid headline in the supermarket check-out lane. *Entertainment Weekly* began with a breathless, worshipful review of the show followed by a pious thanks to the Man Upstairs in recognition of the Banshees' achievement.

"It was the greatest concert I've ever seen," Ted Paxton said on KCLU, exhausted but happy. "I didn't get to interview 'em, but I sat in the fifth row, and folks, I don't know how to explain this, they weren't a day older than the day they died!

"Most of my listeners weren't born when that happened, but I was. It came right after the deaths of Otis Redding, Janis Joplin, and Morrison. But the Banshees were different. For one thing, it was an accident. Their plane went down in heavy fog. It wasn't as if they were shooting up speedballs ..."

O O O

The burgundy Cadillac approached an agricultural inspection station marking the Nevada/California border.

"Turn off the radio," said the man with the beautiful voice.

A man in Department of Agriculture khakis wearing a campaign hat and aviator's glasses signaled them to stop. Lebed lowered the window.

"You gentlemen carrying any fruit, vegetables, or live animals including snakes, insects, marsupials, or primates?"

Lebed grunted no. The inspector looked at him more carefully. Two inked-out palookas and someone in the back seat whom the inspector could not see because of the tinted windows.

"Sir, please pull your vehicle up to the indicated spot and turn off the engine."

"What for?" Lebed said truculently. The man in the back seat wanted to rip off his head. Stupid oaf.

"Because I said so."

Lebed rolled up the window and proceeded to the indicated spot.

"Do exactly as he says," said the man with the beautiful voice.

"What if he asks to look in the trunk?"

"I'll handle that."

The inspector followed them, trailed by a California highway patrolman on foot, hand on pistol. Lebed lowered the window and handed the inspector his license. It was a New York driver's license belonging to Fyodor Lebed with a Coney Island address. Everything was up to date.

"Please step out of the vehicle, sir. You too, sir."

Sighing, Lebed and Yomnosko got out. The inspector stuck his head in the driver's side window and looked into the back seat. The man sat in shadow, nearly squeezed to the door by carefully fitted suitcases and boxes that took up most of the back seat.

"You too, sir."

Van Horn opened the right rear door and got out smiling. The inspector opened the left rear door and looked at the cargo. "What's in those boxes?"

"Souvenirs," Van Horn answered. "CDs. We're heading to Los Angeles. I'm a promoter. The Banshees? Perhaps you've heard of them?"

His carefully modulated baritone sounded almost musical and caused the inspector to hang on his every word. Van Horn looked at the inspector's badge. "I'm Cyril Van Horn, officer. These two boys are Russkis, in case you hadn't noticed. First road trip for all of us."

"A-huh. Would you mind removing that top box and opening it?"

"Not at all," Van Horn answered, reaching into the back seat and grabbing the box. The inspector wondered how he stayed so cool wearing a white turtleneck and Navy blue blazer. And those shades—he hadn't seen a pair like that since the sixties. The man effortlessly removed the bulging box and set it on the hot tarmac. Even in the shade it was over a hundred degrees.

"Open it," the inspector said. The CHP stood next to him arms crossed. A show of force in case the box revealed a family of marmosets. The suave dude in the retro costume removed a folding knife from his pocket. The CHP slapped the butt of his gun and took a step back. Van Horn smiled and sliced the packing tape holding the box shut. He opened it up. Inside were hundreds of tightly packed CDs. He pulled one out and handed it to the inspector. The inspector looked at it. *Beat the Manshee*s was the name of the record, and it showed two longhaired maggots glowering at the viewer and making the sign of the devil. The inspector turned it over. There were two more maggots on back, one clutching a bottle of green piss.

He looked at the edge. It said, BANSHEES. The title was *Beat the Manshees*. "Oh," he said. "Wait a minute. I get it." He handed the CD to the state trooper. "You know these guys, Hank. The satanic rock band that keeps killing people."

"Yes," said the suave young dude in his oddly compelling voice. "But last night at Red Rocks nobody died. They broke the curse."

"My kid would like this," the trooper said.

"Keep it," Van Horn said. He reached in the box and pulled out another one for the inspector. "Would you like us to open the trunk?"

"No, that's all right. You can go now. Thank you for the CDs."

"Our pleasure, officers."

The inspector and trooper watched the three men get back into the Cadillac and leave. The Cadillac stopped in Needles so Lebed and Yomnosko could indulge their newfound passion for fast food. They had stopped at a different place every time.

McDonald's, Arby's, Wendy's, Culver's, Carl's Jr., Popeyes Chicken, A&W. America was an inexhaustible buffet. This time they chose a Subway, and they were not disappointed.

Van Horn sat in the courtyard on a concrete bench, elbows resting on a round concrete table smoking a cigarette. He drew the smoke in deeply and exhaled through his nostrils. He stared into the distance through his groovy shades. Lebed and Yomnosko emerged with their wrapped subs. His pit bulls. Loyal, brutal, and efficient but devoid of imagination. They sat at the concrete table and unwrapped their subs.

"All these happy people," he said. The pit bulls grunted and chowed down. "Legislating niceness while indulging in the basest hypocrisy."

"Fucktards," Lebed said with a full mouth trying out a word he'd just learned.

"That's exactly right, Fyodor," Van Horn said in soothing tones. "Their happiness is my misery. Their freedom an illusion, their leaders' cheap demagogues, their values empty with sentimentality. It is no small thing to remake a world, boyce, but we are well on our way. And when that happens you will rule at my feet with absolute power. You may fuck whomever you please. You may implement the *auto da fe*. You may drown litters of puppies in rock-filled sacks."

Mesmerized by Van Horn's voice Lebed and Yomnosko chewed and nodded happily as if they were listening to their favorite rock band.

"And who is the biggest fucktard of them all? Why none other than my beloved Oaian's own son Ian, for the lad hath cocked his hat and tithed his heritage toward preventing the transformation. I would not think such a frail vessel could punch so hard. How are the ribs, Fyodor?"

Fyodor looked up with angry little pig eyes and grunted. "I'll take care of him, boss."

"I know you would, my friend, but I reserve the right to deal with Mr. St. James personally."

It was 110 in the shade. The only other people out on the street were some Mexican day laborers, a couple of board punks and a sweating mailman in shorts and short-sleeved shirt.

Lebed and Yomnosko finished their sandwiches. Wordlessly they returned to the car and headed north. No one spoke. They drove beneath an enormous sun on a straight-line highway. They passed a slow-moving truck with a pickle on the side.

Van Horn stared at the Razr he'd purchased at a Wal-Mart the previous day. Five miles out of town Van Horn said, "Dirt road in one kilometer. Turn right."

The barely discernible tracks led north into the desert. The big car rumbled north leaving a dust cloud hovering at knee level. The land dipped and undulated. Soon they entered a depression out of sight of the highway. The bleached lifeless land stretched in every direction beneath a merciless blue sky.

"Stop here," Van Horn said.

The vehicle ground to a stop. Lebed opened the trunk from the driver's seat and all the men got out. Lebed and Yomnosko together removed the bulky, heavy duty yard bag. They laid it on the sand. They eased out the body of a young man, one of the ushers, according to his neck badge, one of the last to leave the park. His bike was jammed in the trunk too, broken into several pieces.

"Quickly now," Van Horn said. They had to hurry because of the heat. After a night and day in the trunk the body was beginning to turn. Yomnosko retrieved one of the suitcases and opened it on the ground. It contained dozens of specialized blades including filet knives, butcher's cleavers, bone saws, forceps, pincers, items that looked like a dentist's tools. A fire ax.

Lebed grabbed the fire ax and went to work.

Buzzards circled at three thousand feet.

onnie and St. James landed at John Wayne Airport in Orange County on the morning of the first. Serafin sent a limo that took them to the Hotel Crabbe. The limo driver handed Connie the FedEx shipment containing the flute. Connie skipped her apartment, which she hadn't seen in twelve days.

Nothing had changed between them, and everything. On the flight from Denver they'd sat side by side and held hands. Privately and together they cringed at what they'd done and celebrated. Everyday St. James seemed to acquire more confidence and become more like the man Connie wanted.

What have I done? she asked herself. No worse and certainly a damn sight better than some of the men she'd bedded. Connie hadn't slept with an interviewee in four years. Until now. St. James was part of the story. That was a no-no. Her own rules. But rules were made to be broken, weren't they? What was *In Crowd* but a finger in the face of the Man? At least, that's how it started. That had been its reputation. Now it *was* the Man.

She handed him the boxed flute in the limo. "Here. You keep it."

As they were checking in Connie turned to St. James and said, "I'm going to take you shopping."

St. James looked down at his Dockers and Hawaiian shirt. "Wot?"

They met in the lobby a half hour later and walked down Sunset to a trendy little glitter hole called Lee's where Connie picked out a dazzling white shirt with a pointed collar, a gray silk sport jacket and twilled pants with a crease that could cut cheese. She put it on the *In Crowd* card. By the time they returned to the hotel it was almost time for the interview.

Connie went to her room and checked her phone. Serafin had left her a message that one of the Red Rocks ushers was missing. She used her Blackberry to go online. News of the usher's disappearance had traveled far and wide and the conspiracy buffs were on it like a school bus full of third graders on a sugar high.

"YOU CAN'T KEEP A GOOD CURSE DOWN!" trumpeted TMZ.

Drudge had the flashing lights.

Connie's television silently showed riots. For an instant the screen showed a bearded man outside Pacific Arena holding a sign predicting the apocalypse. Connie leaped for the mute button but the parade had passed.

St. James and Connie reconvened in the lobby. It was four o'clock. The band had agreed to meet them in one of their two bedroom suites. Connie had her laptop and recording equipment. St. James had a notebook and a pen.

She was nervous. But her poise was infallible.

Connie looked at her watch and at St. James. "Let's do it."

They took the elevator to the fifth floor, walked down the hushed corridor and knocked on the door. Paddy opened it almost immediately.

"Come in," he said, stepping aside. He wore clean, tight-fitting blue jeans and a Mastodon T-shirt. Behind him, Cunar sat on the bed listening to an iPod, Oaian was on a chair sipping an iced tea. Cunar wore a white wife beater showing inked arms. A room service cart sat in the middle of the floor with the remains of breakfast: smeared egg yokes, some shredded potatoes, a fingerling of sausage.

Oaian rose as the two entered.

Oaian walked to Ian and embraced him. St. James felt awkward, hands automatically encircling this stranger whom he'd never known. Oaian was muscular and bony. He smelled of lime aftershave with the faintest undertone of rot. Oaian backed off, holding St. James by the shoulders. St. James was taller than Oaian.

"I've been dreaming of this moment all me life," Oaian said.

St. James didn't know how to reply. "'Ow are ya, Dad?"

Oaian beamed. "Never better! When we're done with this tour it's my hope you and me can spend a little time to get to know each other." His gaze was fathomless, pupils the size of pinheads.

Connie sat on the sofa setting her equipment before her. She held the tape recorder up, turned it on, and set it down.

Oaian and Paddy sat on the sofa. St. James and Cunar pulled their chairs into the circle. St. James offered his hand to Cunar.

"Ian St. James"

Cunar shook his hand and said, "RAWWWWWK!" Like a parrot.

"You'll 'ave to excuse Cunar," Paddy said. "'E thinks 'e's a bird!"

"RAWWWK!"

St. James looked around. "Where's Kaspar?"

"Kaspar's inspecting the venue. It's just you and us. You may fire when ready, Gridley."

* * *

THE *IN-CROWD* INTERVIEW: THE BANSHEES

Connie: So who are you guys really?

Paddy: We're the Banshees, Ducks. We're the original band.

Connie: How come you all look like you're in your twenties? If you're the original band, shouldn't you all be in your late sixties?

Paddy: We took a time out.

Connie: How is that possible?

Paddy: Through Lucifer Our Lord, all things are possible. LOL!

Connie: Do you mean Lucifer in the Biblical sense?

Paddy: 'Ere's only one Lucifer, Ducks. Also goes by the name of Scratch, Diabolus, the Antichrist, Prince of Darkness, Satan, Beelzebub, and George Soros.

Connie: Paddy, people aren't going to believe this. Why don't you tell us the truth?

Paddy: Oh they'll believe it ol' roight. Trust me on that. Why the old fiend might even make an appearance at our concert.

St. James: Do you remember dying?

Paddy: Oi remember the plane going down. Fact is we were so fucked up on smack it was loik a roller-coaster ride, y'know, and then, nothing. Darkness.

St. James: How were you resurrected? Where were you resurrected?

Paddy: As to the 'ow, I don't know. I wasn't there. We woke in an old stone castle. All three of us. I think it was in Belarus. Kaspar was the first person we saw, and he gave us a long rap on the means and the ends, but to tell you the truth I woke up with a headache and couldn't remember a word of it.

Cunar: RAWWWK!

St. James: If you guys worship Satan, who's Lord Rathkroghen?

Paddy: 'Oo?

St. James: Do you know a Professor Klapp?

Paddy: 'Oo?

St. James: We dug up your coffin. Do you know what we found?

Paddy. No. Wot?

St. James: A mangrove root and a bone flute.

Paddy: Oi wouldn't know. Oi wasn't around.

Connie: If you worship Satan you must acknowledge the existence of God.

Paddy: C'mon, Connie. There is no God. We sing about it!

Connie: How can there be a Satan if there is no God? Was he not once Lucifer the Archangel who stood at God's right hand?

Paddy: Ah yes. "How are thou fallen from heaven, O Lucifer, son of the morning!"

Connie: Is that scripture?

Paddy: Isaiah.

Connie: How peculiar. You know the Bible?

Paddy: Bits and pieces.

St. James: And what do you hope to accomplish with this tour?

Paddy: Y'mean asoide from gettin' stinkin' rich? Which is always a good thing in Lucifer's book. We hope to usher in a new age, get rid of the deadwood, start fresh, that sort of thing.

St. James: Where? Here? England?

Paddy: Everywhere, laddie. Dream big Oi always say.

Connie: Does Satan require blood sacrifice?

Paddy: Nothing good is ever free.

Connie: So murder is no big deal to you guys.

Paddy: Wha—? Come on, Ducks! When 'ave Oi got toim to murder someone? The only laws we broke are smoking in the club. We don't even do drugs.

St. James: What about Kaspar? Are his hands clean?

Paddy: Love that man! Best manager we ever 'ad.

St. James: Do you think he can withstand a police investigation?

Oaian: Look, Ian, we're a band. We're touring again for the first time in forty years. Readers aren't interested in a lot of superstitious mumbo-jumbo. They want to know our plans, when the new record'll be out, what's on it, and where can they see us.

St. James: No, Oaian, they want to know if you're a satanic rock band from hell and how many lives you're going to claim.

Paddy: Every one of those so-called deaths can be explained.

We had nothing to do with any of it.

Connie: What about the man and woman who disappeared in a sea of blood in Berlin?

Paddy: The coppers never even talked to us! No bodies, no crime. That Kaspar 'e's a genius at the little touches, y'know? Keepin' the legend alive?

St. James: And you had nothing to do with Rulon Wexler?

Paddy: Wot are you complainin' about? You made out like a sweet'eart on that one.

Connie: What's he talking about?

St. James: He's referring to the fact that Wexler and I were not exactly close friends, but I never wished him dead.

Paddy: Didn't you?

St. James: Back off, Paddy! I have nothing to do with whatever deal you made with whatever fuckin' nightmare you worship!

Oaian: There will be twelve songs on the new album. We're recording the last three at Pacific Arena.

Connie: And you guys are going with Melchior?

Paddy: It's great to be back workin' with our first and best producer.

St. James: What do you know about this missing usher?

Paddy: What missing usher? We travel in a womb. We've barely got time to shit. Oi don't watch the news. Oaian, you watch the news?

Oaian: Nope. Too depressing.

Paddy: Cunar?

Cunar: RAWWWK!

St. James: What about the flute?

Paddy: Oi, we keep puttin' it out, but Ian Anderson's never in the audience.

St. James: Aren't you really waiting for Lord Rathkroghen?

Paddy: Oi don't know whatcher talkin' about. Look at the toim! We've got to get ready for the party. Thank you for coming it was a lovely interview.

Connie: I have more questions.

Paddy: They'll 'ave to wait, Ducks. Oaian, Cunar, you comin'?

Oaian: Ian, Oi'd like to speak to you in private for a minute.

Connie: I'll see you at the party.

Cunar: RAWWWK!

CHAPTER SEVENTY

St. James followed Oaian into one of the bedrooms. Oaian shut the door behind him and turned to embrace Ian. Oaian felt cool through his shirt and smelled of citrus. "Flesh of my flesh, blood of my blood," he whispered. Ian hugged him back, somewhat embarrassed.

There were a pair of Toca conga drums on the floor as well as an electronic drum pad set up with a Pignose. No laptop, no cell phone, no iPad. Oaian sat on the bed and idly picked up a pair of drumsticks with which he used to strike the drum pad making a soft thwacking sound.

"Ian, I'd like to apologize for leaving you like I did."

St. James didn't know what to say. They were carrying this farce to absurdity. St. James regarded the young man on the bed with the shaggy black mane, the same clear blue eyes he saw when he stared in the mirror. Except for that crackle—that dried lakebed of crevices around the eyes.

He felt fear, exhilaration, and yes, a twinge of love for this man who claimed to be his father. It had always been there, long before the Banshees were born again. It was instinctive. Mapped in the genes passed down from parent to child. St. James was too old to crumble emotionally, and the twin poles of belief and bullshit ripped him apart.

"What was my mother like?"

"Dora? Lovely girl, not too bright. She was supposed to drive that night, 'er being pregnant and all, but wouldn'tcha know it,

Dora could never turn down a party. We were both pretty scuppered when we got in the Jag."

"Do you miss her?"

Oaian lay back, hands behind his head and stared at the ceiling. "Not really. There've been so many women in my life. To tell you the truth I didn't know 'er that well. I missed you more."

"But you never knew me!"

"Doesn't matter. Yer me son, Ian. Yer me flesh and blood. What's moin is yours. And I loik to think, what's yours is moin. When all this settles down I expect I'll buy a place out here in Hollyweird, and you an' me can get to know each other. Would you loik that?"

St. James was shocked by the rush of emotion that overwhelmed him. He wanted to hug this man he'd just met. He also wanted to slug him. It was as if some part of his life had been missing—the hot steam in the pipes, and suddenly one cold morning the hot steam filled the pipes, and the house became a home.

St. James couldn't explain it. He shied away from the implications. All he knew was that out of the blue God had graced him with family. He looked around. Oaian reached over to the bed stand, snagged a mini-packet of tissues and tossed it to him. St. James blew his nose.

St. James sat on the bed next to Oaian. "How come we never see you with any women?"

"We took a vow of chastity until we got to a certain point. That's all about to change. That's what this party's all about! Time Melchior earned his salt! We're 'opin' to get laid tonight."

"So you've reached that certain point, eh? What is it?"

Oaian patted St. James on the arm. "Oi don't know—Kaspar explained it once, it's all about numbers and demographics, y'see."

"Oaian, for God's sake, why did you play those tiny venues? You could have filled a stadium with your first American appearance!"

"Again, I bow to management. Something to do with building anticipation because from now on we're going to play the biggest stadiums we can foind. We're makin' up for lost time, eh? S'posed to be some bigshot TV 'ere tonight. 'Oo knows where we'll end up."

"This is so hard for me to accept …"

"Think of it as a gift, loik. So. You and the girl reporter. She's a real hottie, that one."

St. James blushed. Was it that obvious?

"We 'ave no secrets among us, Ian. Paddy offered you a deal."

"I didn't agree to any deal."

"Yes, you did. You're reapin' the rewards, aren't you?"

St. James flashed on Wexler's Borsalino lying in a canyon next to the writer's shredded body. His miracle cure. Connie in his arms. Yes, he was reaping the rewards all right. But he'd never agreed to any deal!

"Paddy said I was to write what he told me. But he hasn't told me anything."

"Of course 'e 'as! What do you think that Q&A was all about." Oaian sprang to his feet. He could have been Ian's son. "Now go on with you. Oi've got to get ready. C'mere. Let me give you a kiss."

St. James rose and embraced the younger, shorter man who kissed him square on the lips.

CHAPTER SEVENTY-ONE

The party took place in the John Muir Pavilion behind the hotel. Paparazzi camped out on Sunset and in the bushes as a steady stream of limos and exotic automobiles disgorged their passengers. A dozen security people ran interference between celebrities and lenses.

Guests passed through the art deco lobby and took the stairs or elevator to the third floor which opened on the back grounds, bungalows, and pavilion. St. James and Connie walked up the concrete steps to the lawn on which the pavilion had been pitched. Serafin stepped out from under the tent to greet them.

"How'd the interview go?" Serafin said.

Connie slowly shook her head with her mouth open. "You'll have to hear it to believe it. They claim Satan brought them back to life."

Serafin clapped his hands together and rubbed. "Great!" He grabbed St. James' hand. "Good to see you, Ian. It's been years."

"You too, Richard."

"Connie tells me you put on quite a show in Colorado."

"She's too kind."

Grinning goofily, Serafin looked from one to the other and pointed his finger. "Are you two ..."

"Sort of," Connie said.

"Well, all right!" Serafin turned to Connie. "When can I expect copy?"

"Tomorrow afternoon."

"Okay you two. I gotta go play host."

Serafin headed toward the head of the stairs to greet Jody Foster. The smell of grilling meat made St. James' stomach rumble like a panzer division.

"Fancy something to eat?" he asked Connie.

She put a hand on his arm. "You go ahead. I have to talk to people." She reached up and planted a kiss on his cheek.

St. James headed toward the back of the pavilion where a couple of men in chef's aprons and white toques labored over a huge charcoal grill made from an oil drum cut in half length-wise. A table contained buns, utensils, condiments, and linen napkins.

A fresh-faced young woman in a Hotel Crabbe blazer popped up behind the table. "Yes, sir. Can I help you, sir?"

St. James cast his eye on the grill. Next to a dozen grilling hamburgers were a dozen grilling Polish sausages. He lost his appetite.

"Just browsing, thanks."

"Well, we're here if you need us."

St. James went to the bar and got a 7-Up for himself and a white wine for Connie. She was standing with a tweedy young man in a jacket and glasses, with curly brown hair and a mustache. The man was showing Connie something on his iPad. St. James came up to them and handed the drink to Connie.

"Oh, hello, Ian. This is Randy Birch, our Managing Editor."

"Pleased to meet you, Ian," Birch said shaking hands.

"Randy was just showing me some of the fallout."

"Really nasty article about some geezer who claims the Banshees ruined his life. Saw 'em in England in '74, got stinking drunk, rolled his car, ended up a paraplegic. Blames it on the Banshees. Of course he's suing."

"In case you haven't noticed, Ian," Connie said, "that's how you get rich in America."

"Did you know Pacific Arena is under construction?" Birch said.

"What?" Connie said. "Does Melchior know?"

"I assume so. I drove past this morning, and the place was swarming with construction workers. And there were a half dozen loons out front protesting the Apocalypse."

The pavilion filled up. Paddy and Oaian showed up in their official showbiz uniforms, black blazers, black silk tees, shades, and black jeans. They were immediately engulfed by big shots, actors, and well-wishers. St. James hovered at the outer rim of this little galaxy picking out famous faces. There was the once-promising actor whose career had been saved by an embarrassing reality show, eager starlets ready to jump into bed with whomever, a famous plastic surgeon, a rapper.

Paddy and Oaian signed autographs.

"It's for my daughter," one man explained.

Paddy looked up, saw St. James, and nodded. St. James sidled over.

"So what do you want me to write, Paddy?"

Paddy did not look up from what looked like a spanking new CD edition of their first album. Where had that come from? "Tell the truth, Ian. That's ol' Oi ask."

"You mean about owing your resurrection to Satan and so forth?"

Paddy looked up with a devilish glint in his eye. "That's it."

"We're running that interview verbatim. We have some follow-ups."

"Not 'ere old twig. This is a party. People are supposed to relax and have a good toim! Why don't you go get yourself a nice gin and tonic?"

St. James looked up and spotted Kenny Grace and Woody Nuringer rising from below. St. James knew them from before the fall. Grace carried a guitar case and had a girl on his arm, vanilla parfait in a white strapless evening gown. Jaded roués followed her progress toward the bar. A string trio set up on a prefab wooden stage and began to play a Paganini etude.

Where was Melchior?

St. James went over to say hello. He'd performed on a couple of bills with Charon. "Yo, Kenny," he said approaching.

Grace looked at him with an expression of contempt. "Stay away from me you old burnout."

St. James was left standing with his hand out and his face red. Several of Grace's friends snickered. Stunned and hurt, St. James looked longingly at the bar. One drink.

No way, me larripin' lad. One's too many and a thousand's not enough.

St. James found Serafin shaking hands with Charlie Sheen and his date, a stunning brunette in an oxblood dress. Serafin introduced them.

"Pleased to meet you," St. James said.

Sheen had St. James' hand in a Vulcan death grip and fixed St. James with his laser eye. "Tiger blood."

"Roight."

"I'm Rosily," Sheen's date said.

"Pleased, Oi'm sure," St. James said.

Sheen spotted someone and pulled the lovely Rosily with him. St. James said, "Where's Melchior?"

"Can't make it," Serafin said. "He's planning his own little shindig for tomorrow night. You're invited of course."

"Crikey, is partying all you do out here? How can you stand it?"

"You've got to pace yourself."

"Me old man used to go into training for these parties. He'd down a fifth of gin, smoke some reefer, snort a gram, and hey presto, you're good to go. Every noight."

It's a miracle he's still alive.

Serafin laughed.

"Did you know Pacific Arena is under construction?"

Serafin looked startled. "What?"

"So says your boy Birch. Says he went past this morning and there was all sorts of construction going on."

Serafin pulled out his space needle and phoned Melchior. He turned on the speaker so St. James could hear.

"What?"

"My editor drove past Pacific Arena this AM. Says it's under construction."

"Don't worry. They'll be finished tomorrow."

"What kind of construction?"

"Just some bullshit repairs, shoring up the roof or whatever. Don't worry about it. How's it going?"

"Going great, Burkie-boy. You really should come down here."

"I have to read four scripts before nine AM. I'll see you tomorrow night."

St. James ran into all sorts of people he used to know when he was a promising young jake. Most seemed glad to see him. Others greeted him with embarrassment.

He looked around for Connie. She was talking to some hotshot producer. *No. Wait.* St. James came closer.

She was talking to the Silva-thins Man.

CHAPTER SEVENTY-TWO

As St. James joined them he noted that the newcomer appeared to be in his late twenties with chestnut hair to die for, worn fashionably disheveled and a three-day stubble beneath a Clark Gable 'stache. The best of both worlds. The type of face *People* chose for "The Sexiest Man Alive."

He looked vaguely familiar. St. James must have seen him on the telly, maybe in a movie.

"Ian," Connie said taking his hand, "this is Cyril Van Horn."

They shook hands. Van Horn's grip was firm and cool.

"Saw your performance at the Mish. Rockin'." Van Horn spoke with a faint East European accent.

"Thank you. What do you do?"

"I'm a singer/songwriter," Van Horn said down low and smooth.

"Listen to that voice," Connie said. "Where can we hear you sing?"

"Tomorrow night. Burke's asked me to sing a few songs."

"You know Burke?" St. James said. The dude looked awfully young. But Melchior's business was built on the young. Young stars, young audiences. Certainly this dude was cosmetically correct and his clothes were top drawer. He wore a Breitling on his left wrist.

"Just signed with him. I'm recording my first record now."

"So what's your music like?"

"Psychedelic rock."

"What's it called?"

"Lizard Dick."

"Oi loik it. 'Oo do you fancy then?"

"Pink Floyd, Grateful Dead, Pillbugs."

"Oi love me some Pillbugs. Do you have a band then?"

"Sometimes. Sometimes I wing it solo."

"You like the Banshees?"

"Love them," Van Horn declared with a psychedelic gleam in his eye. "May I speak to you for a minute? Connie, will you excuse us?"

"Of course."

Van Horn put his hand on St. James' shoulder and steered him toward the edge of the lawn, behind a trellis alive with wisteria and frangipani, to an oblique view of Sunset between the hotel and an office block. Beyond the trellis lay a four-foot strip of lawn, then a three-foot drop off held in place by a stone hedgerow.

St. James faced Van Horn.

"Wot?"

"You know, Ian …"

Van Horn brought his knee up savagely into St. James' groin, a sledgehammer blow that lifted St. James a half inch. A thermonuclear bomb detonated between his legs shooting jagged glass shards to his toes and into his brain, pain so intense it obliterated reason and turned St. James into a pitiful mewling creature with no control. St. James fell to his knees, then to his side, drawing himself into a fetal position as waves of nausea radiated from his balls.

Van Horn put his hands on his knees like an excited spectator and looked down smiling. "How do you like it?"

A tendril of drool gathered at one corner of Van Horn's perfect mouth rendering it sinister. A bolus of saliva dropped and splatted on St. James' cheek. A whiff of sulfur.

St. James gasped, tears rolling down his cheeks, staring at Van Horn's custom-made Italian loafers mere inches from his face. Part of him seemed to hover overhead taking it all in from a disinterested perspective.

Why?

What had he ever done to Van Horn?

Knock it off you bloody wanker!

Van Horn crouched and spoke in a mellifluous, soothing baritone. "I don't like you. Who are you to interfere with my plans? I will take everything you love. I will turn your life into a seeping wound. I will make you pray for death. Don't like it? Kill yourself. Do it now."

He held out his perfectly manicured hand and a black capsule fell on St. James' cheek and stuck there.

Van Horn stood and stomped St. James savagely in the ribs with his heel. St. James felt something crack. Van Horn walked away.

CHAPTER SEVENTY-THREE

St. James lay on his side breathing deeply, waiting for the waves of nausea to subside. It hurt to breathe. Somehow, the pill lay six inches from his nose. Gradually he became aware of the gay cackle of voices beyond the hedge, the string trio sawing away. He stared at the flawless Kentucky blue grass between his nose and the drop-off. He got to a sitting position. He got to his knees. He stayed that way a long time and finally, using the trellis for support, he got to his feet.

He looked down at the black capsule. He crushed it beneath his heel.

He brushed himself off and ran his fingers through his hair. Sticking to the perimeter and trying to attract no attention, he haltingly made his way to the bar in back and got a glass of ginger ale. The bartender gave him a second glance, but then immediately looked down. St. James stood at the bar sipping until the final strains of nausea departed. He looked around. No sign of Van Horn. No point in calling the coppers. It was his word against Van Horn's.

Who was Van Horn? What had St. James done to offend him?

A smiling Connie emerged from the crowd and approached with her empty glass. Her smile turned to a frown.

"Are you all right?"

"Just slipped and bonked meself. No biggie. Wot happened to your pal Van Horn?"

"I haven't seen him since you two went off. What did he want to talk to you about?"

"Big fan. Just music stuff."

A stirring in the force drew their attention to the pavilion entrance where a number of people clustered around a wizened homunculus in a tuxedo supported by his twenty-something wife who was a foot taller in her spiked stilettos.

"It's Darrell Cavanaugh!" Connie said.

Darrell Cavanaugh, one-time head of MGM, legendary producer and director whose after-Oscars party was the most sought after ticket in town, and had been for going on thirty-seven years. The entourage passed Connie and St. James on the way to the stage.

"Where are those Banshees?" Cavanaugh said in a surprisingly strong voice. "I saw 'em in England in '74, and I want to see if it's the same guys."

Agents, actors, lawyers, and writers in tow, the procession moved through the big tent until it came to the wooden platform where the string trio had just stopped playing. Valets and guests hustled to set up a row of folding chairs facing the stage for Mr. Cavanaugh and his entourage which included three Academy Award winners.

Cavanaugh sat with his cane between his legs. "Boys! Bring me the Banshees."

And here came Paddy striding up the aisle, turning and facing the great producer.

"'Ow are you, sir? Been a long time, innit?"

Cavanaugh extended his hand and slowly shook the young man's hand, peering at him through glasses the size of a Jeep's windshield. "Paddy, you don't look a day older."

"Neither do you, sir."

The old man brayed, and so did everybody else.

"So you gonna play 'Makin' Bacon' or what?"

"We're not all 'ere, sir."

"You can play anything with a guitar. Have you met my darling Elizabeth? Liz, Paddy MacGowan, lead singer for the Banshees."

"Delighted to meet you, Paddy."

"Come on, boy. Do it for the lovely lady."

Paddy shrugged. "'Oo's got a guitar then?"

And someone called out, "Kenny Grace's got one!"

"Where's Kenny?" the old man cried. "Bring that bad boy up here!"

One did not defy the King of Hollywood, and Kenny appeared before the old man.

"Kenny, give Paddy your guitar so he can sing something."

"With all due respect, Mr. Cavanaugh," Kenny spat poison, "this is my guitar. I'm sure Mr. MacGowan would feel the same if someone wanted to play Cerberus."

"Not at all, Kenny," Paddy said as innocent as cream. "You can play Cerberus any toim. Come by the concert on the 4th, we'll jam."

All eyes on Grace as he was forced to hand over his guitar, a very nice Gibson, with a scowl. Paddy looped it over his neck, tested the strings and found them to be in tune. "Oaian!" he yelled. "'Ow's about you and Cunar 'elpin me out?"

A moment later he was joined onstage by Cunar with a six string Epiphone, and Oaian with the set of bongos from his room. They huddled together briefly, turned to the audience, Paddy tapped it down with his foot, and they broke into "Here Comes the Sun" with flawless three-part harmony as if they'd been practicing for weeks. They did "Because," "You Never Give Me Your Money," "Sun King," "Mean Mr. Mustard," "Polythene Pam," "She Came in Through the Bathroom Window," and finished with "Golden Slumbers."

St. James looked around. Grace's parfait girlfriend clasped her hands together and stared at the band with rapture. Grace shot daggers from his eyes. Everybody else was enthralled, and when the last chord died out the audience roared and clapped.

Cavanaugh surged to his feet. "That's them! That's those boys!"

St. James heard a smack of flesh on flesh and turned just in time to see Grace's parfait girlfriend, head tilted to the side, touching her reddened cheek and grimacing. Her boyfriend shook with rage, hand drawn back to deliver another.

St. James steamed toward them but Paddy beat him to it.

"Hey, fuckwad!" Paddy declared, and when Grace turned Paddy socked him on the jaw causing Grace to stumble back into the condiment table. People jumped in on all sides to restrain the combatants. Cunar and Oaian held Paddy. Woody and some producer held Grace.

"Well this is awkward," St. James whispered to Connie who was just putting away her camera.

"I didn't see any signs, did you?" she said.

CHAPTER SEVENTY-FOUR

Grace was escorted from the party.

Connie put a finger on St. James' arm. "'Scuse me, Ian. I've got to work." He watched her head toward a group of executives by the bar. He'd had a lot of birds in his day, not so much lately, and Connie was definitely the best of the bunch. He wasn't crazy how she kept running after every celeb in the joint but that was her job. At least she had a job.

Crikey. She wasn't going to post that video, was she? Not if she wanted to keep her job.

The string quartet returned and played Mozart.

St. James filled a platter with potato salad, chopped liver, crackers, and jicama (jicama!) and found a seat. He was just polishing off his dinner when he looked up to see a middle-aged man with a semi-famous face approaching with a look of delighted disbelief.

"Ian? Ian St. James? Christ! It's been years!"

St. James racked his brain. *Who the fuck?* He stood and offered his hand. "How are you?"

"Nate Pistol! We did Isle of Wight together, and then that thing up in Marin County. 1992, '93, something like that. Don't you remember? We both got so fucked up on coke and booze we were gonna rob a gas station, don't you remember that man?"

A hideous memory crept down from the attic. Up for five days on a coke-fueled binge of bad crazy. They had guns. They had actually procured guns and ammo and in their extreme state of fucked-upedness, were preparing to commit a felony. The only thing that stopped them was the realization at the last minute that neither of them could drive.

"Of course, Nate. How are you?"

"What's this bullshit about that drummer being your old man? It's a joke, right? I mean I'm old enough to be his father."

"It's kind of hard to explain, Nate."

"You going to the show on the fourth?"

"Absolutely. You?"

Pistol made a pistol with his hand and aimed it at St. James. "You betcha. See you there. Ahmina get a drink."

"Nice seeing you, Nate."

St. James watched him go. He had to get out of there or he was going to start drinking. He went up to Oaian who was explaining a paradiddle to two awe-struck young women.

"Oaian, Oim gwinter bed."

Oaian stood and embraced Ian. "Sleep well. We'll talk in the morning."

As St. James walked away he heard one of the young women say, "Is that your father?"

St. James glad-handed his way around the tent finally spotting Connie having an intense conversation with Serafin. About the video no doubt.

"Connie, I've 'ad it. I'm turnin' in."

"Goodnight, Ian. I'll see you later."

St. James hung there for a millisecond before recovering and heading for the exit.

What was this? A one-night stand?

He stewed all the way to his room, and he stewed in the room. The servy bar mutely beckoned. It couldn't hurt to open the door and look at the selection, could it? St. James used his room key to unlock the servy bar which contained three tiny bottles of Johnny Walker, three tiny bottles of Absolut, and a large can of Guinness.

He was being comped. He wouldn't have to pay the outrageous prices, what, seven ninety-five for two ounces of vodka, are you fuckin' kidding me? He slammed shut the door, picked up the remote and turned on the television. A hotel spokesperson spoke loudly about the hotel's many amenities until St. James found the channel button. Up the ladder he went, settling at last on CNN. He hit the mute and fell back on the bed, piling up three cushions for a back rest.

Fuckin' bitch.

Well face it old sod, it's not as if you're catnip to the ladies. What use does a gorgeous, talented twenty-something have for a has-been like him?

Maybe she felt sorry for him.

That made St. James want to turn into a black hole and implode. There was no ball too small for him to curl up in. He'd been making a fool of himself his entire life.

When was he gonna learn?

He looked at TV, read the scroll running across the bottom of the screen. It seemed as if the world had gone berserk. Riots in the Sudan, Egypt, Lebanon, Syria, London, Zurich, New Jersey. A volcano blew in the South Pacific forcing thousands to flee. Still no sign of the missing usher. A publicity photo of the Banshees appeared briefly onscreen. A brief clip of protesters and counter-protesters outside Pacific Arena.

Maybe the apocalyptics are right, he thought. Maybe it really is the end of the world, and the Banshees are harbingers. It made as much sense as anything else just then. He flicked off the TV in disgust and lay on top of his bed staring at the ceiling, the only light coming from the bathroom.

Well fuck it, he thought. *I'll get up early and have a nice run, maybe a workout in the gym. Who needs that silly bitch anyway?*

He tossed and turned and finally fell into a shallow sleep around four AM. He dreamed he was all alone at the back of a theater and onstage, the only light in the place, a spotlight directed on a silver flute. How it gleamed.

St. James feared the flute. Feared what it could do and the man who played it. Footsteps echoed from the wings. A man came onstage and picked up the flute. He turned toward St. James but before he became fully visible St. James woke up.

CHAPTER SEVENTY-FIVE

Wow, Shelly thought. *I've never been fucked like that in my life! I'm sorry Kenny honey, but you just made a bad mistake.* Besides, that slap was only partly for show. Kenny had had a bee up his ass since being told he was to open for the Banshees.

In the six months Shelly had been Kenny's girlfriend it had been a wild ride with concerts in England, Sweden, Germany, and Poland. She'd inhaled more pharmaceutical coke than nine hundred dentists, been wined, dined, feted, and kissed, worshiped by teenage fan boys who stepped on their tongues.

Yeah, it was swell.

But Kenny could be a real prick. He was like really old—fifty or something—and used to getting his own way. He liked to hurt her during sex. He expected Shelly to come when he whistled. Well Little Shelly never was very good at that game, growing up on a farm outside Fond Du Lac with six other siblings. Shelly had learned at an early age she had to grab her lamb chop fast if she expected to eat. Told since kindergarten how beautiful she was, she cultivated beauty as her calling inspired by the likes of Anna Nicole Smith, Heidi Pratt, and Kim Kardashian, smart women who had parlayed their looks into glittering lifestyles.

Shelly did the photographer and then did the photos. The pictures were always better when they thought they were in love with you. She was good looking enough to audition, but thus far no one had called her back for anything other than a blow job. At least with Kenny it was over and done within minutes.

Kenny had a hair trigger at both ends. All that booze and blow didn't help. Shelly started to panic when she left the party with Paddy. Kenny was holding her stash. But of course a notorious partier like Paddy would have some.

He took her to his bungalow from which the party was a distant rumble of music and laughter. He shut the door and turned to her.

"Got any blow?" she said.

"Sorry, Ducks. I no longer touch the stuff. Got booze if you want it."

Shock. There was always the shit in her purse. It scared her.

"'Ow 'bout it, Shel? My bar is yours."

Shelly demurred. If this was what Kenny wanted, she'd grit her teeth and get it over with. She could always say she fucked Paddy MacGowan. But a funny thing happened while they were making love. She forgot all about the coke, the booze, and Kenny. She forgot about everything but the incredible sensations this man was bringing to life. She clung to him like a life preserver, seeing that she had been only half-alive, indeed, sleepwalking through life in the gravity of a fifty-year-old adolescent narcissist.

Well screw you, Kenny! You fuck like an adolescent too.

There was only one problem. The pictures. The pictures she'd permitted Kenny to take one long rainy weekend when they were up at Big Bear. The pictures were no worse than anything you might find in an XXX skin rag, but Hollywood being the font of hypocrisy that it is, Shelly knew those pictures could sink her. Big time.

So for now, she had to do what the man said, distasteful though that may be. What a shame. Paddy was twice the man as Kenny. She turned on her side and regarded the sleeping Banshee snoring lightly, his lithe young body half covered in a sheet. It was only the eyes that looked old and they were shut now. He looked like a sleeping boy.

He was actually very sweet in contrast to the horror stories. Little Shelly had done her homework. She knew all about the crazy parties, the excesses of the old days. Paddy, at least, had matured.

But there was one thing she didn't understand. If these guys were the original Banshees how could they look so young? Kenny told her they were freaks and fakes, the product of plastic surgery. Maybe, she thought. But Paddy was wise beyond his years, both gentle and fierce when required.

A real man.

Time to perform one last task for the tedious Kenny. Shelly gently depressed the mattress next to Paddy's head several times to see if he would wake. The sonorous drone of his breathing remained steady. Carefully Shelly swung her long legs over the side of the bed and got up. Grabbing her purse, she went into the bathroom and relieved herself. As instructed, she looked through Paddy's shaving kit for any drugs. No drugs. A little velvet bag filled with crunchy stuff. She opened it up. Inside were some tiny stones, some ash, and a little white bone from some small mammal. She knew what that was. A mojo. All these white guitarists worshiped the blues.

She put it back.

Slipping out of the bathroom she went through the bedroom to the living area and slowly, carefully shut the door. Enough light drifted in from the full moon that she was able to see the sofa cluster in the center of the room and the odd, keyhole shaped case that contained Paddy's guitar. Cerberus. Guys had to name things. Kenny named his dick Mighty Samson. She thought of it as Pee Wee Herman.

Paddy's wallet lay on the credenza. Why not? It was his bungalow. Shelly picked it up and went through it. It contained several hundred dollars in cash and a business card from an Escorts place in West Hollywood. No driver's license. No credit cards. No pictures.

What a weirdo, she thought, carefully replacing the wallet. She opened her purse and removed a package of Marlboro Lights. She shook one out and lit it with hotel matches. Carrying her chic little hand-bag she went to the big black guitar case, laid it carefully on the floor, knelt, and undid the latches.

As she opened the case the faint glow of the exterior light reflected off the massive plexiglass slab and stabbed her in the eye with a vision of such cosmic mayhem her breath caught in her throat.

What was *that*?

Suddenly she felt like puking. She felt her smallness measured against the universe and the existential abyss. An Arctic-like wind blew through her soul. She shivered and hugged herself.

She looked again. Cerberus was impressive, but it wasn't transmitting.

"Get a hold of yourself, girl," she muttered quietly, unconsciously echoing her father and many of her boyfriends. The big black case contained cubbyholes and drawers fitted all around the guitar like an old-fashioned clerk's desk. Removing the tightly folded baggie filled with white powder that Kenny had given her from her purse, she opened the middle of three deep drawers—like a jewelry cabinet—rooted up several boxes of picks and buried the baggie in the bottom.

Quickly she closed the case, snapped the clasps and returned it to its upright position. She mashed out her cigarette in the sink at the wet bar and slipped back into the bedroom.

As she slid into bed Paddy's arm reached out and cupped her breast, his erection stiff against her behind. "'Ow you like Cerberus, then?"

CHAPTER SEVENTY-SIX

S t. James woke with a splitting headache. He touched his waist. The fuckin' hernia was still gone. Bleedin' miracle. He got up, put on his track shoes and outfit, and headed out through the lobby moaning softly under his breath. It was good to be back running even on the hard concrete of Sunset Boulevard. Every footfall sent a jolt of pain through his skull, but he knew from experience that if the cure was difficult, it was foolproof.

Plenty of weirdos at that hour: agitated transvestites, Viet veterans in electric wheelchairs and big beards, crow-like youth, lean in black feathers dragging ass back to their encampments beneath the freeway.

He'd lived out here back in the eighties. Lived like a king for about six months until the bubble burst. Now he didn't live anywhere. He was three months in arrears on his apartment in Soho and had already mentally forfeited his meager belongings, including a Triumph Bonny for which he still owed two hundred quid.

Man without a country.

Man without a bike.

And now, apparently, without a bird. Well he'd know more later, wouldn't he? St. James despised himself for the jealous images marching through his mind. Not really worthy of him. He hoped. There was always that fear he wasn't the man he imagined he was. Was, in fact, a loser. Fell into the whole Banshees thing, really. Right place, right time.

Well at least he'd reunited with his father.

St. James laughed out loud startling a wino sleeping on a bus bench. Rationally he couldn't accept it. But the blood spoke otherwise. St. James felt as if he'd been living a dream ever since Prague and would wake any minute in his Spartan three-room apartment, stifling this time of year, landlord pounding on the door.

Instead, he turned around and headed back. He estimated he'd run about five miles. Not bad for a geezer. Returning to the hotel pleasantly out of breath St. James took a shower and got dressed. His eyes fell on the FedEx box. His headache came roaring back.

What was he supposed to do with it? He took it out of the box. It felt warm to the touch. Hesitantly, as if he might contract graveyard cooties, he held it to his lip. St. James had tried his hand at most instruments including drums and flute. He was one of those people who mastered instruments effortlessly. There'd been many offers for him as a session man in the old days.

Trying to remember his first form embouchure, he blew over the hole. The bone flute issued an eerie whistle. It was more like a recorder in that there were no moving keys, just six holes to vary the tone. The tone he summoned forth was much louder than he'd anticipated and he dropped the flute. He stooped to pick it up and it was almost hot. St. James used a face towel to pick it up and lock it in the room safe.

He descended to the lobby half expecting to find Connie waiting for him, but of course there was no such thing. He thought about calling her, but it would only make him seem pathetic. St. James used his room card to enter the business center where he went online.

His Facebook page was dormant. He checked his usual sites and went to Drudge. The flashing red and blue light was on. The headline was in 26-point type:

BANSHEES SUICIDE PACT

Two young men who lived together had committed suicide through a combination of alcohol and barbiturates. An ancient vinyl version of *Beat the Manshees* was still turning and clicking on their turntable when a relative insisted the super unlock their apartment following three days of unreturned phone calls.

The article, lifted from a Sioux City newspaper, claimed that the young men had been subject to continuing ongoing harassment because of their homosexuality.

Beneath it a smaller headline read: "Cryogenics?"

St. James' phone rang. It was Connie.

"We have to talk," she said urgently.

"I'm in the business center. Meet me in the cafe for breakfast."

Ten minutes later a grim-looking Connie strode toward him with her backpack over one shoulder. She sat down opposite him in the booth and ordered coffee. As soon as the waitress moved on she folded her hands in front of her and fixed St. James in an intense gaze.

"Richard told me when you play the record backwards it contains incantations."

St. James shrugged. "Everybody knows that. We used to get 'igh and play it backwards 'til somebody complained."

"What does it mean?"

St. James shrugged. "Fuck if I know."

"Ian, this is serious. Richard told me Melchior had the incantation translated. It's ancient Sumerian—where Iran lies."

"Oi know me geography."

"The incantation warns of a day of wrath when a demon defeats his white-robed enemy, which could be either Jesus or Muhammad. It warns of a darkening of the skies."

"Oh, fuck."

"Ian, this is serious."

"Did you sleep with him?"

Connie blinked and leaned back. "You don't own me. Just because I choose to go to bed with you doesn't mean we're boyfriend and girlfriend. Look, if this is how it's going to be, I can see that you're not going to be much help with the rest of the article."

"What article? Nobody's asked me to write a bleedin' thing!"

"Ian, you caught a big fat break with this story and you know it. I like you. I really do. But if you want to finish off this ride, you had better trim your sails and tack to windward. Don't fuck up a sweet deal."

St. James sighed and seemed to deflate. "What do you want me to do?"

Connie removed a manila envelope from her backpack. "Here's a copy of the letter. Talk to Oaian. Ask him what it means."

"Don't you think, luv, that we ought to consider calling off the concert?"

Connie went white. "Yes. But we can't! Don't you understand? This thing is out of control! Or if it is under control, it's not Melchior's, or Serafin's, or anybody we know. We've got to stop it, Ian. The only way we can do that is to convince someone much more powerful than us that something awful is going to happen unless we call it off."

"Phone in a bomb threat. Works every time."

"What good will that do? They'll just reschedule, and even if someone phones in a bomb threat every day Melchior will sue to have the concert go on. He stands to make a ton of money."

"Don't get between a dollar and Burke, 'at's for sure. Any ideas? Short o' shootin' the boys that is."

"That didn't work out, did it?"

"Wanker couldn't shoot."

"Ask Oaian what it would take to derail this train."

"'Oi'll try, but he's not what you'd call the solicitous sort."

Connie sipped her coffee and set it in the saucer. "There's something else." She reached into her bag and took out her smart phone, folded out the screen and cued it up. "This is the footage I shot last night of the fight between Paddy and Kenny." She turned it on and handed it to St. James. He squinted, found the light and watched fascinated at the ferocious Kenny in the aftermath of the slap. Something moved toward him, a gray blur. He distinctly heard, "Hey, fuckwad!" The blur moved like an overexposure on old film, and Kenny reeled back as if struck.

"Jayzus Christ," St. James said.

Connie reached across the table and took the camera out of his hands. "Yeah.

"Gotta go. Gotta edit that interview. See you tonight." She stood. "Can you find another ride?"

"Yes, luv. Oi'll find another ride."

"You're sweet," she said and walked away.

"Thanks for the mercy fuck," St. James muttered.

Chapter Seventy-seven

Klapp knew he was on a ship from the rhythmic rocking motion and the creak of the hull. *Wolin*, he guessed, *with access to the Baltic.* They'd picked him up in Berlin, two members of the Mad Monks. They didn't bother to hide their tattoos. They spotted him walking along Bernauer Strasse on the way back to the youth hostel. The big Mercedes squealed to the curb ahead of him and Klapp, his mind elsewhere, dimly registered skullduggery at work. Perhaps they were going to smash the window of that jewelry store.

It was a very nice car for common burglars.

He never expected them to grab him and hit him behind the ear with a lead-loaded leather sap. They must have hit him with the ether too because he didn't regain consciousness until hours later, locked in a tiny storage room.

Klapp came to lying on hard bags of uncooked rice. A headache like a tree cutter's wedge split his brain. His hand went to his beard and drew comfort from the talismans therein. He meditated. Fifteen minutes later he felt well enough to slowly get to his feet and search the parameters of his dark and lonely cell. About eight feet by six feet. He found the door. Locked. He found the light switch.

A baleful forty-watt bulb lit up in its own tiny shark cage descending from the ceiling. The room stank of vomit and disinfectant with a subtle underlay of raw fish, borscht, and potatoes. Clever. They knew he was a Druid. By keeping him at sea they cut him off from a major source of his power, the earth itself.

"Old fool," he muttered to himself. They'd known who he was. He'd given himself away by being too sedulous. What did he think would happen, that they'd fail to notice the gnome at the edge of the stage eyeballing their every move? He had aroused suspicion, most likely their thug manager. They had learned his identity through their criminal enterprise whose tentacles extended from Coney Island to Kamchatka.

He had been too active on the web. They may have traced him through their own website which he had foolishly accessed. It was possible the band themselves had recognized him from their early years when Klapp had ridden his old BMW motorcycle with sidecar across Europe following their first tour. His relentless inquiry into the nature of Satanism and its many variations may have tipped them. He'd signed his name at libraries from Stockholm to Alexandria.

As a young man he'd been too rational to trust his instincts. That was his German heritage. Long after the band's demise Klapp came across Dead Sea scrolls that confirmed what he'd long suspected, that a terrible evil, banished from the Earth for centuries, was about to return using the seductive force of music.

Sex, drugs, and rock and roll lights the way to each man's soul.

Why hadn't they killed him? There was only one answer: his death would bring them great power but it had to be done according to the rituals. The rituals were vast and arcane, hiding within their own absurdity. But for those who had a clear vision of the religion, the rituals were an operating manual to turn humanity into a blanket of suffering whose sounds and aromas would please their satanic ruler.

Klapp had written his doctorate about Satanists' will to power from Nebuchadnezzar II to Hitler. Rasputin. Aleister Crowley. There were German ministers and American senators who were closet Satanists. It was Klapp's thesis, which eventually got him in trouble, that this Satan worship predated Judaism. Klapp's Satan was not the fallen angel of the First Testament, but a malignant, ambitious intelligence that had existed since before the dawn of civilization patiently waiting for the apes to evolve into humans so it could do its work.

This Satan, or Baal, Old Scratch, whatever people chose to call him, fed off misery and despair. This Satan, for reasons known only to the Mad Monks and perhaps not even to them, had chosen the Banshees as its instrument to power. The reason was not difficult to discern: the Banshees chose Satan before Satan chose them.

There were always young persons, mostly boys, in which the will to evil overpowered all else. The murder of small animals. Bed wetting. Setting fires. That path was well known. It had always been there.

Klapp's throat felt like forty miles of bad road. He looked around and found a six-pack of Finnish Glacier Water, twisted one out, twisted off the cap, and drank it down. Those Finns were at it 24/7 with blowtorches melting their glaciers for Finnish Glacier Water. Another sign of impending doom.

Klapp was hungry and had to empty his bladder. He looked around, found a plastic container filled with pistachio nuts. Perfect. He poured the nuts out onto one of the burlap potato bags, urinated in the container and sealed it. He sat down to crack and eat the pistachios. The sound of foghorns penetrated the hull. Klapp heard feet walking the deck above.

How long had he been their prisoner? Klapp glanced at his wrist—they'd taken his watch. They'd emptied his pockets as well, removing his wallet, knife, and passport. They'd taken his belt and the laces from his shoes.

But they hadn't touched his beard.

Klapp had studied many ancient rituals and understood the difference between Major and Minor Feats. He was, in fact, well versed in Minor Feats by way of Hoodoo, the Rituals of Thune, Atlantis, and the Scorpolonus Path. Klapp stroked his beard and found power therein.

Woven among his gray hairs were strands from the Shroud of Turin, several of Rasputin's gray hairs, tendrils of figwort, and silk from the Magician/Emperor Kang Wu. Woven among his beard was hair from the heads of Jimi Hendrix, Jim Morrison, and Janis Joplin.

Of course all these rare elements were worthless without the one ingredient that drove all the black arts, blood. The question thus became, whose blood? The professor preferred that of his captors, but he was no fighter. There were ways to disable and even kill his captors, but they would exhaust his very limited beard of tricks and he would still be on the boat.

A deep, throbbing vibration emanated from the bowels of the ship. They were about to embark. They would perform their bloody ritual and drop his body into the Baltic never to be seen again. The further the boat traveled from shore the more difficult his escape.

"It's now or never," he sang giving it a little of the old Elvis magic. He removed his laceless left boot, gripped the swiveled heel tightly and twisted, revealing a hidden compartment from which he withdrew a tiny folded carbon fiber Boga, a short Japanese style knife with a serrated edge. *You'd think a bunch of ex-cons would know how to conduct a body search.*

Klapp had little time. Any minute now the harbor director would clear the ship for departure. Klapp looked around for a piece of wood. There was nothing. He'd have to do it on the hard bag of rice. Klapp composed himself and envisioned the place he'd prepared. It was a storage locker in Leipzig. They would never think to look for him there.

He imagined the locker just as he had set it up, with its shrine to the Baby Jesus, the devotionals, the icons he'd purchased on the black market, and many of the mystic and sacred objects he'd acquired over the years.

Yes, that's it. I see it now, he thought. *I can even smell the incense.*

Placing his right palm flat on the bag, he pressed the Boga to his little finger.

CHAPTER SEVENTY-EIGHT

When St. James returned to his room after breakfast there was a message from Oaian to call him.

"We're headin' out for the sound check around two. Want to roid along?"

Why not? St. James was eager to see the freak show outside the arena. That was part of the story. "Sure."

They agreed to meet in the lobby at two. St. James phoned Connie and left a message. He took out his guitar and tried to write.

St. James was seated in the lobby at two when Paddy, Cunar, and Oaian exited the elevator. Paddy and Cunar carried their axes in ancient, battered cases covered with band stickers. All three Banshees wore sunglasses. St. James rose to greet them.

"What? No Kaspar?"

"'E's already out there," Paddy said. "Johnny on the spot, that one."

Oaian clasped St. James. "It's loik a family outing, innit?"

A limo waited for them in front of the hotel. The rear seat had a complete entertainment system, including video. Fascinated, Cunar twisted the dial, stopped on Green Day.

"RAWWWK!" he declared turning the volume up.

Paddy leaned over and turned it back down. "Behave yourself, Cunar."

They headed south on the I-5.

"What should I write, Paddy?" St. James said.

Paddy displayed his wolfish grin. "You've got most of it."

"Tell me about Lord Rathkroghen."

"He has many names. That is the one we know him by."

"In the 16th century?"

"Yes, Ian. We knew him then. And before that in lands that time forgot."

"And what do you hope to gain by this?"

"This wot?" Paddy said. "We're entertainers."

"Drop it, Ian," Oaian said. "You're me son. No harm will come to you."

"Two young men committed suicide yesterday. They found your record on their turntable. How do you feel about that?"

"Wot do I care if two poofters off themselves?" Paddy said. "They're doin' the world a favor, roight?"

"RAWWWK!"

There were several hundred people milling outside the entrance to Pacific Arena as the limo cruised slowly past. St. James looked out through the tinted windows at the tent city, young men playing hacky sack, a juggler, several mimes. As the limo passed several onlookers saluted with the horned devil sign.

On a portion of the sidewalk directly in front of the arena, cordoned off by police sawhorses, a group of several dozen sober-looking men and women paraded in a circle carrying signs: "SUICIDE IS NOT A FAMILY VALUE," "BANSHEES GO HOME," and "WE DON'T NEED NO STINKIN' BAN-SHEES."

A man of the cloth inveighed against the band while waving a Bible. Cunar lowered the rear window and stuck out his hand with the demon horns. "RAWWWK!"

Some of the onlookers cheered and then the limo was beyond them and turned onto a service road leading to the back of the stadium. As they approached they saw several service trucks, a large flatbed with one or two iron girders, and a steady string of men in hard hats like worker ants going in and out of an entrance labeled R3. Two cops stood outside a City of Long Beach police car with their arms folded.

The limo stopped in the service parking lot and they all got out, Paddy and Cunar hefting their guitar cases.

"Kaspar's settin' up me drums," Oaian said, clasping Ian on the shoulder. They approached entrance R4.

The security guard said, "Gentlemen" and signaled to the two cops who uncrossed their arms and sauntered over. A salt and pepper unit, salt short and squat, pepper tall and lean with a brush mustache.

Pepper went right up to Paddy. "Sir, may I take a look in your guitar case?"

Paddy looked surprised. "Wot's this then?"

"Sir, I would like to see the inside of that guitar case."

"Wot for?"

"Sir, I'm asking you to cooperate. This is strictly a routine matter."

"If it's routine why don't you check 'is case?" Paddy said indicating Cunar.

"RAWWWK!"

Salt said, "We'd like to see that too."

Ian said, "You don't have to show them a thing, Paddy. Not without a warrant. Maybe you should call Ninguna."

"Sir," Pepper said, "you're perfectly within your rights to ask for counsel, but you have not been charged with anything and we are asking you to cooperate voluntarily. If you do call counsel it could be some time before you get inside the arena."

Rolling his eyes, Paddy set the mammoth guitar case flat on the limo hood and undid the clasps. He opened it up. Cerberus reflected the sun like a giant mirror throwing light everywhere and momentarily blinding everyone.

The police gazed fascinated.

"Wow," said Pepper.

"Would you take the guitar out of the case please?" Salt said.

Paddy reached down and picked Cerberus up, cradling it like a baby. Beneath the guitar on the black velvet surface lay a sheet of paper with their play list.

"Would you mind opening the compartments please." Not a question.

One by one Paddy removed the little drawers which contained picks, kapos, harmonicas, spare screws, and steel guitar strings, until only one drawer remained. He opened this and showed it to Salt and Pepper. It was filled with picks.

"Would you empty the drawer please?" Pepper said.

Holding Cerberus around his neck via the strap Paddy upended the little box over the guitar case. Out fell the picks followed by a folded plastic packet of white powder. Pepper picked it up, undid the seal, stuck in his finger and brought it to his lips.

His eyebrows arched in surprise.

"Oi loik to use me own creamer in me coffee," Paddy explained.

Chapter Seventy-nine

P addy, Cunar, Oaian, and Ian entered the stadium via R4. To their left the area surrounding the entrance to R3 had been cordoned off with sheets of plywood behind which emanated banging and the occasional high-pitched whirr of a screw gun.

"Don't worry," Paddy said. "They'll be done tonight."

"What are they doing?" Ian asked.

"Oi don't know, filling holes."

"Halloooo!" Kaspar called coming toward them from inside the arena. "This way!"

"You're looking right chipper, Kaspar," Paddy said as the group joined him. They followed Kaspar down a concrete corridor that emerged in back of the stage which rose ten feet off the ground. A metal stair mounted on a dolly led up. As the band climbed the stair, Ian walked around to the front. The stage faced the side of the oblong stadium for maximum exposure. Speaker towers rose ten feet above the stage, mammoth black boxes poised to atomize the ear. Oaian's drum kit was ready. Box speakers near the footlights were aimed back at the band so they could hear themselves.

Ian paused twenty rows back and sat at the end of a long row of fold-up seats as the band plugged in, Paddy running a Flamenco riff, Cunar thumping out a bottom, Oaian picking up the beat, and suddenly they were playing something Latin and lovely. A sound man in a booth ten rows behind Ian fiddled with volumes and frequencies, talking to the band via the PA.

The band broke up as individual players worked with their sound. St. James got up and headed toward the nearest exit, G1. He emerged in the interior on the other side of R4, also sealed with plywood. Ian found stairs going up and went all the way to the top where the skyboxes surrounded the field, solid mahogany doors marked with brass plaques indicating sponsorship. St. James walked down the corridor reading the plaques. Pepsi. Sony. Wirtz Distribution.

"Excuse me."

Ian turned. A young man in gray coveralls with a white security badge and a curly beard approached.

"What are you doing up here?"

"Ian St. James. Me dad Oaian's drummer for the Banshees. We're gonna be up here somewhere watchin' the show."

"Oh," the young man said. "Oh! You won't believe this, but I have your record! This is a real pleasure, Mr. St. James."

Ian couldn't believe his luck. "So you're one of the twenty-five people who bought it."

The man laughed. "Phil Farnsworth. I'm with security. What do you want to see?"

"Burke Melchior's box. That's where we'll be sitting."

"Come with me."

Ian followed Farnsworth down the gently curving corridor until they came to a door marked Third Eye Blind Productions. Farnsworth pulled out a key ring and unlocked the door. "A whole bunch of people use this."

Ian went down two steps to the luxe skybox equipped with La-Z-Boy recliners, a rich brocade carpet, a complete wet bar, private bath, and a refrigerator. The room could comfortably seat two dozen. Ian plopped into the catbird seat, a leather recliner closest to the out-tilting window looking down on the field. Tiny Bose speakers clung to ceiling corners. The window was hinged at the top and could be cranked open.

Faint guitar and bass barely penetrated the double-pane glass. Farnsworth flipped a wall switch, and the tune-up invaded the room via the speakers. He flipped it off.

"We're tripling our security detail tomorrow night," Farnsworth said. "The cops are gonna have officers stationed throughout the stadium."

"Anybody phone in bomb threats?"

"Nope. Funny, isn't it? So many people are up in arms about this, especially the Christian right. I mean, get a life! It's a rock band for Chrissake. It's not the apocalypse."

Ian had seen enough. He got up. "What are they working on down there?"

"I have no idea. We were just told to stay away and let 'em work. Hey, I gotta kick you outta here. I've got rounds."

"'Preciate it, young Farnsworth. Will you be here tomorrow?"

"Are you kidding? I wouldn't miss it for the world."

They exited the skybox, and Farnsworth locked the door. St. James headed for the nearest stairway. As he reached it his phone chirped. It was Kaspar.

"Ve are leafing in five minutes."

"Thanks, Kaspar old sport. Oi'll be right down."

And I ain't forgetting you tried to kill me.

St. James emerged on the ground floor on the opposite side of the plywood, but a narrow walkway had been left on the outer perimeter. Pounding and ratcheting continued to emanate from behind the barrier. Men shouted at one another in what sounded like Russian. In the narrow corridor between plywood and outer wall St. James encountered a hard hat going the other way carrying a steel toolbox in one hand.

"'Scuse me," St. James said.

The man stopped.

"What are you building in there?"

The man looked at St. James. In shock they recognized each other. It was the thug who'd tried to grab Connie's camera.

The man abruptly turned and moved on.

CHAPTER EIGHTY

Melchior looked out through his home office window at the big pavilion tent that had been set up on his vast lawn. Last night had been for the industry. Tonight would be for him. Rachel Kropenski was, at that moment, shopping for a knockout evening dress on Melchior's dime.

Melissa who?

His eyes dropped to his computer where Professor Elwood Bonner had forwarded a news item:

> London, England—*A robot explorer has revealed ancient markings inside a secret chamber at Egypt's Great Pyramid of Giza. The markings, which have lain unseen for 4,500 years, were filmed using a bendy camera small enough to fit through a hole in a stone door at the end of a narrow tunnel. (Snip) The markings take the form of hieroglyphic symbols in red paint as well as lines in the stone that may have been made by masons when the chamber was being built. According to Peter Der Manuelian, Philip J. King Professors of Egyptology at Harvard University, similar lines have been discovered in a Mayan pyramid in Belize. They depict a horned figure playing a flute surrounded by winged demons bearing people aloft.*

Melchior didn't see how the news clipping was relevant. He sent the professor his thanks.

The caterers had begun to arrive. Seventy-five squabs, a ton of fresh crab meat, Spanish mussels flown in from La Coruna, Melchior's party was going to make last night look like a kindergarten recess.

For the second time that hour he summoned Stanton via the PA system he had set up for the night's festivities.

"Stanton," boomed throughout the house and grounds, down the canyon until it was lost in the scrub. Minutes later the faithful amanuensis appeared in the door looking frazzled and holding a clipboard.

"Systems check," Melchior said without looking at his assistant.

"Liquor, check. Bartenders, check. Parking lot attendants, check. Entertainment, check. Ambulance, check. Food, check. Florists, check. Everything is copacetic, chief."

"What about Kennedy and Schaefer? Did they RSVP?"

"Yup. They'll both be here."

"What about Geffen?"

"Not yet, chief."

"Make sure that ambulance stays out of sight. I don't want the guests freaking." On several past occasions guests of Melchior had suffered overdoses at his parties, through no fault of his own. He did not supply drugs, nor did he use drugs, except for Viagra.

"Chief, my daughter's down from the Bay. Is it all right if she comes by tonight and meets the band?"

Melchior swiveled and gave Stanton the fisheye. "Do you think that's appropriate for a girl of her age?"

Stanton wrinkled his nose quizzically. "Chief, she's twenty-two."

"Oh. I guess it's been a while. Sure. You keep an eye on her, do you follow? What's her name again?"

"Beryl."

"Yeah. Okay."

"Thanks, chief."

"Come with me." Melchior heaved himself to his feet. He wore a burgundy velour jumpsuit with gold piping and Itasca Lakewoods. Gold chains peeked out of the curly hair where the top was unzipped. Melchior danced down the broad stone steps with the bounce of a man half his age. Stanton, who'd been sleep deprived as long as he'd worked for Melchior, was hard-pressed to keep up.

They went out through the patio doors, around the rectangular pool to the tent on the lawn. Cases of Cutty Sark stacked behind the rolling bar. The long buffet draped in white linen and stacked with China plates, silverware, linen napkins.

"We gonna have enough ice?" Melchior said.

"I believe so."

"We run out of ice we're fucked. I might as well take my dick out of my pants and wave it around."

"Chief, we're solid on the ice."

"We'd better be." Melchior walked up to six green Porta Potties lined up near the canyon rim. "Are these clean?"

"You bet."

Melchior opened the door, stuck his head in and took a whiff. Faint odor of chemicals overwhelmed by the floral lozenge hanging from a metal bracket. "These better be outta here by noon tomorrow."

"They will be."

"What about towels? We got enough towels someone wants to go for a swim?"

"Check."

"Where ya gonna stash the ambulance?"

"A half mile up on Brier Lane. They can be here in five minutes."

"Just pray nothing happens. This tour has been meshugga from jump street."

"Chief?"

"What?"

"What's the story on these guys? They're not the real Banshees, are they?"

"If they aren't they'll do 'til the real thing comes along."

"How is that possible? Wouldn't they have to be in their sixties?"

"You know what I think?" Melchior said pulling a fat Havana from the jumpsuit's breast pocket. "Cryogenics. The fuckers faked their demise, probably to get out of their contract with me.

They crashed a plane filled with winos or gypsies or whomever, and they went to Russia, the world leader in cryogenics. They've been frozen for forty years. When the truth gets out it'll revolutionize medicine."

"Do you really think so?"

"There is no other explanation. Tomorrow I intend to have a serious sit-down with Sinaiko about the process and how I can get in on it."

"You're not thinking of freezing yourself."

"No, of course not. But once this gets out, millions will. People suffering from terminal illnesses or perhaps just people who are sick of the present world and would like to see if things improve in another fifty years, do you follow?"

Melchior checked his Tissot. "They'll start arriving in two hours. I'll be in my office. When that cunt Rachel arrives send her up."

"Yes, sir."

"And go check the street—see that the caterers aren't blocking the road. Last thing I need's another complaint from the neighbors."

Stanton walked around the stone manor to the front yard where most of the caterers were arrayed on either side of the long paved drive. The entertainment was just pulling up in a black and yellow Hummer.

CHAPTER EIGHTY-ONE

n the way up the canyon in the Banshees' limo St. James asked Paddy, "What happened to that bird you saved last night?"

Paddy smiled. "Now, Ian, a gentleman doesn't tell."

"Since when are you a gentleman?" Oaian said.

"RAWWWK!"

"I've heard about Burke's place," St. James said, "but I've never seen it. Old English manor house brought over here and rebuilt stone by stone by Chad Goodrich who later hung himself."

"S'posed to have a dungeon in the basement," Oaian said, "you know, for keeping the locals in line."

"S'posed to have a home recording studio," Paddy said. "His first hit was with the Almondines. Great girl group, catchy as 'ell."

Oaian sang a few bars of "Biker Boy" in flawless falsetto.

"That's the shit," Paddy said. "They don't make that kind of music anymore."

"You could make that kind of music," St. James said.

Paddy looked at him with amusement. "Oim just a vessel. The music comes through me, and I give it to the folks."

"Who's the composer? Lord Rathkroghen?"

"Oi don't know 'boot no Rathkroghen. What about it, Oaian? Ever 'ear of this bloke?"

"Never 'ave."

"You guys," St. James said sitting back in the plush upholstery. At least Kaspar had not accompanied them. The dude gave St. James the creeps and not just because he suspected Kaspar had deliberately put him in that car crusher. The dude looked like he was going to explode at any minute. St. James could not conceive a more unlikely prospect to bargain with Burke Melchior. Ninguna was a horse of a different color. Spanish sable, to be specific. The lawyer was smooth enough to play George Clooney.

"Wot's up with you and Connie?" Paddy said with a mischievous grin.

Waves of anger and shame washed over St. James. It had always been this way. Virtually every relationship. Crazy jealousy. Either he had it or she did, and in the end it wrecked the relationship.

St. James had thought he'd got it all out of his system but the truth was he hadn't had a serious relationship in fifteen years and wondered if he were even capable. On the other hand—and here came the rocky shoals of rage—didn't he have every reason to be furious with the two-faced bitch, not only casually tossing him like used eyeliner but taking up with that fucking creep?

Paddy stared at him with just a hint of malice. "She's a nice one, oy? Shame to let that one slip away."

St. James looked out the window. Oaian stifled a chuckle.

"RAWWWK!" Cunar said.

They rode the rest of the way in silence.

Fifty or more guests milled around the park-like property by the time the Banshees arrived at a quarter of nine. Stanton met them at the front door. "Welcome, folks, you can park any personal stuff in the first floor office, there will be somebody there at all times, and if you're doing anything illegal Burke asks you to be discreet. There are places for that sort of thing, you just have to look. Or ask."

A stunning brunette in a gray pleated skirt and cashmere sweater joined Stanton on the stoop, taking his hand. "This is my daughter Beryl."

"I've been dying to meet you!" Beryl gushed.

Paddy stuck out his hand. "Very pleased, Ducks. Where you been hidin' this one, Stanton, eh? Oi hate it when you 'old out on me."

Mike Baron

Stanton smiled and produced two laminated backstage passes on lanyards. He handed them to St. James. "For you and Miss Cosgrove. Isn't she with you?"

St. James shrugged. "I don't know where she is."

The party, including Beryl, followed the flagstone walkway toward the rear from which they heard Bruno Mars crooning over discreetly placed speakers.

"Would you sign my CD for me?" Beryl asked.

"Oi'd rather soign you, Ducks," Paddy said.

"'E'll sign it," Oaian said, "or Oi'll tell the world aboot 'is sexual peculiarities!"

"RAWWWK!"

"Mr. Odoyle ain't spoke the Queen's English in six months. Thinks 'e's a bird."

"It's the drumsticks," Oaian explained.

They rounded the side of the enormous stone house and beheld the party tent. The last rays of the setting sun magically lit the top of the mountain behind them, fat rays of gold dancing on the Pacific. Waiters in white waistcoats circulated with drinks and *hors d'oeuvres.* St. James spotted several actors even if he didn't know their names. They were all starting to look alike, like the stars of those young vampires-in-love movies.

Guests gravitated to the band, basking in their notoriety. St. James slipped off by himself to view the party from a distance. He circled the Olympic-sized pool, noting the dark rectangle of a window at the deep end, toward the house. He walked up the slope a little from where he had a view of the ocean. A puff of cigarette smoke alerted him that he was not alone.

St. James looked over. A tall man in a blue suit, dark shirt and tie was smoking a cigarette watching the sunset.

"Beautiful view," he said.

"That it is. Ian St. James."

"Dan Kennedy. You any relation to the drummer?"

"He's me dad."

Kennedy looked at him funny. "And what do you do, Ian?"

"I'm a musician."

"Must be rough, having a famous dad. Not that I know anything about it. Before last week I'd never heard of the band."

"What do you do, Dan?"

"I'm a federal inspector."

A thousand possibilities exploded in St. James' head like the Big Bang. He hardly knew where to begin. "Are you concerned there might be another death tomorrow night?"

Kennedy laughed. "Actually, I'm here as a guest. Burke knows how to throw a party. There won't be any trouble."

"Wot about tomorrow night then?"

"Several agencies are concerned and we'll be monitoring the concert very closely."

"How is it under federal jurisdiction?" St. James said.

"We are responding to requests from local law enforcement agencies."

St. James nodded. It made sense. "Do you know what they're building in the stadium?"

"My understanding is that one corridor had problems with falling concrete and that that corridor is to be sealed off during the show."

"If they wanted to seal it off, why not just seal it off? They were still working on it when I was there this afternoon."

Kennedy shrugged. "I don't know. I tell you what. I'll get someone in there before the concert."

"I think that would be smart," St. James said.

"If you'll excuse me, I think I'll get a drink."

"Nice meeting you, Agent Kennedy."

St. James watched Kennedy walk toward the bar. He turned his head to catch a little puff of excitement from the rear patio doors, pretty people smoothly moving to be in the reception line. And here came Connie on Cyril Van Horn's arm.

St. James followed Kennedy to the bar.

Chapter Eighty-two

Three Balmenachs later St. James felt better. A fellow in a rising hip-hop group motioned St. James into the pool house and treated him to a line of blow. St. James could see hip-hop's butt crack above the sagging boxers and the pulled-down jeans. They went up the hill and smoked a joint.

There. That'll teach the silly bitch.

"Man," the dude growled, "there's be some fine bitches at this shout."

"Women," St. James said and spat.

Dude looked at him. "O—kay. Omma try the hook-up. You hang tight, y'hear?"

St. James gazed down through the valley at the blanket of light far away and down below. And beyond that the ocean. He looked up. Here in the hills you could actually see stars. He looked around. His new best friend was gone. Drawn by the lights and music St. James gravitated toward the lawn gaily lit with Japanese lanterns. He arrived at the rim of a cluster of excited voices. In the center of the group stood their gracious host with his new-found poopsie on his arm, barely able to believe her luck.

St. James stared stupidly. What happened to that girl he'd brought to Axton's? Then he remembered. The week had passed in a psychedelic haze. Nor had he been doing drugs. Not until tonight. Was any of it real? What was he doing here, at a party "up the canyon" attended by industry heavyweights? It all seemed very remote and unimportant.

Van Horn and Connie bobbed to the front, Connie with a death grip on Van Horn's arm. St. James felt a bolus of concrete form in his gut and edged away. He did not want them to see him. He was afraid what he might do. And he was afraid period. Van Horn scared the shit out of him. St. James wondered if the standard weapons would work: gun, poison, clubbing.

It hadn't worked on Rasputin.

"Folks," Melchior boomed without aid of mike. "Gather round. It is my very great pleasure to present for your amusement and edification, the Magnificent Merino!"

And there he stood as if by magic in his white jodhpurs, crimson jacket, and black top hat, the beautiful Isabella by his side. Merino doffed his hat in a low sweeping bow, was about to replace it but stopped and peered inside in surprise. He reached in with his free hand and withdrew a dozen red roses which he presented to the blushing Rachel.

"For my next illusion I shall require a volunteer!" the Magnificent Merino called, Isabelle posing this way and that with hands on hips. Merino's eyes fell on Connie.

"Ah, the beautiful and courageous Connie! Would you do me the honors again?"

Connie turned paper white, whispered something urgently in Van Horn's ear, her hand gripping his bicep like a vise.

"Not tonight," Van Horn crooned. Merino looked at Van Horn with something approaching death. Or had St. James imagined it?

Beryl Bridger, Melchior's personal assistant's daughter, raised her hand. "I volunteer!"

Connie glared at her in horror, pulled away from Van Horn, and walked toward Beryl, but Van Horn grabbed her arm and pulled her back. Van Horn whispered in Connie's ear, and she nodded once, that line over her eye more pronounced than ever.

St. James wondered if he should say something.

That's right, you old soak. Make a complete and utter jackass of yourself before the industry leaders because let's face it, boyo, in your present condition you couldn't unzip your pants and take a whiz. St. James felt paralyzed.

He knew he was fucked up. Too fucked up to make sense. His only hope of preserving his dignity was to lay low and hope nobody noticed.

Merino took Beryl's hand. "Excellent! You are a young woman of uncommon grace and beauty. If you'll come this way please ..." Merino gestured toward a lone porta-potty set on a promontory overlooking the canyon, about ten feet back from the edge.

"Gather around my friends. Look all around the structure. Peer inside. There is nothing untoward, it is a portable lavatory such as you have seen many times. This one, by the way, is brand new."

He pulled open the spring held door and invited the audience to peer inside, which some did. Merino doffed his hat, reached inside and withdrew a can of Glade which he sprayed inside the booth. Everyone laughed.

He escorted Beryl into the Porta Potty. "Courage, my dear. This will only take a second."

He shut the door and turned the latch. "Now, ladies and gentlemen, if you would be so kind as to surround the booth and join hands, thus insuring that there shall be no ingress or egress in three dimensions."

"Tunnel under the toilet!" yelled a hip-hopper under contract to Melchior.

"I say thee nay, my cynical friend!" Merino sang in his East European accent. "You may upend the Porta Potty just as soon as we vouchsafe the brave Miss Beryl. In the meantime, it would behoove you to shut up and sit down!"

Everyone laughed but the hip-hopper.

St. James joined the group surrounding the porta-potty. Connie and Van Horn were not among them. They had drifted back toward the pavilion. St. James estimated Merino's crowd at about a hundred.

Merino stood in front of the Porta Potty waving a wand with a giant gemstone at one end. "Abra cadabra, ollie ollie oxen free, by the power of the spheres and the twelve lions, in the name of Alhazred the Mad Arab, and according to the ancient Masonic texts unearthed in Ethiopia during the plague of locusts ..."

Screams, shouts, a disturbance in the force on one side of the old stone manor.

"Hey!" someone shouted. A tall man with a wild mane of hair jerked himself free from one of the security guards and strode purposefully toward the crowd.

The circle around the Porta Potty let go of each other's hands and turned to stare. The tall man stumbled and went to his knees. It was Kenny Grace. St. James could tell by the way Kenny staggered to his feet that he was three sheets to the wind and wondered how in the *hell* he'd managed to drive up here from the City, or if someone had given him a ride. By all rights Grace should have been lying in a ditch with a cracked skull.

Kenny looked around with mad eyes. "Where is she?" he croaked.

"Where's 'oo, Kenny?" Paddy appeared out of nowhere.

"Shelly, you fuckin' fake-ass punk!"

"She's in the loo, mate. There's quite a line as you can see."

"You lyin' piece of shit."

"It's the truth, Kenny. Go take a look"

Kenny strode to the porta-potty and practically ripped the door off its hinges. For a minute no one could see because Kenny blocked the entrance. Motionless. He reached inside and pulled out Shelly.

CHAPTER EIGHTY-THREE

By the time St. James returned from the bar Grace and Shelly were gone. St. James stumbled and fell on his ass, spilling his drink all over his pants. *Well that's a new one on me*, he thought. He could use another bump. He looked around for his pal the hip-hopper.

Here came Stanton, Melchior's toady boy. St. James pitied the man.

"Have you seen my daughter Beryl?" Stanton asked with a worried expression.

"Sorry, old chum. Not since she went in the porta-potty."

Stanton stalked off. Where had his daughter gone? With the elephant, probably. St. James somehow got to his feet and returned to the bar. Got himself another Scotch and headed for the main house. *Always wanted to look inside, bit of old Blighty and all that.*

St. James entered through the patio doors and heard laughter and music from several sources. He wandered through the vast chilly kitchen and found a hall in back with six doors. Had to be a bathroom somewhere. 'Cause nobody was going to use those porta potties now! St. James turned a knob and pulled open a door.

"Hey!" a man shouted bent over a woman on a bed. They were both naked. St. James recognized a movie producer.

"Sorry," he said shutting the door.

Careful old chum. It really wouldn't do to go poking your nose into other people's business. He wondered in which room Connie was fucking Van Horn. There's a shocker, eh? As if he couldn't have seen that one coming.

Behind another door he heard the unmistakable snork of coke intake. He knocked softly.

"Go the fuck away!" called a woman.

"It's Ian St. James. I only want a bump."

Furious discussion. After a minute the door opened revealing a glamorous middle-aged redheaded studio exec and her European boy toy. St. James vaguely remembered meeting them earlier.

The woman shook a line out for him on the marble bath counter top. "Help yourself."

St. James accepted the sterling silver coke straw, bent down and hoovered it up. *Well that was a bit of all roight.* Feeling chipper already. Quite good enough to drive down the mountain himself if need be.

"Madame is most gracious," he bowed at the waist.

"Don't tell anyone," the woman said. "Burke doesn't like people to do blow in the house, as if he never does."

"Fucking hypocrite," said the boy toy.

St. James excused himself. He headed back through the kitchen. As he was about to pass from the kitchen into the mudroom, a wooden door to his right slowly, silently swung open. St. James looked at the dark rectangle, feeling an arctic breeze emanate from the depths of the house.

The cellar stairs. A bolus of panic rose in his chest, and he shivered. All because of that time he stayed with the Varley clan for three months, three long hellish months. Not because of Mum and Dad Varley. They meant well. Good Church of England types eager to extend a helping hand to a lad in need.

The Varley's natural son, Dirk, was another story. He was a bully, a loud, obnoxious blowhard who literally threw his weight around and delighted in humiliating Ian. The Varleys had had other foster children before Ian and likely had others after him. All lived in fear of Dirk and his sadistic practical jokes.

The Varleys lived on a small farm east of Cardiff. On a November Sunday when the senior Varleys had gone to church,

Dirk unveiled his masterpiece. St. James should have guessed something was up by Dirk's absence throughout the morning. St. James was reading *Lord of the Rings* in his garret under the eaves when Dirk's heavy tread ascended the old farmhouse's wooden steps like the march of the Gestapo.

St. James quailed, a twig-thin boy who had not yet begun to fill out, already familiar with Dirk's fast hands and filthy mouth. Dirk leaned in the door leering.

"There's our young prince! 'Allo, Ian. Ever seen the old man's military uniform? Oh yeah, Perry was a right proper soldier in Cyprus. Got a bayonet, a drawer full of medals, even kept his old service revolver."

What boy could resist touching a gun? Not even St. James, although he remained suspicious. "Where is it?"

"It's in the basement. Come on. I'll show you."

"Why don't you bring it up here?"

Dirk took two steps to the bed, seized young St. James by his outsized ear and dragged him out into the hall. "Go on, you bloody twat! What are you, afraid of the dark?"

Dirk kicked and shoved the hapless St. James down the pyramidal stairs, through the kitchen to the basement stairs, leading down into darkness. St. James had been there a couple times since he'd arrived, but always with Mrs. Varley, whom he helped with the laundry. The basement itself was always dark despite a pair of windows at ground level and some weak bulbs screwed into ceiling mounts.

St. James stopped at the head of the stairs. "You go first."

Dirk wrapped his meaty arm around St. James' head and held him down in a headlock. "You little wanker! Get your ass down there!" Dirk threw St. James down the stairs, causing him to stumble and roll painfully, the edge of the wooden stair digging into his back. Near the bottom St. James looked up. Dirk grinned.

"Have fun!" And he slammed the door shut and locked it.

For the first time St. James noticed that no light was coming in through the two basement windows. Dirk had blocked them with blankets. The faintest light shown around the edge and at the top of the stairs, but not enough to navigate.

St. James sat on the bottom stoop breathing hard. There was nothing to be afraid of. It was just a dark cellar. Why did he even subscribe to this irrational fear? Wasn't his old man a consort of Satan?

St. James sat there for several minutes before he became aware of the sound. A minute scruffing. There it was. Then it stopped. St. James' hand crawled up the rough stone wall to find the light switch at the base of the stairs, but of course Dirk had removed the bulbs.

Then came the breathing, shallow rapid breathing with an undertone of rage. It came from one of the far corners of the room. St. James held his breath, afraid of making the slightest noise.

That steady whistling rasping. What was it? St. James' imagination conjured demons from the deep. Quietly he rose to his feet. The rasping increased like some marine engine revving up. As quietly as he could St. James climbed the steps, carefully placing each foot next to the wall to avoid the slightest noise.

Halfway up the rasping emitted a high-pitched squeal and came at him. St. James panicked, taking the stairs two at a time, hurtling into the door with sufficient force to break the old hasp and slam it open. St. James didn't stop, running by Dirk sitting at the kitchen chair doubled over with laughter, right out the kitchen door into the yard.

One second later Dirk screamed and followed, kicking madly behind him at a mass of fur with its fangs sunk in his ankle. St. James watched in astonishment as Dirk stumbled across the yard trying to shake his assailant loose.

Dirk had located a rabid badger and somehow put it in the basement.

It was Dirk who had to receive six extremely painful anti-rabies injections through his stomach, but it was St. James who carried with him a horror of basements for the rest of his life.

Chapter Eighty-four

St. James braced himself, seized the basement door, and pushed it firmly shut, hearing the spring-loaded bolt slam home with a satisfying click. Instantly he felt warmer.

And stay shut, you fuckin' nightmare.

He exited behind the kitchen and found himself by the pool. He stumbled, finding a wrought iron bench semi-concealed by flowering bougainvillea clinging to an arched trellis. Ouch. Bit hard on the old tailbone. From here St. James had a gauzy view through the vines of the party against the star-splashed sky. He looked down. Still had his drink in hand. Who said he'd lost his touch?

He lifted the highball glass to his lips, ice tinkling. "Cheers," he said.

"Bottoms up," said a voice so close St. James rose two inches nearly losing his drink.

He looked over. A pale, thin man with long flaxen hair and a proboscis like the conning tower of a submarine sat next to him staring out to sea. The man wore a pale blue bowling shirt with the word "Goodie" stitched in red and jeans stuffed into cowboy boots. He had an enormous pistol stuck in his belt.

"Wot's with the gun, mate? You're not gwineter shoot somebody, are you?"

"Hardly. I like guns. I've always carried guns. An armed society is a polite society."

"Wouldn't know. 'Ow you know Burke?"

"I've known Burke a long time," the man said. "I sold him this house."

"Cor. You ain't Chad Goodrich?"

"Call me Goodie."

St. James chuckled. Why the fuck not? Enough drink and blow you're apt to see Bill Shakespeare.

"I like you Ian. I've always liked you."

"'At's funny 'cause Oi don't remember you at all."

"It doesn't matter. It's good that you're here. Do you believe in God, Ian?"

"I'm not having this conversation."

"I do. I always did. No matter what was going on in my personal life, I always went to Mass and I confessed. Oh yes, I confessed, Ian, and in all the history of Catholicism, few have had as much to confess as me. Short of your mass murderers, there is. I'm not bragging, it's just the way it was. I was the original party animal. Partied with your old man, London, 1974. Ask him about it."

"Oll roight."

"If there is a Satan, and I believe there is, there must be his opposite, are you with me?"

"Oim with you, Goodie. Keep goin'."

"I was such a sinner I did all I could to atone. I gave generously to the Archdiocese. I even had the archbishop bless my swimming pool, for a suitable donation, of course. Absolution every time I took a dip."

Goodie grinned cadaverously. "The absolution solution. I thought if I was a good enough Catholic in the daytime, I could do what I damn well wanted at night. Then I shot that girl. I didn't mean to, but then again, I did, if you know what I mean."

"'Aven't a clue, Goodie. But keep goin'."

"Frigid bitch, a real cock-teaser. Been stringing me on for weeks. So one night after I treat her at Papayo's and buy her a diamond tennis bracelet and an eight ball of coke, she laughed at the size of my dick. So I shot her. You can understand that, can't you?"

"Oi certainly can, Goodie. If there's one thing Oi know, it's back-stabbing, lying ass bitches."

"That's the spirit! But I confess, not all my atonement could erase the evil that resides in these walls."

"What walls?" St. James said.

Goodie gestured toward the house. "These walls that belonged to Laird Melchior, who tore down Castle Rathkroghen and used the blood-drenched stones to build the house. Rathkroghen's stones. Melchior Manor."

"Aha!" St. James said. "Now we're getting somewhere. So you know this Lord Rathkroghen."

"He is but a manifestation of an ancient evil that goes by many names. If you burn the house with Rathkroghen in it you'll likely kill the curse, at least for the foreseeable future. These things never really go away. Not entirely. And I don't mean just anyone, laddie-buck. I mean you personally because of the blood tie."

St. James nodded. "Makes sense. Makes as much fuckin sense as anything else out here. Why's it so bleedin' cold all the time? You got the AC on?"

No answer. St. James turned. He was alone. He looked down the slope to spot Stanton still searching for his daughter. Melchior stormed out of the house, followed Stanton until he was within range and hurled a shot glass at him. It struck Stanton in the middle of his back. Stanton stiffened and turned.

"WE'RE OUT OF ICE YOU STUPID SON OF A BITCH! YOU'RE FIRED! GET THE FUCK OUTTA HERE!"

CHAPTER EIGHTY-FIVE

Van Horn picked Connie up in a chauffeured limousine. Inside there were flowers and champagne, Sinatra singing "The Summer Breeze" through the Harmon Kardon speakers.

"Wow," Connie said. "You like Sinatra?"

"The greatest singer of all time."

"How old are you?"

Cyril smiled. "Old enough."

"I can see that." In fact, Connie saw a great deal. Cyril Van Horn was uncommonly relaxed in his own skin with no need to impress. Yet impress he did, as Connie observed whenever she was around him. He exuded a natural authority. Charisma was the word for which she was searching. With his looks and his voice Connie had no doubt Van Horn would go all the way to the top.

It would be thrilling to share that ride. Was he a rock star? Hard to tell. She'd only heard him sing once, at the previous night's party, and only doing back-up. Even so his mellow baritone anchored the group.

"Are you going to sing something tonight?"

"We'll see."

"Well as of this morning Charon was still on the bill," Connie said.

"Melchior coughs, everybody jumps."

"Are you with him?"

"I haven't signed with anyone."

Where did he get the money for the clothes and the limo? The way Van Horn conducted himself he had to come from old money, possibly in the east. He had those prep school manners.

"Where did you go to school?"

"Oh, I jumped around a lot. King's College, Grinnell, Colorado State, University of Dusseldorf."

"You don't happen to know a Professor Klapp, do you?"

"Never met the man. Probably before his time."

Connie grinned. "You're pulling my leg."

"I wish I were."

Connie swatted him on the arm. "You devil!"

By the time they arrived at Melchior's it was full night and the long driveway was double-parked on either side with Bentleys, Ferraris, Mercedes, Porsches, Royce's, Beemers, two Teslas, and a Veyron. The driver drove beneath the *porte cochère*, hopped out, and held the door for Connie. Van Horn let himself out. They walked through the chilly hall toward the rear.

"Brrrr," Connie said. "Why is it so cold in here?"

"Retains the atmosphere of its native Scotland, I should think."

They exited through the patio and went to the bar where Connie ordered a White Russian and Van Horn an Odell's Myrcenary, which Melchior had delivered along with 128 other local brews by a truck that drove through all contiguous 48 states for that purpose. Connie looked around. Lots of actors, producers, and directors. She spotted Quentin Tarantino talking to Meg Ryan. Rod Stewart with a stunning redhead.

"Connie!" Connie turned around. Fred Arnold, who played a young vampire in love in *Young Vampires in Love*, was there with Mira Hofsberger, one of the new *X-Factor* judges.

"Hello, Fred. Hello, Mira. I don't believe we've met. I'm Connie Cosgrove and this is Cyril Van Horn."

Van Horn shook Arnold's hand, took Mira's. "You were superb in *Ghost Rider IV*."

"Thank you."

"What do you do, Cyril?" Arnold said. "Please tell me you're an actor."

"I'm a musician, unfortunately."

"That's too bad. I'm casting a film and you are the look, man. You've got it nailed. Any interest?"

"Perhaps if you let me sing a song in the film."

"We can talk about it."

"How do you know Burke?" Arnold said.

"I don't, actually. I'm with the Banshees. Just a friend."

"Can't wait to meet them," Mira said.

"Oh, look," Connie said. "Here he comes."

They turned to see Melchior plant his feet in front of the tent. "Folks," Melchior boomed without a mike. "Gather round. It is my very great pleasure to present for your amusement and edification, the Magnificent Merino!"

Connie's heart stopped. Van Horn looked at her solicitously. "Are you all right?"

She swallowed, nodded, squeezed his hand like a vise grip.

And there he stood as if by magic in his white jodhpurs, crimson jacket, and black top hat, the beautiful Isabella by his side. Merino doffed his hat in a low sweeping bow, was about to replace it but stopped and peered inside in surprise. He reached in with his free hand and withdrew a dozen red roses which he presented to the blushing Rachel.

"For my next illusion I shall require a volunteer!" the Magnificent Merino called, Isabelle posing this way and that with hands on hips. Merino's eyes fell on Connie.

"Ah, the beautiful and courageous Connie! Would you do me the honors again?"

Connie began to hyperventilate, her abdomen twisting in on itself like a Moebius strip. She felt as if she were literally being ripped apart. She stumbled and gripped her stomach.

What was he doing here?

"Cyril," she whispered in a barely controlled voice, "I have to get away from here."

Van Horn calmly led her away from the crowd. There was a slight look of disappointment on the magician's face. They went up the slope from whence they could see the ocean, tiny lights of freighters far out at sea.

"What's wrong?" Van Horn said.

"I ... I don't like magicians. I had a bad experience once."

"I've been following you on Twitter and *In Crowd*. That's quite a piece you turned in yesterday."

"All I did was ask questions and transcribe."

"They're very clever with their publicity, don't you think?"

"I've never seen anything like it. Plus, there's this whole backstory about Rasputin and black magic and Rathkroghen."

"I read that. What a crock."

"I'm glad to hear you say that, Cyril. I thought I was losing my mind."

They sat silently and held hands. They watched as Grace crashed the party, caused a scene, and yanked Shelly out of the porta-potty. The deejay put on Arcade Fire.

"Want to see Melchior's Ego Wall? It's really special."

"Sure."

Van Horn got to his feet and pulled Connie up. They went in through the patio, around to the main entrance and up the winding stone staircase to the second floor gallery. Walls that had once held portraits of Melchior's ancestors were now plastered with gold records, band posters, and photos of Melchior with a virtual Who's Who of showbiz going back to the seventies.

Melchior with Burt Reynolds, Raquel Welch, Faye Dunaway, Freddie and the Dreamers, Eric Clapton, band after band, face after face. And the certificates! Melchior had spread his largesse among dozens of grateful charities from the United Way to the Save the Androgynous Skink Society.

"Are you sure it's all right to be here?" Connie could practically see her breath. Outside it was in the mid-seventies. Why did Melchior keep his house so cold?

"Certainly. What good is this wall if no one sees it? Look at this." Taking her hand, Van Horn led Connie down the corridor and opened a heavy, intricately carved wood door.

"This is a guest bedroom. All this furniture, the tapestries, straight from the Tudors. Our Burke fancies himself an English gentleman rather than a vulgar, grasping Jew."

Connie blinked. He'd said it so delicately, almost like reciting haiku. "You're not a Jew hater, are you?"

"I save my scorn for individuals. I'm sorry if I offended you. Some of my best friends are Jewish."

Connie laughed. She searched for a glint of humor or irony in Van Horn's eyes.

"What about you? What are your dreams and aspirations?"

Hooo-boy. Van Horn looked good but he spoke like John Barrymore in *Dinner at Eight*. "I want my own TV show."

"And you shall have it. You have the talent, the beauty, and heaven knows you've got the brains! I was beginning to despair of ever encountering an intelligent woman out here."

That's more like it.

"I like the way you write."

She turned toward him with just the slightest hint of acceptance, and he cupped her head lightly, one hand in the small of her back and kissed her. Her hands went around his neck. Forget that Jew stuff. This was the real deal. Van Horn knew how to kiss—he didn't just slobber over her lips, he moved with delicacy and precision, tongue like a rapier.

They sat on the high bed and continued to kiss. They fell sideways on the bed and continued to kiss. Van Horn traced the contours of Connie's body. Through his silk shirt Connie felt tight muscles. The dude worked out. Then she felt his fingers at the buttons of her shirt and her own hand came up to gently grasp them.

"First date, first base is all you get, buster. We'll see about the rest."

Van Horn pulled back grinning. "Class will tell. Will you be my guest at the Banshees' concert tomorrow night?"

"I can't do that, Cyril. I'm working. I'll be all over the place. If you're Burke's guest, I'll be using his skybox. So will Serafin."

A vague unease insinuated its way between Connie's shoulder blades. Something else was supposed to happen tomorrow. What was it?

"Then we'll set something up for after that ..."

Van Horn sprang to his feet and offered his hand to Connie. "Shall we walk among them?"

They came down the curving stair just as Oaian and Cunar carried a comatose St. James by the shoulders, his loafers dragging on the marble floor, toward the front door. Connie froze, squeezing Van Horn's hand. Sensing her caution, he froze, too. They watched silently as the Banshees dragged St. James out the front door toward a waiting taxi.

CHAPTER EIGHTY-SIX

S t. James was in hell. His entire body was in revolt, from the freak waves cascading through his skull to the wolverine chewing at his guts. His face felt like someone had held it to a grinding wheel. It was the rough twine-like carpet against which he lay.

A metronomic jack hammering thundered throughout the room, every blow detonating a pain bomb in St. James' swollen head. His temples throbbed, blood elbowing its way through the constrictions like a diamond drill bit.

BOOM, BOOM, BOOM.

Luther nailing his theses to the cathedral doors.

Diet of Worms.

St. James' stomach rolled over like a lazy cat.

BOOM, BOOM, BOOM.

He opened one eye. From where he lay he could see the *Los Angeles Times* which had been shoved under his door, and the bottoms of two feet. Disconnected synapses met up, joined hands, and a trickle of current flowed through his brain.

Someone was pounding on the door. It was *déjà vu* all over again.

Prague. I'm back in Prague. Any second now that bitch is gonna yell, "You stay you pay!"

It was a relief, in a way. It had all been a bad dream. The Banshees, Connie, the whole megilla. It was also a disappointment.

Here he was, plastered to the floor in his own vomit, flat broke, the butt of jokes. At least in his dream he'd cleaned up and got laid.

Moment of truth, old sod. Keep on like you're keepin' on you're gonna wake up dead.

BOOM, BOOM, BOOM.

"Mr. St. James! Open up!"

St. James jerked his head off the floor and nearly lost it. Steady. He looked around. This wasn't Prague. This was far too nice for Prague. And then he remembered. He was at the Hotel Crabbe. The party last night. Oh God, he'd tied one on and made a complete ass of himself.

"I know you're in there, Mr. St. James!"

The voice was familiar, but St. James couldn't quite place it. "Hang on," he croaked, feeling the full effect of his desiccated esophagus. He sat up. The room gyrated like the Wild Mouse at Kennywood Park. His gorge rose. He crawled on his hands and knees into the white tiled bathroom and heaved it all into the porcelain god with great gorging vomit sounds. Over and over until his stomach churned like the starter motor on an old Ford.

His visitor heard him. His visitor was patient. St. James felt somewhat better after the massive upchuck. Gripping the counter, he got to his feet, flipped on the switch and beheld himself in the mirror.

Behold the vampire!

His eyes were sunken, the skin dark, nasty stubble, eyes angry red planets. St. James turned on the cold water, soaked a cloth and splashed himself in the face. He filled a bathroom glass with water and drained it three times. Wiping himself with a hand towel he stiff-walked to the door and peered through the spy hole.

He didn't recognize the older man in an Oakland Raiders hoodie with the hood up.

"What the fuck you want," St. James rasped through the door.

"It's Professor Klapp! Open up."

St. James managed to open the door before staggering backwards and collapsing on his ass. Professor Klapp entered the room and shut the door. He was a far different man from the jovial garden gnome they'd encountered in Berlin. Klapp looked like he'd lost thirty pounds and had shaved off his luxurious beard. With the hood up he looked like a white supremacist down from Idaho for a rally. His right hand was bandaged with a telltale rust spot.

Klapp looked at St. James and sniffed. St. James saw the disappointment in his face.

Foin. Add your name to the list.

"It's today, Mr. St. James."

"Wot is?"

"The turning. The new dark ages. An inconceivable evil. The end of hope. Only you can stop it."

"Me? Woy me?"

"Because you're flesh of their flesh, blood of their blood."

St. James groaned. He hated this nepotism shit. It never did him much good. Sure, he got his foot in the door and his own talent got him a contract, but what had it done for him lately?

"Wot the fuck happened to you anyway?"

"They nearly got me. I was forced underground for a time, but I outwitted them and here I am."

"What happened to yer hand?"

"I cut it escaping. Now hurry. There's no time to waste. Get in the shower. Do you need some help?"

Klapp grabbed St. James by the arms and pulled him to his feet. St. James groaned again. Jayzus, he wished he were dead. He allowed the elderly professor, surprisingly strong for his looks, to guide him into the bathroom where he sat on the toilet and stripped. Klapp turned on the shower.

St. James got in and sat on the floor. His nostrils stung. He remembered doing coke but he hadn't the slightest idea how he'd ended up in his hotel room. Somebody was looking after him.

When he came out of the shower wrapped in a towel, Klapp handed him one of the little whiskey bottles from the servy bar. "Oi, you've got to be fuckin' kiddin' me."

"I am not, sir. Hair of the dog. Drink it."

"Bottom's up as me old pal Goodie used to say." St. James tossed it back. Within seconds he did feel better although now his stomach had switched to hunger mode and the panzers were on the march. Fickle organ, that.

"Let's grab some victuals downstairs and you can fill me in."

"There's no time for that, Mr. St. James! The concert begins in one hour!"

"Wot? What time is it?"

"It's six PM. Get dressed. I have a car."

St. James threw on fresh jeans and a Badger T-shirt. "What else do I need?"

The Professor's eyes flicked to the wall safe visible through the open closet door. "The flute."

"'Ow you know about the flute?"

"I did my homework, Mr. St. James. They held me for a time. They had no reason to think I could escape them. Their arrogance is their blind spot. Theirs is not the only means to an end. Lord Rathkroghen will appear at the event to eat his blood pudding, and when he does, darkness and confusion will rise in men's hearts and he will rule by acclamation."

"What blood pudding?!" The imagery roiled his gut. He wished it would make up its mind.

"The blood pudding this whole tour was designed to create!"

St. James knelt by the safe and tried to remember his personal code. Eight, thirteen, seventy-five. The day the Banshees died. The door popped open and St. James grasped the flute, wrapped in a hand towel, and brought it out.

Klapp went bug-eyed. "May I see it?"

St. James extended the flute. "Careful. It's hot."

"It's only hot when you play it." Klapp took the flute, marveling at the smooth finish, the intricate runes worked into its design.

"We 'ad it tested. It's from a twelve-year-old girl."

Klapp sighed with sadness. "I was afraid of that, but had it not been created according to their vile charter it would have no effect."

"What's it do?"

"Let's go. I'll tell you in the car."

CHAPTER EIGHTY-SEVEN

Klapp opened the door. St. James followed him down the corridor to the elevator. When they exited the lobby into the street St. James was shocked. The sky was overcast, the color of burnished steel. Klapp gave the attendant his parking ticket.

"Crikey, maybe it'll rain."

"It won't. The sky is a manifestation of the turning."

A carhop brought up Klapp's battered Dodge Neon. On the rear bumper was a sticker: GOD'S BACK AND SHE'S PISSED! Klapp tipped the man a dollar. St. James reluctantly slid into the passenger's seat.

"It was cheap," Klapp said defensively. "I only need it to bring you to the arena."

"It's foin. Crikey, me head feels like it was struck by a comet."

"There's food in the back seat."

St. James twisted and found a paper grocery sack. He dug out a cold can of Coke, a package of beef jerky and one of shelled sunflower seeds. St. James dug in.

The on-ramp to the 405 was choked. They moved at glacial speed. Klapp kept shaking his head.

"Don't hit the bleedin' horn," St. James said. "Someone'll shoot us."

The car lacked air conditioning. The windows were wide open admitting that peculiar mix of air, exhaust, and bullshit unique to the West Coast.

"How'd those fuckin' Russians get involved anyway?"

"Sinaiko's father was their pilot."

St. James looked at the wizened homunculus in astonishment. "What?"

"Yes. He was a WWII Russian ace. Shot down three Stukas and a German bomber. Defected in '61. The Mad Monks have had this in the works since Rasputin."

"Since Rasputin what?"

"Since the days he held power in St. Petersburg."

"But they're not bringing back Rasputin! It's this Rathkroghen wanker, innit?"

"They have been tricked, my friend, by the master trickster. When we get to the arena we have to find Rathkroghen and stop him. Don't let him partake! Once he tastes the blood pudding his power will increase a thousand fold. Do you believe in God?"

"Aw Jayzus," St. James said with his mouth full. "Here we go again. Yer not gonna hit me with that holy roller shite, are ya?"

"Shut up and listen. The flute is only effective if you believe in God! Otherwise it's useless."

"All roight, let's say for the sake of argument I believe in God. What happens when I play the flute?"

"He'll stop whatever he's doing and come for you. He cannot abide the sound of his flute played by a believer."

"Well, you know my image of God ain't exactly an old man with a beard, no offense. More like a spiritual entity that can't be envisioned."

"That's fine."

"It's a big fuckin' stadium. How'm I gonna find him?"

"He'll come for the sausage."

"And how will I find the sausage?"

"It will be obvious."

They drove south on the 405 at thirty miles an hour surrounded by low-riders pumping enough bass to trigger the San Andreas Fault.

"We've got plenty of time. Charon's opening, remember?"

"You haven't heard?"

Ice cold water dribbled down St. James' spine. "What?"

"Kenny Grace piled up his Maserati driving back from Melchior's party. He's dead, and so is his girlfriend."

St. James looked at the lowering sky through the windshield. The city smelled of sulfur.

How could anyone let Grace drive in his condition? Why had no one stopped him? Where was security or his friends? Where was Woody?

God help us. There were no atheists in foxholes. St. James gripped the flute like a short sword. Traffic picked up, and soon they were going forty but at that pace it would still be an hour before they reached the stadium.

"Did Stanton find his daughter?" St. James said.

"I don't know a thing about that. I pray we're in time."

St. James consoled himself with the fact that bands never started on time. Particularly the Banshees. With Charon gone Melchior had to have booked a last-minute opening act. He doubted an arena audience would sit still for Merino the Magnificent. St. James looked past Klapp's face. Several miles to the east thick smoke rose from two locations.

The *whup-whup* of a chopper closed in from behind. They looked up as a big civilian job hovered over them heading southwest, carrying the Banshees to their gig. St. James read the distress on Klapp's face. The traffic slowed to a crawl again. Up ahead cars exchanged gunfire.

From far behind came the *whoop* of emergency vehicles, louder, louder, until they appeared behind them on the inside service lane, three police cars, lights strobing. The Neon was in the left lane. As the last of the three cop cars *whooped* past, Klapp yanked the wheel, pulled onto the service lane, and laid on the gas.

"Are you bonkers? They'll arrest us!"

Klapp hunched white-knuckled over the wheel. "No they won't. Whatever they're rushing to, it's far more important than us."

St. James gripped the ceiling handle and snugged his seat belt. He wondered if the relic had air bags. He hadn't been inside a church in twenty years. He offered up his second prayer in as many minutes.

St. James spoke through gritted teeth. "What do you mean they had you?"

"They caught me in Hamburg, the Mad Monks. They thought they were resurrecting Rasputin. I tried to disabuse them of that notion, but they're so mired in their narrative they can't conceive of another, older power."

St. James looked out the window. Passengers in cars to his right were alternately flipping them the bird and cheering them on. "How did you get away?"

"A little luck, a little divine intervention, and a little DNA." Klapp held up his and, and for the first time St. James noticed that the pinkie was missing, the stub covered with a bandage.

St. James stretched his head to look behind them. Great. A police car was a hundred meters back and closing fast. There was literally no place for the Neon to go other than forward. The lane to their right was bumper to bumper.

Abruptly the cars stopped altogether as a number of highway patrolmen had halted traffic to clear a path for the emergency vehicles all the way to the right and the Lakewood Boulevard off-ramp. Policemen yelled and blew their whistles. One jumped in his car ready to give chase, but another cop pulled him out, pointing to the cop car right behind them which blew through at 110.

Hunched over the wheel like a senior citizen on his way to the VFW, Klapp kept the pedal to the metal. It must have been one of those souped-up Neons because it was going 110. They followed the screaming cop cars all the way to Pacific Arena where a scene of utter chaos greeted them.

Klapp didn't even slow. He veered right between the orange plastic stanchions into the vacant lot across the street from the stadium that had been turned into a tent city. It had grown exponentially since yesterday. There were now thousands of people on the big lot and another thousand across the street. Numerous loud arguments echoed up and down the road.

From further south came the roar of dozens of unmuffled Harleys. St. James climbed a billboard advertising *Pirates of the Caribbean IX*. The Insane Assholes were arrayed against a group of Christian bikers who were every bit as filthy and as tough. Two blue uniformed highway patrolmen parked their Kawasakis between the two gangs trying to keep them apart.

St. James counted five news copters circling the stadium. Five points of a pentangle. Thousands of people lined up outside the main entrance, pressing to get in. The police had their hands full, so no one followed Klapp and St. James into the lot.

St. James climbed down and retrieved his backpack. "What now?" he said to Klapp.

"We've got to get in there."

The front was a mad house. St. James waited for a break in the traffic and headed across. "We'll have better luck in back. I've got a backstage pass."

They worked their way through the mob to the sidewalk and headed south.

CHAPTER EIGHTY-EIGHT

The police had cordoned off the rear. The work trucks and workers were gone. As Klapp and St. James approached the barrier a uniformed cop said, "There's no access back here, gentlemen."

St. James showed the cop his laminated backstage pass for the Banshees at Pacific Arena signed by Burke Melchior. Even a beat cop knew that name.

"Okay, you can go. What about you?" he said to Klapp.

"I have no pass."

"Sorry, sir. No one gets in here without a pass."

Klapp shrugged philosophically. "I'll meet you inside."

St. James squeezed between two sawhorses.

"Just a minute," the cop said. "Open your backpack."

St. James unzipped his backpack and held it open for the cop. The cop reached in and pulled out the flute. "What's this?"

"It's a flute."

"You're a musician?"

"Yes, sir."

"Well go on. I doubt a flute can be heard over the noise they're going to make."

St. James was relieved to see three ambulances standing by. A highway patrol motorcycle was parked near the rear entrance. The sky seemed even lower, a lousy night for fireworks, but at least there was no rain. St. James had seen it before like this. Not often, but often enough to know it would blow over without showering a drop. A thickset man in a wife-beater, arms covered with tats, checked passes at the door.

As the man mulled over St. James' pass, St. James noted Rasputin's image emblazoned on the checker's bicep. The thug handed back the pass and grunted. St. James was inside the stadium. His first thought was to go to the skybox, but Klapp had said the sausage factory was on the ground floor and it would be obvious.

The interior was gelid. Angry buzzing, as if from a million yellow jackets, filled the air, scraping nerves raw. St. James looked up half expecting to see them. The ceiling was bare.

St. James looked down the corridor and was surprised to see the plywood edifice from the day before still in place. Above and beyond the angry buzzing, and the screaming and honking that slipped in off the street, he heard the grunt and gasp of humanity on the other side of the plywood. Curious, he approached.

The unmistakable *kerrang* of Cerberus echoed through the great hall.

What the fuck? The sound check was yesterday! St. James looked at his watch. The Banshees weren't due to perform for another fifty-five minutes. Something else was odd. The concession stand to his right was closed. There should have been a lot of people back here. Where were they? Why wasn't it open?

And if the arena was sold out, who was in that that long line snaking back from the main entrance? Had they oversold? Melchior of all people knew that was a no-no.

The angry buzzing reignited his headache from earlier. He had a sudden urge to bolt for the men's room, but enough was enough for Christ's fuckin' sake! He swallowed the bolus of nausea, took a deep breath, and headed for the barrier. Suddenly a man appeared, blocking his path. St. James recognized the little pig eyes alive with fury. The Russian would love nothing more than separating St. James' head from his body. St. James instinctively glanced at the man's biceps looking for Rasputin.

The thug started toward him.

St. James did a U-turn and ran down the aisle to the main floor. Even on his worst days he could outrun some muscle-bound palooka, especially now with the hernia taken care of.

Write what we tell you. Everything will be yours.

He stepped outside onto the field and looked around. Several thousand people were seated throughout the stadium but it was far from full. Where were all the people? The sky looked like crumpled aluminum, the *whup* of the choppers drowned out by the band playing a fast blues, Paddy singing but the words were indecipherable. They didn't sound English.

A horrendous fireball smote the sky. St. James looked up. Two of the news choppers had collided and were falling to earth in an entanglement of death, trailing black smoke. An instant later the expanding sphere of gas knocked him to the ground. The helicopter disappeared behind the rim of the stadium with a sickening report. It landed on the Pacific Coast Highway accompanied by screams, the shriek of metal on metal, and the blaring of horns. Sirens wailed. Three helicopters converged to film the damage, oblivious of the danger. The audience surged and moaned toward the exits. They hadn't signed on for this.

St. James looked around like a mad dog. No one had taken them seriously, and now it was too late.

The plywood edifice masking the tunnel's terminus—the one they'd been working on—was still up. Paddy ended his blues with a blood-congealing howl. In the momentary lull St. James heard screams and groans coming from behind the barrier. The sounds of madness. The band launched into Rick Derringer's "Let Me In." St. James picked up the pace. Paddy elicited great pealing stadium riffs from Cerberus, bent backward in an ecstasy of destruction.

St. James ran. He ran up to the plywood barrier where one side had been crudely fastened to the next, seized it by several knotholes and with a strength he didn't know he possessed ripped the wall away exposing a scene from hell.

A human sausage machine.

The corridor ended in a stainless steel grate divided into thousands of one inch squares through which people were oozing, driven by pressure from the back of the line. That's what the workmen had been installing. It was fixed to the concrete with massive steel bolts. St. James was struck dumb and inert by its ingenuity and its cruelty. This is what the whole tour had been about as the band built buzz.

Streaks of black air shot out a foot from the grate. They rose, grew, twisted, and turned into flapping leather carnivores flitting over the panicking crowd looking for meat.

The late day sun sidled down and out of the arena. St. James looked around for cops, security, anyone. A black flapping thing snatched a woman, screaming, from the stands and lifted her into the air on crenelated wings. A man strolled around the corner whistling the theme to *The Andy Griffith Show*. His pitch and tone were perfect, clear as a bell.

Van Horn wore his shades but smiled at St. James and gave a little wave as he headed toward the grate through which people oozed like hamburger.

CHAPTER EIGHTY-NINE

St. James ran at Van Horn and tackled him. For an instant Van Horn was inert and went down like a cheap lawn chair. St. James straddled him and wailed away, striking the beautiful face again and again until his fists ached. A terrible squealing scraping noise caused him to look at the grate. An eye oozed from its socket like an egg yoke. Flesh and fiber mixed together under the relentless pressure from the rear. Faint screams could be heard through the barrier of flesh.

Van Horn turned over, got his foot into St. James' gut, and blasted him like a human cannonball ten feet through the air. St. James landed hard on his back, the wind knocked out of him, his backpack digging painfully into his kidneys.

Aw Jayzus, don't break the flute.

Van Horn stood breathing heavily and glaring, his face a mask of hate behind the bug-eyed shades which had somehow survived the beating. Van Horn composed himself, straightened his shoulders, and turned toward the grate. St. James grasped his backpack and yanked out the flute. He got to his knees. Van Horn surveyed the enormous oozing rectangle like a tourist at a Las Vegas buffet.

A foot from St. James the turf exploded showering him with a sprinkling of dirt. St. James twisted, his gaze going to the top row on the opposite side of the stadium where a figure sat on the top bench carefully sighting through a scope as he brought his rifle to bear. The setting sun reflected off his wrap around gold shades turning them red.

St. James juked sideways, brought the flute to his mouth and tried to blow. He had no breath. His throat was as dry as the Gobi. Van Horn reached out and seized a gobbet. St. James found some air deep down in his lungs and pushed it out over the mouthpiece producing a surprisingly clear tone.

A bullet smacked through the grate into impacted flesh.

Van Horn shuddered and whirled. Again he composed himself and straightened up, uncurled his claws and drew his hands through his thick hair.

"That's my flute," he said sweetly.

Using his shadow for a guide St. James moved so that he was in a direct line between the rifle and Van Horn. "How's it yours? Did you make it?"

"It was made for me." Van Horn held out his hand. "May I have it?"

St. James brought the flute to his mouth and rippled through the keys searching for a system. Van Horn subtly hardened and came toward him. St. James bobbed, weaved, blew a piercing blast and segued into "Soldier of the Cross." Something flapped overhead, and out of the corner of his eye St. James glimpsed a black and leathery creature rowing through the air bearing aloft a shrieking Goth girl. A barrier had been breached. Other black wraiths rose on leather wings all around the perimeter sending concert-goers screaming into the aisles where they scrambled over one another in a mad dash to get away.

St. James played the song loud and clear. Van Horn stiffened, bent at the knees, clapped his hands to his head, and howled, a rising ululation of pain and rage that rose and rose until it was the volume of a jet afterburner drowning out the band, the flute, the very sky.

St. James continued to play. A bullet ricocheted off the steel grate with an eerie whistle.

Spaced evenly around the arena rim, five pyrotechnic stations erupted sending gouts of flame into the sky, singeing the bottom of a low-flying helicopter. St. James caught a glimpse of the LAPD logo before the chopper erupted into an expanding ball of white-hot gas that knocked St. James to the ground. The helicopter plummeted, whirling blades sweeping the top row of the stadium slicing through flesh and tossing blood. St. James watched in awe as a tiny black object hurtled through the air like a Hail Mary pass, landed on the infield, and rolled to a stop at Ian's feet.

It was a head, sightless eyes staring at the nightmare sky. It was the thug with the Rasputin tat who'd checked his pass. His neck had been cleanly severed exposing the white spine, the mass of arterial tubes, the ooze of blood, like something in an open-air butcher shop in Tunisia. St. James had seen dead bodies when he'd worked as a gravedigger. They'd been embalmed. He swallowed fighting a gag reflex. Breathe in, breathe out.

The burning helicopter crashed into the infield melting metal chairs. A wall of heat enveloped St. James. He thought his clothes would catch fire. St. James fell to the ground and rolled. Outside the stadium sirens raged.

Van Horn whirled and ran for the grate. St. James bounced to his feet and blew a piercing blast just as Van Horn reached the oozing mass of flesh, reached out, and jammed something into his mouth.

St. James felt a divine strength fill him, his lungs filled with air, and he advanced with flute to mouth piping like Hubert Laws. Van Horn whirled, hands to his ears. His sunglasses fell off, and for an instant, like a subliminal frame in a movie, revealed his true face. Its sheer hate-filled ugliness struck St. James like a hammer blow. He reeled back, knowing that he would never be able to exorcise that image as long as he lived.

Shutting his eyes, he bent over his flute and made the bone sing loudly, clearly, and now it was the flute he heard, pure as morning's first light even as his lungs inhaled the scent of burning aviation fuel and human flesh.

A hideous, metallic ripping sound filled the air. St. James opened his eyes. The awful steel grate that had been grinding people up bulged outward at the top. An instant later it slammed to the ground with a muffled bong, and dead people spewed from the vile sewer.

Van Horn was nowhere to be seen.

CHAPTER NINETY

The LAPD chopper crash sent a shockwave through the arena felt by every sentient being. Ticket takers, concession clerks, and ushers abandoned their posts. Confusion reigned. A mushroom cloud of dense smoke rose from the arena.

Professor Klapp entered amid the flood of people trying to get out. He was inside a human transistor going the other way. Klapp put his hands together in front of him palm to palm, fingers pointed forward. He called it the Wedge, and it worked. With the Wedge leading, Klapp made his way through the panicked crowd, down the long corridor onto the arena floor. He was directly opposite the gate, unable to see past the fiery wreck of the helicopter. A black leathery thing flapped close, didn't like what it saw, and flew away.

Dire wraiths. The vermin of Lord Rathkroghen's world pouring into ours through the conduit of the blood sausage. Klapp prayed that St. James held up his end. Klapp couldn't do a thing about Rathkroghen—that was St. James' particular cross to bear. But Klapp knew how to deal with the dire wraiths. He had to get above them.

Klapp turned back to the seats, up the concrete stair to the rows of benches and climbed steadily toward the top tier. Inside one of the skyboxes would have been better, but Klapp didn't have the time to go back inside the arena, climb the stair, and find one that was open. Grimly determined, he put one foot in front of the other, feeling every minute of his sixty-eight years, the backpack weighing heavily. He paused panting at Row 25. An intact bottle of mineral water lay at his feet where it had been abandoned. Klapp reached down, opened the bottle and gratefully upended it.

An hysterical scream assaulted him. Klapp whipped around to see one of the flapping creatures carrying aloft a thin young man. The creature had him by one arm, its black talons digging deep into flesh. As the man struggled he rained objects: cell phone, wallet, keys. Klapp instinctively reached out to grab him but the man was too far away. Klapp watched the creature carry its burden over the rim.

Klapp resumed his climb. There was no time to waste.

Finally, he reached the top row, beneath the overhang of the skyboxes. A young man and a woman lay huddled trying to squeeze beneath the bench. The man had long hair and horn-rimmed glasses. The woman's face was buried in his chest. Klapp acknowledged them with a cautious motion.

"Stay down," he said. The arena floor was a nightmare. Charred bodies smoked where they'd fallen from the chopper. Molten metal lay twisted and intertwined with human remains; those unlucky enough to have been in the chopper's path. Confused first responders stood in the tunnel entries wondering which way to turn. Smoke from the chopper crash cut visibility to a dozen feet.

Klapp sat heavily on the top tier and opened his backpack. He removed a Hohner harmonica that had once belonged to Paul Butterfield. He removed a turtle shell guitar pick that had once belonged to Michael Bloomfield. He removed a pint of Southern Comfort—half full—that had once belonged to Janis Joplin. He removed a tube of mascara that had once belonged to Freddie Mercury. He removed a comb that had once belonged to Eddie Cochran. He removed a Mason jar, and he removed a butcher's cleaver he'd purchased at Bed, Bath & Beyond.

Opening the Mason jar, Klapp poured in the whiskey, added the guitar pick and the mascara and stirred it with the comb. He said the ancient words, Latin, Sumerian, and Mayan. He placed his right hand flat on the bench before him and gripped the butcher's knife in his four-fingered left hand.

"Little by little, Lord," he muttered, "You are whittling me down to size."

He looked to his side. The young couple huddled on the floor stared at him. "What are you doing?" the man said.

"I'm trying to stop the dire wraiths. Sir, I would appreciate it if you could give me a hand."

"What do you want me to do?"

"Come over here, and when I say the word, take this jar and fling the contents out over the stadium as far as you can."

One of the flapping things hovered with a sound eerily similar to the helicopter. Klapp gestured with the knife, and it took off in search of easier prey. The man scrambled to his knees, then to his feet. He came over hunched as if expecting a blow.

"What the fuck are those things?" the man said with a thin edge of hysteria.

"Dire wraiths. Wait until I give the word," Klapp said, positioning the knife.

"What the fuck are you doing?"

Klapp winked at him. "You think magic is easy? Comedy is easy. Magic is hard."

Klapp bore down with all his might, neatly severing the little finger on his hand launching a fire bolt of bone-flattening pain up his arm, throughout his body, and into the stadium itself. He picked up the severed finger and put it in the mason jar.

"Now!" he grunted.

The man picked up the Mason jar and with a grunt flung its contents in a wide arc.

Klapp picked up the harmonica with his and and placed it to his mouth. Putting the pain from his hand in a little box he shut the lid and placed it in the attic of his mind. Somewhere Klapp found breath and played a bluesy riff.

The black things twisted in agony, some dropping their prey, as they went into death spirals, turning to smoke before they hit the ground.

Chapter Ninety-One

A trickle of first responders appeared: firemen, EMTs, and cops. Soon there were dozens bringing out every portable fire extinguisher from the stadium and their vehicles. Someone opened a motor gate and ambulances entered adjacent the stage.

The crashed choppers sent a column of black smoke which rose eerily to the top of the stadium before swirling into eddies and arabesques. The heat had diminished but it was still close to 130 degrees on the ground, and smoke made it hard to see. Bodies lay in heaps and pieces in the stadium where they had been crushed by those trying to escape or struck by whirling helicopter parts. People lay or crawled on the ground screaming for help. The pyrotechnic stations continued to spew flame into the air and a clinging ash began to fall.

A woman thudded to her death at St. James' feet, bouncing slightly. He looked up. The wraith that had born her fell, whirling like a maple seed.

The music had stopped. Of the Banshees there was no sign.

Where was Connie?

Where was Klapp?

Grabbing his backpack St. James sprinted for the backstage exit. Inside the concrete stadium, echoing with screams, grunts, sirens, and the sounds of violence, St. James ran up five flights taking the stairs two at a time. At the top, a City of Long Beach policeman lay in the concrete corner, head twisted at an impossible angle.

St. James hesitated, eyeing the officer's automatic pistol snapped in its black holster. He stooped, unfastened the holster, and removed the pistol. A 9mm Glock. Ted Nugent had once showed him how to fire a pistol at a rock festival in Alabama. St. James flicked off the safety and jacked one into the chamber. Moans issued from behind a handful of doors as St. James ran down the curving corridor to the closed door of Third Eye Blind. He tried the handle. It was open.

He stepped down into the skybox and stopped cold. Angry buzzing permeated the room but it was not caused by yellow jackets. Literally thousands of obscenely glossy blue/black flies feasted and hovered over the mound of red meat parked in the catbird seat. The smell of a human being turned inside out was worse than that of burning flesh. Acid roiled his sinuses. The only way St. James could tell it had once been Melchior was by the man's gold Rolex lying on the floor beneath his bloody limb.

Richard Serafin was pinned to the wall by a mike stand through his heart and hung between a photo of the Los Angeles Lakers and one of Melchior posing with the President.

A groan alerted St. James to a figure slumped in the corner, arms covering his head. "No more," the huddled figure gasped.

St. James went to the man and knelt. "It's over. Who are you?"

"Stan Schaefer," the man gasped. "The Banshees—they came in here—they did this—"

"Was Connie here? Connie Cosgrove?"

"Yes. Help me. I'm on fire. I'm burning up."

"Where did she go?"

"The band took her. Help me!"

The man did not seem to have any visible wounds. "I'll send someone up," St. James promised and bolted from the room. There was only one place they could have gone, but how was he going to get there with the streets impassable? He took the nearest stairwell. As he neared the third floor, two heavy sets of treads approached from below. St. James flattened himself against the wall and brought the Glock up in both hands.

Lebed came first, his face a comic mask of shock as he confronted St. James' unlikely figure. With a snarl of rage Lebed reached for something in the small of his back and St. James let him have it, three shots right in the center, three claps of thunder filling the stairwell top to bottom.

His thumb hurt. St. James saw where the grip had pistoned through the base of the thumb. He'd forgotten about that. He'd have to adjust his grip.

St. James advanced behind his pistol. Sinaiko grabbed Lebed's automatic from the small of his back and brought it up with a thunderclap. Sinaiko's bullet ripped the Glock from St. James' grasp and *splanged* it against the wall where it fell fifty feet to the main floor. St. James' hand went numb. There was a purple welt but no bleeding.

Kaspar advanced grinning, stepping around Lebed's body, sprawled on the steps with one hand touching the landing. "This time when I kill you, you'll stay dead."

"Now Kaspar, what's Oaian gwinter to say if you kill me?"

A ripple of dismay flashed across Kaspar's skeletal face quickly replaced by a sardonic smile. "He will say too bad! That's what he deserves for trying to interfere with our glorious return. Please tell me. How did you get out of the automobile compacter?"

St. James had backed all the way to the concrete wall. Kaspar stood five feet away, too wary to come within grappling distance. The gun never wavered.

"If I'm gwinter die, tell me something, Kaspar old sod. Why are you doing this? Lord Rathkroghen isn't Rasputin."

Another wave of anxiety. Kaspar grappled with deep theological issues. "For power, you fool! Why else does anyone do anything? The Mad Monks will rule the world through the Skorzny Group! Lord Rathkroghen must have his gang, yes?"

"Then what're those black things carrying people off?"

Kaspar stared at him blankly. He looked confused. "I don't know what you mean. How did you get out of the trunk?"

St. James knew that the moment he satisfied Kaspar's curiosity he would die.

I can't die! Not like this! Where's God? I'm doing Your work! Can I get a hand here?

Lebed's hand twitched. St. James saw it out of the corner of his eye but was afraid to take his eyes off Kaspar who might interpret it as a sign of revolt or submission and open fire. St. James heard himself say, "I used the jack to pop the trunk," and steeled himself to leap. If he was going to die he would do his damnedest to take Kaspar with him.

Kaspar saw him tense and took a half step back.

Lebed's hand closed around Kaspar's ankle and, with his dying strength, pulled. He was trying to pull himself up. Kaspar half turned in surprise, and St. James rushed forward, shoved Kaspar's gun hand to one side and, as Kaspar turned back, head butted him on the bridge of the nose. The old Glasswegian Kiss. Kaspar staggered back, stepping unwittingly over the stairs, and fell. St. James followed him down the stairs kicking. One kick sent the automatic skittering out of Kaspar's reach. The second kick thudded into Kaspar's ribs. St. James thrilled to the feel of snapping bone.

Kaspar contracted into a ball and stood with his back to the wall, coming forward in a fighter's crouch. Blood poured from his nose. Kaspar snapped a kick aimed at St. James' knee but St. James was an old footballer and checked it by raising his leg. Kaspar rushed again, and St. James lowered his head and met him like a bull—the key to rugby was a low center of gravity.

The Battle of Dunkirk was won on the playing fields of Eaton.

Kaspar grunted and staggered. St. James kneed him in the groin, stepped aside, and grabbed the Russian by the back of his shirt and his belt, and gave Kaspar the bum's rush over the iron railing. Kaspar screamed all the way down until he struck the concrete with the sound of a dropped watermelon.

St. James leaned over the rail. Kaspar's body lay broken and twisted into a swastika. St. James experienced an instant of vertigo. He gripped the rail tightly and went to his knees. He couldn't seem to get a breath.

Forcing himself up, St. James bolted down the stairs three steps at a time. He didn't look at Kaspar's body as he left the stairwell.

On the first floor he buttonholed a cop. "There's an injured man in skybox 512."

"Got it," the cop said.

St. James ran for the back entrance. Outside was mayhem. Bodies lay around the stadium's perimeter like dead crows, too many to count. The sawhorses had been knocked down or pushed aside as emergency vehicles crowded the service lot. Men carried stretchers that stank of aviation fuel. Ambulances hit the lights and sirens and peeled out.

The highway patrol motorcycle had been left unattended next to the wall.

Fuck it, old sod. The only way out of here's by bike. He pulled his sunglasses out of his backpack.

St. James threw a leg over the heavy Kawasaki and was gratified to see the key in the ignition. He turned it on, found neutral, and brought the big bike to life. Nobody gave him a second glance until he was in second gear headed for the street.

"Hey! Hey!" someone yelled behind him, but then the voice was gone. Even the side streets around the stadium were in full gridlock as people tried to flee the neighborhood. Thick columns of smoke rose not just from the stadium but to the east as well. The two helicopter disasters must have seemed like terrorist Armageddon. St. James found the bike's lights and siren and turned them on.

He rode the shoulder past stupefied motorists, got on the Pacific Coast Highway, and headed north up the service lane toward the 405. A lowrider had pulled out in front of him. St. James ripped the microphone from its perch and keyed it on.

"Get that car out of the way. This is a fuckin' emergency."

The startled gang bangers immediately inserted their left front fender into the glacial flow of traffic. Soon St. James was doing eighty, two feet from the concrete lip. No margin for error. If he went down he'd look like the ground meat at the end of the tunnel.

As he turned onto the 405 more helicopters buzzed toward the smoking stadium. Several columns of black smoke were visible from all over the city and far out at sea. Traffic on the 405 was at a crawl. St. James roared up the service lane. He cut west on the 10. The sun cast long shadows. Traffic thinned, and St. James cut the lights and sirens. It was dark by the time he reached the bottom of Selden Canyon. St. James shook although he could still feel the heat of the stadium. Carefully he turned onto Selden and headed up the canyon. The motorcycle's headlight picked out a coyote crossing the road.

Burn the fucker with him in it, that's what Klapp had said.

Where was Connie?

A debilitating sensation of dread sunk its screws into his gut. They hadn't been able to stop the slaughter at the stadium, what made him think he could save Connie? Twelve miles up the canyon St. James turned off onto Siddhartha Parkway and rode up to the entrance to Melchior's long driveway. He turned in between the brick pillars. The lawn was chewed up on both sides of the smooth blacktop. A black and yellow Hummer and a burgundy Cadillac were parked beneath the *porte cochère*. A few dim lamps glowed from behind mullioned glass. The massive front door was slightly ajar.

Why did I drop the fuckin' gun?

Now all he had was the flute. Holding it close to his side he pushed the door wide and stepped inside. It was eerily quiet inside the house. And cold. His breath formed a white cloud. Why did he keep it so cold?

St. James was afraid to call out, to shatter the stillness, afraid of what might answer. A coat of arms hung in the foyer next to a pair of crossed cavalry swords. Cautiously St. James roamed the first floor, through the living room, dining room, several dens, several baths, the massive kitchen, its larder which was larger than St. James' abandoned apartment, a mudroom, etc. Not a sign of life.

From upstairs, ever so faintly, he heard "Sunshine of Your Love." Oaian always did love Jack Bruce. St. James headed for the stairs, feeling every bruise from his encounter with Van Horn. He stiff-walked up the broad stone steps to the vast art gallery landing. Several gold records and certificates were knocked askew or lying on the floor as if there had been a scuffle. St. James heard rustling from behind a door at the head of the stairs.

He opened it and stepped back. Cunar Odoyle launched himself from the utility closet swinging a Hoover Tornado like a baseball bat. "RAWWWK!"

St. James got an arm up but the impact knocked him backward against the marble banister. Odoyle jumped on him with both hands around St. James' neck. The bigger, stronger St. James merely pushed his forefinger into Odoyle's throat, and the bass player backed off gasping. St. James followed that with a goal-winning kick to Odoyle's crotch.

Odoyle smiled. "RAWWWK!" He charged.

St. James sidestepped, seized Odoyle by the back of his shirt and pants, and heaved him over the balustrade. Odoyle fell to the marble foyer with a sickening crack. St. James looked down. Odoyle lay on his back with his head at an unnatural angle, limbs twitching.

"'Allo, Ian," Paddy said behind him.

CHAPTER NINETY-TWO

S t. James whirled clutching the flute. At the end of the gallery Paddy stood with Cerberus around his neck. The guitar looked as if it were made of the thinnest ivory and contained a powerful light bulb.

"Where is she?" St. James said in a surprisingly calm voice.

"'Oo? Your bird? She's around 'ere somewhere, but be careful what you wish for, old sod. That's my flute, by the way."

"Did you kill her?"

"'Oo? Connie or the girl I made that flute from?"

"The girl."

"Oi didn't kill her. Oaian did. That was 'is specialty like. I'd like me flute now please."

St. James brought the flute to his mouth and blew, breath visibly shooting from either end of the bone tube.

Paddy grinned. "You can blow 'er all day. Won't affect me. Oi made that flute. Now it's my turn."

Paddy's hand fell to Cerberus and flew from neck to neck faster than the eye could follow. The backbone of the earth cracked exposing the marrow. The sound of a high-speed car wreck amplified a thousand times. The house absorbed the guitar's impossible peals and increased them a thousand fold bringing pressure on St. James' skull. Augers bit into both ears trying to join in the middle. St. James fell to his knees covering his ears and grimacing. The flute lay on the ground before him.

The soul crushing arpeggios died out leaving a vast booming silence in his skull. His head felt hollow. He saw Paddy's lips move, but he couldn't hear him speak. Paddy came closer. Grabbing St. James by an ear he bent down and yelled, "'OW YOU LIKE CERBERUS THEN?"

St. James grabbed Paddy's hair and yanked him face first onto the floor. Paddy landed on top of Cerberus with a metallic bong. St. James stood and kicked Paddy in the ribs as hard as he could. Paddy rolled to the side, scrambling to release the strap around his neck. The strap came loose and Paddy leaped up snarling. St. James stomped on the guitar and was rewarded with the sound of breaking wood.

Paddy charged, ramming his head into St. James' gut, bowling him over and down. They struggled on the cold marble floor. Paddy kneed St. James in the crotch. Nausea exploded behind St. James' eyes. He curled into a ball like a contracting watch spring. Paddy reached for Cerberus. St. James threw himself on top of the guitar and Paddy punched him viciously in the kidney. St. James rolled over to protect himself and heard something crack.

Paddy picked up the guitar and strapped it on. St. James looked at the flute. It lay in two pieces. St. James picked up a half and held it in his hand like an injured sparrow. It had broken at an angle creating a sharp bone point. As Paddy adjusted his guitar St. James lunged, plunging the half flute point into Paddy's neck. Blood gushed like a burst water main, rhythmically splashing St. James down the front of his shirt. Paddy swayed, mouth open in shock, one hand going to the protruding bone. He gripped the flute and pulled it out, followed by a wild gush of crimson.

Paddy fell to his knees, Cerberus striking the floor with a clang. A heavy, evil droning filled the house—the yellow jackets were back. No. It was feedback. Cerberus glowed from some internal power source. St. James reached down and flicked off the power. The lights faded away along with the light in Paddy's eyes.

St. James found the other half of the flute and fit them together. The break had been a simple fracture. All he needed was some Super Glue. Ears buzzing, St. James opened the next door and found Melchior's office. He went into the darkened room drawn by the glow through the window. He looked out the window. South and East Los Angeles were burning. He saw the orange glare reflecting off the steel-colored sky. He went to Melchior's desk and went through the drawers. In the top right drawer he found a tube of Super Glue. Sitting in Melchior's chair St. James delicately applied the glue to one half the flute then squeezed them forcefully together for a minute.

It worked. The flute was restored. St. James blew a tentative tone. Good to go. An ancient text popped into his head from a time when foster parents made him attend Bible class.

"Even though I walk through the darkest valley I fear no evil for you are with me. Your rod and your staff—they comfort me." Psalm 23.

Clenching the flute before him like a divining rod St. James left the office and searched the floor. The next room was dark. St. James felt along the wall for the switch. It illuminated a single Tiffany table lamp next to an impossibly tall and heavy four-poster bed covered with an equally ponderous brocade. Gold thread glinted in the pale light. St. James' breath hung in the air. An armoire that looked like it weighed a ton jutted from one wall. An antique French make-up table with a mirror and a settee, a coat rack heaped in coats and jackets, a full bath beyond the armoire. The closet was stuffed to overflowing with clothes, both men's and women's, the floor thick with shoes. The room was deserted.

"Not my style," breathed a reedy voice on St. James' neck. He cried out and whirled, pointing the flute like a sword. Chad Goodrich stood before him in blinding white tennis whites, shorts, and a LaCoste shirt, feet in white Nike tennis shoes, slightly transparent.

"Where's Connie?" St. James croaked.

"She's around here somewhere, but don't be surprised when you find her. All women are whores including my mother."

"Why are you even 'ere, Goodie? I mean ghost-wise."

"Sinister forces out tonight. Oh, it's a night for the ages, Ian, one we won't forget. I have seen demons spread their wings across a gibbous moon. I have seen fanged slugs slither from sewer grates to seize children and small dogs. Babies stillborn with but a single eye in the middle of their foreheads. And that business at the stadium. Terrible."

"How do you know about that?"

"I watch television. It's on in the pool house. Just terrible. People didn't behave like that in my day."

"Well Goodie, it's been noice chattin' with ya, but Oi've got to get going."

"Sure. Remember what I said. Oh. And one other thing."

"What's that?"

"What was the name of the Banshees' first album?"

"*Beat the Manshees*. Wot of it?"

But there was no one there.

Chapter Ninety-three

St. James massaged his throbbing temples. His headache had returned along with the buzzing drone. It had become impossible for him to separate the imaginary from the real. He couldn't trust his own body. Was the buzzing in his head? Like all rockers, he suffered from tinnitus. Had he tripped some internal trigger, some stray nerve like a loose wire in a jury-rigged control board that amped up the tinnitus so that it filled his head like helium in a balloon?

Why was it so cold?

His breath hung in front of his face then whisked away like a cartoon double-take.

His hearing crept back. The angry surf retreated. The great house sighed and creaked, adjusting its ancient bones. The very walls had once been soaked in blood. How could Goodie think he could bring it over and live without consequences?

If you believe in God, you must believe in Satan.

If you believe in good, you must believe in evil.

Leaning on the marble balustrade St. James opened the next door. The room was a film museum with framed posters of everything from *Birth of a Nation* to *Chinatown*. Rows of files held scripts. An immense shelving system held thousands of DVDs. A pair of Barcaloungers sat before a 52-inch flat screen TV. Opposite the DVDs was a wall of LPs arranged alphabetically by artist beginning with Abba and ending in Zombies.

St. James stuck his head out and looked down the gallery. Paddy and Cerberus were gone. St. James rushed back to the broad gallery. A smear of blood led to the stairs as if someone had dragged Paddy's body away. He looked over the rail. Cunar was gone.

Oaian?

Where was Connie?

He cupped his hands to his mouth. "CONNIE!" The stone walls played his words back to him until they marched off into the distance.

St. James turned his back on the blood and went down the hall. Bathroom. Staff office. Around the corner and down a short hall lay the massive, intricately carved door to the master bedroom. The carving showed a satyr leading a flock of children toward a cliff while playing a flute. St. James put his hand on the iron door handle, and his flesh stuck. It was like touching dry ice. Holding the flute in his fist by his chin St. James opened the door with a desiccated shriek.

A faint glow emanated from around the corner. From where St. James stood the bathroom was on his right and the bedroom straight ahead. He became aware of a rhythmic squeaking sound. A hand closed around St. James' throat. Like a man lost in nightmare he walked toward the bedroom unable to stop himself. The short hall seemed to elongate before him. He forced himself through the gelid, viscous air, a man struggling against nature. It took him forever to reach the corner.

He stepped into the bedroom proper, a dark chamber with a vaulted roof and exposed beams. The faint light came from a dim table lamp in the corner with an amber shade.

Squeak, squeak, squeak.

St. James looked at the massive four-poster bed with canopy and drapes, and saw a pale orb rising and falling in the middle of the bed. He stepped closer.

"Hey," he said.

The man on top turned toward him quizzically. It was Oaian. Connie brought her head up beneath him.

"Ian," she said stupidly.

"'Scuse me, old sod. Bit of privacy please?"

A mule kick to the gut. Oaian straightened, turned, pulled out a dick like the Queen's scepter, and sat on the edge of the bed. "Ian, lad, would you mind leavin' us alone for a few minutes? There's a good boy." His ten-inch penis bobbed like a metronome. A demon's face had been tattooed on the head.

"GET AWAY FROM HER!" St. James roared running forward and smashing his father in the face with his left hand. Oaian fell to the burgundy Persian rug and lashed out with his foot, buckling St. James' leg and causing him to stumble back and land on his ass.

Oaian bounced to his feet, seized a stoneware bowl from the sideboard, and smashed it over Ian's head. He kicked Ian under the chin causing his jaw to slam shut with an audible click and bringing stars to his eyes. Oaian's second kick sent the bone flute flying. It hit a wall tapestry and slid to the floor.

Oaian picked up a free-standing ashtray made of turned walnut and brought it down on Ian who barely managed to get an arm up. His arm took the brunt of the blow and turned numb. Ian scrabbled backwards on his ass as Oaian advanced swinging the heavy stand, dick flopping between his legs. Ian backed hard into the sideboard sending a porcelain container to the floor. The lid fell off and spilled a delta of gray ash onto the carpet.

Oaian wanged the ashtray off Ian's left thigh sending a shock wave across his body. Without thinking Ian grabbed a handful of the chalky dust and hurled it in Oaian's face. Oaian stepped back choking and rubbing at his eyes.

St. James stood, pulled a heavy wooden drawer out of the sideboard, lifted it above his head like the Ten Commandments, and brought it down on his father with a resounding *thunk*.

Oaian staggered. Ian kicked him between the legs. Oaian went down groaning. Ian looked at Connie who was sitting up with a satin sheet drawn over her breasts. "Put something on. We've got to get out of here."

Connie looked at him dazed. He'd seen that look on junkies. She shook her head slowly. "What?"

St. James found her clothes in a heap at the foot of the bed and tossed them to her. "Get dressed! We've got to get out of here!"

Connie did a double-take, eyes going to the writhing naked man on the floor, back to Ian. Wordlessly, she grabbed her clothes and put them on.

Where was Van Horn? If he let Van Horn go it was all for naught. Connie slipped on her shoes and stood. Ian took her hand and pulled her out of the room, shutting the door behind him leaving his old man writhing on the floor.

"Have you seen Van Horn?"

Connie looked at him with startled eyes. "Van Horn? He was in the skybox. We were all in the skybox. I don't understand. What am I doing here?"

"Come on, luv." He pulled her down the long hall to the blood smear at the top of the stairs. Connie inhaled sharply and stepped around the blood. They went down the stairs avoiding the trail of blood that did a sharp U-turn on the main floor and headed for the kitchen.

St. James pulled Connie out of the house and led her to the burgundy Cadillac. It was unlocked. The keys were in the ignition. "Sit here. Do you have a phone?"

"My purse!"

"You can't go back in there. I'll get it. Take this." He handed Connie his phone.

"Call 911. Tell 'em there's a fire. Whatever you do, don't go back in the house, do you understand me?"

St. James looked at his hands, bewildered.

Connie began to cry. "What's happening?"

"What the professor warned. Fuckin' Armageddon, can you believe it? But if I can catch that bastard in the house, Oi'm gwinter finish 'im off."

"Wait!" Connie wailed.

St. James turned and headed back into the house.

CHAPTER NINETY-FOUR

he walls pulsed blackly. St. James felt it in his skull like a heart murmur a nanosecond behind his own. *Lub-dub. Lub-dub.* Each beat sent a sliver of tin into his eyes. Van Horn was in the house. St. James could feel him like an infected tooth. He sprinted up the stairs and ran down the corridor to the master bedroom. Oaian was gone but Connie's purse remained on the floor next to the bed. He grabbed it, looked around, found the flute half under a bureau, snatched it, ran downstairs dumping the purse in the massive foyer then turned and followed the blood trail to the kitchen. The trail disappeared beneath a heavy, un-ornamented wooden door. St. James pulled it wide and saw the smear continue between shelves laden with foodstuffs to disappear beneath another door set directly beneath the stairs.

The door to the basement.

St. James opened the door. The stairs descended forever, lit by three evenly spaced red light bulbs in iron cages. Like looking into the wrong end of a telescope. The walls were uneven plaster, rich with whorls.

A wave of vertigo washed over St. James. He shut his eyes and sat on the top step, leaning between his knees. Breathe in, breathe out. Breathe in, breathe out. Gradually he got his reeling equilibrium under control. Thought about getting the hell out. Just torch the fuckin' place, and be done with it!

But if Van Horn were in the basement, and St. James knew he was, the fire would fail. Van Horn had to burn to bring things full circle. St. James clasped his hands.

"Lord, I've been a sinner, God knows. You know. I don't even know if you're there. Like to think so. I've gotter confront that rank bastard who used to stand at your right hand, and frankly, I could use some help. Not for meself, but for everybody. So if you, like, want to just take care of business, take care of that rotter your Own Bad Self, give me a sign, wouldja?"

St. James looked up hopefully. The red light bulb near the bottom of the stairs blinked out. Not exactly a ringing endorsement. Gripping the iron banister in one hand and the flute in the other St. James descended as quietly as he could. Halfway down, he paused to listen.

The old house groaned and creaked around him like it was trying to get comfortable but from the basement, nothing, nothing save for a cold, damp exhalation. St. James reached the bottom of the stairs. There was a door here, too. He opened it onto utter darkness, the feel of a vast underground chamber. He felt along the wall for a light switch, found one, one of the old fashioned knobs you rotated, and turned it. A series of feeble light bulbs lit a big room filled with boxes and furniture, much of it covered with tarps. The pulse of evil was stronger here, waves of nausea rolled through him right to left.

St. James turned right. The blood smear was thinner but still pointed toward the back of the big room, where St. James saw a horizontal strip of light shining beneath a black door. As he approached he gasped. The entire back wall was made of cuneiform-covered marble. The door itself served as the mouth of a massive demonic face contorted with fury. An underground mausoleum.

A voice began to sing, a baritone with overlays and undertones. Slowly with vibrato.

I went down to the Crossroads, fell down on my knees
I went down to the Crossroads, fell down on my knees.
Asked the Lord for mercy, save me if you please.

Ian felt through his pockets and found a book of matches

from the hotel. With all the junk in the basement the mansion would go up like a grain elevator, and whoever was in that mausoleum would go up with it. He found a stack of old newspapers and clumped them at the base of the door.

A steel guitar string looped over St. James' neck and tightened cruelly, cutting into the flesh and squeezing shut his esophagus. He tried to struggle, but whoever held the garrote was too strong for him. His legs scrabbled for purchase on the dusty floor but his assailant had him bent backward.

His father said softly, "Boy, Oi troied to protect you. Oi warned Kaspar to leave you alone. Who do you think saw that you got home safe last night from the party? Oi thought you'd have enough sense to cut your losses and walk away."

St. James struggled trying to dig his fingers beneath the choking wire. Oaian relented just enough for St. James to draw a breath. "Do you think Oi want to kill me own flesh and blood? You're loik some fuckin' Staffy terriers don't know when to quit! You coulduv had that bird again. Now you've got to doi."

St. James tried to say something but the wire inexorably tightened. A band of pain encircled his neck. Like a Christmas goose.

A sudden jolt and the pressure lessened. St. James slid to the floor landing painfully on his tailbone. The world swam, darkness edging in. Darkness claimed him, then spit him out. St. James regained consciousness on the floor of the basement and looked behind him. Oaian lay curled on his side with a ceremonial short sword protruding from his back like a shrimp on a toothpick.

Above him stood Stanton, Melchior's personal assistant, grim as death.

"Have you seen my daughter?" he asked in a harsh, guttural voice, breath forming a cloud.

CHAPTER NINETY-FIVE

St. James struggled to his knees choking. His hands went to his throat in an effort to soothe the pain. A red line encircled his neck. He cleared his throat several times looking for his voice.

"She might be behind that door," he said, coughing and pointing. He looked for the flute. He picked it up. "You might want to dig that sword out. Thanks ..." *COUGH, COUGH* "... for saving me life by the way."

Stanton had dressed for battle like a character in one of Melchior's movies: black trousers, black turtleneck, and a watch cap. St. James looked at the wool cap with envy, his breath tracing contrails in the frigid air. Stanton had a massive revolver tucked into his pants. St. James had seen that gun before, but he couldn't remember where. Stanton gripped the sword in both hands, braced a foot against Oaian's back, and pulled it out with a squeaking sound that scraped St. James' nerves to the bone.

St. James had hoped to set the fire and get out, but now the possibility existed that Beryl was behind the mausoleum door. Like everyone else within a half mile of Melchior's place last night, he'd heard the producer blow up at his personal assistant. He felt an acute sympathy for Stanton, who had been too loyal by half. Melchior's reputation was widely known. It was a miracle Stanton had lasted as long as he had. St. James was glad to have an ally. He put his finger to his lips. Stanton reached into his pocket and handed St. James a pack of Spearmint Certs. St. James gratefully put one in his mouth.

The singing had stopped. Frigid silence flowed through the narrow slot at the bottom of the door. *Was it possible to feel evil?* St. James wondered. Icicle waves emanated from behind the door, rippling through his flesh causing his joints to throb. St. James got to his feet rubbing his hands together. He shoved the flute down the back of his pants gangsta-style.

"You feel that?"

Stanton nodded solemnly. "I should have quit years ago, but the money was good and I had to put Beryl through college. The things I've seen him do ... he should have been locked up for life."

"'E's dead. Van 'Orn killed him at the stadium."

Stanton shut his eyes and breathed deeply. "He offered to help her, you know. I couldn't allow that. I know what his help meant."

"Oi guv'nor, we need a plan. Can you shoot that thing?"

Stanton gripped the revolver and pulled it out resembling a Robert E. Howard character with a gun in one hand and a saber in the other. "I can shoot."

It was one of those Dirty Harry guns. Being a Brit, St. James assumed every American could shoot. "An armed society is a polite society," he murmured to himself.

"What?"

"Nothin'. What do you want to do? Yank the door open and go in with guns blazing? What if he's hiding behind your daughter?"

Stanton froze.

"Do you know what's behind that door?"

Stanton shook his head. "In all my years I've only been down here twice. I never saw that door before." Stanton looked at the wall, and an element of fear crept into his eyes. He stepped back and tottered like a fighter who had just taken a left hook to the temple.

He found resolve. "I'm not leaving without my daughter."

"They know we're here," St. James said

The men faced the door which opened inward.

"Roight," St. James said softly. "You take the left, and I'll take the roight. First we'll open the door, and then see what happens."

The men took up position, Stanton holding the revolver next to his chin in both hands, St. James gripping the sword in his right and reaching for the knob with his left.

"Careful!" boomed a good-natured voice in an East European accent. "It might be a trap."

They jumped. Merino the Magnificent stood next to the stone wall resplendent in sparkling red waistcoat, white jodhpurs, shiny black boots, and top hat.

Stanton stepped away from the door into a shooter's stance aiming the pistol at Merino. *"Youuuu ..."*

St. James watched Stanton's fingers contract. "NO!" he shouted.

Too late.

Stanton squeezed the trigger, cracking the stone and launching a gout of flame. He couldn't miss.

As the smoke cleared Merino remained standing, but he was no longer next to the wall. He'd shifted four feet without motion. He held up one hand in a traffic cop's gesture.

"I am not responsible for your Beryl any more than you are responsible for my Isabelle."

St. James suddenly understood Merino's change of heart.

"How do we kill him?" St. James said.

Merino motioned. "Come away from the door."

CHAPTER NINETY-SIX

Merino led them to a dark corner beneath the stairs where they huddled, heads close, voices low. An immense wine rack held hundreds of dusty bottles. Lace-like frost clung to the bottoms.

"What happened to Isabelle?" St. James said softly.

"He took her for the blood," Merino said. He pronounced it "bludt." "To resurrect his favorite band. Again."

"What's behind the door?"

Merino shrugged.

"Why are you with him?" Stanton hissed.

Merino looked down. "I made a bad bargain. There's no hope for me, but Isabelle may yet go free."

St. James felt the bottom drop out of his heart. "What kind of bargain?"

"I went down to the Crossroads ..." Merino softly sang.

He stared at the floor.

"He promised me things, and in my greed and hubris I accepted," he said bitterly. "I should have known. You who are raised in the enlightened West cannot understand this. Those of us who grew up in parts of Eastern Europe ... our faith is misplaced. No, our faith sought other paths. I never thought he would take Isabelle!" he added piteously.

Like an electrified frog's leg the magician shook himself, and his shaman showman face popped into place. Up close St. James could see the pancake make-up, the rouge on his cheeks, and the eyeliner. Merino was older than he first appeared.

"A man told me Van Horn could be burned," St. James said.

"I have heard that as well," the magician said. "Compared to this damnation my gifts are pitiable, but they yet may serve. Music will mesmerize him. Flame will obliterate him."

"What if Beryl and Isabelle are in there?" Stanton said, hand on his gun. Merino's eyes went to the big six-shooter.

"Are the bullets silver?" he asked softly.

"Get the fuck outta here!" St. James said. "That too?"

"We can only pray," the magician winced on the word, "that the women are still alive. He took them for their blood, to keep his precious band alive."

A great weariness settled over St. James at the prospect of having to kill Cunar again, not to mention his father. Who'd been shagging his bird.

"I tackled him," St. James said. "He was strong as an ox. We're no match for him physically."

Merino doffed his top hat, reached inside, and withdrew a sterling silver flask bearing the red, gold, and blue seal of the Soviet Army Corps of Engineers. "This contains Everclear. It's pure alcohol. Do you know how to breathe fire?"

"I'll be playing the fuckin' flute. You breathe fire."

The magician went pale. Bullets of sweat popped on his forehead. "It's no good unless you get right up close to him," he said more to himself than the others. He paused, looked deep within himself and located a nugget of courage. "I'll do it."

St. James clapped him on the shoulder. "Good man! Now wot's the plan? Do you know what's behind that door?"

"I have no clue," the illusionist said.

"What if they're waiting for us?" Stanton said, holding the pistol at his side.

St. James looked from one to the other. "All roight, who wants to go first?"

Beat.

"I'll go," Stanton said.

"We'll be right behind you," St. James said. "Merino, go right. Oi'll go left."

Solemnly they walked back to the door. They stared in silent disbelief at the pool of blood where Oaian had fallen mere minutes before. A trail of blood led under the door.

"Are you fuckin' kidding me?" St. James said.

"Isabelle has some magic," the wizard said choking. "Her blood is strong."

St. James hugged the wall on the left, Merino the right. St, James looked down. Billows of condensed air puffed from beneath the massive oak door. He looked up. The demon's eyes were fixed on him, the pupils black. St. James shook himself and looked again. It was an inanimate frieze.

Stanton said, "One, two, three," turned the knob, pushed the door open, and stepped inside. St. James did not hesitate. He followed on Stanton's heels and backed along the wall to the left. An instant later Merino entered clutching his flask and stepped to the right.

The air was stale as if the room had been closed for decades, with traces of blood, offal, the skunk smell of hashish. The long, low room was lit by fluorescent fixtures set flush with the acoustic tile ceiling. The floor was covered with a thick oxblood shag rug stained in places. The furniture was black naugahyde beanbag chairs and two sofas with chrome fixtures. Gold records and framed black and white photographs decorated the wall. KLH box speakers were mounted at angles in the four corners of the ceiling. A glass bong sat on the black-lacquered coffee table next to old copies of *Billboard*. A larger than life poster of Little Richard covered a portion of one wall floor to ceiling.

Opposite the door a glass window with a door on the right sealed them off from the recording studio.

Paddy bent over Cerberus, his hand a moiré pattern. Cunar boomed bass. Oaian hovered over the drums; though nothing could be heard through the thick glass. In a booth to St. James' left sat Van Horn turning the dials on ancient analog equipment, racks of reel-to-reel tape covering the back wall. Van Horn seemed bemused.

There they fuckin' were, fresh as the day St. James first laid eyes on them. They kept coming at you and coming at you, and no matter how many times you killed them they bounced back stronger than before.

This time when I kill you, stay dead.

Behind the musicians in the sound room a horizontal window framed an aquamarine rectangle. The pool lights were on and cast a bluish tint in the studio.

Van Horn looked up and flipped a switch. Sound erupted from the speakers. Stanton staggered. He raised the horse pistol in both hands, sited in on Van Horn, and squeezed the trigger. The crack of percussion cut through the heavy metal din, a 310 grain slug smacked against the recording booth glass and hung there in the center of a vast spider web of cracks. The glass had to be an inch thick.

The flute felt cool in St. James' grasp. Even if he could get in there he had as much chance being heard as a fart in a tornado.

Where were the women?

Driven mad by the deafening music St. James looked around for something, anything, with which to break through to the studio. His eyes fell on a gold and red naugahyde bowling bag next to the sofa. It was monogrammed: CGJ. He picked it up. Heavy. He opened it. Inside was a gold bowling ball with "CGJ" in diamonds. The G was bigger than the framing letters. Chad J. Goodrich. That's how they printed it back then. With the surname in the middle.

Sticking the flute in his belt St. James gripped the bowling ball like a basketball. The bag fell to the floor. St. James inserted his fingers in the holes and recalling his hammer throw spun counter-clockwise three times, releasing the bowling ball on a trajectory directly at the center of the cracked glass.

The glass wall shattered into a million pieces falling on both sides of the waist-high sill. The band stopped and looked up. A curl of feedback hung in the air. Stanton rotated and squeezed one off at the guitarist, but Paddy ducked and the bullet struck the back window and stopped in the center of another spider web.

Almost casually, Oaian gripped one of his brass cymbals by the rim and flipped it with a flick of his wrist. It sliced through Stanton's neck severing the carotid artery. Stanton's fingers went numb and the pistol fell to the shag with a thump followed by

Stanton, blood spurting like a schoolyard bubbler.

Van Horn spoke through the PA system in his musical baritone. "This is it, boys. This is where the magic happens."

St. James dove for the gun.

Chapter Ninety-seven

St. James looked up from the prone position, hoisting the pistol in two hands

Are the bullets silver?

The bass drum sailed out of the studio like a depth charge straight at St. James, who got his arms up just in time. The drum collapsed his grip and the pistol flew from his hands. To his right, back against the recording room door, Merino chugged from the flask, whirled one hundred and eighty degrees, and let fly right in Cunar's face as the bass player was about to step over the ledge holding his solid body Fender by the neck.

"RAWWWK!" he screeched backpedaling, face dripping with Everclear. Merino snapped his fingers and flame appeared—a kitchen match.

"Die, hellspawn."

Merino tossed it at Cunar's chest. Cunar erupted like a desiccated spruce. He spun backward spinning and shrieking. The bass player fell to the hardwood floor, curled up, and died smoking.

St. James recovered the pistol and got to his knees. Merino flung Everclear at Oaian, gripping the flask in his right hand. Oaian dodged but caught several ounces. Merino fumbled with his matches. Oaian leaped the sill, heedless of the jagged glass digging into his palm, and slammed a drumstick horizontally into

Merino's ear, killing him instantly. The drumstick poked red from the opposite side.

St. James got to his feet and raised the pistol toward his father. "Sorry, Dad!"

Oaian smiled and started to say, "I am too ..."

The report erased whatever hearing St. James had left. The slug caught Oaian dead center of his chest. His father staggered back until his ass hit the sill. He looked down at the hole in the center of his chest. No blood. He poked his index finger into the hole and drew it out dry. He held it up and made a whirling motion.

"Ring-a-ding-ding."

St. James drew a box of Hotel Crabbe matches from his pocket, lit four in a cluster and tossed them at his father who gaped stupidly for an instant before they landed on his shirt and burst into flame. Oaian fell to the floor grunting through his teeth and rolled. St. James held the revolver muzzle against the back of Oaian's head and squeezed the trigger twice before the hammer fell on a spent chamber. The bullets exploded through Oaian's frontal lobes leaving his face a mass of mangled meat. Like that other mass of mangled meat. St. James turned away.

Paddy smiled grandly, teeth smaller and sharper than before. Cerberus caught the overhead light and played it back, a rainbow in plexiglass. St. James was freezing. He struggled to control his shivering.

"Well it looks like it's just you an' me, laddie-buck!" Paddy declared.

"Where are the women?"

Paddy arched his eyebrows. "The women? Oi, they're around, but if you want to foind 'em, you an' me got to have a little cuttin' contest. You know what that is, don't you Ian?"

"What? Me on flute and you on that thing?"

"Play anything you loik."

St. James glanced at the control booth. Where was Van Horn? There didn't appear to be any way out of the tiny booth, which jutted into the sound room from one corner.

A sudden burn caused St. James to whip the flute out of his waist, yet it was merely warm when he held it. He tucked it beneath his arm to absorb the heat.

Well I guess it wants me to play it. She. She wants me to play it.

St. James brought the flute to his lips and blew over the hole. A foghorn split the air.

Where the fuck did that come from?

Paddy's arm semaphored releasing a monster power chord.

St. James stood in front of Paddy, hands flying over the bone eliciting Rimsky-Korsakov's "Flight of the Bumblebee." Paddy matched him note for note, that vulpine grin, hands blurring between Cerberus' three necks. Faster and faster they went until it seemed as if one or the other would drop from exhaustion when St. James snapped the flute in two and slammed the pointed ends into Paddy's ears, just as Oaian had done to Merino.

Me old man did teach me a trick or two.

Cerberus' strap broke, and the guitar fell to the floor cracking one neck. Paddy's eyes bulged as his hands fumbled at his belt. "You have ... beat ..." His buckle came loose. He unzipped his fly. His pants fell to the floor. He wore no underwear. St. James could not believe what he saw.

"... the Manshees," the hermaphrodite sighed, collapsing.

The control room door clicked open.

CHAPTER NINETY-EIGHT

The beautiful young man stood in the doorway to the recording booth with an expression of crazed glee like an excited dog, flickering. Parts of him blinked on and off, an imperfect hologram, so that looking at him imparted a sense of vertigo.

"I am going to break every bone in your body," he said melodically. "Then I'm going to find your woman and impregnate her with my seed."

"Why don't you just fuck yourself like the other hermaphrodites?" St. James said yanking out the two pieces of flute.

Van Horn took a step into the room. "You think you're clever, don't you, preventing me from feeding. But I had a taste! Just a taste, that's all I need until I can bring forth another band of acolytes."

"How're yer gwinter to do that, Rathkroghen? Your Russian gangsters have gone all to pieces. Must have taken decades to put this job together, at least that's what I heard."

Rathkroghen's eyes turned to burning pools of oil.

His jaw dropped open turning his mouth into a saucer-sized hole rimmed with thousands of tiny sharp teeth. A column of blue bottle flies burst forth striking St. James in the chest with such force they turned to blackish yellow goo. St. James threw his arms up to cover his head and fell backwards. He scrambled back on his ass still clutching the bone shards and bumped into Paddy's corpse. Warm blood seeped through St. James' seat. It got on his hands and his pants.

Rathkroghen continued to belch flies.

St. James scrambled to his knees, slipping in blood and mashed flies, barely able to make Rathkroghen out through the swarm. They settled on his head like a shroud, crowding his eyes, nostrils, mouth, and ears. Trying to get in. For an instant St. James thought he would go mad. He lashed out in all directions snarling incoherently.

This is too much.

He felt the pointed end of the bone digging into his palm. He had the bones! St. James got to his feet and charged his tormentor clutching the twin shards, teeth shut against the flies. He plunged the shards down like twin daggers. Rathkroghen caught him by both wrists and pulled him close so that St. James could smell his breath, a wind from hell, the stench of diarrhea and vomit and all foul things.

Rathkroghen showed St. James his true face, an atlas of malice built on a hatred of all living things. St. James gasped and turned his head, and Rathkroghen threw him to the ground with incredible force. St. James' head bounced off the red shag floor, and he saw stars. He groaned, covering his eyes.

"Oh, open your eyes, Ian," said the beautiful voice. "You don't want to miss this."

St. James opened his eyes. The gold bowling ball lay by his head. He sensed Rathkroghen's position from his voice, not daring to look. One more look would drive him mad.

His imagination scurried through the cupboards of his mind looking for an answer. What did Goodie say? Remember the name of the album! *Beat the Manshees.* What did it mean, that the Banshees were all hermaphrodites? Banshee meant a female spirit. That had always bothered St. James. Hadn't they known?

Klapp had told him that only fire could destroy Rathkroghen. But Klapp was wrong! Just as album title reversed its meaning, so did the method of execution. It was not flame that would destroy Rathkroghen. It was water.

Seizing the bowling ball St. James rose in a spiral, whirled, and released it with a grunt, not at Rathkroghen but at the back window looking out on the pool. The bowling ball hit the lacework cracks off-center, but it was good enough. With the sound of icebergs calving, the glass wall bulged momentarily inward then exploded, releasing a rush of warm pool water into the room.

Water blessed by the Archbishop.

Rathkroghen's scream was worse than his face. St. James watched the waters engulf the demon in a hissing column of steam. The steam cleared leaving one black claw grasping at nothing

St. James rode the surge of water through the door into the outer room until he slammed into the hard oak door. The scream broke into a hissing, choking sound. St. James stood with his back against the door to the basement and waited for the waters to subside.

CHAPTER NINETY-NINE

Where were the women?

St. James shivered uncontrollably. At the same time, he was aware that the unnatural chill of the house had receded. He was wet, cold, and exhausted. He gasped for breath, bracing his hands on his knees until he could stand and breathe normally. His back and sides throbbed. He'd busted a rib.

His back against the door, he looked all around the room and registered the wall-size poster of Little Richard. The water had peeled back the bottom portion revealing a door. St. James waded through the knee-high water to the wall and ripped the poster down. It floated on the surface. St. James gripped the knob in both hands and pulled the door open against the force of the water. Water rushed into the darkened chamber.

The smell of sheared copper slapped St. James in the face. His hand felt along the wall and found the light switch. Harsh white light illuminated the long narrow room. A two-lane bowling alley running under the garden. The headless body of Isabelle hung from hooks through her Achilles tendons fastened to ductwork in the ceiling. The gutter beneath her had turned pink in the swirling water. St. James' eyes fastened on the ball return mechanism. Isabelle's head lay next to a bowling ball, her face turned away.

Another body lay on the cheap plastic bench, back to the room—a young woman, her hands bound behind her with gaffer's tape. St. James feared she was dead. He waded through the ankle deep water and touched her shoulder. Beryl twitched like a Mexican jumping bean, turned to look with terrified brown eyes that melted into relief when she saw him.

St. James sat on the bench and carefully removed the gaffer's tape sealing her mouth. "Water," she croaked. St. James remained where he was patiently unwrapping the tape from her hands and ankles. Shivering, she sat Indian-style on the bench clutching herself. St. James stood, found the bathroom off the bowling alley. He filled a paper cup with water from the faucet and brought it to the exhausted young woman who drained it in two gulps.

St. James got her another cup. She drained that, too.

"Can you walk?"

"I think so," Beryl said, teeth chattering. St. James looked around. An old black and red satin bowling jacket lay at the end of the bench. He picked it up. "Goodie" was stitched in gold on the breast. He draped it over Beryl's shoulders and helped her to her feet.

They came to the studio door. St. James put a hand over Beryl's eyes and said, "Don't look. Just let me guide you." They waded through the diminishing water to the basement door. Stanton's and Merino's bodies shifted in the draining flood. Of the band or Rathkroghen there was no sign.

St. James opened the door to the basement. The water had spread over most of the floor, seeping into the old cardboard boxes. There must have been drains because there was no standing water. Beryl leaning on him, St. James helped her slowly up the stairs trying to ease the pain in his ribs.

The long ascent seemed to take forever. St. James counted thirty-six steps. They stepped into the pantry and out into the kitchen. St. James was surprised to find the house and yard bathed in sunlight. As he helped Beryl to the front door it burst open, and two Los Angeles County Sheriff's Deputies rushed in and split to either side holding service automatics before them.

"Don't shoot!" St. James cried. "I've got an injured woman here!"

For a moment the cops remained in their shooter's stances.

"Are you St. James?" one of them said.

"That's me. I could use some soddin' help."

One cop holstered his weapon and came forward taking the still stunned Beryl from St. James. "Who's this?"

"Beryl Bridger," St. James said. "She's Melchior's assistant's daughter."

"Who else is in the house?" the cop holding the gun said.

"Bridger and Merino, the magician, are in a recording studio off the basement. That's all you'll find. The others sorta melted away."

"*What?*" the cop with the gun said.

"Nothin'."

Two EMTs entered the foyer carrying a fold-up stretcher. The cop holding Beryl said, "Over here." The techs quickly unfolded their stretcher.

The deputies turned their attention to St. James. "What happened?"

"Fuck if I know," St. James said, collapsing in a heap.

CHAPTER ONE HUNDRED

St. James woke in crisp hospital cotton, torso encased in tape, an IV in his wrist, and a bandage around his head. He was in a private hospital room with a TV hanging from the ceiling, a cantilevered table next to his bed, and a pile of softly snoring rags in a chair. It took St. James a minute to realize it was Professor Klapp, looking like a homeless person with his bulging Gladstone at his feet, both hands swathed in bandages.

The TV was on some local news channel, muted, showing the aftermath of what appeared to be an urban war zone. An image of Melchior briefly flashed before they cut to an insurance ad.

St. James was parched. He reached for a tall cup of iced water with a straw, straining his bandages and setting off a bright red warning signal in his ribs. He gripped the plastic cup, pulled it to him, and slurped it down. He lay spent for a minute, waiting for the throbbing in his side to recede. Two weeks ago he'd been at the end of his tether in Prague. Now he was grateful to be alive.

How could it have happened?

St. James thought of himself as rational, took pride in his sophisticated worldview. Not for him the boobery of the superstitious masses marching to their churches and temples and mosques every Friday, Saturday, or Sunday, like primitive cargo cults waiting for the planes to land. Not for him the doomsday cults preaching Armageddon.

St. James hadn't been to church since he was sixteen. His last foster family was determined to choke, shriek, and beat the devil out of him. He hadn't thought much about God over the years, or the existence of good and evil. Good? Evil? Come come, old chap. Don't be ridiculous. Those people who strap bombs to their children have legitimate reasons. The lunatic who guns down the congresswoman thinks he's killing a dragon. The millionaire socialist who rapes a hotel maid justifies it by the "greater good" he is doing all of mankind—simply by being there. St. James placed each of these on a graph like a power point presentation. "On a scale of one to ten, how would you describe the evil you are experiencing?"

There were shades and degrees of evil in all of us, just as there were shades of good.

Sometimes evil so colors the soul there is no shade of gray. Most such creatures exist on the fringes and are often the engines of their own destruction. Occasionally they rise to prominence depending on the degree of good, evil, and apathy among those who surround them. Sometimes they rule nations.

Rarely do they arrive as a literal manifestation of the Devil. If not the Devil, then some*thing* that predated and hated man. Some malignant, unknowable race that hated mankind as an aging diva hates her replacement. A curdled, acidic hate beyond the ken of your garden variety haters.

I have battled Evil and won.

Without God, there is no Devil. My victory is not mine, but God's.

God, Gaia, Alvin. Whatever you want to call it.

A higher power.

Thanks, Big Fella.

He might have to go to church one of these days, nothing too strident, maybe an all-faith chapel. As soon as he thought it he dismissed it knowing the warm palliatives of an all-faith chapel were useless against the forces of evil.

Give me that old time religion.

A song popped into his head like a burst blood vessel. He looked around for a pen and pad. Straining against the tape and grunting in pain, he reached over to the nightstand and pulled open the top drawer. Inside was a pen and a note tablet from

Heartland Ford in Mill Valley. He pulled them onto his lap and wrote, "Little did I dream when I began to revel, that I would end this song staring down the Devil."

His script trailed off the pad onto the blanket.

Fuckin' pain meds.

A chuckle bubbled to his lips. He was on the dole, no home, no prospects. The recording contract died with Melchior. The *In Crowd* gig died with Serafin.

Had he really talked to Chad Goodrich? Or was it the booze? Trying to separate the real from the imaginary made his temples throb.

The very fact of waking in hospital made him doubt all that had gone before. What if he'd been in some kind of accident and bumped his head and was just now coming out of it? What if he were still in Prague?

One glance at the TV evaporated the idea.

"No such luck, you old tosser," he muttered to himself.

Then there was Connie. All that had happened had happened because of Rathkroghen. The Connie he knew would never dream of bedding his old man, for the sake of her career if nothing else. Never mind the ten inches. Maybe he had been a little possessive, but they'd all been under Evil's influence to some degree. Surely she would understand that.

Face it, old sod. You're too fuckin' old for her.

He didn't even know if she was alive.

She had to be. He'd gotten her out of the house, hadn't he? She wouldn't have run back in, would she? Not even for the biggest story in the world.

St. James was having a hell of a time bending his mind around it. What would the press say, and what would people believe? The words "terrorist attack" scrolled across the bottom of the news feed.

Some things never change, he thought. He laughed because, really, what else could you do?

Klapp shook like an old dog coming in on a cool day and looked up.

CHAPTER ONE HUNDRED-ONE

Y ou're up," Klapp said.

"What do you keep doin' to your hands, professor?"

Klapp held them up and stared at them as if seeing them for the first time. "I chew my fingernails. It's a terrible habit."

St. James groaned feeling the soft buzz of painkillers. "What day is it?"

"It's Monday. You've been out for 36 hours. There's a policeman in the hall."

"Why?"

"In case the Mad Monks try to retaliate. I explained that wasn't going to happen. The debacle triggered a power struggle. So far, fourteen dead. Two other gangs are contesting the Monks from Belarus to Brighton Beach. Look at this."

Klapp unclasped the bulging briefcase and withdrew the *Los Angeles Times*. He stood, walked to the bed, and held the newspaper up so St. James could read the 32-point headline:

212 DEAD IN STADIUM CRUSH
12 DEAD IN HELICOPTER COLLISIONS
23 DEAD IN RIOTING

St. James took the paper and scanned the fine print below the fold. Mass hysteria, poor planning, bad drugs, gang rivalries, and irresponsible and dangerous pyrotechnics had led to the multiple tragedies. There was no mention of Satan nor terrorism. The media was sampling narratives to see which the public would buy.

The cops pinned the skybox murders on the Russian mafia. The Justice Department was investigating the Skorzny Group's role in the tunnel slaughter. Nadio Ninguna had decamped for Spain. Justice sought extradition.

St. James scanned the front page then turned to the jump. He flipped through all the pages of the first section. Not a word on the Melchior Estate.

"How's Connie?" he croaked hoarsely.

"She's fine. They insisted she spend the night here for observation. She checked out yesterday. We're in Mt. Sinai Hospital in Ventura by the way. How did you do it, Ian?"

"The pool was full of holy water. I smashed the window into the studio."

Klapp's bushy eyebrows did an elaborate *pas de deux*. "It could not have been holy water, which requires certain oils. Perhaps it was blessed water. An apocryphal story about Goodrich had him donating to the church in exchange for certain eccentric absolutions. How … how did you know?"

"Goodie told me, good Catholic that he was." St. James flexed his limbs.

"Chad Goodrich? I don't …"

"His ghost, professor, or one hell of a drunken hallucination."

Klapp nodded. "There have been several sightings over the years."

"Where're my clothes? I'm out of here."

"Well they're in the closet, but where will you go? Mrs. Serafin wasted no time rescinding all *In Crowd's* comping privileges while she goes over the books."

St. James lay back, realizing he had no place to go. No money, no recording contract, no byline.

He was not without prospects.

He knew how these things worked, better than most.

The offers would be lining up as soon as they knew where to find him: books, TV, recording contracts. You become famous overnight—for eating a thousand hot dogs or murdering your family—publishers and producers could work with that.

It's all showbiz, he reminded himself. He'd have to get an agent and a lawyer.

Klapp's cell phone played *The Ride of the Valkyries.* He stood. "Excuse me," he said, opening the door and going into the hall. He shut the door quietly behind him.

St. James found the remote on the bed table and rotated through channels until he found CNN. Video showed the devastation from the stadium, the scorched concrete where the helicopter had crashed onto the highway, the burnt infield, the terrible scarring, and stains outside the tunnel. St. James left the sound off. Commentators fell all over themselves with explanations like six blind men describing an elephant.

St. James hoped the Crabbe hadn't thrown his guitar and meager belongings out on the street. He reached for the house phone, called 411 and got the Crabbe's phone number, but when he tried to call a voice informed him that he was not authorized to make long distance calls from that room and to contact the operator to make other arrangements.

Fuck it.

He was lucky to be alive.

He had to take a piss. Carefully, like a geriatric getting out of a bathtub, St. James eased himself to the cold tile floor, grabbed the chrome stanchion holding his IV, and pulled it with him into the large lavatory, the tubes and hooks sounding like wind chimes.

He relieved himself, washed his face and hands, and searched the closet, the chest of drawers, and the nightstand. He found his clothes and his knapsack.

No flute.

The police would have taken that as evidence.

That was all right. If he never saw a flute again that would be all right, too.

Someone knocked twice on the door.

"Come in."

The door opened, and Connie slipped inside wearing black and that old pink sweater. She carried her backpack containing her laptop at her side. She sat on the bed, leaned over, and kissed St. James on the mouth. She smelled of jasmine.

An electric surge crackled from St. James' scalp to his toenails. One kiss was worth a thousand words, and in that kiss all doubt evaporated.

"We're going to write the book, Ian. You and me."

On a warm August evening St. James and Connie drove up Poudre Valley in a rented Mustang convertible. St. James was playing his first official gig in six years, and this time he was the headliner. They'd just signed a contract with a big publisher and split a $500,000 advance. Connie trailed her left arm in the wind, pulling it in when they passed cars coming down the narrow canyon road. Families packed up following picnic dinners the length and breadth of the wild river.

At seven-thirty the canyon was already in deep shadow.

Sherkoff had roped off one of the precious parking places for them. The remaining parking was taken by motorcycles. A group of inked bikers in black leather hovered by their bikes as Connie and St. James approached the front door.

A bearded behemoth did a double-take when he saw them, turned to his cohorts, and said something. They all turned, two making the sign of the devil with their hands, another holding out a fist.

"Right on, brother."

"Righteous, dude."

St. James bopped fist with the Insane Asshole and opened the door. Inside, the club was already packed, with the shuttle bus bringing more. Matt Sherkoff was working the bar. He put his towel down when he saw them, came out from behind the bar, and embraced St. James, then Connie.

"Really looking forward to tonight. Anything you need, just ask. You guys can use my office as a dressing room."

"Who's usin' the trailer? Grand Punk Skateboard?"

"Grand Punk had to cancel, so we had to find someone fast. This fellow came very highly recommended, and he says he knows you. The Druids? Heavy metal band out of Germany. Ever heard of them?"

"Yeah," St. James replied. "Can't wait to see Herr Professor play bass with eight fingers."

Connie took his arm. "He's a wizard. He can do anything."

Acknowledgements

I would like to thank the following for contributing to *Banshees*: Bob Garcia, Peter Brandvold, Val Mayerik, Al Zuckerman, Franklyn Peterson, Judi K-Turkel, and Joe Comstock.

About the Author

Mike Baron is the creator of Nexus (with artist Steve Rude) and Badger, two of the longest lasting independent superhero comics. Nexus is about a cosmic avenger 500 years in the future. Badger, about a multiple personality, one of whom is a costumed crime fighter, from a resurgent First Comics. Baron has won two Eisners and an Inkpot award and has written The Punisher, Flash, Deadman, and Star Wars among many other titles.

Baron has published four novels, *Helmet Head*, *Whack Job*, *Biker*, and *Skorpio*. *Helmet Head* is about Nazi biker zombies. *Whack Job* is about spontaneous human combustion. *Biker* is hard-boiled crime about a reformed motorcycle hoodlum turned private investigator. *Skorpio* is about a ghost who only appears under a blazing sun.

If You Liked ...

If you liked *Banshees*, you might also enjoy:

Skorpio
Mike Barron

Working Stiff
Kevin J. Anderson

Enter the Janitor
Josh Vogt

OTHER WORDFIRE PRESS TITLES BY MIKE BARON

Skorpio

Whack Job

Helmet Head

A Brief History of Jazz Rock

Our list of other WordFire Press authors and titles is always growing.
To find out more and to see our selection of titles, visit us at:

wordfirepress.com